IN WONDERLAND

IN WONDERLAND

A NOVEL

JOYCE MAYNARD

Published by Little A, New York

www.apub.com

Amazon, the Amazon logo, and Little A are trademarks of Amazon.com, Inc., or its affiliates.

EU product safety contact:
Amazon Media EU S. à r.l.
38, avenue John F. Kennedy, L-1855 Luxembourg
amazonpublishing-gpsr@amazon.com

ISBN-13: 9781662540899 (hardcover)
ISBN-13: 9781662541230 (paperback)
ISBN-13: 9781662540905 (digital)

Cover design by Zoe Norvell
Cover illustration: © David Baker

Printed in the United States of America

First edition

*This book is for my friend Tami Vezina, who has taught
me so much more than the game of tennis.*

PROLOGUE

If you've never seen a dead person, here is one of the things you might not know. Dead people look different from living ones. This remains true even if they didn't get run over by a truck or die as a result of some long illness that caused their body to waste away. Just the fact that their heart no longer beats, their lungs don't take in air, their brain has ceased to register any emotion—just that—is enough to transform the look of them.

For this reason, even to someone who knows the dead person well death may have rendered her almost unrecognizable.

I was not quite fifteen years old the first and only time I saw a dead person. She had probably only been dead a few minutes. Thin as she was—a condition that had nothing to do with lingering physical illness—she had no need to accentuate her cheekbones further, but she'd evidently applied blush. She had changed from the outfit I'd seen her wearing an hour or two earlier into a silk nightgown. Knowing her as I did, I imagine it was chosen with great care for its particularly flattering shade of peach and the way the folds fell over her nearly skeletal body. Every rib visible.

She was a person who cared a lot about this kind of thing. Her hair lay arranged across her silk pillowcase in a manner that made you wonder if she'd actually fanned it out that way before she set her head down that last time.

You might say she looked beautiful, as she always did. But she didn't look like herself.

One thing about the sight surprised me, other than the fact that she was dead. She had applied her lipstick perfectly—as always. Her lips were slightly open, almost as if she were about to offer up one of her discourses to us on something we didn't do that we should have, or something we did that we should not have done, or simply a way in which we might improve ourselves. Until the moment of her death, she invariably had something to say, and it was seldom affirming.

No words came out of her now, of course. But here came the most shocking aspect of what I saw that night: At one corner of her mouth, just barely visible—some people would have missed this, in fact—I could spot a trace of what I recognized as the smallest residual crumb of Boston cream pie. Until that night, I doubted she had let anything of the kind touch her lips in decades, if ever. This, more than any of the rest of it, served as indication that an event of huge and unprecedented proportions had taken place that night: A woman who counted every calorie that entered her body had eaten dessert.

I've pointed out already that up until the moment of her death, she was a person who liked to have the last word. She insisted on that. In fact, it could be said that even now she was delivering a final message to those who survived her. Dead as she was, she had somehow managed to point her long bony finger directly at the object of her greatest love and her greatest contempt. She might as well have been aiming a gun.

I was fourteen years old the night I found her body. It took me thirty years to recognize that it wasn't all my fault—not only her death, but everything that had happened over the three short months I think of as my Wonderland summer.

1

Bad Moon on the Rise

June 1986

The drive from my family's apartment in New Jersey to the Emersons' summer place in Maine took seven and a half hours, but I wouldn't have cared if it lasted a month. I got to sit in the front seat next to Forrest. What else mattered?

It was a little after one o'clock when Forrest pulled up in front of our building, meaning he must have left Lake Catherine before sunrise. I could hear the music blasting from the Porsche a block away—Creedence Clearwater, music I knew from listening to my father's old vinyl. Never mind that it was drizzling. Forrest always had the top down.

He and my father had been friends since they were eleven years old. That summer, when everything changed, I was fourteen going on fifteen—stuck in a box called Hubbard, New Jersey, the only child of two parents so occupied with waging war against each other they seemed to have forgotten I existed. Then Forrest Emerson showed up to take me to Maine, and it felt like my life was finally going to get interesting.

I wasn't wrong about that.

Back when Forrest and my father were growing up in the neighborhood, he went by his original name—Howie. My father, Henry, went by Hank.

My dad had filled me in on the basics. His family lived in the apartment one floor above where Forrest grew up—three kids to a room, rice and beans the staple for dinner, a belt on the behind when they got out of line and when they didn't. Nobody had any money, and they had even less in the way of prospects for the future.

"When you grow up in the projects like I did," my father said, "it's hard to picture getting out of there. That's all you know."

The two of them, Hank and Howie, had been like brothers, my father said. They got into lots of trouble together but had fun doing it. Then there was the other part. Howie could barely read or write. He struggled so badly in school, he never would have graduated if not for my father, who sat next to him when they took tests so Howie could copy off his paper.

"He isn't stupid," my father said. "There's just something about Howie's brain. Words on paper don't make sense to him. When he tries to write, it looks like what you'd expect from a very young kid."

Still, Howie was the one who got out of Hubbard. He changed his name to Forrest when he married Regina. Except for visits with my father, he did not look back.

My dad was still Hank. Still living within five blocks of where he started out. Also still drinking. These days he and Forrest only saw each other once a year, when my parents and I made our annual visit to Forrest and Regina's house in Maine, Wonderland. As differently as their lives had played out, though, Forrest still called my father his best friend. Now here he was, back in the old neighborhood.

He got out of the car like Erik Estrada, my first crush, on the show that used to be my favorite when I was younger, *CHiPs*—hopping over the driver's-side door of the convertible instead of opening it like a normal person. He looked like a movie star.

We were only three days into June but already Forrest had a tan. He was wearing shorts and a Ramones T-shirt that said "Too Tough to Die." He kissed me on the cheek, then opened the trunk and tossed in my suitcase—an old red Samsonite bag that my mother had bought for her honeymoon, to Florida, with my dad.

"This all you got?"

I nodded. I was ready to become a whole new person. Hard to accomplish that in your same old clothes.

The offer to spend the summer in Maine had come out of the blue on the last day of ninth grade, just four days earlier. (They'd had to cancel the last two weeks of classes on account of a broken water line that flooded the whole first floor of our school, causing a giant mold problem. That was my neighborhood for you.)

Sometime that year my parents had stopped speaking to each other. The two of them moved through the small, dark rooms of our apartment as if there were some kind of radioactive field around the other person's body—careful not to brush up against each other. I huddled in the corner, trying to keep out of range of the hate waves. When one of them needed to get a piece of information across to the other, they used me as the message bearer.

Tell your mother.

Ask your father.

"I'm not your secretary," I told my father one time. Not that this had any effect.

My parents and I had been sitting at the kitchen table in our apartment, finishing dinner—television on, no conversation, picking at a reheated casserole that wasn't any good back on Day One—when the call came, with Forrest's job offer. The au pair they'd hired had just canceled on them. Did I want to join his family at Wonderland as their mother's helper?

Was the sky gray? (In Hubbard, the answer was always yes.)

"Can you imagine?" my mother said—a rare moment in which she seemed actually to address my father. "With Regina in the shape she's in? Some spoiled French girl decides she has better things to do and leaves the family without a babysitter the week before the children's school gets out?"

The shape Regina was in.

Regina was Forrest's wife, of course. It was never clear what her problem was, only that she had one. I used to think she was just drunk a lot—a condition I knew well—from the slurring of her speech as the day went on, but though she definitely took prescription drugs, Regina never touched alcohol.

She was very skinny. And she was always knitting something. She explained it to my mother one time. "If you're holding knitting needles, you're not so likely to reach for a snack." She held those knitting needles a lot. If she did eat, it was probably celery.

"The thing about dealing with Regina is recognizing she's just not a normal person," my father said. He was the one who held out a little sympathy for her. My mother? None.

How Forrest put up with her was a mystery. There was her money, of course—the brownstone in Back Bay, Boston, where they lived the rest of the year, their Florida vacation home, right on the ocean. (We'd never visited there, but every Christmas we got a card with the four of them—Forrest, Regina, Hayward, and Jilly—pictured in front of a giant white tree with matching ornaments. Blue one year, purple the next.)

But the place that occupied my imagination was their lake house, Wonderland. If you asked me to dream up what heaven might look like, that would be it.

"I'd probably marry a psycho too," my mother said, "if they came with a maid and a cook and a handyman to take care of everything."

According to my father, none of that mattered much to Forrest.

"The guy loves his wife," he said. "They've got this thing going on between them. It must make him feel good, taking care of her."

That summer I thought he'd take care of me too.

Now the two of us leaned against the side of the convertible. Forrest stood there taking it all in: The street where he grew up, with its boarded-up storefronts and graffiti, stray dogs and winos, the smell of rotting trash. The windows of my family's shabby apartment two floors up.

"I'll just run up and say hello to your old man," Forrest said.

A look passed between us. As early in the day as it was, my father would have started in on the vodka. One look at my face and Forrest put away the idea of a visit.

Then I was buckling into my seat beside him, and we were heading toward the highway—the wind in my hair, like an actress in a commercial.

"You want the top up?" he asked me. I shook my head. Everything was perfect. It wouldn't matter if I never laid eyes on Hubbard, New Jersey, again. Forrest Emerson was delivering me to my future. I might have thought—though I wouldn't have said this part out loud—that Forrest Emerson *was* my future.

"What do you say we hit a casino in Hartford on our way north?" he asked me. Before I had time to respond, he slapped his thigh. "Damn. I keep forgetting you're just fourteen years old. I was all set to teach you how to play blackjack. Give you a hundred dollars and see how far you get with it."

"I'll be fifteen in September," I reminded him.

"Oh, well then. That makes all the difference," he said.

2

AGAINST THE WIND

Of the many things I loved about Forrest—how much fun he was and that he always had great ideas for things to do and the energy to do them—this was the best: He paid attention to me. He may have been the first person in my life—the only one, my parents included—about whom I could have said this.

Up until now I'd only gotten to see him once a year—but that had been enough to secure his position as my favorite person. For as long as I'd known him, which was all my life, Forrest had wanted to know what I was up to, who my friends were, what I cared about. Where some adults would ask you, *How's school?* and never bother to wait for the answer, Forrest always listened. The questions he asked were never the obvious ones. He wanted to know: Did I ever skip school? And if I were to do that, how would I spend the day? He asked me what music I listened to and if I had an interest in skateboarding, or if I ever thought about getting a tattoo. Would I walk naked for two blocks down the main street of my town if I got paid a million dollars to do it? Would I do it for a thousand? Where was the cutoff?

He might also inquire about my favorite flavor of ice cream, then pull over at the next exit to buy a pint of it.

The last time I'd seen Forrest—Labor Day, the summer before—he asked me if I believed in God. Then again, he wanted to know if I ever shoplifted.

"Just one time," I told him. "OK. Three."

That was the thing about Forrest. You could tell him something like that and he wouldn't deliver a lecture. No doubt he'd shoplifted plenty himself when he was my age.

"Whatever you took, I hope it was the expensive brand," he said.

Now here we were, just the two of us—Forrest and me—out on the highway together. He put on a Bob Seger tape—more music from back in the day. Never mind that the sound of the cars we passed drowned out our voices.

"Living by the sword . . ." I had no idea what it meant; I just loved shouting the lyrics as loud as I could as we raced over the highway. There was this feeling as we drove north that something big was going to happen that summer.

Somewhere in Connecticut, when we went through a toll, Forrest said the woman in the booth looked like she'd had a rough day, so he gave her a fifty-dollar bill without waiting for her reaction.

"We're going to have ourselves some major fun this summer," Forrest told me as we headed back out on the highway. We'd been listening to the Casey Kasem countdown of the hits of 1973. "Tie a Yellow Ribbon Round the Ole Oak Tree" came on.

"Oh man," Forrest said. "We're in big trouble now."

Trouble? Us? I thought everything was perfect.

"We'll never be able to get that awful song out of our heads."

When we stopped for gas—in New Hampshire now—Forrest picked up a couple of matching hats for us that said "Live Free or Die." There was a store with a fake totem pole out front where he decided to buy moccasins for the whole family, including me. He didn't need to say this, but I felt it: I was part of this family too.

3

Queen of the Lake

It was ten o'clock at night by the time we reached Wonderland, but we could see the lights of the house from all the way down the long gravel driveway. Then came the familiar old elm tree, where Forrest showed me the tree house he'd started to build for Jilly the previous fall, and beyond that a long run of granite steps leading up to a wide door with a pair of marble dogs guarding the entry.

I knew this place well. But always before, I'd made the trip with my parents—and only for our annual Labor Day weekend visit that I used to look forward to all summer. Three perfect nights. Then the long drive back to New Jersey, knowing a whole year would pass before I got to return. Now here I was with a whole summer at Wonderland stretching ahead of me.

It was dark now, but in the moonlight I could make out the vast rolling lawn where we played croquet and badminton, the rose arbor, the massive stone barbecue where Forrest roasted steaks, the firepit where we made s'mores, and beyond that, the dock, with a Sunfish and a couple of Old Town canoes, along with Forrest's pride and joy, his Chris-Craft, named for Regina: "Queen of the Lake."

"It's about time I taught you how to water-ski," he said to me.

A picture came to me, of how it would be out on the boat that summer with Forrest. Me in my swimsuit—a slimmer, more shapely version of myself, baby fat gone, my breasts filled out enough to look good in a bikini—holding on to the rope. No sign of the children or Regina in this picture. Just Forrest and me with the sun shining down on us.

I didn't know yet that Forrest had a way of promising things he might not deliver.

He carried my red suitcase up the walk. I was still wearing the "Live Free or Die" hat. In his other hand Forrest held the boxes of moccasins.

"Honey, I'm home!" he called out. Just like a dad in a TV show.

In the family room, I could make out the sound of the television set. The children were still up, probably because nobody told them to go to bed. On the screen, a man and a woman were lying on a bed together, kissing with their mouths open. A couple of empty bags of Cheetos spilled out onto the floor. Orange powder on the couch.

Regina lay on a chaise lounge, wearing a long white gown, her hair up in a bun, a string of pearls around her neck. There was a pair of knitting needles in her hands and a blanket over her shoulders.

"You brought Frances," she said to Forrest—her voice low and whispery. She said this as a person might acknowledge he'd picked up milk on the way home, or a dozen eggs.

Regina scanned my body up and down. Something in the way she looked at me made me know she recognized my terrible secret: I was the only girl in my grade who hadn't gotten her period.

This was when Jilly raced over to us in her pajamas, carrying an American Girl doll. Watching her leap into her father's arms as she did, I registered the faintest stab. *Imagine what it would feel like, having Forrest for your dad.*

"Did you bring me something?" Jilly asked him.

"Boy did I ever," he said. "I brought you Frances."

She didn't seem impressed.

Regina glanced over at me again, taking in my ratty haircut, my red suitcase. Her mouth formed something that resembled a smile, but with Regina you got the feeling it was more like her imitation of a smile, as if she were reminding herself to turn her lips up at the corners. She placed a long, thin, elegant finger on her forehead—that place between her eyes, as if rubbing the spot might make the crease there go away.

"I tried to get the children to bed, but they never pay any attention to me," she sighed. She nodded in the direction of my suitcase. "Hayward will take that upstairs for you. We'll talk in the morning."

Hayward was the Emersons' son—a bratty little boy I'd never paid much attention to before. I'd figured he was probably nine or ten by now, but the first thing he did as he emerged from the TV room was tell me he was twelve—uncomfortably close to my own age. In the year since I'd seen him last, he'd grown to the point that he was now the same height as me, possibly taller. Nobody would have called him fat, but there was a softness to his body that spoke to a life spent on the couch, watching TV shows and playing video games, drinking sodas and eating Cheez Doodles.

In my hazy memory of him from past summers, I remembered Hayward playing with He-Man figures and watching cartoons. The person who stood in the doorway now had the hint of a mustache on his upper lip. Just the finest hair, but this was disconcerting. I was supposed to function as this boy's babysitter for the next three months, and here he was, beating me at puberty.

"Hey." He seemed to be staring at my chest. His voice cracked in the way a boy's voice does when he's on the brink, and you never quite know any more than he does what octave the sounds will be that come out.

"We got *Legend of Zelda*," he said. (Low octave to start, then back to high.) "We could play if you want."

"Frances must be exhausted," Regina pointed out, though she was the one who sounded that way. "She probably wants to see her room."

I followed Hayward to the stairs. Even from behind, without catching a glimpse of his face, there was something about the way he strode down the hall that made me uneasy.

4

Every Day a Special Occasion

The staircase at Wonderland was the kind you'd see in a movie, with some beautiful woman descending in a gorgeous evening gown. At the top was a long, wide hallway that led to the rooms that housed each of the children—also (strangely, to me) separate bedrooms for Forrest and Regina.

Photographs of the Emersons lined the hallway—the children mostly. In one of the few pictures featuring the parents, Forrest looked handsome and happy—not so different, in fact, from how he looked still. The surprise was Regina. You couldn't have called her expression joyful, but it conveyed something that was missing in Regina as I saw her now: hopefulness. In the picture she was looking up at Forrest with an adoring expression. I might not have recognized her as the same person who spent her days on the chaise, letting hours go by without speaking, her knitting needles always clicking, staring out at the lake.

On past visits, my parents and I had stayed in a guest suite at the end of the hall, but at the moment, these were unavailable, Hayward explained to me. "My dad started this company where he was going to South America all the time, buying baskets to sell to department stores to put things like chocolate and fancy pears inside for Christmas presents," he said. "But it turned out nobody wanted to buy them, so we ended up with all this junk." He waved his arm in the direction of the bed I'd slept in the previous summer, piled high with unsold merchandise. "Typical," he said. That grin again.

At the far end of the hall stood another door, one I'd failed to notice in the past. I figured this must lead to the room where I'd be staying and reached for the doorknob. Hayward flung out his arm, blocking me. His voice took on a force absent until now. Anger or fear, hard to tell.

"Don't even think about going in there," he hissed.

"You keep poisonous snakes or something?" I asked him. I thought I'd make a joke.

"It's my mom's stuff," he said. He pointed to a narrow set of stairs leading to the third floor. "Your room's up there."

He set my bag down just outside the door. "Word of advice," he told me. "Don't ask my mom about that other room, the one with the lock. It makes her act weird." He paused for a moment. "Like she isn't already, right?"

The bedroom they'd prepared for me was probably the smallest in the house, not that I minded. I liked that the ceiling sloped down over the wooden daybed, with a skylight overhead. A second window looked out toward the lake and the boathouse. With the window open, as it was even now, late in the evening, I could hear the sound of the water lapping against the shore, the hum of a single motorboat.

A small chest of drawers sat alongside one wall. As few things as I'd brought with me—my bathing suit, naturally, three pairs of shorts, two sleeveless cotton shifts, underwear, and some other basics—I wouldn't need more than a couple of drawers.

My clothes were all wrong. But what mattered was just being here. Everything about the room where I'd spend the summer felt like a dream—the bedspread with its matching bolsters and cushions, milkmaids and cows marching across the wallpaper. In the corner was a desk painted robin's-egg blue. I pictured myself writing stories there, and letters to my friend Martha back home, though only if I had time. I might be too busy having fun. A person could do anything she wanted in a room like this. In her mind, anyway.

It was all so beautiful. Outside now, a pair of loons called out to each other. Lace curtains fluttered at the window, moonlight glittering. From the other side of the lake, someone was setting off fireworks for no particular reason except that at Lake Catherine every day felt like a special occasion.

5

"You're Going to Be a Beauty Someday"

Forrest was already up, standing at the stove with an apron over his tennis shorts, when I came downstairs the next morning.

"I hope you like pancakes," he said. "Prudence does a great job of feeding us here, but nobody knows how to make flapjacks like I do."

Prudence was the housekeeper, who showed up most mornings a little before lunch and stayed until dinnertime. I knew her from past summers—a quiet woman who seemed to take in everything and said almost nothing about any of it. I gathered she'd been working for Regina's family long before Forrest came on the scene—since Regina was a child, probably—alongside Billy, the handyman, and a couple of gardeners who showed up several times a week to mow the lawns and tend to the hydrangeas.

Nobody else seemed to be up yet, so it was just Forrest and me sharing our breakfast at the counter.

"This is my favorite time of day," he said. "Before all the action gets underway." He set a plate in front of me with a tall stack of pancakes on it and passed me a pitcher of maple syrup.

As part of the self-improvement project I'd planned for that summer, I'd told myself I'd stay away from high calorie foods, but I made an exception that first morning. Being around Forrest did this to a person.

He never seemed to feel the obligation to deny himself pleasure, not that this seemed to have had any ill effect on his body. Now I poured a thick river of syrup over my pancakes.

"Glad to see someone around here has a healthy appetite," Forrest said, as I reached for the butter. No need to explain he was referring to Regina. As for me, nobody would have called me overweight, but I hated the little roll of baby fat on my belly. Nights in my bed, I ran my hand over the spot, searching for my ribs.

I took a bite of my pancakes, trying to chew as slowly as possible.

"You probably don't know this yet," Forrest said, "but you're going to be a beauty someday." Simple as his words were, I felt warmth come over me, as real as if I'd stepped out of the shade into a patch of sunlight.

We finished our breakfast. Still no sign of Regina. In the den, I could make out the sound of the television. The children were up. I started to clear away the dishes, but Forrest waved me away from the job.

"Prudence takes care of that," he told me. "I thought I'd bring you down to the club. The kids take tennis lessons over there three days a week. Then there's sailing and golf practice. I can't even keep all the things straight that Regina signs them up for. Basically, all you need to do is drop them off and make sure nobody gets arrested."

6

Such a Good Husband

The Lake Catherine Country Club sat at the end of a long private road landscaped with alternating colors of begonias (red, white, red, white) and a statue of the club founder at the entrance—a great-grandfather of Regina's, it turned out. Along one edge was the golf course—rows of carts lined up, men in pastel shirts and plaid pants out on the links, some of them accompanied by younger men carrying their bags.

"Welcome to the club," Forrest said, as we pulled into his parking space. **Reserved for Staff.** Forrest was never one to pay attention to rules.

"They've got a Jacuzzi and a sauna and a great pool," he said to me as we toured the building. "There's sure to be plenty of kids your age."

For a moment then, I let myself imagine I could be one of them. I pictured myself in my faded one-piece swimsuit, sitting around with a group of girls in bikinis. I had no idea what they'd talk about. Boys maybe. Makeup. Parties. Shopping.

"I might not fit in," I suggested.

"Who wouldn't want to be your friend?" Forrest said. "And if they don't, screw them all."

A girl about my age was just coming in as we entered the clubhouse. She had a tennis outfit on—white, with pink piping along the hem, and a matching shirt and visor. A few steps behind, a woman who must have been her mother carried a bag that contained the girl's racquet—several racquets, from the looks of it.

The mother knew Forrest. She smiled when she spotted him.

"You devil," she called out. "You didn't even let me know you were back! I wasn't expecting you until the Fourth."

"We wanted to get a jump on the summer," Forrest told her. "It's always too short."

"You're looking good," the woman said. Phyllis was her name, evidently. She had on a necklace that spelled it out.

"You could stop by for a drink later," she went on. "Terry's out of town, and Olivia's having a sleepover. I'll be all by my lonesome."

Was my imagination taking over—when did it not?—or did she turn her body very slightly at this moment, in a way that made her breasts appear more prominent?

"Regina needs me at the house," he said.

"God, why do you have to be such a good husband all the time?" she said. "Maybe you'll give Terry a few lessons."

"I want to introduce Olivia to Frances," Forrest said, gesturing in the direction of the girl my age wearing the tennis outfit. "She'll be spending the summer with us."

I was grateful that he had not presented me as their family's mother's helper. For all either one of them knew, I could have been a relative, with a cute tennis outfit of my own back at the house and a bagful of racquets.

Olivia looked me over. *Not likely.*

There was something about the look of a girl who grew up going to a country club, and something about that of the one who didn't. You could pore over the pages of *Seventeen* magazine all day. It wouldn't help. When a girl came from the place I did, she brought it with her wherever she went.

"Maybe Olivia could show Frances the ropes around here," Forrest said.

"You never know," Phyllis told him. "But she's pretty busy with her tennis these days."

Forrest put an arm on my shoulder. I felt its warmth. This was what it must be like having a father who looked out for you. A father, or a boyfriend.

"Stop by if you can," Phyllis called out after him. "There'll be a Manhattan waiting with your name on it."

I studied Forrest's face as he watched her head toward the tennis courts. They were red clay, not asphalt, like tennis courts in public parks, if you even lived in a place where there were parks. I watched as a couple of men in white uniforms moved up and down along the length of the courts, rolling out the clay for the players.

For a moment, the sight of those men rolling the red clay left me transfixed. Or maybe what fascinated me was the life of a girl like Olivia, for whom they were preparing the playing surface now—a girl for whom this place was as familiar as, for me, it was exotic and magical.

"I don't think that girl wants to be my friend," I said to Forrest. He'd seen it all, of course. The way that mother took in the sight of him. Her daughter's disdain when she'd looked me over.

"Pay no attention to her," he told me. "The main thing is, we're going to have a more interesting summer than the lot of them."

We were a team then. We understood each other and the world. It was as if we had a club all our own with only two members.

Afterward, Forrest brought me to a place called the Caboose. He wanted to buy me a milkshake, but I said no thanks.

I ordered a Diet Coke. Forrest introduced me to the manager. Anytime I wanted, he said, I could come by with or without the children for ice cream or snacks. He did the same at the little grocery store down the street from the Caboose, where the vegetables were set out like jewels, and gourmet cheese from France filled one entire wall.

"Whatever this girl orders, just put it on our account," Forrest said.

I could have whatever I wanted. Nobody had ever suggested this before.

"In case you hadn't noticed, we're not in New Jersey anymore," Forrest told me, back at the house.

He took me to where a row of bicycles was lined up in a rack. He reached for one.

"You're going to need to get around town," he said. "Do errands. Take the kids places. Normally, the girls we hire for the summer have their license, but since you don't, it seemed like a good solution to pick this up for you."

He had bought me a bike—yellow, twenty-one speeds, with a basket on the front. "For when you go pick up the croissants," he said. "Or just . . . have an adventure."

I never had a bike like this before. I owned a very old one for a while, back home, but someone stole it.

"It will be good exercise for the kids, riding their bikes to the club along with you instead of getting driven around all the time," he said. "Those two spend way too much time in front of the TV set."

I couldn't speak, the bike was so beautiful.

"I think this baby deserves a name," he said. "What do you want to call her?"

It just came to me. "Buttercup," I told him.

7

A Training Bra, a Box of Tampons, a Journal

It had occurred to me on the drive up from New Jersey that my breasts might develop enough over the course of the summer—finally—that I'd need a bra, an item I'd be unlikely to procure without the embarrassment of asking for a ride to town. Weighing on me even more heavily was the question of how I'd deal with it if I got my long-overdue period that summer.

Regina Emerson was not the type of person you'd ask to drive you someplace, and though Forrest would have taken me to the store, no problem, that would mean sitting next to him on the way home, in the front seat, with the bag containing tampons on my lap.

Now, thanks to the gift of the bike, I had my own transportation.

That first morning, before setting off for the club, Forrest had reached into his wallet and peeled off a bunch of bills—a hundred dollars' worth, it turned out, when I counted them later. "Anytime you need more, just let me know," he said.

Now I stuffed a few dollar bills into the pocket of my shorts and jumped on Buttercup, heading downtown to pick up supplies. Along the way I passed the houses of the Emersons' neighbors—vast family mansions along the lakefront and then, as I made my way from the water, more modest homes, though still way nicer than where I'd come from. There was a plant nursery, a dog grooming establishment, a beauty salon, an ice cream parlor. At the top of the hill sat a wonderful old stone building, the Lake Catherine Library.

All told, the ride to town took no more than fifteen minutes. With my hands placed squarely on Buttercup's handlebars, I was in no rush. I tried out all the gears, threw my head back to feel the wind rushing past.

MacDougall's stocked pretty much everything. I spent fifteen minutes walking the aisles, getting up my courage to make my purchase, and when I did, I added toothpaste and bobby pins and Kleenex to my basket to make the presence of that box of tampons less obvious. While I was at it, I picked up a training bra.

Back at the house, up in my little attic room under the eaves, I placed the box of tampons in one of the drawers, concealed under my three T-shirts. I put on my training bra and stuffed toilet paper down the front, one clumped-up piece on each side. I almost looked like a regular teenager.

The family was in the sunroom—Regina with a book, the children playing Chinese checkers, though only Jilly seemed invested in the game. Hayward looked up when I walked in. Maybe I was imagining things, as I did so often, but it seemed as though he was staring at my chest again. A smile came over his face. Not the good kind.

"It's Forrest's poker night," Regina said. Slowly, like a person in a dream, she rose from the sofa and drifted over to the table, where Prudence had set out the meal. "So it's just the four of us tonight."

I hoped I'd concealed my disappointment. Without Forrest around, things were a lot less fun. Standing over the table, she turned to me with that odd look of hers that never seemed focused on anything in particular.

"That new bike will come in handy for taking the children to tennis," she said.

Jilly, feeding the contents of her taco to her doll, made a face. "Our old babysitter drove us places," she said.

"It will be fun riding your bikes to the club." Maybe Regina was trying to invest her words with enthusiasm, but it wasn't working.

"You're lucky," Hayward said to me. "All you have to do is sit around waiting for our lessons to finish up. Our tennis teacher makes us run all over the place."

This was Hayward's view of life, it occurred to me. Getting away with doing as little as possible, unless it involved playing video games. Over dinner he had talked about becoming a rock star when he grew up, and there was an expensive-looking electric guitar leaned up against the wall of his bedroom, but I saw no evidence that he ever picked it up to play.

"Something looks different about you," he said to me.

"I probably got a lot of sun today," I told him. But I knew he'd noticed. It was the bra. The toilet paper stuffed inside. He was onto me.

After dinner I went back to my room. I said I needed to get my things organized, though the truth was I hardly had any things to organize.

I had just hung up my one blouse and a pair of too-short pants when I heard the knock. I opened the door. Regina stood there. She was holding a package wrapped in silver paper with one of those stick-on bows that appeared to have been salvaged from some other gift.

"I brought you something," she said, extending her long, thin arm, those spidery fingers placing the package in my hands. "To welcome you to Wonderland."

Inside was a notebook. The cover had been hand-tooled, with a pattern of birds and trees.

"It's a journal," she said. "Every girl your age should have one."

"I never kept a journal before," I told her.

"There's so much going on for you right now," Regina said. "One day you'll be glad you keep a record of what you experience. If I remember, you're interested in writing."

She wasn't wrong about that. The odd part was, I'd never told her. Now I ran my finger over the leather cover of the book, the thick, creamy pages inside—paper so expensive-looking I wondered whether anything I came up with would be important enough to write on it.

Regina seemed to know my thoughts. "Don't hold off using this just because you think you don't have that much to say," she said.

"I'm always thinking up stories," I told her. I wouldn't have thought I'd confide in Regina about this. It just came out. "But I don't usually write them down." I did not add that the ideas I had were way too secret and embarrassing, even for the pages of a journal.

"One thing about a journal," she said, "it's just for you. Nobody else needs to know what you write in it. You don't ever have to wonder if what you're putting in it would upset anybody, or shock them, or make them think you were stupid or strange. You get to say whatever you feel like writing down."

I fingered the leather cover of my gift. The idea of actually committing my secret thoughts to its pages was scary but also thrilling.

"I wish I'd kept a journal when I was your age," Regina said. "Sometimes, as you grow older, you can lose track of who you used to be. It gets harder, finding that person. Getting back there and rediscovering what used to matter to you. Your dreams. The people you cared about. Remembering the person you used to be."

A look came over her. But fleetingly.

"Of course you can leave it blank if you want," she said. Her voice returned to its customary flatness. She was already turning to go. "You can do anything you want." This was the second time that day that someone had told me this. The second time in my life.

After Regina left, I stood there, holding the gift of the leatherbound journal. This wasn't one of those diaries that gave you a page for every day of your life, with just enough room to record what you ate for breakfast and how annoying your parents were, or the initials of some boy you had a crush on. The pages of this journal contained no preprinted months or dates to limit the length of my entries. In a journal like this one, a person might write as many words as she felt like putting down. You only had to discover what they were.

That night, propped on the pillows of my small, cozy bed, I opened my journal to the first page. I sat there for a long time, trying to come up with something.

There was so little of interest to say about my life, and what there was to say seemed to concern everything that was missing, everything that was wrong. *I hate my clothes. I hate my stomach. I hate my parents. What if I never get my period?*

And blah blah blah.

I considered writing about the ride up to Maine from New Jersey with Forrest, the moment Forrest placed the "Live Free or Die" cap on my head, the glow of happiness I'd felt passing through my body when we pulled into the diner where we sampled the homemade pies.

"I shouldn't eat this," I'd told Forrest, when our waitress set the plate of lemon meringue in front of us, right after we'd polished off the pecan. "I'm trying to slim down."

"You're perfect the way you are," he told me. "Don't change one thing about yourself."

What I really wanted to say on the first page of my journal was that I wished I could stay in this place forever. I could be a whole different girl here. Have a whole different life. But even in these pages, those words felt too dangerous to commit to paper. Each thing you wished for presented a new possibility for disappointment, if you didn't get it. Every good thing you got brought with it the prospect of loss.

That was the perspective I'd been raised with, and it had kept me from pursuing large dreams, the same way it had for my parents. As boxed in as I'd been in our sad, dark apartment with the hum of the fan that never managed to cool things off and the dark cloud of my father and mother's unhappiness hanging over us like the smell of cigarettes and last night's dinner, in my imaginary life I knew no limits.

I held the pen over the page, considering. I began to write, and because, for me, the world had suddenly opened up, I let my thoughts take me wherever I wanted.

8

Hear Everything

The next morning I got up early again. Forrest was making the coffee. "Looks like mornings will be our time together," he said, pouring me a glass of orange juice, freshly squeezed. "We're the only two people in this house who know how great it is to catch the sunrise."

I knew this about Forrest: He was not the kind of person who felt a need for a lot of small talk. He got right to the important topics, but in a way that never felt as though he was fishing around for gossip.

"Listen," he said. "I know your mom and dad are going through some difficult things. I bet it's been hard on you. That was part of my thinking when we invited you up here this summer. To give you a break from all of that."

As was often the case, I didn't know what to say. I also knew that with Forrest I didn't have to say anything.

"To be honest, it's not like things are ever easy between Regina and me either," he said. "I know it's no secret. She's had . . . problems. I can be a real idiot sometimes.

"Certain things happened," he said. "Life isn't easy for Regina. The people who judge her don't know her story."

Neither did I. But as forthcoming as Forrest could be, particularly about himself, it was plain he wasn't saying more about that, and I had nothing to contribute.

"Regina and I have an unusual kind of relationship," he said. "It might seem more obvious that she needs me, but the truth is, I need her too, and not just because it's her money that pays the bills around here. We actually love each other."

This was Forrest for you. I'd never known anybody before who talked to me as if I was a person who mattered, not some random kid.

"I'm hoping we can show you a wonderful time here this summer," he told me. "But more than that, maybe, I'm hoping that this can be a time for you to discover that you're in charge of your own destiny. After a point it doesn't even matter so much who your parents are or what they do. You can find your own path, same as I did."

I spread a dollop of jam over my toast. At that moment it felt like too much to meet his eyes.

"You're a wonderful girl, Frances," he said. "You deserve to have an amazing life."

I was glad there was toast in my mouth; that was my excuse for not responding. Young as I was, it had seemed that for me the horizon had always sat low. How was I ever going to get myself beyond the confines of my parents' dark, quiet, anger-filled apartment, our dirty little neighborhood? In the books I checked out of the library, I could read about other kinds of lives people might live. I just never saw myself as having a life like that. More than anything, I wanted to believe that what Forrest said to me now was possible.

I had a blue desk. A yellow bicycle. A leatherbound journal in which to write whatever I wanted. A whole other family, almost. For ninety-two days, anyway—the number I'd get to be at Wonderland. I was keeping count.

That night I wrote in my journal again. I told the story of how, at dinner, Hayward had looked up from his hamburger and said to me, "I hate to tell you, Frances, but your epidermis is showing."

For a moment there, I'd felt my cheeks grow hot, wondering which body part I'd left exposed.

"I know what you were thinking!" A burst of laughter came out of him then, like Woody Woodpecker. "It's just your skin, stupid!"

After closing my journal, I lay stretched out in my little bed under the eaves, looking out the skylight to the stars. I heard a noise that sounded for a moment like some kind of animal.

But it was just snoring. It was Forrest in the spare bedroom. That was where he slept, alone. Directly below my bed. Where I could hear everything.

9

A Tight Ship, a Red Typewriter

Regina took a lot of pills. It was Forrest's job to keep track of them all. Every few hours he'd be there with a glass of water and another pill—more likely a few of them. Sometimes she protested. "What does it matter, anyway?" she'd sigh. "Whether I take this or I don't, I'll still feel bad."

Times like that, he'd just put his arm around her and stroke her hair. She basically ignored this—though sometimes, too, she treated him like a fly buzzing too close around her head. Flicked him away.

I'd never be like that if it were my hair he stroked.

He never stopped trying. If the two of them were out on the patio together, or in the living room, he'd rest a hand on her knee or adjust the shawl around her shoulders. He kept checking to see if she needed anything. Water, shade, her book, her knitting, something to put her feet up on. The way some new parents are with a baby, that was Forrest, overseeing Regina. If she was there in the room, his eyes looked over to where she reclined. If she was out of the room, he went to check on her.

"What do you think I'm going to do, jump out a window or something?" she snapped at him one time, when she'd left the table in the middle of dinner and drifted down to the high ledge above their wide stone patio.

Maybe he did think that.

But here was a surprising thing about Regina. As tuned-out and depressed as she appeared to be most of the time—as many pills as she appeared to ingest—she ran a tight ship at Wonderland. The children's schedules—tennis lessons, sailing lessons, golf clinic, swim class, play-dates—were set out on the breakfast table, with stars in blue marker for Hayward, pink for Jilly—along with a menu for Prudence, laying out what foods she should prepare for them every day of the week but Sunday, her day off. Alongside this, she had laid out instructions for Forrest—shopping lists, meetings of the country club board, the Library Foundation, her massage appointments and visits to her various doctors. He drove her to those. Every day's list featured reminders to drop off and pick up dry cleaning and prescriptions. Those, especially.

Regina didn't just scribble her lists down on a notepad, like other people. She typed them. She did this on a beautiful red Italian typewriter that sat on her desk in a corner of the kitchen. An identical typewriter sat in her bedroom, evidently. I hadn't laid eyes on that one yet. But from the first morning of my time at Wonderland, the typewritten instructions began to appear. Regina communicated with everyone in the family this way, including the children.

REMINDER TO FAMILY: Drink plenty of water. And *Hayward: Two Reese's Pieces, maximum.* Even for Jilly, who was only just learning to read, the word *FLOSS*.

The list Regina provided for me every day was the most detailed. Along with the time of every one of that day's commitments, she'd include suggestions for what clothes Jilly should wear and instructions concerning how many minutes Hayward was allowed to play video games—a number she calculated based on his behavior the day before. Along with this she offered running commentary.

Playdate for Jilly at the home of her friend Laura. Laura's a tattletale, and her mother babies her. Name: Annette.

Hayward hasn't been taking his daily shower lately. Bad smell!!

She included suggestions for me as well, even on Day One: *I notice your hair is looking a little greasy. I left out a brand of shampoo that may help you with this problem. Also, if you stop at the Caboose after tennis, remember french fries are high in calories. Look out for Coca-Cola. Check out the diet sodas.*

Every day I read through my list before stuffing it in my pocket. I consulted it throughout the day to make sure I didn't forget anything. The next morning, a new list would await me on the breakfast table. I never understood when Regina got around to writing them, but she must have done this late in the night, because the list was always waiting next to the box of Honey Nut Cheerios when I got up. (Calorie count for the Cheerios also provided.)

Regina used carbon paper when she typed her lists. One copy for herself. One for Prudence. One for Forrest. One for me. Every morning Forrest and I read our lists, side by side. It felt like one more thing we shared. Sometimes, reading them over together at the start of the day, I'd hear him chuckle.

"Be sure Jilly's vitamins are sugar-free," Forrest read out loud from his list. *"Also, Hayward needs new shoelaces."*

"My wife is an amazing woman," he said. "She thinks of everything, doesn't she?"

10

How to Get Thin

It was a few days into my time at Wonderland. The children were off at the club for a golf clinic. I was down by the water. I'd fallen asleep with my book. I woke up to find Forrest standing over me with his shirt off. Tanned and handsome as always, bare chested, in his shorts.

"You looked so peaceful and happy there I almost didn't want to wake you," he said. "But it's a perfect day for a ride on the lake."

I'd ridden on his boat before, on summer visits with my parents, but this was the first time it was just Forrest and me.

"What we have here is a classic," he explained, stroking the wheel of the Chris-Craft as we headed out onto the open water. "There's plenty of faster boats around, and just about every one of them is easier to maintain. This one here is wood, not fiberglass. But for my money, what we have here is the sweetest ride on the lake."

I had no basis for comparison, never having ridden in any other boat, but I agreed, naturally.

"The thing about a Chris-Craft is the lines," he told me. "The motor's inside the body, not stuck on top like every other boat. That's why it's so quiet. In a boat like this, you could come up alongside the shore, and the birds wouldn't even take off.

"Then there's the upholstery . . ."

The way he stroked the leather, it was almost as if he were touching a woman. I knew little about how a man touched a woman—I'd just seen a few movies and TV shows—but I'd cooked up scenarios in my head.

Forrest was right about the day. There was something about the way the sun hit the water that afternoon. A heron circled over our heads. A girl on a Sunfish drifted by. As much fun as it looked, I wouldn't have traded places with her.

"My kids are spoiled," Forrest told me. "This little baby's a prime example. You know what a Chris-Craft like this one goes for, if you can even find one for sale?"

I knew Forrest wasn't expecting me to guess. All I had to do was listen.

"But Hayward thinks a Chris-Craft's not fast enough. Just the other day he started in on me that we didn't have a Glastron GT-150."

I figured that must be a boat. An even more expensive one.

We were motoring past a stretch of houses along the eastern shore of the lake, most of which, like the Emersons', had been in the same family since the early 1900s. Each one situated to take full advantage of the sunset.

"When I was my son's age, I was picking cans and pop bottles out of the trash to redeem them for pennies," he said. "If I held back some of the money instead of giving it all to my father, there'd be a belt on my backside. Even if I gave him my whole take, I'd probably still get the belt. My dad never needed a reason for hitting me."

I heard no particular bitterness in his voice; he was just stating a fact. That was Forrest. He didn't dwell on difficult experiences. Forrest was a man who saw himself as lucky. Which he was, of course.

"Then you've got Hayward," he said, grinning. "My son's idea of hardship is not having a wide-screen TV in his room."

We stood side by side at the wheel of the Chris-Craft, looking out toward the island. It was a perfect day. Not just because of the weather.

"Want me to show you how to drive this boat?" he asked.

He stood behind me with his arms encircling my body then, so both of us had our hands on the wheel. He took his baseball cap from his head and placed it on mine, then placed his large hand—surprisingly rough—over the fingers of my right hand as he showed me how to work the throttle and guided me as we changed the gears.

For a moment, I could forget about my parents, at war with each other back home in New Jersey, and the way that tennis mother had looked at me at the tennis court, and Jilly, when I'd told her it was time to put her pajamas on, throwing her Teddy Ruxpin across the room, and Hayward's eyes, looking me over when I wore my training bra.

I put away thoughts of my own disappointing body and the unopened box of tampons in my drawer, the girls at the tennis court with their cute little pleated skirts and their brand-new sneakers, huddled over their Cokes at the snack bar, giggling together, while I zipped Jilly's racquet into its bag and then searched around the pool for the floatie she'd left there, crawling under the lounge chairs as they painted each other's nails. To the girls at the country club, I didn't exist.

"Next time I take you out on the boat," Forrest said, "we're getting you on water skis."

I'd heard this before. But I always believed him.

"Regina's still the queen around here," he said. "But I'm making you my princess."

If I could have stopped time forever right then, I would have done it. Very soon Forrest would be turning the boat around and heading back to the house, where Jilly would be wanting to play Candy Land with me, or set up another tea party for her American Girl dolls. But in that moment, I wouldn't have changed anything.

I might not have been an actual part of the Emerson family, but there I was, and the next day I'd be parking my wonderful yellow bicycle in front of the Lake Catherine Country Club and pushing open the big wooden doors into the beautiful sunny lobby, with its daily arrangement of fresh-cut roses. I might not have been an actual member of the club, but the woman at the desk nodded to me when we came in these days. The man who cleaned the pool smiled when I walked by, as did the men who rolled the clay on the courts. I knew where the dispenser was that held the ice water with the lemon slices floating in it, and the table with the basket holding thick cream-colored towels with the club insignia ("LCCC") woven into the plush. In my own way, I had become a regular.

A regular. I liked the sound of those words.

Sometimes in these moments the thought would come to me, clear as an acorn hitting my head or the sound a tennis ball makes when somebody hits it just right: *This is what happiness feels like.*

11

A Library Card

I had hoped—briefly—that I might get to know some of the kids at the club, but it became clear from my first day there that I was not about to be included in their circle of friends. The tennis girls seemed to come from a whole other planet from me—as far removed as the models in *Seventeen* magazine.

Never mind, I told myself. I knew the place I could always go to when things were difficult.

All my life, the library had been my place to escape. That first day, I'd pedaled past the beautiful old stone building with the sign over the lintel: **Lake Catherine Township Library**. I took it in as a welcome sight, the final confirmation of how perfectly everything was turning out that summer.

Sometime around Week Two, I parked my bike in front of that wonderful old stone building again and stepped inside.

"I'd like to get a library card," I told the librarian.

"Are you a resident?" she asked me.

"I'm here for the summer," I told her. "I work for the Emersons."

"In that case, there's no problem," she said, taking out a stiff white card and a pen. "They're some of our biggest supporters. We'll keep this on file for you."

I made my way into the stacks, breathing in the familiar library smell, and headed over to the section labeled "J through M" to choose a new selection from the Stephen King shelf. Not even a mile down the road, the tennis girls would be hitting balls out on that red clay court. But here was the place I always fit in.

I reached for a book, scanning the description on the inside flap. *Sex. Money. Murder.* All I needed. Some forms of adventure didn't require a membership fee. They took place in your own imagination.

Outside, I set my selection in my bike basket and made my way back to the club. It was time to pick up the children.

Once I saw how little interest the other kids at the club had in getting to know me, I started bringing a book along with me to read during lesson times. The story was so gripping, I wouldn't have minded if the children's lessons had gone on for hours while I was reading it.

Sitting in my usual spot on the hot tar next to the tennis court, bent over my book, I could hear the thunk of tennis balls hitting racquets, the voice of the pro calling out pointers.

"Follow through, Jessica."

"Eye on the ball, Walter."

"Samantha! Watch your grip."

From further off came the sound of children splashing in the pool and mothers calling out to them to stay in the shallow end. In my book, *The Stand*, the family of a security guard was frantically trying to get out of a town overtaken by a deadly virus. A butterfly landed on my thigh. I imagined that someday I'd write a book myself, for some girl like me to read.

Now came the voice of the tennis coach. "That was a perfect shot, Gabrielle," he called out. "I think you just got yourself some topspin."

As compelling as the story I'd been reading was, I had to look up. I had no idea what topspin was, or why the players sometimes used the word *love* when calling out their scores.

People spoke a whole other language in this place.

An unopened can of tennis balls sat on the bench next to me. I popped it open and took out a ball and rubbed it over my cheek, feeling the fuzz. Wilson Number Three. For no particular reason, I stuck it in my bookbag. I wanted that tennis ball, was all. Or what it signified.

12

"I Was a Test-Tube Baby"

Something was compelling me to break rules. Nothing really bad, like the kinds of trouble my father and Howie used to get into when they were my age. I just wanted to try out being a different kind of person. A year or so back, I'd slipped a tube of Revlon "Love That Pink" lipstick into my pocket. I didn't even like wearing lipstick. After I got home, I threw it in the trash. More recently, I'd told Hayward I met Madonna once, at Bloomingdale's in New York City, and she complimented me on my outfit. I'd never even been to Bloomingdale's, and only once, ever, went to New York City, for a class trip to visit the Statue of Liberty.

Now, as Hayward stood at the side of the court, zipping his racquet back into its case, something compelled me to offer up a story. I just felt like doing this. It wasn't even as if Hayward was someone I cared about impressing. I just wanted to see if he believed me, if I was a good enough storyteller. Like Stephen King—but in life, not a book.

"You probably don't know it, but I was a test-tube baby," I told Hayward. "My father had a tragic problem involving his reproductive organs that kept my parents from having me the normal way, so they went to this lab where they put the sperm and egg together in a petri dish."

My story about meeting Madonna hadn't made much of an impression on Hayward, but this one piqued his interest.

"That's why I don't have a belly button," I told him.

This was where I slid the waistband of my shorts down just far enough to reveal a strip of bare skin on my midriff. An inch lower down and I would have revealed my navel, but he bought it.

"I bet you could have got on Phil Donahue or something if you'd let someone know about it," he said.

"It was all hush-hush," I told him. "My parents signed a nondisclosure agreement."

I didn't know what that was exactly, but I'd heard the phrase.

"I guess that explains why you're so weird," Hayward said. But I knew I'd impressed him.

That night in my room, under the eaves, I took out the tennis ball I'd brought back with me from the court that afternoon. Lately I had taken to standing in front of the mirror in my room, in my training bra, stuffed with a couple of socks, imagining how I might look if I ever developed breasts.

I tossed the tennis ball into the air above my head. Just that. I didn't know anything about how to swing a racquet, even less about how to play the game. There was just something about holding that ball in my hand and launching it into the air and catching it without ever losing sight of the words on the fuzzy green surface: "Wilson 3." My goal was simple: to keep the ball from touching the floor. If it did, Forrest—in the bedroom below me—might have heard and wondered what I was doing up in my room. This was my secret. The first one, maybe.

13

AFTERNOONS WITH STEPHEN KING, AND HANKY-PANKY

Eighty-two days still remained. There was a rhythm to how we spent them, and far from feeling bored that this was so, I loved the consistency of it all, the way those happy summer days played out, steady as Forrest's crawl stroke as he made his way out into the lake every afternoon, steady as a tennis rally between a couple of players who knew what they were doing, as the children did not. Breakfast with Forrest—sometimes bagel, sometimes croissant—then tennis at the club ("Little Hitters" class for Jilly, "Racquet Maniacs" for Hayward), followed by a stop at the Caboose, then home.

After lunch, Hayward and Jilly went off to their sailing lessons. These took place at the yacht club, which was close enough to Wonderland that we could walk over, though sometimes Forrest dropped the children off in the boat. We could usually count on one of the other mothers to bring them home afterward.

This left my afternoons gloriously free, most days. I was still waiting for Forrest to take me out on the boat again for my waterskiing lesson, but meanwhile, there was plenty to occupy me. Down by the water, I might read or go swimming—take a nap, swim some more, work on my tan, toss my tennis ball, imagining I was out on the court myself, like the country club girls, racquet in hand. In the fantasy version, I played better than any of them.

Now and then Prudence might ask me to fold some laundry or carry out the trash or bring afternoon tea to Regina and clear away her cup afterward, but that was about as demanding as my job ever got. Prudence always set a cookie on the tray with the teapot, but Regina never touched it. That cookie was mine to savor with whatever book I'd checked out of the library most recently. Luckily, Stephen King had written enough books that I didn't have to worry about running out.

Every time I finished one—as I did every few days now—I'd hop on Buttercup and ride back over to the library. If it was a rainy day, I'd settle into a cozy chair there to read for a while. On sunny days, I took the long way home, stopping in the village to look in shop windows or get a Diet Coke. I could almost imagine this town was my actual home.

It was late in the afternoon, the sun low on the horizon. Regina was sipping her club soda. Forrest had fixed himself his gin and tonic. The two of them sat on the patio glider together, Forrest's hand resting on Regina's thin white shoulder. The strap on her sundress had slipped. He rearranged it for her. It slipped again. Their eyes met. I registered something, though I wasn't clear what.

"Why don't you take the children out to the Caboose for fried clams," Regina said to me.

"Count me out," Hayward said. "I'm sick of fried clams."

"You heard your mother," Forrest said to him. "It's still light enough the three of you can ride your bikes."

The children and I headed out the French doors toward the rack where we kept our bicycles. Jilly, holding her Molly doll, ran ahead.

"You know why they said that, right?" Hayward said to me.

I looked at him. I didn't, actually.

"Hanky-panky," he whispered, grinning. "Every now and then my mom lets him fool around with her. It doesn't happen very often," he told me. "Maybe they watched a sexy video or something last night. *Hubba-hubba.*"

Though it was early in the summer, I'd already learned the best way to deal with Hayward's remarks: Ignore them whenever possible. He wasn't finished, though.

"They sleep in different rooms," Hayward said. "But on special occasions she visits him. You'll probably hear them one of these nights."

He made an odd movement, like a man working a drill—up and down, up and down. He made a series of noises then. Grunting, panting, a small, high scream.

"Don't look so surprised," he said to me. "Don't you know about sex? It makes people go crazy."

Did I know about sex? I wanted to know. I thought about it every day—with horror and fascination, both at once. I wrote about it in my journal at night, as well as a person could who'd never actually experienced it. But as with nearly every other aspect in life, this one left me feeling, once again, like an outsider.

It was as if there were this great party going on to which everyone had been invited—even Regina, evidently. Everyone but me. I stood on the sidelines, wanting to catch a glimpse of what was happening and trying to make sense of things.

More and more over that last year, thoughts about sex kept popping up in my brain like the weirdest kind of public service announcement ever. *We interrupt this program with a special bulletin . . .* I'd catch sight of the pale, bland face of the weather person on TV, and the thought would come to me: When was the last time she had sex? And when she did, what happened, exactly? What was it people actually did when they had sex with each other? I knew the basics, but I longed to understand what it felt like—more so, what it meant, and why people cared about it so much.

I considered the sex question about almost everyone I encountered. It could be a woman at MacDougall's when I stopped in to pick up suntan lotion, or the school secretary, or the man who delivered our mail, the bank teller to whom I'd handed my passbook when I'd deposited my most recent stash of babysitting money. Nancy Reagan. Barbara Walters. My social studies teacher. A woman who'd shown up at our apartment wanting my dad to fix her toaster.

It started a year or so before this, but since I'd come to Wonderland, I seemed to be on fire. All of a sudden sex was everywhere. Everywhere I looked, I saw it. The possibility of sex, anyway. And its effects on people. Either because it was going on in their lives or, for some of them, because it wasn't. Until that night when Forrest and Regina sent us off to the Caboose, I had believed they were in the no-sex category, but Hayward's remarks had revealed a new layer to the mystery. Even Regina had sex. Not very often, maybe. But she did.

I figured I must be a freak. Was I the only person who thought about these things? What was happening to me?

Stop it, I told myself.

Only I never could.

And now came a realization that might have been comforting, only it wasn't. I was not the only person who thought about sex. So did Hayward Emerson, the biggest loser boy, ever, which probably made me the biggest loser girl.

14

I See You

Other than worrying I'd never need to open the box of Tampax in the bottom of my top drawer, life felt less stressful than I could ever remember. I felt no pang of homesickness for my parents or my life back home. I didn't miss the sound of the vodka bottle hitting the trash bin in the night, or my mother's silent death-ray looks when she found it there in the morning. In the days since I'd been at Wonderland, my parents hadn't called. This was good news.

When I woke up in my little bed under the skylight to the sound of Forrest down in the kitchen mixing the batter for pancakes, or the smell of French toast on the griddle, I couldn't believe how lucky I was just being in this place. Every night, after I did my sit-ups and practiced my pretend tennis serve in the mirror with the stolen Wilson Number Three ball, I said it all over again in my journal.

June was going by fast. Eighty-one days remained in my Wonderland summer. Eighty-one more days I got to spend in the company of Forrest Emerson.

"Earth to Frances," Forrest said. We had finished our breakfast. The two of us had gone over our typewritten instructions for the day from Regina. We were just sitting there—Forrest filling the day-of-the-week compartments of Regina's pillbox, me off in that other world I went to sometimes, the one in my head. It was an odd thing, but at random moments, I'd find myself thinking about tennis, picturing myself out on the court, with Forrest on the other side of the net.

I could hear the sound of Jilly's Teddy Ruxpin upstairs, reciting the line that emanated from his furry stomach if you pushed the button and the batteries hadn't given out yet: "Can you be my special friend?"

Forrest snapped the pillbox shut. Mission accomplished. Soon enough Regina would have more jobs for him. "Where are you?" Forrest said to me.

"I was thinking about something," I said. I didn't add, thinking about him.

Of the two of them, Regina and Forrest, the one who mattered to me was always Forrest—he, the one who saw me for the girl I was; he, the one who offered attention, affection, tenderness, and what felt to me like the first real love anyone had ever shown me. In my nighttime life, it was Forrest who occupied my brain.

But in the daylight hours, with the exception of those breakfasts Forrest and I shared, it was Regina who kept an eye out for me.

Forrest would promise a waterskiing lesson. Had done so a number of times, in fact. And no doubt he meant to make good on his promise. He just wasn't all that reliable.

Cool and detached as she invariably seemed, Regina was the one who made sure I put on sunscreen. It was Regina who asked me—in one of her notes—whether I'd had a tetanus shot and made an appointment for me to get one. *Last summer I found a nail sticking out at the dock,* she had typed, on one of her notes, early on. *We don't want you ending up with lockjaw.*

It was Regina, not Forrest, who had remembered my birthday every September for as long as I could remember—even the year my own parents forgot. Though the date fell just after Labor Day—the week following my family's annual visit to Maine and her own children's return to school in Boston—Regina never failed to put a package in the mail for me.

She sent the strangest, most random-seeming gifts, but they had a certain unexpected magic to them. One year my present was a hand-carved owl and a book of poems by Emily Dickinson. She sent an amaryllis bulb, a book about dolphins, a pair of fishnet stockings. I was ten years old, and my mother called the gift ridiculous and inappropriate, but I loved them. One time—I doubt I was older than six—an extremely heavy box arrived at our apartment, containing a block of clay and a card with just two words: *Make something.*

Last year, she'd sent a vinyl recording of a singer I'd never heard of, named Maria Callas. This, at an age when I and every girl I knew was listening to Madonna.

You seem like someone who would understand what makes Maria Callas so different from everyone else, Regina had written in the note that accompanied the record. I had no idea how she came to this conclusion. Those times we visited, Regina and I barely spoke.

And if you don't understand yet, you will, she'd written. *Once you get a little more life under your belt.*

It was Regina who, on one of my family's visits a few summers earlier, had rented a VCR tape of a French movie about a young boy growing up in Paris, who was misunderstood by his parents and then his teachers, accused of crimes he did not commit, and sent to juvenile detention. What other adult would show *The 400 Blows* to a nine-year-old, just barely old enough to read the subtitles?

"Frances will like this one," she'd said to the others, who decided they'd rather sit outside on the patio with their gin and tonics than watch with the two of us.

She was right, of course. I knew what it was like to be that boy in the movie.

Here was an odd thing about Regina and her gifts to me. As much time and thought as she appeared to give to considering what I might like and what it was I might want or need that I didn't have, she never seemed that interested in her own children.

One night when I was in the living room, reading my Stephen King book—Regina on the opposite couch with her knitting—Jilly came bouncing into the room with a medal around her neck. She'd won a prize at sailing camp that day. She wanted to show it to her mother.

The way Regina looked at her, it was almost as if she were watching through one-way glass. She took in the sight of her daughter, twirling her plastic medal, but said nothing. When Jilly landed in her lap, I saw her wince.

A person might have thought that Forrest would have appeared irritated or resentful, witnessing his wife's strange, distant, and downright cold behavior toward just about everyone around her. It wouldn't have seemed surprising if he'd grown distant himself. What amazed me, as a person accustomed to seeing married people exchanging hostile remarks, if they even spoke to each other, was how amiably he accepted everything Regina did, and more so, everything she didn't do—the hours she spent on the chaise lounge, the way she brushed their children aside, not to mention him, when he'd lean in to stroke her hair, as he did now. But Forrest held steady. He never seemed hurt by the bored look in Regina's eyes.

Jilly did. Jilly worshipped her father, of course. On this particular occasion, she deposited herself firmly in Forrest's lap, confident of the affection and enthusiasm she'd find there. He picked her up and spun her around, pulled up her Care Bears T-shirt, and pressed his mouth against her stomach, making fart sounds and tickling her.

"Da-ddy!" She always pretended she was annoyed, but I knew she loved it.

"Your daughter just had a root beer float," Regina said, sounding wearier than ever. "If you aren't careful, you'll make her throw up."

But Jilly was already asking him to do it again. "I'm worn out," Forrest said, feigning the kind of exhaustion Regina conveyed twenty-four seven. "Can't you see I'm an old man?"

Not even close.

I sat there watching as if this were a movie. Only I got to be in it, as an extra, anyway. Unlike Jilly, I kept my adoration for Forrest hidden. It was a secret little flame burning hot in my heart.

Then what do you know, he turned to me.

"Our Frances," he said, reaching my spot on the couch and shaking his head with a look of wonderment, as if he could hardly believe it that I was actually there. I felt the same thing, but more so. How was it possible that this god of a man shared my opinion?

"Our Frances!" he said again. "I don't know how we ever got along without you," he said. "You know you're part of the family now."

I tried not to show how thrilled I was, hearing the words. I looked down at my lap.

My cheeks burned. In that place I could not name, the one I'd begun touching in my bed at night, a warm feeling coursed through me.

I looked over at Regina then. Her face didn't look mad or jealous in the way girls' faces got when somebody got asked to the dance by a boy they hoped might ask them instead. The look on her face was just sad, that was all. The saddest look I'd ever seen on her maybe—like she was a dead person, back on earth just long enough to pay a quick visit to the living before heading back to wherever it was dead people went once their hearts stopped beating.

In my journal that night, I didn't write about Regina's coldness to Jilly, or Jilly's disappointment. I wrote down Forrest's words to me: *Part of the family.*

15

Picking Up After People

Forrest and I were down at the water, gathering up empty bottles of bubble solution and popped water balloons left by Jilly and her friends. I'd learned by now that children at Lake Catherine—not just Hayward and Jilly but their friends too—left a wake of candy wrappers and pop bottles and abandoned toys behind them when they got bored with playing. It never seemed to occur to them that there wouldn't be someone to pick up after them, and they were right.

Forrest was scraping up the last bits of Silly String on the lawn furniture when his friend Evan appeared, still wearing his bike shorts and helmet. Evan had a habit of stopping by around cocktail hour. This time he had a brochure with him.

"The club's sponsoring a triathlon," he told Forrest. "Raising money for some good cause or other. I can never keep them all straight. You should sign up."

"I don't know," Forrest told him. "I can handle the biking and running, but that two-mile swim across the lake might do me in."

"It's not till Labor Day, buddy," Evan said. "You've got the whole summer to train. Think what it'll do for your abs. You don't want to start getting a beer gut, do you?"

Forrest had no beer gut. No doubt he wanted to keep it that way.

"I wasn't bargaining on spending the summer in training," he told his friend.

"Look at it this way," Evan said. "It'll keep you from dying of boredom."

I was out on the dock—having moved on to picking up the children's towels, as I did every afternoon, along with the empty chip bags and juice boxes strewn near the water—while the two men discussed the triathlon plan. Forrest never treated me like an invisible person, but Evan appeared not to have noticed I was even there.

Now, hearing his suggestion that Forrest might find his life lacking in excitement, I registered a momentary stab. To me, it was enough just being in this amazing place, getting to spend time together. Those early mornings when Forrest and I got to talk over breakfast, and odd moments throughout the day when he'd ask about the book I was reading, or check my bike tires, or fix me his special Power Smoothie in the Vitamix, I never got the impression that he felt restless. I wanted to believe he was having as great a time as I was. Not simply with his family. *With me.*

"All that training, man. It's a great excuse for getting out of the house," Evan said.

"OK, sign me up," Forrest told him. "Just no training before seven thirty. Early morning's reserved for Frances and me."

"Frances?" his friend said.

He hadn't noticed me. But Forrest always did.

When I opened my journal that night, flipping to a new page, I wrote down what Forrest had said to his friend. *Early morning's reserved for Frances.* After I'd written down the words I read them over a few times. That single sentence looked lonely all by itself on the page, so I thought I'd write something more, even if it was just wishful thinking.

I think Forrest loves me.

16

A Little Dog. A Redhead.

It was never easy getting the children out the door to go to the club for their tennis lessons. It was the job of Prudence to clean up the kitchen after serving Hayward and Jilly's breakfast. This left me to pack up their things (tennis racquets, water bottles, insect repellent, sun visors, ziplock bags filled with Goldfish crackers, Fruit Roll-Ups, and M&M's) and get them out the door for our bike ride to the club.

You could pretty much count on Jilly to have misplaced one of her sneakers or complain that she didn't have the right socks. She needed hair ornaments to match that day's outfit, or she'd decide she didn't want to go to the club at all and have a tantrum because I told her it wasn't a good idea to bring her American Girl dolls to tennis with her on account of how, the last time she'd done this, she'd lost one of the shoes and I had to spend an hour looking for it.

Getting Hayward out the door presented a different set of challenges. From the moment he came downstairs in the morning, he'd be sitting in front of the television with his bowl of cereal beside him, eyes glazed over, playing a game—the sound of popping guns and miniature characters drowning out whatever anyone tried to say to him. Sometimes I'd have to speak to him three or four times before he answered.

"Tennis sucks," he said. "I don't see why I even have to go to these lessons."

"Your grandparents paid for them," Regina said. Words that carried little effect. *You have no idea how lucky you are,* I wanted to tell Hayward. *What I would give to take tennis lessons, to grow up with a father like yours.*

Once we got out the door, things generally got better. I let Jilly lead the way, followed by Hayward. I'd bring up the rear, calling out to the two of them to slow down if a car was coming.

I loved our bike rides to the club—the perfect green lawns and the smell of cut grass in the morning, the neat, well-tended gardens and the happy-looking neighbors, trim and tanned, who waved to us as we pedaled past while they walked their dogs. We made our tires wobble on purpose, pretending to be drunk, going no hands (just Hayward and me) on a particular flat stretch. One time Jilly had us all singing "Rainbow Connection" from *The Muppet Movie.* Even Hayward chimed in.

It was late June. Seventy-eight days left in my Wonderland summer. We were partway to the club—our bodies bent over the handlebars, standing up on the pedals of our bikes, pumping for all we were worth—when a small dog darted out in front of us. Hayward managed to avoid him, but Jilly wasn't as steady. Swerving, her bike tipped over. She landed hard on the gravel sidewalk, letting out a wail as she went down.

A redheaded woman appeared, coming from the same direction as the dog. She ran to the spot on the ground where Jilly lay, her arms stretched out, with a dribble of blood on her knee.

"Oh my god!" the redhead called out. "Is she alright?" From the sounds coming from Jilly, a person might have thought she was dying. I set down my bike to investigate.

The woman got down on the ground next to Jilly, patting her leg. I wasn't good at guessing grown-ups' ages, but she looked younger than most of the mothers at the country club. She had long rust-colored hair and was wearing a pair of short-shorts.

"He was just so confused!" the woman explained, speaking of her dog, evidently—one of those miniature breeds, small enough to fit in a pocketbook. Later I'd learn the name of the breed: a shih tzu.

"My husband and I just drove up today to spend the summer. Pumpkin spent five hours in his dog carrier. The minute I let him out he took off before I had time to stop him."

The woman patted Jilly on her leg some more. From the way she did this, I got the feeling she wasn't a mother, though she was playing the part, more or less. "You're going to be alright, honey," she said, before turning to me as the closest there was at the moment to an authority figure. "My husband and I are renting a house here for the summer. I guess you live nearby?"

Jilly had quieted down by this point, though she was still sniffling. When she stood up to take a step, she limped dramatically.

"Tell you what," the woman said. "We'll leave your bikes at our place, and I'll drive you home. My husband can bring the bikes back later."

When I told her where we lived, she looked excited. "Oh my god. Wonderland? You can't see much of that house from the road, but when we passed this morning and I saw the sign, I told my husband I'd give anything to see it up close," she said.

Sitting in the front seat of the woman's car, I realized she hadn't told us her name. When we pulled up in front of the house, she just stood there for a moment, staring at the wide front door and the marble dogs on either side. Jilly had been sniffling quietly. Hayward, in the back seat with Jilly, seemed to have taken an interest in the dog, Pumpkin, who'd jumped into the car for the ride and was now licking his face.

Then Forrest appeared. He was wearing his running gear, having embarked on his training regimen for the triathlon. Jilly ran to meet him, displaying no further sign of injury.

When he reached the redheaded woman's car, he reached out a hand. Smiling, as usual.

"Forrest," he said.

For a second she looked baffled. Maybe she thought he was referring to the trees around the property. More likely, she was taken by the man.

"That's my name." He laughed. "How about yours?"

"Brenda," she said. "I'm Brenda. Brenda's my name." She seemed to be having trouble speaking. This often happened to women when they met Forrest. Once she'd collected herself, she explained what happened. The dog. The bike accident. "Thank god your little girl wasn't too badly hurt," she said, waving an arm in the direction of Jilly without taking her eyes off Forrest.

"Some people might say it's too early for a drink," he told her. "But if you ask me, now is a fine time for a Bloody Mary."

Just lightly, he placed his hand on Brenda's back and led her up the granite steps into the house.

"Darling!" he called up the stairs, to where Regina was probably napping. "We've got company."

I didn't know it, but that was the beginning.

Over drinks on the patio, Jilly recounted for her parents the details of her collision with Pumpkin. Hayward informed them that, for his birthday, he wanted a shih tzu. Regina reminded him she was allergic to animal hair. Hayward asked why everyone else he knew except him got to have a dog. Then it was Forrest's turn.

"The good news is, if it wasn't for my daughter's unfortunate run-in with your little dog, we never would have gotten to know you, Brenda," he said, looking into her eyes.

"Close call," said Regina. I wasn't clear if she meant Jilly's accident, or the possibility that she and Forrest might have missed out on meeting Brenda.

She had to go, she explained, looking regretful. An old fraternity buddy of her husband's was passing through town, and they were having a cookout.

"We need to meet him too!" Forrest said. I figured this meant her husband, not the fraternity buddy, though with Forrest, you never knew. He was always open to making friends. "What do you say you two come by for cocktails next week?"

"What can we bring?" Brenda asked.

"An appetite!" Forrest told her.

After she left, Regina's face took on the look of a person who's just discovered an invasion of bedbugs in her home.

"Who are these people anyway?" Regina asked Forrest, over dinner on the patio. As was generally the case, she'd been off somewhere—on her bed probably—during much of Brenda's visit.

"They're up from Connecticut for the summer. His father owned a car dealership that closed down recently, so he's between jobs. His wife says he's 'assessing his next move,'" Forrest told her.

"Translation: unemployed," Regina said. "I bet they're staying in that dump across the lake, with the mold problem, that nobody wanted to rent."

"Brenda's pretty," Jilly offered.

Regina made a sound like humming. A look passed over her face.

When dinner was over, Forrest scooped up Jilly, and the two of them headed toward the stairs. "Let's see what old Ramona Quimby's gotten into tonight," he said. Hayward disappeared into the TV room. This left Regina and me by ourselves at the table.

"Forrest wants everyone to like him," Regina said. "That's his big thing. It probably has something to do with him growing up poor, not having a college education. Let's be honest: The man barely knows how to read or write. This is how he compensates."

"He can read," I said, feeling a wave of fierce loyalty. At this very moment, for instance, he was upstairs on the bed with Jilly, reading a Beverly Cleary book to her.

Regina just shook her head. "Forrest never feels like he really belongs here," she confided. "He's got to try harder than everyone else. You wouldn't think it to look at my husband, but he has a massive inferiority complex."

Partly I liked it when Regina talked to me this way—as if I were a girlfriend of hers, a confidante. But I felt guilty too, listening to Regina speak critically about Forrest. As if simply by listening, I was betraying him. Because there was no doubt in my mind on this: I was on Forrest's team, not Regina's.

17

A Made-Up Boyfriend

Down at the Clam Hut having lobster rolls, Jilly was telling a story about a boy in sailing class who picked his nose and ate what he found there. Regina said that wasn't dinner table talk.

"We're not at the dinner table," Hayward pointed out. "We're at the Clam Hut."

It was Forrest's poker night again, so he wasn't with us, which always made things less interesting. We sat there chewing for a while.

"Why don't you have a brother or sister?" Jilly asked me. Her question came from nowhere. Boredom, probably.

"I just don't," I said. "I'm an only child."

"You're lucky," she said. "My brother's a pain. I wish I had a sister instead. Or nobody."

"Don't talk with your mouth open," Regina said. "Finish your dinner."

"My mom's an only child too," Jilly said to me. "Sort of."

A wave of tension came over us at the table then. I looked at Regina. I knew not to respond. I figured Regina would say something, but it was Hayward who spoke.

"Shut up, Jilly," he told her. "You know what Mom told you." Then he turned to me. Somebody needed to change the topic of conversation—this was clear.

"When's your birthday anyway?" he asked me.

"September."

"Mine's October. I'll be thirteen." He reached for a fried clam. "So we're practically the same age."

Not exactly, I wanted to tell him. But he'd made his point. I could see why a boy barely two years younger than me would have a hard time taking me seriously as his babysitter. I had studied his face more closely by this point. Enough to confirm that he definitely had the beginnings of hair growing on his upper lip.

"My mom's two years older than my dad," he said.

"Woo-hoo," Jilly shrieked, pointing at the two of us. "You and Frances could be boyfriend and girlfriend." This may have been the first time she actually used my name.

I could feel my face turning hot. Hayward seemed to register no embarrassment. He just looked at me.

What I said next surprised nobody more than my own self. Maybe, like Hayward, I wanted to shift the conversation to a different topic from the one that appeared to have had such a strong effect on Regina, the part about her not always having been an only child. But also, the part about Hayward and me. The horrible image of the two of us as boyfriend and girlfriend.

"I'm going out with someone back home," I announced to them. I hoped I'd made my voice sound cool and mysterious.

Where did that come from? Speaking the lie had been surprisingly easy, like shoplifting a lipstick and—more so—further proof of my future career as a writer of fiction. Only my announcement unleashed a torrent of follow-up questions, requiring me to embellish my story.

"What's his name? Do you kiss him?" Jilly again.

"Open or closed mouth?" This was Hayward's contribution.

Regina came to my rescue. "Some things are private, children," she said. "Whatever Frances wants to do with her boyfriend is her own business. She's allowed to do what she wants."

"Even if they get naked together?" Hayward had that smile on his face again. "Even if they have *S-E-X*?"

This would have been the moment for Regina to reiterate her warning about what constituted dinner table conversation, but she said nothing. This was Regina for you. There were times when the simple act of responding to Jilly's or Hayward's remarks appeared to be more than she had the energy for.

"Finish your meal, children," she said, getting up from the table. She hadn't touched hers. It was just the three of us then—Jilly, Hayward, and me, chewing our food in silence. But it seemed to me that they looked at me differently on account of the boyfriend story. With a certain air of respect.

"What's his name anyway?" Jilly asked me. "Your boyfriend."

"Julio," I told her.

"He's Mexican?"

I gave her a look meant to convey mystery, inscrutability, enigma.

"Life is complicated, Jilly," I told her.

18

Made-Up Stories

Once I'd mentioned my nonexistent boyfriend to Regina and the children, the floodgates opened.

I could make up any story I wanted. That's when I started to do it.

As I had done every night since Regina first gave me the journal, I took it out of its place in my drawer, under the T-shirts and the tampon box and an old issue of *Town & Country* magazine that I found in the living room, and settled onto my bed under the eaves. I opened it to the page where I'd left off.

This time I didn't write about what we'd had for dinner, or the boring hour I'd spent with Jilly pretending the American Girl dolls were paying a visit to Disneyland, or the annoying way Hayward had of sticking Cheez Doodles in his nostrils. So what if Prudence made strawberry rhubarb pie? Why bother with any of that anymore? I thought about Forrest's words to me after I first got to Wonderland—that I deserved an amazing life—and it seemed more and more like a waste of my time, occupying my mind with any of this. If I hadn't started having my amazing life yet, at least I could pretend I had.

Propped up on the gingham bolsters in my perfect little bed, I considered, briefly, constructing a story about my pretend boyfriend back home. I could give him a name, a leather jacket, great hair. I could model him on Bruce Springsteen, maybe, or the boy at the Caboose who scooped our ice cream into our cones. He'd be older than me—sixteen or seventeen. Maybe he owned a car. He'd write poetry or play the guitar. (Really play a guitar. Not simply keep one propped up in his room, like Hayward.)

But the idea of a boyfriend back in New Jersey failed to capture my imagination. I couldn't summon a picture that moved or excited me.

When I tried to conjure a male figure playing the starring role in my fantasy, a different person came to mind—one who drove a Porsche and a Chris-Craft and performed magic tricks by the bonfire and played the ukulele. More importantly, he looked into my eyes in a way that let me know he understood me.

He slept in the bedroom directly below mine. Alone. He had called me one of his favorite people and told me I'd be beautiful someday.

Never mind the difference in our ages. We came from the same place. "I'd better break it to you now, Frances," he'd told me that day. "We're never letting you go home."

He'd put his arms around me on the boat. "You're perfect," he said.

That night I wrote only a single word in my journal, but I wrote it over and over—in block print letters and cursive, very tiny letters and large ones, underlined, with shading, and a row of exclamation points.

Forrest. Forrest. Forrest!!!!!!

I must have written his name a hundred times before I finally fell asleep.

I crossed the line so easily. After that night, I abandoned my previous practice of offering up tedious accounts of my daily activities in the pages of my journal. I'd moved from the realm of predictable G-rated autobiography to romance fiction. The odd thing was that what I wrote now, even though I made it up, felt more true than anything I'd written before. True to my feelings, anyway. If it wasn't true to how I lived or who I was at the time, it was true to who I wanted to become.

There's this way Forrest looks at me across the breakfast table when I'm having my cereal, I wrote. *It's like he's looking directly into my soul. I'm looking directly into his too!*

I found out yesterday how old Forrest is, I wrote. *Thirty-seven! That might sound old, but the older I get, the less it's going to matter. When he's forty-seven, I'll be twenty-four. When he's fifty-five, I'll be thirty-two. Thirty-two! By then I'll be old too!*

Something happened when he passed me the peas tonight, I wrote. *His hand brushed against mine. I felt something like an electric shock. He felt it too, I could tell. Nobody else noticed. But my eyes met his. It was as if everyone in the world disappeared but us.*

Back when I first arrived at Wonderland, Forrest had occupied the space of the uncle I never had, or even my dream dad. Forrest was the husband I wished my mother had married. Then came the guilty part, but also the source of my secret thrill. The leap was easier than I might have expected, from one form of fantasy to another, from the longing for a father to the longing for a lover—possibly because I knew so little of what it meant to have a lover, or be one. All I knew was my longing for love.

I was still doing my sit-ups, tossing my tennis ball in the air in front of my mirror, and making regular stops to the library on my yellow bike, working my way through the shelf of Stephen King novels, but what consumed me more and more, as the days passed, had less to do with reading and more to do with writing. I started looking forward to the end of the day, when I got to climb into bed and make up that night's journal entry. Now that I no longer felt constrained by sticking to the ordinary details of my real life, every night's exercise brought a new level of excitement.

Everything was different then. Everything stayed the same.

Every day I still checked my underpants for a sign of blood. *Nothing.*

Nights alone in my little room under the eaves, with my shirt off, I studied my reflection in the mirror. A few strands of hair had sprouted in my armpits, and in that other place whose name I could not speak, where I touched myself under the covers on a nightly basis now.

Something was happening inside my body. But no blood came.

Every night I thought about the man who was probably downstairs in the family room at that very moment, having a beer and watching the Red Sox, or giving Regina her final doses of pills for the night. If it was late, he might even be asleep, in the bed one flight down, in the room directly below mine. Lying awake himself, like me.

Now came my nighttime life—the secret world I entered, alone in my bed at Wonderland. I imagined Forrest Emerson's scratchy beard rubbing against my skin, his strong back, his arms encircling my body as he did when he picked me up that first day, and that other time, out on the boat.

Sight for sore eyes! he'd said. *You're just my kind of girl.*

I unbuttoned my pajama top and climbed into bed. I opened my journal. I began to write: *As we were clearing up the dishes in the kitchen after dinner, he leaned over and whispered in my ear, so nobody else could hear him. "I wish I could take you out on the lake tonight," he told me. "Just the two of us in the moonlight. I think about you all the time."*

This was Pretend Forrest talking. Now came Pretend Frances's response: *"I'd love that too," I said. "I never stop thinking about you."*

"I want to wrap my arms around you and never let go," he said.

Leaning up against the headboard of my little single bed under the eaves, I gripped the open covers of my leatherbound journal and scribbled hard.

He pressed his mouth against mine, I wrote. *I'm glad I don't wear braces, like some of the girls down at the club. I could feel his tongue. It was like we were one person.*

For over a year now, my mind had been occupied with thoughts about bodies—mine, and those of other people around me, and what people did with each other in their bedrooms, or wherever else sex took place—as much as I could imagine any of this with my own extremely limited understanding of what that might be.

I didn't just think about it anymore. I wrote it down. I was on the yellow bike, no hands, racing down the steep hill all the way from town. No brakes.

After that, there were no more journal entries about the Emersons and me playing Trivial Pursuit by the firepit, Forrest making up funny songs and pulling quarters out of Hayward's and Jilly's ears. If I wrote about Forrest roasting s'mores now—and I did—the focus of my story had nothing to do with heartwarming family times. What mattered to me about that event was how Forrest had picked out just the right stick for me to roast my marshmallow on. Most significant of all was what Forrest had done afterward, the tender way he'd wiped chocolate sauce from the melted Hershey's bar off my cheek.

In my real life, that part actually happened. In the version I created for my journal, he hadn't just wiped the chocolate sauce from my face. He'd licked it.

Of course I'd fallen in love with Forrest Emerson. Who wouldn't?

19

Gin and Tonics

I invited that nice woman who brought the kids home to stop by for drinks tomorrow with her husband," Forrest told us. We were all out on the boat, taking in the sunset. Even Regina had come, which was unusual.

"You could have checked with me first," she said.

He had his hands on the steering wheel of the Chris-Craft. But he took one off just long enough to pat her leg. "You're right, darling," he said. "Sometimes I'm an idiot. I just thought it would be fun to make new friends."

No comment from Regina.

The Barnetts showed up a little after five o'clock the next afternoon. Forrest had the gin and tonics ready. G&T's, he called them. Before that summer, the only alcoholic drink I knew was vodka. That and beer. Though in the weeks I'd spent at Wonderland, I'd learned about others.

Brenda Barnett had the kind of hair you might expect to see in a shampoo commercial. The day I met her, I thought she was beautiful, though on closer examination, a lot of this had to do with makeup. Her skin was unusually white, and she wore a great deal of foundation. Regina's skin was not so much white as pale, almost gray.

"Sunscreen is my religion," Brenda told Regina, not that Regina had said anything about her complexion.

"Good for you," Regina said. I knew how much she'd been dreading this event.

"I love your dress," Brenda added. This was the moment I knew not to trust a word Brenda Barnett ever spoke from that day forward. She couldn't possibly have meant what she just said. Regina's dress was awful, not to mention unflattering—a sort of floaty tent dress you'd think a person would choose because they were fat, though in Regina's case the opposite applied. Maybe she hoped it would make her look less scrawny, but it didn't. This as opposed to Brenda's dress, which wouldn't have seemed all that distinctive on anybody else, but which allowed her to accentuate more of her breasts than most of the mothers I'd observed at the club did. All of them, in fact. Then again, I'd been right about this part: Brenda wasn't a mother.

The couples made their way into the living room, facing the French doors that opened onto the lake. The children were installed in the den, watching a video, as usual. I headed to the kitchen to retrieve the platter of cheese and crackers Prudence had prepared, while Forrest poured the drinks.

The four of them gathered on the patio. I floated between worlds: the den, where the children were glued to their video and calling for refills on the chips, and outside, taking in the late afternoon sun over the lake with the adults—Brenda looking ridiculous in a New Jersey Devils cap she'd borrowed from Forrest to protect her skin. I could tell she thought she looked adorable in it.

Passing the tray of appetizers, I mostly just listened, my eyes returning to Forrest more than any of the others—his calf muscles, the hair on his chest just barely showing under his shirt, unbuttoned partway. At one point Hayward passed by the French doors on his way to get another soda. As he walked by me, he whispered, "Va-va-voom," under his breath. I ignored him.

Brenda offered the opinion that the cheese—cheddar from the local market, nothing special—was amazing. "I try not to eat dairy," she said. "But sometimes I can't resist."

"It doesn't look like you've got a problem," Forrest told her. Eyes on her cleavage.

An odd little smile flashed across Regina's face. Not one to smile often, she did this now less with an expression of pleasure than with wry amusement. She looked like a person who's been on this train before and knows where it's heading.

Forrest's eyes remained fixed on Brenda. This was a different gaze from the one with which he looked at Regina as she instructed him on the correct method for barbecuing salmon or the one with which he looked at me when he asked me about school or friends or the music I listened to or my views on the existence of God. The way he looked at Brenda was more like how a dog gets when you take a steak out of the refrigerator and set it next to the grill.

Kyle Barnett seemed oblivious. He was studying the Red Sox game through the window, soundless on the big-screen TV. But Regina hadn't missed a thing.

"I hate to be rude, but I'm not feeling so well. I need to go lie down," she said. "Don't let me break up the party." She rose slowly from her chair and headed toward the stairs.

The Red Sox must have scored a run just then. From where he sat, Kyle Barnett let out a celebratory yelp.

"I'll help you clear away the dishes," Brenda told Forrest. Under normal circumstances, with Prudence off, this would have been my job, but the two of them disappeared into the kitchen. In the TV room, I heard the children arguing about who got to choose the next show. I figured I'd better check on them.

The voices of Forrest and Brenda were still coming from the kitchen. I couldn't make out what Forrest was saying, but whatever it was, an annoying machine gun sound followed from Brenda. Her version of laughter.

Then silence, and all I heard was the sound of the ball game. A few minutes later, the Barnetts were gathering their things—Brenda's summer wrap, a bottle of whiskey Kyle had brought over and seemed to feel entitled to bring home with him. (Even I understood this wasn't how it worked at Lake Catherine.)

I went to the kitchen to finish loading the dishwasher. I could make out Brenda's voice as she stood in the doorway, gushing over something else. (The doormat maybe. Or the light fixture? The crackers?) "We have to do this again sometime," she said. "Tell Regina I hope she feels better soon." Then they were gone.

There seemed to be nothing so unusual in any of it. Except for the look I'd seen on Forrest's face. As little as I understood about life at that point, it struck me that Regina may have been well acquainted with that one.

20

The Locked Door

It came to me, as I made my way down to breakfast, that there were lots of secrets in this house. Every day when I came down the stairs, I passed the padlocked door at the end of the hall and the forbidden room behind it. I knew that this was not a topic to bring up.

I kept thinking about the look on Prudence's face when I'd asked her about the room and she'd told me—with unprecedented sharpness—that I should leave that one alone, the same warning Hayward had delivered that first night I'd arrived, when I reached for the doorknob on the mystery room.

There were all those pills, and the care with which Forrest oversaw their use. The look on Regina's face when, during the Barnetts' visit, Forrest had brought up a time Regina used to play doubles tennis down at the club. The look on Forrest's face after he said this. This was a forbidden topic evidently. One of many.

I had my own secrets too, of course—all the things I wrote down in my journal that never exactly happened. I just wished they had. My secret feelings for Forrest, which went beyond the affection a girl feels for an old family friend. And the unopened box of tampons lying in my drawer. What would happen to me if I never became a woman? What would happen to me if I did?

Then there was Forrest's story, and in some ways, this one felt the most mysterious of them all. The man I had known and loved for as long as I'd been alive, the one with whom I'd always been able to talk about almost anything, had seemed to me like the most loving husband a woman could ask for, devoted to his family, and in particular, to his wife. Then I'd seen what happened to him when Brenda Barnett walked in the house—the way he'd looked at her on the patio, the way his eyes had followed her out the door. I'd seen the way Forrest charmed women at the country club, but this was different. That had felt like a game, a dance. What I'd witnessed, watching Forrest's behavior when he was with Brenda, felt totally different. As if an unprotected electrical wire dangled down from the ceiling, giving off sparks.

I was up in my room at Wonderland now—eyes fixed on the milkmaid wallpaper, my bluebird rug, my small blue desk. My capacity for constructing stories had been unleashed, and I let myself go to another place. If I couldn't uncover the secrets in this house, I could make up stories whose resolutions I'd invent.

I pictured myself grown up. Eighteen at least. Possibly twenty. Beautiful at last—slim, but not scrawny like Regina. It would be summertime. No longer a mother's helper, I was back at Wonderland.

In the story I constructed, Jilly and Hayward were away someplace—boarding school probably, or (this being summer) camp. Prudence was absent. No need for her now.

It was just Forrest and me alone together. Just the two of us on the boat, motoring off toward the sunset, pulling up to the island he'd pointed out to me—the one owned by Regina's family—only this time, we'd dock the boat and step off onto the land, lay a blanket down for the two of us.

I had a new picture to add to the story I dreamed up now. I imagined the two of us playing tennis. Forrest, tanned and golden. Me in a white tennis outfit, returning every shot he hit. And after our game (unclear who won), the two of us would share some kind of fancy drink together at the clubhouse. Paper umbrellas in the glass. His arm over my shoulders.

You were amazing out there, he'd tell me.

I never knew it could be like this, I'd tell him. (Like what? I didn't know, actually. As much interest as I possessed in what happened between women and men, when they fell in love with each other, or simply got into bed, I understood just about nothing of what it was they actually did about that.)

Now Forrest is unbuttoning my shirt, I wrote.

I could see him doing this. He would undo the buttons one at a time, slowly and reverently, looking into my eyes as he did so.

He takes his time.

Rewind. I liked the scene better another way.

He rips off my shirt. He can't keep his hands off me.

"Do you have any idea how long I've been waiting for this moment?" *he asks me.*

"Me too."

"We shouldn't."

"We have to."

"I can't help it."

"I know."

He gasps for breath. I reach for the zipper on his jeans.

Now came the place where I set down my pen.

Writing my journal entries, as they had evolved to become, proved surprisingly easy, with one exception. The problem was that even in my fantasy world, there remained a single image I could not summon. I knew what the face of my fantasy lover looked like. It belonged to Forrest Emerson. I knew his arms and his chest, his strong calves, his rough hands, which were so gentle when they touched me. But one part of him caused me to draw a blank.

I didn't know how to describe a man's naked genitals because I'd never seen any. I could write about Pretend Forrest unbuttoning the shirt of Pretend Frances. But when I got to the part where he pulled down his zipper and stepped out of his shorts, I had no pictures for what came next. In the little movie theater I had constructed in my brain, this was where the screen went dark. All I knew was the deepest form of longing to be touched.

I knew about feelings. Not bodies.

Say the word, I told myself. *Write the word down.*

The story always stopped there.

21

It Makes You Want to Get Naked

D o you think Brenda Barnett would still look good without makeup?" Regina asked me. It was a couple of days after the Barnetts' visit—Forrest was off training for the triathlon. Her question caught me off guard.

"I don't know," I told her. "I didn't pay that much attention." Regina had brought down her nail kit. On her list for me this morning, she'd typed, *Get a pedicure!* Now she was giving me one. She had suggested I might benefit from tweezing my eyebrows too.

"That woman's got the kind of face that won't age well," Regina said, jabbing a metal stick under my nail bed while I kept an eye on Jilly and her friend Emma, playing in the water. Hayward lay on a towel with a comic book.

"If you ask me, without eyeliner and blush and lipstick, nobody would look at her twice," Regina continued. She was not finished with the topic of Brenda Barnett, evidently. "Great hair, of course. I'll grant Brenda that much."

"She probably uses some really expensive shampoo," I offered.

Regina said nothing more for several minutes. She was focused on my toenails. But I got the feeling she had more to say on the topic of Brenda Barnett.

"I can't really blame Forrest for taking an interest in her," Regina went on. "My husband's a man with a significant appetite. I know I can't fulfill all his needs." She dabbed the color on my big toenail and drew the brush slowly over the surface like a professional.

I thought she'd leave it there, but she didn't. "I'm referring to sex," she said.

I didn't look up. She was on to my third toenail now. With one whole foot still to go. At the rate we were going, I'd hear Forrest and Regina's whole story before we were finished with my pedicure.

"You're too young to understand, but a man has his needs," Regina said. "Women do too, of course, only I'm just so tired all the time.

"You wouldn't know it to look at me now, but in our early days we were all over each other like a couple of puppies," she told me. "Sometimes we made love three times in a day. In all kinds of places too. The boat, of course. The gazebo. One time Prudence walked in on the two of us when we were having sex on the kitchen floor. I was setting things up to make pancakes and he came up from behind and started kissing me and rubbing my back. I left the mixer on. Batter was flying all over the place."

I tried not to show my surprise, but the scene she described was hard to imagine.

I said, "Wow." All I could think of.

"Prudence was shocked, but we didn't care. We were just so in love. But not just that. We couldn't keep our hands off each other."

This was a feeling I didn't know about. When I thought about sex, I—not yet fifteen years old—thought about someone paying attention to me. When I thought about actual touching, I didn't get further than imagining a man's arms around me—one man's in particular, his hands stroking my skin. I pictured him looking at me. That was as far as I could go.

"You know the island out there where Forrest likes to take the boat?" she asked me. "My parents own it. There's this place we used to go to that nobody knows about. You've got to hike in a ways from where you dock your boat, but once you're there, it's like you're in the Garden of Eden. In all the years I've been coming here—long before I met Forrest, even—I never ran into anybody there. It was our secret spot. Forrest's and mine."

A look came over her. For a moment, I could understand what my father meant when he said Regina had been beautiful once.

"There's all this moss growing there. It makes you want to take off your shoes to feel it." She seemed to have forgotten about the nail polish, my toes.

"It makes you want to get naked," she said. "That's what we always did. Before the kids."

I looked out to the water—Jilly, calling out "Marco" in that high, screechy voice of hers. "Polo!" her friend answering back. Of the two of us—Regina and me—I knew I was the one who'd better keep an eye on the children. They were good swimmers, but I understood that if anything happened to one of them, it would be up to me to save them. Regina was off in her own world a lot of the time.

"I think Jilly might be swimming too far out," I told her. "Maybe we should call the girls in."

"Oh god," Regina said. "I'm such a hopeless mother. It's a wonder my children have survived me this long."

"You do other things," I told her. "You're the one who makes all the lists for us."

"Oh, those lists," she sighed. "I could spend my whole night typing up lists for everyone, but what does it matter, really? Most of the things you really need a person to do for you can't be put on a list. Mostly they're things you have to do for yourself anyway. Or leave undone.

"The really important things," she said to me, "are the ones you can't put on the list. Like 'find excitement in life again.' Or 'be happy.'"

The way she sighed then, it was as if someone had let all the air out of her. More air than was contained in her lungs. Air enough to fill Jilly's swan float, possibly. So much air leaked out of her, her whole body seemed almost to deflate as it happened. It was a sigh that went on longer than any sigh I'd ever heard.

Regina turned to look at me, her nail polish brush suspended in midair. "Pills can only do so much," she said.

I didn't know how to respond, so I said nothing.

"When you think of it," she said, "you could wonder how Forrest puts up with me. Why he doesn't just pack up and go. Only there's the children, of course. And this place." She waved her nail brush in front of all we beheld, like an artist.

"Forrest could never think of leaving Wonderland," she said. "It's as simple as that. And he will never leave me. Wonderland and the children and me. We're a package deal."

22

THINKING OF YOU TONIGHT

That night up in my room, when I opened my journal, I wrote about Brenda and Forrest.

I did something new in what I wrote there that night. The crossing of another line. This proved surprisingly exciting.

As I wrote, I let myself pretend I was Brenda Barnett. I'd been the one with the cleavage bursting out of my dress that night. I'd been the one in the kitchen with Forrest, clearing away the dishes.

As I was rinsing the dishes, he came up from behind me, I wrote. *He pressed his body against mine. I could feel him, pressing hard against me.*

What would that feel like? I didn't know exactly. All I had to go on were boys in my class, times I'd noticed something appeared to be going on with their penis—and how, when it did, they'd grab a notebook or their sweatshirt and hold it over the crotch of their jeans. As difficult and embarrassing as it was being a girl, at least the things that happened to girls—the sexual things—took place under cover. Nobody could see. Where for a boy there was no concealing it.

Take Hayward, for example. As annoying as he was, I could almost feel sorry for him, with his voice in the middle of changing, never knowing when he opened his mouth what sound might come out.

But that wasn't the worst of it. The picture came to me of him on a recent afternoon at the club when a girl named Jennifer dove off the high board and her top slipped. I had looked at Hayward then to see if he'd noticed, and he had, evidently. It was as if a small animal woke up in his swim trunks.

Was he embarrassed, or proud?

I turned back to the journal page I was writing on. Back to the scene in the kitchen. With myself in the role of Brenda Barnett.

I was trying to wash a glass, I wrote. *There were lipstick marks on the rim. He took my hand, which was holding the sponge, and moved it away from the sink. It was as if there were no muscles in my arm. I let him move my hand like it was a part of his body, not mine. Like he owned it.*

He turned off the water and set the glass on the counter. Then he guided my hand to his . . .

My pen stopped moving. Writing the word, even in my journal, felt scary.

He pressed his mouth against mine. I felt his tongue going deep. And further down, something else, pressing against my body.

His finger made its way down my neck and my chest. Then further down.

"Don't ever change," he told me. "I love you just the way you are."

"I'll be thinking of you tonight in my bed," I told him.

That part was true.

Did I actually believe Forrest and I would become lovers that summer?

I was young, but I wasn't crazy. If the man who was my father's oldest and best friend ever actually did any of the things I dreamed up in the scenes I played out in my brain and wrote down in my journal, I wouldn't know what to do. If he kissed me, I doubt I could kiss him back.

Part of the appeal of Forrest Emerson, to my almost-fifteen-year-old self, rested with the knowledge that mine was an unattainable fantasy.

Forrest could take up residence in my brain—and he had—without any risk of embarrassment or failure. Forrest Emerson, as I brought him to life in the pages of my beautiful leatherbound journal that summer, was like a character I dreamed up in the hope that he'd rescue me from my profound loneliness. Constructing romantic scenes between the two of us—Forrest and me—felt dangerous and safe at the same time. So long as the stories just happened on the page—like the stories I read in my Stephen King novels—nobody could ever get hurt.

23

Breakfast, Solo

The next morning I came downstairs for my typical breakfast with Forrest.

For the first time since I'd been at Wonderland, he wasn't there. Regina's typewritten instructions were waiting for me as expected, indicating that despite being under the weather earlier, she'd still gotten up in the night as usual. This morning's note included a reminder about a birthday party Jilly and Hayward had been invited to. *Select a present from the Birthday Present Cupboard,* she'd written. (Who else had a special cupboard designated for birthday presents?) *Price range: $10–15.*

There was a second note on the counter for me. This one was in Forrest's handwriting.

Went for a Bik Ride. I dee frosted a bagle for u.

I was accustomed to his terrible spelling, but the disappointment I felt in reading his words caught me off guard.

One nice thing: A small bunch of flowers lay on the napkin at my place—marigolds from the pot by the door. Nobody had ever given me flowers before.

When Forrest finally came home after his training session that after-noon, he looked different. Knowing the look of him as well as I did and the way he acted—and maintaining the consuming interest I had in every aspect of his life—I tried to figure out what it was that had changed.

The only comparison that came to mind was to my father during the one period in which he'd told us he'd stopped drinking. A couple of weeks after that, he had entered our apartment through the back stairs—the place we set the garbage—and set a box there that he cov-ered up with an old comforter. You didn't have to move the comforter to know there was a case of vodka underneath. You didn't even need to smell it on his breath. He had this look on his face. You knew he'd gone off the wagon.

That was Forrest when he came back from what he told us was his five-hour bike ride.

He asked me if I'd slept well the night before—the kind of question people ask when they just feel a need to ask you a question. He wanted to know if I'd found the bagel he'd left out for me.

"The Van Burens are throwing a party this weekend, if I'm not mistaken," he said. "Should be a blast."

Parties at the club were never a blast. Forrest knew this. Nothing he was saying sounded like his real self.

"Regina did my toenails," I told him. I pointed to my foot, still in sandals. It turned out she'd been right. The opalescent pearl she'd picked out had been a good choice.

"That's great," he said. But he didn't look down.

The next morning he was gone again when I got up. Another note was waiting for me. Briefer this time.

Gon 4 bike ride. Help self to serial. (His spelling.)

The surprise was seeing Regina at the counter, up even before I was this time—Regina, who seldom got out of bed before ten, and sometimes not until noon. She was wearing her bathrobe, her hair a tangle. She looked as though she hadn't slept. For once she had not typed up any lists for us.

"So it's started," she said.

24

Like a Virgin

Forrest and Regina had taken the kids to see a movie in Bangor, with a stop to pick up an Uncle Sam costume for Forrest. Prudence had the day off. I was alone at Wonderland. Other than running a load of laundry, I had nothing to do.

I fixed myself a peanut butter sandwich. (Peanut butter—not on my approved foods list. I told myself I'd make it up by not eating dinner.)

In the laundry room, I heard the sound of the dryer winding down with the load of laundry I'd put in that morning. There would be clothes to fold and put away.

I put on a Madonna CD. Not the music of choice at the Emersons', but I could play whatever music I wanted now. As loud as I wanted. The song I wanted to hear: "Like a Virgin."

I started in on the laundry, dancing. Hayward's clothes first. He favored oversized T-shirts, no doubt to conceal the pudginess of his body, and boxer shorts. It felt odd, folding the underwear of a boy so close to my own age. Even when it was freshly washed, I didn't like touching his underwear.

Jilly's clothes were less problematic. She favored pink and mauve, and shirts with glitter on them—Care Bears, Barbie, Teddy Ruxpin, Wonder Woman, *The Little Mermaid*—though Regina said those weren't appropriate for the club. She had tiny shorts in every shade of pastel. Ruffled socks. Day-of-the-week panties. Someone—it must have been Jilly herself; Prudence would know better—had tossed a few of her American Girl doll outfits in the laundry with her own clothes. I lifted a tiny red sweater from the pile, real wool, belonging to her Molly doll, shrunk to half its original size.

Jilly would cry when she saw it. But only briefly. They'd buy her another one.

The laundry I studied most closely belonged to Regina. She—or possibly Prudence—had placed her panties and a couple of bras in a special bag, meant to protect the delicate fabric. The panties were silk, bikini cut, each with a rosebud on the front. The bras—tiny cups, see-through lace—featured matching rosebuds.

After I finished folding, I brought each person's stack of clean and folded laundry to their room. I left Regina's for last. In the weeks since I'd first arrived at Wonderland, this would be the first time I'd ever actually entered her room. I held one of the bras up to my body, allowing myself to pretend I was Regina. This proved more than my imagination could accomplish. Even though I had no breasts, Regina's bra was too small to go around my body and fasten.

I set the bra back in the pile.

All I had to do was set her things on the foot of her bed as I'd done with the others.

But nobody was home.

I opened the top drawer of her dresser.

If this had been one of the stories I cooked up for my journal, now would be the moment I'd make some shocking discovery: Letters from a lover. A pair of handcuffs. A whip. I'd heard about this kind of thing from my friend Martha at school, whose father had a collection of X-rated videos. One time, when her parents were out of town and the older brother who was supposed to be watching her was off someplace with his girlfriend, we'd gotten to watch one, but only for about a min-ute because they came home.

All Regina's drawers contained were more pairs of panties. All pretty much the same, just slightly different shades of silk. Light beige, white, light pink. Same with the bras.

I opened the closet. I was familiar with much of Regina's wardrobe, but one dress called out to me. I'd never seen her in this one.

The dress was silk, long and slim, a shade of silver like a sardine. Judging from the size, she must have bought it a long time ago, when she wasn't quite as skinny. I'd fit into this one.

I slipped it off the hanger and pulled my T-shirt over my head, stepped out of my shorts and underpants. (Mine were the old-fashioned kind. Cotton.)

I hadn't put my training bra on that day, so all I had on was my undershirt. I took this off too.

The fabric of the dress felt like a cloud. I shimmied into it and fastened the zipper. I stood in front of the mirror.

Next to the bureau was one of those brushes people use to remove lint from their clothes—for the type of people who care about lint on their clothes. I picked it up and held it to my face as if it were a microphone. I looked in the mirror.

The CD was still on. Madonna was singing a different song now. "Material Girl." I wasn't singing along with Madonna so much as I was pretending to be her.

Or maybe I was just pretending to be the kind of girl who would dance in a silver sardine dress with no underwear on, belting out a song to a few thousand fans. But it was enough being alone in a house on the shore of a lake in Maine, just singing to myself at the top of my lungs.

25

How to Talk like a Doll

The four of us were playing badminton out on the lawn—Jilly and Forrest on one side of the net, Hayward and I on the other. Regina was off on the sidelines with her knitting, half-watching from her spot on the recliner. I'd been feeling relieved that, after that one uncomfortable time when she'd confided in me over her feelings about Forrest's sexual needs, Regina had made no further mention of the topic. In the days since the Barnetts' visit, Brenda's name had not been spoken again. If anything, Forrest seemed more attentive to Regina than usual. That was saying a lot. But he had been gone a lot more than usual too. Training for the triathlon took a lot of time, he explained.

Suddenly he put down his badminton racquet and shot off toward the house so fast you might have thought he'd smelled smoke. When he returned a few moments later he was carrying a glass of ice water and one of Regina's many pill bottles. In my days at Wonderland, I'd come to recognize how many of these there were, and the care with which Forrest kept track of them all.

"I should have brought you these back at lunchtime," he said, leaning over her, almost as if she were a sick child. "I hate it when I mess up the schedule."

"What does it matter?" she sighed. "Whether I take these or not, I'll still feel like shit."

What could you say to that? He didn't try, just rubbed her back and rearranged the cushions under her feet.

"Just give it a few minutes," he said. "I won't be late with these again."

Some men—my father, for instance—might have shown annoyance at a moment like this. (More accurately, my father would probably have broken a plate, if one had been within reach.) Not Forrest. It occurred to me that as annoying as it must be, looking out for Regina in all the ways Forrest did, some part of him seemed to love his role as her protector. Maybe it made him feel needed.

After the game was over, I'd put away our badminton racquets and doled out the kids' Popsicles. I was leaning on the counter in the kitchen, flipping through a J.Crew catalog and sucking on a Popsicle of my own, when Regina came up alongside me, so quietly that when I heard her voice, I jumped.

"I like watching you play with the children," she said, in that oddly flat, whispery voice of hers. "I like seeing them having a good time with someone. Even if the person isn't me. Which it never is."

"I'm not very good at badminton," I told her. "I never played it before."

"But you know how to play," she said. "I'm not talking about a particular game. You know how to *play* is all. You know how to be playful. I have no clue."

I might have refuted this to make her feel better. But she was right, of course. I'd seen what happened the one time Jilly tried to get her mother to engage in one of those inane scenarios with her American Girl doll—tea parties, discussions of boys or kittens. When she told Regina "you be Molly," Regina went mute.

"I don't know how to talk like a doll," she'd told Jilly. "I don't know what dolls are supposed to say."

"My husband, on the other hand," Regina continued, "there's someone who's a master at playing. Playing may actually be the only thing Forrest knows how to do. To Forrest, everything's a game. The man's got a unique talent for having a good time. That's probably why everyone loves him so much."

I was still standing there, leaning against the counter, licking my Popsicle. I was studying a pair of J.Crew pants I'd never be able to afford.

"It's true about me, isn't it?" she asked me. "I'm just not much fun, am I?"

I wasn't sure what I was supposed to say.

"Everybody loves Forrest," she told me again. "But nobody understands him the way I do. I know everything."

I had finished my Popsicle. Now Regina did a strange thing. (Regina did many strange things, but this was stranger than most of them.) She reached out and took the Popsicle stick out of my hand. She considered it for a second. Then she drew the stick across her neck as if it were a dagger. As if she were slitting her own throat.

"Let me tell you something, Frances," she said. "It's not a gift to be envied, knowing everything. There's such a thing as knowing way . . . too . . . much."

Sometime in the middle of that night, I thought I heard noises in the bedroom below mine, where Forrest slept. I was half asleep. At first I thought there must be some kind of animal in the house, making some kind of high-pitched wailing. Maybe the animal had been injured, and snuck in a window.

I took a minute to realize it wasn't that.

It was Regina, crying out. And a second voice, deep and low. This voice I knew. It belonged to Forrest. This must be what he sounded like when he was making love.

She's trying to hold on to him, I thought.

Then came another thought: *But he's already drifting away. And there's probably nothing she can do to stop it.*

26

The Heartbreak of Jacqueline du Pré

For the Fourth of July party coming up at the club, everyone was supposed to wear something red, white, and blue. Nothing I had with me went with the dress code.

"I'm taking you shopping," Regina said. I might have been wrong, but I got the feeling she needed to distract herself. In all the time I'd been living with the Emersons that summer—a month now—this was the first time I'd seen Regina take the steering wheel of their Jeep Wagoneer. She drove slowly, with both hands on the wheel, and stared straight ahead, sitting up perfectly straight, her back not touching the seat. She checked the rearview mirror regularly.

We didn't go to a mall, or the outlet stores along the highway. She brought me to a place that looked as if it had been in business since before my parents were born. They had a display in the window of women's suits that looked like the kind of thing Nancy Reagan would wear, only cheaper.

"We're looking for a party dress," Regina told the salesperson. "Patriotic theme." The woman took out a dress with cap sleeves, royal blue, with white piping around the neck.

"Our young friend could wear this with a simple red cardigan," the saleslady said, addressing Regina. "Or red accessories. A flag pin, maybe."

Regina accompanied me to the dressing room. Not anticipating this, I'd worn my undershirt, not the training bra, which I'd washed that morning in the sink of my upstairs bathroom so Prudence wouldn't see it in the family laundry. My jeans already on the floor, I pulled my shirt over my head, leaving me in my cotton undershirt and underpants. Regina studied my body the way a visitor at an art museum might consider an abstract painting she didn't understand or care for.

"You haven't hit puberty, I see." Regina sat on a stool in the dressing room, assessing my body. No visible breast development still, and I was holding my stomach in.

"You don't need to do that," she said. Regina missed nothing. "You're going to have a nice body. Just wait. I know it seems uncomfortable now, but things are going to get better for you."

Did they get better for you? I wanted to ask her. I probably knew the answer.

I studied my reflection. The dress the salesperson had selected for me was not the kind I'd pick out for myself, but it didn't matter. I wanted to make Regina happy. I also knew, as her husband did, that this was impossible.

The blue dress was a little long. They would have hemmed it for me at the store, but there was no way this dress would ever look fashionable, so why bother?

In the car on the way home, Regina put on a cassette tape. I knew nothing about classical music, having been raised to a nonstop background of my father's jazz—which I drowned out, when I could, with Cyndi Lauper or the Bangles on the radio, or my one precious Madonna tape. Regina's voice, as she explained what we were listening to, contained an unusual element of emotion.

"This is a cello concerto by a composer named Elgar. It's the saddest piece of music I've ever heard," she said.

We drove without speaking for a while. I got the impression that if she loosened up on the steering wheel even a little, she might crash the car into a tree.

"You're listening to Jacqueline du Pré," she said. "In my opinion, she's the finest cellist who ever lived. She married a great pianist and conductor."

The way Regina said this, I knew she was telling me something important. Important to Regina, anyway.

"Did you ever hear her at a concert?" I asked. My mother took me to see Joan Baez in Boston, the one time ever I can remember doing something like that with her, though this had less to do with my mother wanting me to see Joan Baez than it did with her wanting to be there, herself.

"Jacqueline du Pré stopped performing a long time ago," Regina said. "She got a disease called multiple sclerosis, where she couldn't feel her fingers anymore. She was just in her twenties."

"What happened to her?"

"She can't play the cello anymore. Her husband's off somewhere, leading an orchestra. He's probably got a girlfriend."

Regina stopped talking and rewound the tape a little. "You have to hear this part," she said. "It's like she's making the cello sigh. Then it starts moaning. Then . . . wait for this . . . here it comes . . . the only word I know for the sound the cello makes here is *keening*. You might not know what that means, but listen to this part and you will.

"Then it gets quieter again, but that's the saddest of all. The first time I heard this, it made me cry."

I couldn't imagine that, Regina crying.

At the point Jacqueline recorded the Elgar concerto for cello, Regina told me, she didn't know yet that she had multiple sclerosis, or that her husband would leave after she got so sick. "But it's all in the music," Regina said. "It's like she knew. She understood a broken heart even before she had one."

Regina went silent then. From the tape deck, the Elgar concerto filled the car with the nearly unbearably sad strains of Jacqueline du Pré's cello. A person didn't have to know about classical music to understand.

"You'd probably prefer rock and roll or something," Regina said. "Happy music. I get it. But sometimes it's important to experience things you don't think you'll enjoy. You may discover new parts of yourself you didn't know existed."

The music was growing on me. It wasn't my usual kind of thing, but when Regina offered to stop the tape, I said I wanted to hear the rest.

"It's not such a terrible thing when a piece of music is sad," Regina said. "Life is sad too." For a moment, she was silent. Just driving. "You have no idea," she told me.

In the seat beside her, I fingered the fabric of the blue dress. When Regina had handed over the money for the dress, I had thought, briefly, of all the clothes I'd rather own than this particular item, which wasn't cheap. I had felt a small sting of regret at the time. Now, hearing the story of the great cellist losing the ability to play, none of that seemed to matter.

"There are worse things than feeling sad," Regina said. "Feeling nothing. That's worse."

It was hard to know what she meant. My problem was, I felt everything.

27

Tired Out

I was tying Jilly's shoes, getting ready to take off for tennis.

"Did you know my mom went away one time?" she said. "They took her to this special place where she could rest. That's why I never learned to tie my shoelaces."

The part about the shoelaces didn't make much sense. The part I'd focused on was the other. Regina, going away somewhere.

"I didn't get to see her for a long time," Jilly said. "She couldn't come to my birthday party. She went away in summer. It was cold when we went to pick her up."

"I bet you missed her," I said.

"When she came back, I wanted to show her my new dolls, but she went up to her room."

"She was probably tired," I said.

"That's what my dad said too," Jilly told me. "But I didn't get it. All that time she was gone, they said she was resting. So why did she need to rest some more?"

Then I was at the club, as usual, waiting for the kids' tennis lessons to finish and watching the staff put up decorations for the big party the next night. After the first few days of sitting on the bench when they received their instruction, I'd developed the habit of wandering over to the far side of the courts to watch the lessons of older kids at the club. Maybe I had the idea that if I watched closely enough, I might figure out how to be more like them. Maybe I could fit in better.

Though probably not.

I made a game of it: listening to the pointers of the tennis pro, Jonathan, on the correct follow-through for a backhand stroke, or a forehand, or an overhead shot, and trying to anticipate what he'd say next. One time, up in my little attic bedroom, in front of the mirror, I tried to replicate the motion.

Now there I was on the bench outside the court where Olivia was having her private lesson. As much as I was loving my current Stephen King novel, I found myself studying what was happening on the court instead of the pages of my book.

Olivia was very pretty—with the kind of looks I saw in the pages of my well-thumbed July issue of *Seventeen*. She had a confidence I couldn't imagine possessing—the air of a girl who took it for granted that she'd be invited to parties and taken to the mall with a charge card in her pocketbook to purchase whatever she might spot in the J.Crew catalog and feel like adding to her wardrobe.

She was wearing a new outfit that day. By this point I was familiar with her vast wardrobe of tennis skirts. This one was purple with tiny yellow stars, and a matching yellow top—yellow with purple stars. She wore her hair in a ponytail and tossed it frequently. Her body had filled out in a way mine still failed to do, but I knew from overhearing her conversation with some other girls at the club—about a sleepover party she'd had—that she'd recently turned fifteen.

Even on good days—and despite her mother's obvious dedication to her daughter's future on the court—Olivia was not what you could have described as an enthusiastic tennis student, but that morning she seemed more reluctant than usual to go through her paces. She told Jonathan she had a blister on her heel. Not to mention she had a headache.

"Why don't we just work on your serve," Jonathan suggested. "You won't have to run around so much."

She took her position at the line with about as much enthusiasm as Hayward showed when putting his cereal bowl in the dishwasher, on some rare occasion when Prudence suggested this.

Jonathan tossed her a ball. She took it in her hand, studied it briefly, wrinkling her nose. Olivia never seemed to care one way or another about what took place during her lesson or whether she progressed particularly well. She was stalling for time, was all. The fact that the meter was running on her lesson—something I would have thought about, raised as I was by parents who noted the expenditure of every dollar—never seemed to occur to her. If Olivia was thirsty, she'd amble off the court to get herself a Coke at the snack bar and amble back. She took her time. If Olivia needed to go to the bathroom, she might rebraid her hair while she was in there. Or stop to chat with someone on her way back.

Now came her ball toss, way high and outside. As little as I knew at this point about tennis, or serving, I could tell she shouldn't try for this one. I watched the ball rise up over her head, her arm reaching behind her back first as she'd been taught, then swinging. No contact.

Off to one side by a few feet, with a cartful of balls, Jonathan tossed her another. She did no better with this one. Or the next.

On the fifth try, she managed to connect with the ball, though it went into the net. No luck with the next four or five. She tossed her ponytail. Made a face.

"I hate tennis," she said. "I just do this because my mom makes me."

"Everybody has a bad day now and then," Jonathan observed, his voice calm and even, encouraging.

"I need a break," she told him. "I'm hot."

He pointed out that she had half an hour left in her lesson.

"No offense, but this is boring," Olivia said.

Jonathan gave it one more try, but she was already zipping up her bag and heading off the court in the direction of the clubhouse.

Then there was Jilly, handing me her tennis racquet to zip into the case for her.

"Ice cream time," she said. It wasn't a question.

28

A Really Nice Dad

Do you like my dad?" Hayward asked me. We were sitting on the bench at the club, waiting for his tennis lesson to start. Out on the court, one of the other players' fathers—a man I'd seen around a lot, the dad to a couple of pale, ginger-haired twins—was hitting balls to one of his daughters.

"I like both your parents," I told Hayward.

"But mostly my dad, right?" he said. "My mom just lies around all the time. She never does anything. My dad's way cooler than other people's dads."

On the court, the twins' father was picking up balls with the ball hopper now. From the back, you could see the crack where his bottom started—the kind of thing I never failed to notice. Hayward was right, of course. Nobody else's dad at the club or anyplace else came close to being as cool as his.

"You're lucky," I told Hayward. "You've got a really nice dad."

"And you like him a ton, right?"

No way Hayward could have found my journal any more than Regina could have. And anyway, I doubted he could read cursive. On the court where Jonathan was finishing up another boy's lesson, I heard the sound of racquets hitting the ball.

"That kid's pretty good," I said. Diversionary tactic. Unsuccessful.

"Everyone loves my dad," Hayward said. "Especially girls. All the moms get this look on their faces when he picks us up at swimming. Mason's mom keeps inviting us over for lemonade. Same with Carter's mom."

Hayward fingered the strings on his tennis racquet. He pressed it into his thigh in way that left a mark. As he spoke, he studied his skin. He had taken out a pen, and was drawing tiny squares on it in the spaces where the strings of his racquet had left the marks. He did not look at me as he spoke.

"The moms all know my mom hardly ever goes anyplace. If we went over to their house, it would be just my dad that took me. The mom would tell their kid and me to go outside and play, then she'd try to kiss him or something."

"Your father loves your mother," I told him. "He's just a really nice person. It's not surprising that people like him. Not just your friends' moms. Everyone."

"But the moms especially," Hayward said. More tiny squares on his thigh.

I studied his face. He still wasn't meeting my eyes, but it seemed to me that he was looking for a reaction.

"He likes them back too," Hayward said. Now his gaze met mine. For a second I could see what he'd look like when he was older.

"You ever go all the way with anybody?" he asked me. From the way he put it, I guessed this was not a term he'd tried out before, if ever. "Like your boyfriend back in New Jersey?"

"None of your business," I told him.

"You think I'm just some little kid," he said. "But I did French kissing one time. It was at this girl's birthday party that I know. We were in the basement playing Twister and someone turned out the lights. I put my tongue in her mouth."

"Big whoop," I said. "It's time for your lesson."

"I think she had onions on her cheeseburger or something," he said. "If you know you're going to be doing French kissing, you should probably brush your teeth first."

Jonathan appeared at the edge of the court. "Time to get out on the court, bud," he said.

Taking his time, Olivia-style, Hayward picked up his racquet, but not the way a tennis player does. He held it as if it were a guitar. He strummed the strings and bent his body over the racquet with his face twisted up like a person in pain, the way rock stars did on MTV when they were in the middle of some amazing riff. From over at the court, Jonathan looked on, waiting. This was not the first time one of his students wasted his time. Hayward kept on playing his tennis racquet.

"You like Guns N' Roses?" he called out to me from the edge of the court. "I could play you a tape of them sometime on my boom box."

"You're up, buddy. Time's a-wasting." Jonathan again.

From where he stood, racquet in hand, still in guitar position, Hayward ignored him.

"My birthday's coming up," he told me. "I'll be thirteen, but I'm old for my age."

"Let's see what you got for me today, Hay-man," Jonathan said. People who worked at the country club weren't supposed to lose their patience, but I could see he was getting close. With certain people it was pointless to argue. Not if their family were founding members of the Lake Catherine Country Club.

Hayward made his way slowly toward the service line. But not before turning around first and sticking out his tongue at me, wiggling it like a snake that was slithering out of his mouth.

"French kissing," he called out to me. "You should try it."

29

SWEAT

The next day I was back at the courts again, waiting—as usual—for Jilly and Hayward to finish up with tennis for the day before bringing them back home to get ready for the big night at the club. As was my habit, I wandered over to the court where Jonathan was giving a private lesson with his regular eleven o'clock tennis student, Olivia.

She had on a new tennis outfit, but her attitude remained unchanged. After three shots in a row sailed past her—easy shots, even I could tell that much—Jonathan set his racquet against the net and walked over to her.

"What's going on?" he said. "You could have returned those shots."

"I'm bored," she said. "I don't want to do this anymore."

"Everybody has their off days," Jonathan told her. "You have to power through them."

"I'm sick of tennis," she told him. Off on the side, I could see a group of girls, the ones Olivia hung out with at the club. They all had their fancy drinks in hand. They were waiting for her to join them, no doubt.

Jonathan made one more attempt. "Your mom's paid up for another six lessons," he said. "It was a package."

"Big deal," she told him. "I'll say I had an anxiety attack." She was already off the court when she shot him a quick glance. "Have a nice life."

I studied Jonathan's face. He was probably no more than twenty-two, though to me he qualified as a grown-up. This would not have been his first experience with a kid who had more interest in hanging out with her friends than playing tennis.

As his eyes followed Olivia's departure from the court, they landed on me, sitting on a bench with my book. Jilly and Hayward had taken off for their semiprivate by that point. I picked up my book. I was at the part in *Cujo* where the dog's infection has just started to get out of hand and he kills the neighbor.

"Hey, what's your name?" Jonathan called out to me. "You're always here. You a member?"

"Mother's helper," I told him. "I don't know how to play tennis."

"I've got an extra racquet," he said. "Why don't you give it a try?"

I didn't know what to say.

"I'll give you a few pointers," Jonathan said. "I'm not doing anything anyway."

I knew nothing about the game, just what I'd picked up while watching other people's lessons.

"What do you have to lose?" he asked me.

I stepped onto the court.

Except for times I packed for the children's lessons, I'd never held a racquet. I'd heard Jonathan talk about forehand grip and backhand grip and follow-through, and I knew to keep my knees bent and my feet moving—and sometimes, when Forrest had the television on, watching a match, I'd watch with him. That was the extent of my experience with the game of tennis.

Jonathan set me up at the mid-court line to start with. He hit me a ball. I surprised myself by returning it. He hit it back.

We did this for a while. Then he came over to my side of the net to offer a few pointers on my swing.

"You're doing great for your first time," he added. "Let's get you back to the baseline."

I hit a few wild ones, but after a couple of tries, I started getting the hang of it. We hit like that for another ten minutes. I wasn't wearing the right shoes, but I covered the court surprisingly well. There was a fierce kind of energy in me I hadn't known existed.

A boy showed up. "My next lesson," Jonathan said. I handed the racquet back to him.

"I wouldn't lie about this—I'm surprised," he told me. "You really never hit before?"

I shook my head.

"Listen," he said. "Show up tomorrow, same time. If Olivia doesn't have some amazing change of heart about the game of tennis, which something tells me she won't, you can take her hour. She's got another six paid for. Those can be yours. But you need to look into better footwear."

I could probably borrow sneakers from Regina. She had a closet full of them, and all she ever wore were slippers.

"See you tomorrow," he said.

I walked my bike over to the court where the children were just finishing their lesson.

Hayward seemed to be studying my face.

"Your face is red," he told me. "There's sweat under your armpits. No offense, but you kind of stink. I could give you some deodorant if you wanted."

Something about the way he said this made me uncomfortable.

"I've got my own," I told him. I didn't, actually. I hadn't needed it before. But I hadn't chased after a tennis ball before either.

30

Nobody Else's Story

The Fourth of July celebration at the club had turned out to be almost as boring as one of Jilly's American Girl tea parties—basically just a bunch of people standing around with drinks in their hands, dipping shrimp in cocktail sauce and admiring each other's outfits. Regina had on one of her floaty dresses. Forrest wore a white linen suit with a navy blue T-shirt underneath, like Don Johnson on *Miami Vice*.

I told nobody about my tennis lesson with Jonathan that afternoon. It wasn't much of a story, but for once the story was mine, not somebody else's or made up. I got to be the star of it.

"You're a natural, Frances," Jonathan had told me.

For the first time in my life, it occurred to me that I might actually be good at something.

For fourteen years I'd seen myself as a loser. I had caught a glimpse of a world—just a glimpse—in which I might actually be able to win.

The next day, at the club, when Jilly and Hayward went off for their lessons, I made my way to the court where Jonathan had hit with me.

"Do you have time for me?" I asked him.

He handed me a racquet.

That night I took my journal out from its place in the bottom drawer of my dresser, under my T-shirts. *Jonathan says I've got an instinctive understanding of how to connect with a ball,* I wrote.

No fantasies. Just the truth.

This was how I fell in love with the game of tennis. Three mornings a week now—sometimes four—I'd meet up with Jonathan during the Emerson children's lessons. For fifty-five minutes, right up to the time we had to pick up the balls, he put me through the paces of ball drills and serving practice. Nights in my bed I went back over what he'd taught me and wrote it down. I'd used up Olivia's credit now. But Jonathan hadn't brought this up.

Sometimes I actually dreamed I was playing. Finally, I had something interesting to share in my nightly writing that had actually happened. And it had nothing to do with Forrest Emerson or my parents or Regina or the children. This was all mine.

I needed to find a better place to hide my journal. Writing as I did now, nobody must ever see what I'd set down on these pages. I studied my little room, searching for a hiding place.

Not many options. Only one, actually. I lifted the edge of my mattress off the bed frame and set the journal on top of the slats. Before replacing the mattress, I added another element of security—a row of BBs from Hayward's BB gun that he was always leaving around. I laid these out in a row alongside my journal. Twelve of them. If anyone ever disturbed my hiding spot, I'd know.

31

XXO

Back when Forrest's friend Evan first encouraged him to sign up for the Labor Day triathlon, Forrest had explained to us—with a look of regret—that his participation required serious training of a kind likely to be painful to an old man like himself. But until Brenda Barnett appeared on the scene, I hadn't noticed any big level of commitment on Forrest's part to train for the event.

Now all that had changed. The brief, wonderful stretch of weeks in which I'd had breakfast with Forrest every day seemed to be over. As early as I came down to breakfast now, he was always gone already. His training for the triathlon required him to spend most of the morning on his bike, he told us. Afternoons he alternated between running and swimming. As early as I got up—six o'clock, most mornings—he'd be off on his bike already. He might come home sometime in the late morning, but when he did, it was mostly to take a shower and fix himself a protein shake before heading out again for his swim or his run.

He always left a bagel or an English muffin at my place at the counter; I just didn't have the taste for them anymore. More achingly than I could have imagined, I missed those times we'd had together in the early days of the summer. I ate my toast or cereal alone now. The one small consolation: Every morning without fail I'd find a little bouquet of pansies next to the bowl laid out for me. Occasionally there was a piece of notebook paper set out next to the flowers. No words on it. Just a smiley face or heart, drawn (somewhat unevenly) in pencil. Forrest was such a bad speller, I knew, he probably decided to forgo words altogether and stick to *XXO*.

I brought the pansies up to my room, lifted the mattress, moved the row of BBs, and took out my precious journal. I placed the pansies in the pages of my journal with another book on top to flatten the petals.

None of this was simple. But at that moment, the gift of those flowers meant the world. That little bouquet had been a message. Forrest Emerson still cared about me.

32

Only Friend in the World

It was raining, so we weren't going to the club. The children had gone over to the Olivers' house to work on a presentation they were putting on at the club the next week, a skit commemorating Bastille Day, featuring one of the older kids—Olivia, in a fancy dress and wig—playing the role of Marie Antoinette. At the Lake Catherine Country Club, they were always celebrating something or other.

So I was off duty. I was lying on the couch, starting in on a new book.

My attempts at keeping my calorie intake low over the summer had failed miserably, due to a combination of my daily visit to the Caboose with the kids, the presence of an irresistible assortment of great snacks in the pantry at Wonderland, and Prudence's fried chicken. In spite of this, I'd trimmed down noticeably, thanks to bike riding, and the fact that I was playing tennis almost daily now.

Studying my body as I did, up in my attic room at night—my legs, my chest—I no longer experienced the level of self-hatred that had plagued me in recent years. I often thought about Regina's words to me that someday I'd look beautiful. This was still hard to believe.

My lack of breasts was a continued disappointment. Sometimes, sitting across from him at the table, I'd see Hayward studying my chest, but with a bemused expression, like a sailor onboard ship, looking out to the horizon in search of an approaching vessel and finding nothing but fog. Even more unnerving was the smile he gave me on these occasions. More precisely, a smirk.

I wore my training bra when I could, but not when I had tennis lessons, and I was having tennis lessons almost daily now. The first time Jonathan had worked with me on my serve, I'd worried that one of the balled-up pieces of toilet paper I'd stuffed inside my bra would fall out. After that I'd abandoned my efforts to fill out my appearance. I decided that developing a serve mattered more.

I opened my book. Other than Forrest—Forrest as he was until recent days—Stephen King had become my best company over the course of my Wonderland summer.

Regina had been resting. Or so I thought. Then there she was, settling herself into the lounge chair next to me. She held on to the sides of the chair as she lowered herself. I got the feeling that without the support, she might keel over.

"You probably wonder what's the matter with me," she said. This was Regina for you. She felt no need to enter into a conversation with the usual pleasantries. She got right down to things.

"Nobody says anything, but I know everyone thinks I'm this pathetic, screwed-up nutjob."

"Not really," I said. Though they did, of course.

I reached for my Diet Sprite. I was still holding my book, not sure if it was OK to get back to my reading, though I wanted to. It seemed that Regina felt a need to talk.

"That's a scary one," she said, pointing to my book. "I can't read his books. If you ask me, real life is terrifying enough."

I took a sip from my drink, trying to think of a good response, but Regina had more to say.

"My husband loves me," she said. "Just in a different way from how some people do it. And I adore him, of course. Who wouldn't fall in love with Forrest? That's the problem."

I didn't know what to say. I knew plenty about husbands and wives not getting along, of course, though nothing in Forrest's and Regina's behavior toward each other reminded me of what went on, or didn't go on, between my parents. Other than his disturbing attentiveness to Brenda Barnett that night, it seemed that Forrest remained unfailingly kind to Regina. She brushed him aside like a bug sometimes, but that was about as far as she took it. They never had fights.

A lot of the time Regina gave the impression that she didn't seem to care all that much about anything. Now, though, her voice sounded uncharacteristically emphatic. She seemed to be speaking from some-place very deep in her chest. I got the feeling she'd been preparing for this moment and worked out her speech to me.

"Marriage is . . . difficult," she said. "And then there's sex. Oh god. Sex."

I couldn't look at her. I kept my eyes on a page of my book. But I listened hard. As much time as I spent thinking about sex, nobody had ever talked to me about it.

"People act like sex is so great," she said. "But you know the truth? It's crazy what sex does to people. When you think about it, sex is pretty dangerous, isn't it? Opening yourself up to another person that way. Giving them all that power over you. Letting yourself love someone. Knowing if something goes wrong it could ruin your life?"

What could I say? For all my nighttime thoughts, I knew nothing about what sex would actually be like. I had all kinds of ideas, pictures I dreamed up, but none of them were real. Now here was this woman I'd known all my life, though not really, talking about sex to me as if I were her girlfriend or therapist. Regina wasn't talking about sex the way your gym teacher would, or the school nurse. She spoke about it the way a person might speak about a flesh-eating virus or a tsunami. As something dark and terrifying.

"I'm just trying to protect you," she said, though nothing in the way Regina was looking at me left me feeling safe. "Nobody ever told me these things. I learned the hard way."

Most of the times Regina spoke to me, she looked away, almost as if she weren't speaking to me at all. This time she looked directly into my eyes. Hers had taken on a wild look. The thought came to me: I could see how it was they'd put her in a hospital that time.

"We go through our lives pretending nothing's going on," she said. "Pick up the dry cleaning. Go to the supermarket. But you always know that under the surface people are doing all these crazy things. They just never talk about it."

I doubted Regina Emerson ever went to the supermarket. But I got her point.

"You think the only place to find horror is in one of those books?" She pointed to the novel in my hands, then ripped it out of my hands and waved it over her head.

"Sex can be"—she hesitated—"a catastrophe."

I had no idea what she was talking about now. I wondered whether later, when I was older, her words might make more sense to me, but I doubted it.

"Sex can destroy a person," she said. "When you think about it, it's not so different from murder."

As quickly as it had flared up, the intensity in her voice disappeared then—replaced by Regina's usual low and whispery air of resignation. Now came the words I sensed she'd been waiting to deliver.

"You understand what's happening between Forrest and Brenda, I assume?" she said, her voice cool, almost matter-of-fact.

I nodded.

"Forrest's tradition of summer affairs has been going on for a long time," she said. "The women change, but the pattern stays the same. Every summer a new person. I'm used to it, almost."

What could I possibly have to contribute on this subject? It didn't matter, actually. She was talking to herself again. I just happened to be there.

"You could call it Forrest's summer tradition," she said. "Playing around with somebody's wife at the lake. It usually starts around Fourth of July, and by Labor Day everything's over. We get back to our life. Until the next year."

It seemed important to respond to this. As inadequate as it was likely to be. "That must be hard," I offered.

"This year we were slightly ahead of schedule," she said. "But it's not as big a deal as you might think.

"There's no point taking it seriously. It won't amount to anything. I just thought you should know. You should understand: Nobody's going to break the two of us up. It isn't real. It means nothing."

I guessed this was supposed to be good news, though it didn't feel that way.

"But one thing about my husband: The minute he starts fucking some new woman, the whole rest of the world disappears. It's like he's drunk. He can't think of anything else. I thought I should prepare you."

She used the word *fucking*. Though my mother often used the phrase "fuck you" when fighting with my father, this was the first time anyone had ever used that word when speaking with me, in an actual conversation. The fact that Regina did this now unnerved me.

"Maybe you should talk to somebody," I said. Maybe she'd forgotten I was just fourteen years old.

She laughed. It came out as little more than a low growl. "But I am talking to someone, aren't I?" she said. "I'm talking to you."

She reached out her long, thin arm then. Her thin hand touched my hair. She stroked it. Maybe nobody, ever, had done such a thing.

"You know the crazy thing?" she said. "You may be my only friend in the world."

33

Dip

I was ironing one of Jilly's party dresses for the Bastille Day celebration at the club. Regina was upstairs, taking a nap. Pam Oliver was dropping Jilly and Hayward off from the run-through of their Bastille Day skit. "I thought I'd just pop in to say hello," she said. But there may have been more to it.

When I met Pam at the door, the first thing that hit me was her perfume. She was wearing a lot of it. Also full makeup and a tank top that revealed her nipples and a skirt that came to within inches of her crotch.

"Is Forrest here?" she said. "I know we'll see each other at the club tonight, but I wanted to give him this now." There was a piece of paper in her hand.

"I served him this dip last summer, when he and the kids stopped by. He wanted the recipe."

She held tight to the paper. It was clear her plan was to give it to Forrest. For a moment I was unsure whether she'd place it in my hand. I was definitely not the person she wanted to see.

"He's out on a bike ride," I said. "He's been training for the triathlon."

"Well, tell him Pammy said hi." She turned to go.

It turned out Regina had been on the stairs, watching. Once Pam's car pulled out, she took her place by the window, watching it disappear down the driveway. You could still smell Pam Oliver's perfume in the air.

"Poor woman," she said. The whispery voice with which she'd confided in me about Forrest's affairs had disappeared. Her tone now was hard, businesslike. Sarcastic.

"She keeps hoping to start things up again. Did you check out that little skirt she was wearing? She doesn't even play tennis."

I was still holding the piece of paper with the dip recipe. I could probably toss it.

"She had it all planned out, no doubt," Regina said. "If Forrest had been here, she would have invited him over to help her fix her drain or something. Her husband's always out of town.

"And the thing is, Forrest would have done it too. Not that he knows anything about fixing drains. He just likes to make women happy. But he never carries these escapades of his into the next season."

Nothing about Regina at this moment seemed soft or vulnerable. But for some reason I felt like putting my arm around her—the thing my mother never did with me when I was sad. That probably would have looked dumb to Regina, coming from a fourteen-year-old. Her babysitter. Even though she had recently told me I was her only friend. My guess was she'd forgotten by now.

"I'm sorry," I told her. Not that I'd done anything. I was just sorry about how sad she was, but mostly I was sorry that Forrest Emerson had turned out to be so much less perfect and wonderful than I had wanted to believe. Though his recent and surprising change in behavior had not altered my love for him, it had damaged my respect.

But that wasn't the hardest part. The hardest part was recognizing that with Brenda Barnett's arrival on the scene, it appeared I wasn't Forrest's favorite after all. Not in the way that mattered.

Regina, floating up alongside me in her caftan, seemed to read my mind.

"Don't let it get to you, Frances," she said. "You wait and see. Next summer, it'll be Brenda Barnett that's stopping by with a recipe for my husband. Or some article from the newspaper. Tips for firming your abs, not that he needs them. A quote from Khalil Gibran, possibly.

"And you know the funniest part?" (It didn't sound as if she found any of this funny.) "Forrest doesn't know the first thing about cooking. In his whole life, he's never prepared dip." She made a noise that was probably meant to resemble a chuckle, but it came out more like a snarl.

I could hear Prudence upstairs, reminding the children to get dressed for the club and explaining to Jilly why she couldn't bring her American Girl dolls to the celebration. Regina needed to change too. But it felt as though she wasn't finished talking to me.

"I don't want to shock you, but there was a time not so long ago when I thought maybe I should just do myself in," she said. "I figured it would make everyone's life so much easier. But you know what? Forrest would miss me. The children might not care much, but my husband would.

"I'd miss them too," she said. "You might not believe this, but I love them all. In my way."

Upstairs, back in my room, I got dressed for the Bastille Day celebration, to which I would wear my same blue dress—the second party in two weeks. The five of us piled into the Wagoneer and headed to the club.

The thought came to me, sitting in the back seat, between Jilly and Hayward, as I looked out the window, that for all the discussion Regina and I had that day—about Brenda, about Forrest, about herself, about sex—one character in the family drama she'd never mentioned was me. Maybe because I was never really all that important to anyone here after all.

34

Regina, but Not

They served pâté at the party—a food I'd never tasted before that night—and it didn't agree with me. I must have looked pretty bad, because even Regina noticed and suggested I go home to lie down. Under normal circumstances—how things had been up until recently, anyway—this would have been a moment Forrest would have volunteered to drive me, but as it was, Regina corralled Jonathan, who'd been standing alongside the punch bowl, looking almost as out of place as I was, to bring me home. I couldn't say much on the ride back to the house, but he made a point of telling me, again, how impressed he was with the progress I was making with tennis.

Back at the house, I threw up. That left me feeling better. With the house empty, I took the opportunity to scope things out again. This time, instead of checking out Regina's room, I stepped into the one occupied by Forrest.

Not much to uncover there: a collection of Red Sox caps, a running treadmill, a plastic bin containing a few dozen identical pairs of neatly balled-up white tube socks, and beside those a stack of identical white T-shirts. There was a framed picture of the Buddha on one wall, next to some kind of certificate, also framed. On closer examination, this turned out to be Forrest's high school diploma.

I opened the top bureau drawer. More tube socks, plus underwear, a jockstrap, bike shorts, and a pair of bicycle gloves. The next drawer held a pile of some kind of item I couldn't identify at first, though after studying the writing on the packets, I understood. This was the first time I'd ever actually seen what a condom looked like.

At the very bottom of the drawer—with a dollar bill folded around it, held by a paper clip—there was a photograph. The girl in the picture looked a lot like Regina. This must be Regina, of course, but in a certain way she didn't resemble Regina at all. She was smiling broadly, for one thing. She was tossing her head as if she'd just finished laughing. I studied this picture for a long time, wondering what could have happened to Regina to make her change so much.

Next to the photograph—less well hidden, in fact—was a card, the kind a person would purchase at a Hallmark store, with a rose on the front. The printed message read simply, *Thinking of you and our special moments together.* Below that, someone wearing bright orange lipstick had evidently pressed her mouth against the card, leaving a lip-shaped impression, and below this, a single letter, with a heart around it: *B.*

I felt like throwing up again, though this time it had nothing to do with the pâté.

35

WHERE HAPPINESS COMES FROM

Forty-nine days remained in my Wonderland summer. Life went on just the way Regina told me it would, with little visible sign of change: just the usual round of tennis lessons, ice cream cones, play-dates, sailing at the yacht club, takeout lobster rolls on the patio, riding bikes, boating, and trips to the supermarket, library, or Caboose. Fried-chicken dinners. S'mores by the fire. Biking to the club. Tennis again.

The only part that changed was that Forrest seemed to have slipped out of view. He was still around—though not for our break-fasts together—but even when he was physically present, he seemed distracted all the time now.

This would have been unbearable if it hadn't been for my time out on the tennis court. Jilly and Hayward seemed to regard their lessons as a chore undertaken to please their parents. For me, those fifty-five min-utes on the court with Jonathan had become the high point of my day.

As for Regina, after that one afternoon in which it had occurred to me that she might need to go back to that hospital—and in spite of her apparent recognition that Forrest had now embarked on an affair with Brenda—she actually appeared a little brighter these days, a little less depressed. She was taking fewer naps. She had started wearing makeup, more subtly applied than Brenda Barnett's, and getting dressed in actual clothes, not just caftans. Maybe, with a competitor on the scene, she was trying to up her game, though from the looks of Forrest's many absences ("triathlon-training sessions," he said, and there were more of these as the days passed), her efforts weren't doing anything to keep her husband home with her.

To look at how the days went in Wonderland over those weeks—midsummer now—it all looked pretty good. But I knew that, just as Regina had explained to me, a whole other set of events was taking place, everyone engaging in their own secret activities or just entertaining their own private thoughts that nobody would ever have guessed.

It was true for everyone probably. Maybe everyone who'd ever been born. Who knew what went on in the life of Prudence, when she went home at the end of her long day of cooking? Or my kind and handsome tennis teacher, Jonathan—home for the summer from college to give lessons, and, according to the gossip I overheard at the snack bar among the tennis girls, rumored to have a forty-year-old Argentinian boyfriend in town, even though mothers at the club kept trying to set him up with their daughters. *Imagine having a tennis pro in the family. Lessons whenever you wanted.*

I thought about Pam Oliver, still holding out hope that Forrest might stop by for a replay of whatever activities the two of them may have engaged in the summer before. The picture came to me of Olivia, the rich girl who huddled with her posse every morning at the club, all of them sipping their five-dollar virgin piña coladas. They might only talk about their hair and some model they saw in *Seventeen*, but at the end of the day, Olivia lay alone in her bed too. When she did, what thoughts entered her mind?

Hardest of all to imagine were the secret yearnings of Regina Emerson, but even Regina must have had hers. Or maybe it was the disappearance of yearning, the absence of hunger for anything more, any more, that led a person to the place Regina seemed to occupy now—where it seemed she barely cared if she lived or died.

One thing had changed in my nighttime routine. Where, until recently, I'd filled the pages of my journal every night with make-believe scenes I imagined taking place between Forrest and someone I pretended was me, the story had gone flat. I could no longer write about any of that, or allow myself to concoct our fantasy encounters on the page.

Days went by now that I made no move to retrieve my journal from under the mattress to write a new entry. Brenda Barnett had ruined the thrill. When I pictured Forrest now, her face always appeared—her mean little eyes, and that red hair of hers. The stupid things she said.

I found excitement now when I stepped out on the court to hit the tennis balls Jonathan lobbed to me from across the net.

I was hitting them hard now.

36

A Doll Bill Cosby Might Get for His Daughter

Arriving back at the house on our bikes after our morning activities, the children and I found a long black vehicle, barely smaller than a limousine, pulling up outside Wonderland—a black Lincoln Town Car with South Carolina license plates. The car was unfamiliar to me, but Hayward and Jilly knew who this was. Neither one of them looked particularly happy about it. Nobody seemed in a rush to greet the occupants.

"Our grandparents," Hayward groaned. "They live in Hilton Head most of the time. My mom told me some friend of my grandpa's kicked the bucket. They probably came for the funeral."

A visit from the Cabots was a rare event, evidently. "My grandpa hates my dad," Jilly explained as the three of us parked our bikes.

"Our grandmother's not that wild about him either," Hayward added. "They think our dad just married our mom so he'd get a bunch of their money."

As we approached the house, a more immediate problem concerned me. Ever since the arrival of Hurricane Brenda, Forrest had been gone for the better part of every day. The note he left this morning said he'd gone for a "training swim"—a full seven miles around the lakeshore.

Judging from recent experience, he was unlikely to be home for another hour or two.

That wouldn't be so bad if Regina were up, but her naps had been lasting longer and longer lately. This left the distinct possibility that it would be just the children and me entertaining our guests and having to come up with an explanation for the absence of their parents.

Prudence had let them in. Now the grandparents—Colson and Suzanne—sat side by side on the couch. Though it was just past lunchtime, they had their drinks in hand. Good call on the part of Prudence, who was back in the kitchen now, preparing snacks.

Just when I thought it was going to be up to me to keep the ball rolling, Forrest appeared. Still in his swim trunks, he'd come in straight from the lake, his impressive ab muscles on display. He was still drying himself off on the patio when he spotted them: the in-laws who despised him.

The man who stepped into the house now was either a long-distance swimmer who had just spent four hours making his way around the lake or—more likely—a man who had passed the majority of that time having sex somewhere with Brenda Barnett. You could say that finding his in-laws in his house at just this moment was Forrest's worst nightmare.

I watched him arrange his face. Within seconds he took on the role of genial host, offering a warm welcome to the only two individuals on the planet, possibly, who didn't think he was wonderful. He ran the towel briskly over his still-wet hair and wrapped it around his waist, then extended his hand with his usual open-faced grin.

"Colson! Suzanne! Regina didn't tell me you were coming. Looks like Prudence already got you a drink!"

My weeks at the Lake Catherine Country Club had provided me with an education in the behavior of people like these two, and at the club I'd learned to tolerate them, but I didn't do that now. As hurt as I'd been by Forrest's abandonment, I felt a surge of protectiveness and offense on his behalf. It had taken me about four minutes to conclude that I hated the Cabots.

Forrest cast his eyes in the direction of the kitchen. I knew he'd be praying Prudence would bring a drink for him too. On the double. I could hear her in the kitchen preparing it.

He took a seat across from his in-laws. Forrest was always good at concealing any sign of trouble, but I knew, because I knew him so well, that he'd rather be almost anyplace else—the dentist's office getting root canal surgery, a meeting with the Internal Revenue Service to discuss his tax return, a class in embroidery, cleaning a bilge pump—than where he was, in this beautiful room, in his beautiful house, overlooking a beautiful lake on a perfect summer day, with two people who probably wished he'd drop dead so long as he didn't bleed on the furniture.

Across from them, the children slouched against the pillows of the other couch. Hayward examined his fingernails. Jilly kept her hands in her lap.

"Come say hello to your grandparents," Suzanne instructed them. Jilly approached the couch, offering a gesture resembling a hug. Hayward followed. For Colson, the greeting was a handshake.

"They're getting so big," he observed to his wife. "Aren't you a pretty girl?" he said, addressing Jilly. How was a six-year-old supposed to respond to that one?

"You want to see my Teddy Ruxpin, Grandma?" Jilly said. "He talks."

"Did you get the doll I sent you?" her grandmother asked. The latest American Girl.

"I sent you a thank-you note," Jilly reminded her. Regina would have made sure of this.

"Oh, right. I hope you liked it. I have to say, those dolls are no bargain."

Prudence set out the plate of cheese and crackers. Colson reached for an olive. Forrest took a long sip from the Bloody Mary Prudence had delivered to him in record time.

"So how was your drive?" he asked.

"We stopped in Boston for the night," Suzanne offered. "The Parker House."

"I've had their rolls," I told them. Trying to be helpful. It was meant to be a joke, sort of.

"Getting a lot of golf in this summer?" Forrest asked his father-in-law.

"Not particularly." End of conversation.

Jilly had returned now with the toy to show her grandmother—her talking bear. Hayward had already made his way over to the gaming console. We could hear the sound of a game he'd acquired recently coming from where he sat, *The Legend of Zelda*.

Suzanne cast her eyes over Forrest, bare chested and still dripping on the couch. "Looks like you've been doing some swimming," she observed. Still with his towel around his waist, Forrest reached for his shirt. A damp spot had formed underneath him. No doubt Suzanne would disapprove. Regina was particular about the upholstery. I saw where she got it from.

"I'm training for a triathlon," he said. "Labor Day weekend."

"I never had the time for that kind of thing," Colson said. "Something called *work*. Corporations don't run themselves."

We sat in silence. I reached for a chip. Colson did likewise. Suzanne—not quite as skinny as Regina, but getting there—abstained. Jilly, with her mouth full, pushed Teddy Ruxpin's button. For once I was glad to hear his stupid singsong voice: "Can you and I be friends?"

"I got him for kindergarten graduation," Jilly told her grandmother. "Want to see my room?"

"We have to be heading out, unfortunately," Suzanne said. "Your grandfather and I have dinner reservations. Tomorrow's the service for Harold."

"You aren't having supper with us?" Jilly asked her. They didn't act anything like the grandparents on *The Waltons* reruns she watched on Nickelodeon. But as little enthusiasm as these two demonstrated for the role, they were still her grandparents.

"Maybe next time," Suzanne said. Jilly looked vaguely disappointed. Or maybe just surprised.

All this time, Regina had yet to put in an appearance. Neither of her parents had mentioned this. It was Forrest who did, finally.

"If you're not sticking around for dinner, I'd better see what's keeping that daughter of yours," he told them. He'd brought out his best imitation of the old Forrest, the one I loved, not much in evidence lately. "You know Regina. Always off someplace, up to something."

We all knew the truth. She was up in her room. Regina hardly ever went anywhere.

"I'll be right back," Forrest said. As if his in-laws might miss him.

An awkward silence fell over the room again. Prudence asked Colson if she could refill his drink. "I'm driving," he told her.

This was when Suzanne addressed me for the first time. "So what brings you to Lake Catherine, dear?" she asked. "Are you one of the children's young friends from the club?"

Yeah, right. Almost fifteen years old, and I'm hanging out with a couple of spoiled pip-squeaks. For fun.

"I'm the babysitter," I told her. "I come from New Jersey."

"New Jersey." She considered this for a moment. "The shore?"

"Hubbard. My dad and Forrest grew up together."

Something inspired me to go further with this. Maybe it had something to do with the weird dark side of myself that had been coming out for a while in the pages of my journal. The Bad Girl.

"Forrest was really bad at reading and spelling. My dad wrote his papers for him. Sometimes he'd forge notes for the two of them when they wanted to skip school. They snuck into the movies a lot. One time they watched four James Bond movies in a row."

I studied Colson's and Suzanne's faces as I spoke. *Nothing.* But I was on a roll.

"How interesting," Suzanne said. "I guess we'll be heading back to the hotel." She reached for her bag. She was one of those women who brought her purse with her wherever she went. You never knew when you might have some shopping to do. Or one of the servants might try to steal your charge cards.

This was when Regina appeared at the foot of the stairs. She was wearing one of her floaty dresses. I guessed that Forrest had encouraged her to put it on so she'd look a little more normal, though she didn't.

"Hello, Mother." She drifted over to where Suzanne sat checking her lipstick to receive a kiss.

"Father." He turned his head to receive what passed for a kiss.

"Keeping your figure, I see," he observed. Did he think it looked good, her being so skinny?

"It's too bad about Harold," she said.

"He'd been in the nursing home for almost ten years," Colson told her. "The last time we saw him, he thought I was his father. Miserable life."

"I guess in that case your friend dying could be a relief," Forrest said. "When a person gets like that, it's a huge burden on the family, right?"

Colson gave him a look. You might have called this the evil eye. I could read his mind. He was thinking that this was what his son-in-law's attitude would be toward him someday, when he was the one to kick the bucket. Why would anyone feel otherwise?

Suzanne had her hand on the doorknob now.

Maybe Regina felt a need to make one last try, because she turned to her mother and said, "I've been working on a knitting project." Meaning the white mohair thing that never seemed to progress beyond the fourth row of stitches.

"Too bad you chose white. One drop of red wine and it's ruined," Suzanne said. They were out on the steps now. Short as their visit had been, it seemed like the right thing to walk them to the car. The scene felt so awful, I thought I'd help.

"Jilly loves her new doll," I offered.

"I wish they'd make a Black one," Jilly said. I would not have expected this from Jilly. She was definitely trying to get a rise out of her grandparents. Maybe visits from the Cabots brought out the bad girl in all of us.

"Those dolls are expensive." Suzanne again. "They make them for the type of people who can afford them." Meaning white ones.

"Bill Cosby could afford to buy his kids American Girl dolls," Hayward said. "Same with Michael Jordan, if he had a girl someday. Or Mr. T."

The grandparents had taken their seats in the Lincoln by this point. The six of us stood lined up in the driveway, watching. Regina in her oversized housecoat. Forrest in his towel. Jilly was still gripping her bear, whose recording device appeared to be malfunctioning in such a way that he kept saying the words *special friend* over and over. Even Prudence was there, holding the refill Colson would not be needing.

Suzanne flipped down the passenger-side sun visor to check her reflection. Something must have caught her eye in the rearview mirror. She rolled down the windows. Her voice—which had seemed, for the entire duration of her visit, like that of a person in a commercial—took on an utterly different tone for a moment.

"What's that you've put up in our old maple?" she said. She must have noticed the tree house Forrest had been building for Jilly. Unfinished.

"I thought we took that down years ago," she said. "After—"

"It's a different one," Regina said. "This one's for Jilly."

"I can still remember the tea parties you used to have up there," Suzanne said. "You and—"

"That's enough, Suzanne," Colson said. His wife rolled up the window on her side.

Regina went back into the house without further comment. Forrest and I stood there, watching the Cabots' Lincoln disappear down the long driveway. When we stepped back in the house ourselves a moment later, Regina had gone back to bed.

37

WhAT A MAN Looks Like AfTER He Has Sex

Jilly and I were up in her room, playing with her dolls. She was Molly, her most recent acquisition. I was Samantha, the one whose hair she had cut a while back, before she understood what a bad idea it was, giving a haircut to an American Girl doll.

The dolls were having a fight. Molly had just accused Samantha of being mean. The voice Jilly employed when being Molly was higher than her normal one, the words delivered in something approximating an English accent. Jilly's idea of one.

"I'm not mean, I just have a stomachache," I said, trying to come up with an alternate voice of my own for my doll—Southern, maybe— and having a hard time at it. It wasn't a very inspired response, but I wasn't into the game. I was thinking about Forrest, though not in the happy way I had in the early days of summer. I was thinking about Forrest as he was now. A version of him I still loved, though I wasn't sure I liked him.

That night he took us all out for fried clams. We were sitting at an outdoor table, a giant bowl of clams in the middle. French fries, tartar sauce. All my favorites, with my favorite person at the table. Even now, in the Post-Brenda World—even now that he didn't seem to be too interested in hearing about my life the way he had been previously—I couldn't help feeling good just being around him.

Forrest looked distracted—a little like the way I got, it occurred to me, when Jilly wanted me to play tea party with her and her dolls, and I wasn't really into it. But I told myself this wasn't so bad. He might be cheating on Regina, but he wasn't cheating on me. Our relationship could still be the same. One thing remained the same, anyway: I could still be who he'd told me I was. A girl with an amazing life ahead of her. A girl he considered part of the family.

This was the night I decided I'd tell the Emersons about my tennis lessons. Not that it was the group of them that mattered to me. I just wanted to tell Forrest.

"You remember that girl, Olivia," I said, dipping my clam in the sauce. I wanted to tell Forrest about how she'd walked off the court, and the free lessons Jonathan had been giving me, and what he'd said about my potential as a tennis player. I wanted to tell him how it felt when I was running after the ball so hard I thought my heart might explode, actually connecting with it at the last second—and not just connecting but returning it. Hearing Jonathan's voice calling out from across the net, "Good get." The high five afterward.

I didn't get that far into my story. I was just getting to the part where Olivia walked off the court. Forrest checked his watch.

"I hate to cut things short," he said, "but we've got a full moon tonight. I'm going on a nighttime ride with the guys."

He wasn't fooling either of us. Regina and I both knew where he was going.

Forrest got up from the table. As he often did, he lifted his bike from the back of the Jeep. "You take the car, honey," he told Regina. "I've got my ride."

Jilly protested, of course. Jilly was the one who gave voice to what the rest of us were feeling and not saying.

"Daddy!" she wailed. "Why don't you ever stay home with us anymore?"

"I've got some steep hills to tackle tonight, Jilly Bean," he told her. "You don't want your old man to drop out of the triathlon because he can't keep up with the young guys, do you?"

"I don't care about the triathlon. I just want you," she told him. For once I agreed with her.

There remained one source of reassurance—Regina's words to me that Forrest's affair didn't really mean anything. This would pass, as it had with Pam Oliver and the others before her. I told myself the fact that there had been many women before Brenda was the good news. Forrest's affairs meant so little. This one would be over soon, same as the others.

Meanwhile I was feeling a surprising new connection with Regina. As little warmth as I sensed coming my way from her in the past (even when she gave me the fishnet stockings and the wooden owl, and the Maria Callas album, and the awful Fourth of July dress, and when she played me the Elgar concerto), I'd come to feel something for her—not affection, exactly, but a weird kind of sisterhood that I could never have anticipated. Forrest mounted his road bike. Regina and I exchanged a look, shared a mutual recognition of the fact that the man we both loved was likely to find himself, within the hour, nuzzling the flowing auburn hair of Brenda Barnett.

It was after midnight when Forrest returned. His bicycle made no sound as he pulled up to the house, but for some reason, even though I'd been asleep up until then, I knew he was back, and when I looked out the window, there he was in the moonlight, resting the bicycle against the house, unbuckling his helmet and setting it on the seat of his bike.

He didn't walk into the house right away. He stood there for a moment, facing the lake. From my small bed three stories up I watched him out the window. Even knowing what I did, the sight of Forrest Emerson standing there in the moonlight still lifted my heart.

He ran his hand through his hair. He stretched his arms out wide, as if he was reaching for something. His back was arched, his head thrown back. I couldn't see his face, but I imagined it. His eyes would be closed, as if he was going over in his head everything that happened that night.

The thought came to me. *This is what a man looks like after he has sex.*

38

Forever

It was a few days later—the fourth week in July now.

I'd used up Olivia's tennis lessons a while back, but more than ever I wanted to work with Jonathan. In a matter of weeks I'd become obsessed with tennis.

Regina had recently decided to increase my pay by another thirty dollars a week. I'd started to use this money to cover the cost of my lessons—four a week now, sometimes five. Jonathan probably imagined that, like all the other kids at the club, I had parents footing the bill. That would have been nice, but on the other hand I liked that I was paying my own way. I didn't ever want to be a person like Jilly and Hayward, or Olivia.

After my lesson that day, I biked over to the library. I'd finished *Pet Sematary* and needed to find something new to read.

Between reading and tennis, it came to me that I'd been thinking less about Forrest lately. I wasn't even writing about him so much in my journal anymore. I felt relieved that this was so. I wasn't over my feelings for Forrest, but he no longer occupied the same space in my brain.

Then it happened. Wandering through the stacks, I heard a familiar voice. Just the voice, but I knew right away who it was, though two or three rows of books concealed us from each other. I didn't need to see his face to know who was speaking.

"I think I can get away Thursday night," the man was saying. "The kids have a sleepover at their friends' house. I'll tell Regina I need to head into the city for the day. I need new running shoes."

A woman's voice then. "Oh, darling."

"But what about your husband?" The man again. I knew who this was, of course.

"Kyle's an idiot." Her voice was less familiar than the man's, but it wasn't difficult to figure out to whom it belonged. "He never notices anything if the Red Sox are on."

There was a pause. Kissing, probably. Then the man's voice again. "I don't know how I can wait that long to have my arms around you again. I have to be inside you."

Brenda's voice took on a concerned tone as she said, "I just want to make sure you feel as good as I do about what we're doing. I don't want us to do this if it doesn't feel totally right. What we have is too important."

The two of them had chosen a spot deep in the stacks to meet—someplace that housed books about medieval history or outdated manuals for things like crochet and training your pet. It was a part of the library where vacationers at Lake Catherine were unlikely to venture.

What was she talking about—wanting to make sure that what they were doing with each other was right? How was it ever supposed to be right to have sex with someone else's husband? Not to mention cheating on your own husband at the same time, and lying to everyone while you were at it. Then there was what Forrest was doing, cheating on his wife and his two children. And—this part I kept in the most hidden-away portion of my brain—the way he'd hurt me too.

"How can something that feels this right be wrong?" he said to Brenda.

I probably missed the irony here. It did not occur to me that at least the first part of this scenario was one I had imagined, myself—a version of it, anyway, with me playing the role now enjoyed by Brenda. Like Brenda Barnett, I had constructed scenes of myself in the arms of someone else's husband. This same husband, actually.

In my case, what I had envisioned had unfolded as a fantasy. It wasn't ever going to happen, except in my imagination. What Brenda and Forrest were talking about in the stacks of the Lake Catherine Library was actually taking place.

I held my breath. I stood there with my hand on the spine of the Stephen King book I'd been planning to check out that day. A couple of rows over, I could hear the sound of the two of them breathing heavily. Forrest was whispering. I couldn't make out the words. He was nuzzled up close now, most likely. Her hair muffled the sound.

"I knew the moment I saw you we were meant to be together," she said.

"Me too."

"I feel like we must have known each other in another life."

"I was thinking the same thing."

"It's going to be agony waiting until Thursday."

I might be fourteen years old, but even to me, a kid, their words to each other sounded dumb. *Gag me with a spoon,* Hayward would have said. The two of them talked like characters from one of Prudence's soap operas.

"You know this is crazy, don't you?" she said.

"If this is crazy, I don't ever want to be sane."

Then came more breathing, followed by what was probably the sound of kissing. A book falling off the shelf. A few of them. Nervous laughter.

"We'd better get out of here before we get in trouble with the librarian," he whispered. "You know librarians."

"I don't know anything anymore. I just know I have to be with you."

"You will be, darling," he told her.

This last part was what startled me.

"Forever?" she asked him.

"I've never felt like this about anyone, ever," he said.

"I want to spend my life with you," she said. "We'll figure out a way, right?"

Based on the sounds emanating from their section of the library stacks, it seemed Forrest agreed with her.

I stayed in the stacks for a few more minutes, until I was sure the two of them had left. I got my book and brought it to the front desk.

"You're quite a little reader, aren't you?" the librarian asked me, stamping the well-used copy of *Christine*. "You've become one of our best customers."

"I really like Stephen King books," I told her.

"You work for the Emersons, right?" she said. "You just missed Forrest. What a sweetheart."

A look came over her. The librarian was on the older side, but the thought occurred to me that maybe she had a history with Forrest too, long ago.

"He was picking up a book for his wife," she said. Back to librarian mode. "She's not a well woman, I gather. He's such a caring husband."

Outside, I hopped on Buttercup and headed in the direction of the house. But I couldn't go back there yet. Until this moment, I hadn't fully accepted what Regina had told me about Forrest's affairs. I'd held out a slim hope that she could be wrong about Forrest and Brenda. I might have told myself it wasn't Forrest's fault women chased after him all the time. He was just being nice.

What I felt now, pumping my bicycle up the long hill toward the road leading to the lake—standing up on the pedals, tears coming so hard I could barely see in front of me—was an emotion I had not registered before. Not toward Forrest, anyway. I wasn't just hurt. I was angry.

When Regina confided in me about her husband's summer liaisons, she described them as if they meant nothing. "It's like a sport for Forrest," she'd told me. "Sometimes he plays tennis. Sometimes he golfs.

Sometimes he fools around with somebody's wife. When the summer's over, he's mine again. He's always mine in the end. Forrest isn't going anywhere."

What I'd overheard at the library told me otherwise. To hear Brenda talk—and not just Brenda, but Forrest himself—the two of them seemed to be embarking on a serious all-out love affair. With a future that went beyond Labor Day.

Brenda believed she'd be with Forrest forever.

He had not disputed the idea.

What did I know about love affairs? Nothing beyond what I'd picked up at the movies and in a few books. But nobody could have mistaken the tone of Brenda's voice as she talked about their upcoming get-together as that of a woman interested in nothing more than a casual flirtation. And then there was Forrest. He sounded like a drunk person, but not the kind of drunk I was familiar with. Drunk on love. Or sex, anyway.

I had pedaled Buttercup halfway around the lake now, and up into the hills above Lake Catherine. My legs were sore, and it had started to rain, but I couldn't turn back. I had to calm down first and figure out what to say when I got back to the house and saw Regina.

Was I supposed to keep this new information to myself? The truth was that even after Regina had explained to me about Forrest's summer flings, he had remained my favorite person in the universe—as opposed to her, a woman it was hard to feel affection for. But she and I had become allies now. Regina wasn't the only person Forrest had cheated on.

This was when I discovered what rage felt like. It seemed to me that in addition to having betrayed his not-particularly-lovable wife, the man I loved more than anything had betrayed me, personally. Every kindness he'd shown me—playing me Creedence Clearwater and Bob Seger tapes in the car on our long drive from New Jersey up to the lake, letting me steer the boat, hitting golf balls with me on a driving range in the last light of day, bringing me along in the Porsche to pick up strawberries at the farm stand and eating the whole box in the car on the way home while we talked about my dream of becoming a writer, telling me I was part of the family now and that I had an amazing life ahead of me—all that had been a lie. I was a sucker and a loser to have imagined he ever cared about me.

He probably made fun of me to his girlfriend. "Can you believe our babysitter's in love with me?" he'd say. "That flat-chested little girl who plays with my daughter's dolls?"

They'd laugh. Then they'd start kissing again. Then would come the sex part. The *fucking*.

I said it out loud. Yelled it actually. On my yellow bicycle, pedaling hard, I yelled it. *Fuck him. Fuck everyone. Fuck everything.*

Forrest had conned me. All those questions he'd asked about my thoughts on life were just his way of keeping me on board as someone who'd ensure that Jilly and Hayward stayed occupied while he fooled around with Brenda. I was a dope and a loser to have ever believed otherwise.

It's one thing when people you never trusted in the first place turn out to be mean—people like Olivia. The worst thing is when the person who lets you down is a person you loved more than anyone else in the world.

39

SUMMER LOVE

Something shifted in me. Maybe there was a direct correlation between the level of devotion you could feel for a person, if you believed he cared about you, and the depths of hatred you'd reach if you discovered otherwise.

This was what happened to me then. Over the space of time it took me to ride my bike up the hill from the library, the long way along the lakeshore back to Wonderland—more than an hour—my whole world changed. Where, so recently, Forrest had represented everything good in my life—his approval all that mattered—what I wanted now was for him to feel the kind of grief and pain I was experiencing.

If I hurt this way, so should he.

There was only one person on earth capable of understanding what I was going through: Regina. Unlike to Forrest, for whom it turned out I had been nothing more than an amusing plaything, to Regina I was a respected friend and confidante, an ally.

Regina took me seriously. She'd called me her one true friend. All this time I'd looked at her with a mixture of judgment and pity. Now I understood how brave she was, how wronged she'd been. I understood something else too, an ominous piece of information that Regina had yet to take in. From what I'd overheard at the library, the affair with

Brenda wasn't just a replay of Forrest's usual summer behavior. What was going on was more than a summer fling.

Those two wanted to be together, not just for some stupid version of the summer love fun Olivia Newton-John and John Travolta sang about in *Grease*. They were talking about always. For real. *Forever.*

Brenda had called her husband an idiot. Forrest wanted to leave his wife. There seemed no other way to interpret what they'd said.

I already knew that Regina's appeal for Forrest (not his love for her, maybe, but his desire) had expired a long time ago. She'd said as much herself back when we had our conversation down at the lake.

What I understood now was the hardest part: Forrest Emerson had no real interest in me either. Maybe he did once. Maybe he never did. But whatever little piece of his heart he might have reserved for me in times gone by, I didn't occupy one inch of that place anymore.

I was last year's American Girl doll.

In my fourteen-year-old brain, there seemed only one thing to do now: I would tell Regina what I'd discovered about Forrest. Whatever she wanted to do with that information, I was on her team now.

40

SHE SAID *WE*

I waited a day before I told Regina what I'd learned at the library. I was afraid of what she might do. I'd heard my mother's assessment: *You never know with that woman when the next time will be when she goes off the deep end.* I didn't want that to happen on my watch.

I chose a moment the following afternoon when the children were at sailing lessons. Forrest was gone, of course, off on one of his supposed triathlon-training sessions. Prudence was doing laundry.

I knocked on Regina's bedroom door.

She was typing one of her to-do lists. She seemed so engrossed in it that I had to say her name twice before she looked up.

"I need to talk to you," I said.

She looked up from her typewriter, identical to the one in the kitchen.

"I guess you never saw this room before, did you?" she said.

I looked around, as if studying the room for the first time. There were pill bottles everywhere, plus Regina's record player, with a pile of very old albums strewn across the floor—classical, from the looks of them—along with balls of knitting yarn, a lace shawl, slippers, some kind of animal skin (deer maybe?), and a glass table displaying specimens of exotic insects impaled by pins. There was a photograph of

Regina and Forrest looking young and in love, and a machine that made sounds like the ocean, probably meant to help her sleep. What looked like a very old Barbie doll on a stand, wearing a black sequined evening gown, was poised next to the bed on what looked like a custom-made stand. Beside her, the red typewriter.

I stood at the foot of the bed. She did not suggest I take a seat.

"I was at the library the other day," I told Regina. "I went there to pick up a book."

She didn't rush me. She did not say, as some might, "Cut to the chase."

"I heard these two people talking," I told her. "It turned out to be them, Forrest and . . . Brenda." For a moment, I resisted speaking her name.

"Oh, really?" Regina's voice sounded steady. "I wouldn't have guessed Brenda Barnett as the bookish type."

"I don't want to make you mad," I said. "But they were saying these things to each other. About how much they wanted to be together. They were making a plan to meet up."

My words seemed to have had less effect than I'd expected. Regina reached for the ball of mohair wool she used in her knitting project and stroked it contemplatively.

"Oh well," she said. "I guess we knew about this already, didn't we? It's just Forrest engaging in his usual summertime hijinks. Forrest being Forrest. This too shall pass." She let out a long sigh. She looked back at her typewriter keyboard, ready to resume work on her list, apparently.

I could have let it go there. It would have been easy to let her think that nothing more had taken place at the library that afternoon. But I knew this wasn't the whole story.

And maybe there was something else going on in me that made me push harder. As much anxiety as I'd felt about delivering the news of what I'd learned at the library and as much personal grief as I'd suffered over it, I'd felt excitement about my role as the one person other than Forrest and Brenda themselves who understood what was going on and was in a position to help Regina. This conferred a kind of power on me that was all new.

"They were talking like they were going to be together. The word they used was *forever*."

"Oh, Frances," she said. A look of something between sympathy and pity came over her. "If I'm not mistaken, before you got on this Stephen King kick, you were reading all those Judy Blume books. Wasn't there one with that word for the title, about a couple of kids who think they're each other's destiny or something? I read that one too, long ago. As you may remember, it didn't work out that way."

Maybe she was right. I wanted to believe she was.

"What you overheard at the library between Forrest and this little girlfriend of his was just a couple of not-particularly-bright people getting sex confused with love. It's happened before with my husband— every damn summer, if you must know—and I have every reason to believe it's going to happen again. Maybe the two of them think cheating on your partner is more honorable when you call it love. Whatever their story is, it doesn't matter all that much to me."

"I just thought you should know," I said.

In truth, I couldn't even remember what Forrest and Brenda had said to each other that day anymore. I just remembered the feeling I had hearing them. That I'd shrunk into nothing again. That in the world of Forrest Emerson, in which Brenda Barnett presided as queen bee—a world in which I had seemed, very briefly, to occupy a place of significance—I now meant no more than a bug.

In the world of Regina Emerson, on the other hand, I was important. Never more so than right now.

She had returned her hands to the keyboard of her typewriter, but she wasn't typing. I could see her turning it all over in her mind, considering my words. Maybe they were sinking in. Maybe she was beginning to get it.

Regina said nothing for a surprisingly long time then. She just sat there, stroking the sides of her beautiful red Olivetti.

"They just sounded so serious," I said again.

"Well then," Regina said, her tone still revealing little in the way of concern. "It may be prudent to keep some sort of record. I suppose we need to protect ourselves."

She said *we*. I didn't get the part about protecting ourselves, but the other part I did.

We.

"That husband of this Brenda person—the car salesman, Kyle—is too weak to do anything," Regina went on. The way she named his line of work, she might as well have been telling me he was one of those men who walked along the side of the highway picking up trash. "They're just renters here, you know."

Renters. I knew what that meant. Another breed altogether from Regina and her family. The Barnetts weren't even members of the country club.

"What happens now?" I asked Regina.

"This is where you come in, Frances," she told me. Her voice, which had sounded so hard, softened now. "I'm lucky you're at my side here. My only friend."

Not that there was much competition in that department. I felt flattered that she described me as she did. But it was unnerving too. I had the sense she had forgotten I was just a kid, and as much as I wished I were older, or looked older to the rest of the world, at this particular moment I felt I was way too young for this. I had no idea what any of this had to do with me. Only it did, evidently.

As was often the case with Regina, she seemed to know what I was thinking, even at times when I said nothing.

"I know you haven't even begun to menstruate yet," she said. This was an odd thing to mention—an odd way of putting it, and embarrassing, of course. But she had nailed it: the source of all my problems, my inadequacies, the reason for my inability to be heard or seen or taken seriously. "But even when you were very small, I recognized you were old beyond your years. You understood so much more than they did. More than most people."

As was often the case with Regina, I had no idea what to say. I waited for her to explain.

"I'm going to need your help," she said. "You're actually a key player here. *The* key player."

All this time I'd been standing at the side of Regina's bed. Now she patted a spot beside her, indicating I should sit there. She took my hand. She stroked it as if she were petting a dog.

"I need proof," she told me. "On the chance that I ever feel the need to get a lawyer involved."

A lawyer?

"For the divorce, naturally. If it comes to that. I'm sure we both hope it won't."

There was that word again. *We.* I wasn't following her. But it had an effect. As did the word *divorce.* Until now, it had seemed to me that Regina held tenaciously to her marriage. She might be critical of Forrest (relentlessly so). She might even be disdainful. But I'd never heard the slightest suggestion that they wouldn't be together always.

Now a side of her I'd never seen revealed itself. Her eyes had taken on a steely cast. She drew her lips tightly together as if she were sucking on sour fruit.

"I can't do this without you, Frances," she told me.

In my whole life, I'm not sure anybody had ever said they needed me. Oh, maybe Forrest needed me to take the children to their tennis lessons, and sailing. Prudence needed me to set the table for dinner, or clear off the plates afterward. My mother mostly needed me to keep quiet and ask as little of her as possible. My father needed me to listen to him talk about the novel he was never going to finish, the poems and music I didn't understand. But Regina Emerson needed me to do something that mattered. To Regina, I was *the key player.*

"You're too young to understand all of this, but there's a lot of money and property at stake here," Regina said. "Forrest understands very well that if he leaves me, he'll be penniless. If this woman he's playing around with is foolish enough to throw everything away to be with him, she'll be penniless too." Something like a smile crossed over Regina's face.

"Brenda." She spoke the name as if just saying it out loud felt physically disgusting. As if she had maggots in her mouth and needed to spit them out. And then she laughed.

"I'll do whatever you want," I told her. What was I saying? What did it matter? Did anything matter anymore?

Regina shifted gears then. She was typing.

"You'll be like a private investigator," she said, fingers flying over the keys. "Collecting the evidence."

"Evidence?"

"We need proof of what's going on between those two," she said. "In the unlikely event that Forrest is actually stupid enough to believe that he and his little girlfriend have a future together. I need proof of what Forrest's been up to, in case he ever goes after me for some ungodly amount of money he doesn't deserve so he can start a whole new life with her."

This didn't sound like the Forrest I knew, and it was not how Regina had ever portrayed him to me either. The Forrest I knew never cared much about money. On the other hand, the Forrest I thought I knew never would have said those things to Brenda Barnett that day at the library. Maybe I never really knew Forrest after all. I didn't know anything anymore.

"He'd have to accuse me of being an unfit mother. He'd probably say I'm a drug addict. He'd testify that I have mental health issues. Just to get his hands on my money."

"That's not fair," I said, indignation rising up in me.

When you thought about it, the potential accusations Forrest might make about Regina were not so far off base. Still, it would be pretty terrible for a person to actually raise them.

"You do a lot around here. Like those lists you make." There had to be more. I just couldn't think of it.

"We'll make sure it never happens," she said, patting my hand again. "You'll be my personal detective. Think of yourself like that woman in *Murder, She Wrote*. Or Nancy Drew. Harriet the Spy."

"I never did anything like that," I told her. "I wouldn't know how."

"Oh, but you're a natural," she said. "You've been sitting on the sidelines, watching other people all your life. You notice everything. And you're so good at being invisible.

"See how interested Brenda Barnett is in sticking around," she said, "once her dream lover's sleeping in a double-wide trailer. See if she still believes in forever then."

41

LIFE AS USUAL

An odd thing happened after that: nothing. The day passed with no further word concerning Regina's plan, whatever it was she was cooking up. And another day after that. I'd almost come to believe that her words to me—about my being her personal detective, collecting evidence, the possibility of divorce—were a product of some drug-induced altered state she must have been in that afternoon. Maybe she'd forgotten the whole thing. One way or another, she gave no indication of taking action.

It was a few days later. At dinner that night, served on the patio, Regina wore a surprisingly becoming outfit (silky black pants and a silk shirt, electric blue, in her appropriate size for once. Zero, probably.) She had makeup on, and earrings, and she'd done something with her hair. It didn't seem as lank as normal. She looked pretty.

At the table across from me, seated in the chair he always favored, with Regina on one side, Jilly on the other, Forrest was entertaining us with a story from his swim around the lake that afternoon—a swim neither Regina nor I believed he'd actually undertaken.

"I was just going along, minding my own business, doing my crawl stroke, when who should come up to me but the Loch Ness Monster," he told us.

"You're pulling our leg, Daddy," Jilly said.

"I'm telling you the god's honest truth," he said. "All my life I've heard stories about the monster living at the bottom of our lake, but I never saw him before," Forrest went on. "*Her*, actually. It turns out she's a girl monster."

"Yeah, right," Hayward said. He was affecting his customary bored voice, but you could tell he was at least mildly interested in what his father was going to come up with next. "How were you supposed to know if the monster was a girl or a boy, anyway? What did you do, dive underwater and check out its genitals?"

The way he said it, you knew Hayward was enjoying saying the word *genitals* in front of us all. Me, in particular. Maybe he imagined this would make him seem older. More sophisticated.

"You raise an excellent point, son," Forrest said to him. "In fact, it is a known feature of sea monsters that the female of the species is considerably less colorful than the male—as is true of so many other species of wildlife. Peacocks, for instance. The Guatemalan quetzal. The African mandrill, a variety of monkey."

"You're full of it," Hayward said, rolling his eyes. But I could tell he was enjoying it.

"This is hardly true of the human species, I have to admit," Forrest went on. He was not yet finished with his discourse on plumage, evidently, and none of us was in a rush.

"Take your mother, for example," he said, placing his arm over Regina's shoulders and stroking her hair. "There is no question who the beauty is in this family. And you know the truth? It has nothing to do with this lovely blouse she's got on, or these pearl earrings of hers."

He tapped one slightly, enough that it spun.

"Your mother, children, glows from within."

I shot a look over to Regina, her face softening slightly.

"Do I glow from within, Daddy?" Jilly asked him. That was Jilly for you. Always quick to see where she fit in the story and make sure she was the star of it.

I had no need to ask a similar question concerning myself. As Regina had reminded me that day, my great talent lay in attracting the least attention possible. Though I had briefly known the feeling—and it was intoxicating—of standing in the warm glow of Forrest's attention, that magical and fleeting time was over. I might as well have been eating my dinner in the kitchen with Prudence for all the interest Forrest appeared to take in me now.

"So, what did you do when this monster approached you, darling?" Regina asked. She called Forrest *darling*. Just three days after she'd conjured an image of him living in a trailer after their possible divorce. "Weren't you scared she might eat you alive?"

From his spot across the table from me, Forrest flashed his irresistible grin. He might have grown up in the projects, but somehow he'd managed to emerge from there with the whitest teeth.

"You know I have a way of charming myself out of tricky situations," he said. "I just told that ugly old monster she was looking particularly lovely that day. She batted her eyelashes and took off on her way."

Regina smiled. I had the odd feeling that what I was watching—despite the presence of the children—was an intimate, almost sexual scene between the two of them. Even their children played a role in the drama, but I shouldn't be here. I was an interloper.

Still, I couldn't tear myself away. As out of place as I felt sitting with the rest of them, I couldn't get up from the table. There was something about Forrest that drew you to him and made you melt.

"Did you really meet a monster that lived in the lake, Daddy?" Jilly asked him. "Really, truly, actually, for real?"

"Would I lie to you?" he said.

The next morning, when I came downstairs to the kitchen—the absence of Forrest at the breakfast table no longer a surprise—I found a small package, wrapped in tinfoil, next to my cereal bowl. When I unwrapped it, I found a fishing lure and a hook. A piece of paper was impaled on the hook. No words on it. Just the letter *X*.

Maybe I was wrong about his lack of interest in me after all. No question, he was having an affair with Brenda. But he still had a place in his heart for me.

What was he trying to tell me? What was I supposed to do about this?

42

The Assignment

Another few days passed in which nothing appeared to change. Forrest continued to leave the house just after sunrise, disappearing for hours. I made the rounds of the club, the Caboose, my chaise lounge down by the lakefront, the library. I had a tennis lesson almost every day now, not that anyone but Jonathan took note.

At night I no longer wrote my crazy, dangerous stories of sex and romance. Lying in bed now, I replayed moments on the tennis court, remembering what Jonathan had told me about my backhand grip, my footwork, my serve, my follow-through. If I lifted up the mattress and took out my journal at all now, it was only to make lists of pointers Jonathan had given me that day. I went over these in my head in the moments before sleep.

Regina continued to leave us all her daily lists of typewritten instructions—for Forrest, a reminder to pick up some medication and check the filters on the air conditioner, or that her pearls needed to be restrung and would he please bring them to the jeweler for her. There was a reminder that Jilly had another birthday party to attend and needed a gift. Her most recent birthday offering hadn't gone over well, so Regina had increased the budget to twenty-five dollars.

I've been noticing you seem to have taken off a little weight, Frances, she wrote to me. *Bravo.* She followed this with a reminder that Hayward needed to clean out his earwax.

Other than the exchange of these notes, Regina and I had barely communicated since our discussion in her room. The same was true of Forrest and me; it was almost as if he knew I'd overheard his conversation with Brenda, or simply that he knew I knew what he was doing and couldn't look me in the eye.

I missed him, of course. Even as I was busy trying to hate him. I was never very successful at accomplishing that.

It was August now, and the goldenrod was coming out along the side of the road on our bike rides to the club—an uncomfortable reminder for me that there were fewer days of summer ahead of me at Wonderland than behind. The number was down to thirty-two.

On this particular Saturday—with rain pounding down and no end in sight—there would be no tennis. Hayward and Jilly were happy watching a movie. Forrest was off on his bike. (He said he didn't mind riding in the rain, though Regina and I both knew that where he was going, he probably wouldn't get that wet.)

I was just about to start reading my most recent library book—*It*, by my favorite author, naturally. My longest Stephen King novel yet. Just as I settled in on the couch, Regina came over with a cup of hot chocolate for me. Amazingly, she'd made this herself.

"I've got it all worked out," she said. "Our plan. Come up to my room and we'll go over everything."

When we got there, she closed the door and settled herself on the bed, gesturing for me to take the easy chair closest to it.

Regina took a sip from her tea. I did the same with my hot chocolate.

"I've worked out the details," she told me. "I needed to think everything through."

I sat there, waiting. She'd tell me when she was ready.

"You're an odd girl, Frances," she said. "But I like you. I see who you are and what you're capable of."

For most of my life, my goal had been trying to seem more like other people. But hearing what almost seemed like praise from Regina filled me with unfamiliar pride.

She took another sip of her tea before she continued. "As unlikely as the prospect may be that Forrest will actually follow through with some crazy plan of leaving me—considering that Forrest never follows through with anything—I have decided it's a good idea to assemble a body of evidence. As an insurance policy, you might say. Naturally Forrest must not know we're onto him."

Even now, feeling as disappointed in him as I was, it felt uncomfortable to be colluding with a woman as unlikable as Regina on a plan that could bring down a man I had adored.

"You were right about one thing," she told me. "My husband seems more preoccupied with this little redhead than he's been with his previous summer flings. I find it hard to attribute his obsession to the woman's attractions, which seem negligible at best. But you know men. Or maybe you don't.

"You've probably observed how different things have felt around here lately," she said.

I had, of course. All my life, I'd been that quiet, boring girl nobody paid attention to, standing off on the sidelines, watching, while other people lived their big, interesting lives. I noticed everything. They might not pay attention to me, but I paid attention to them alright. Up until now, I'd kept my thoughts to myself.

I picked up on conversations. I noticed small things nobody else did. For example: That Prudence sometimes stashed an extra twenty-dollar bill in her pocket before she went home at night. That a charm bracelet belonging to Jilly's friend Cookie had somehow migrated to Jilly's jewelry box. That one of the mothers at the country club liked to call her opponent's shot "out" in a doubles game, when it wasn't really.

I'd spotted the copy of *Penthouse* magazine in Hayward's room, tucked behind his untouched guitar. I had studied the issue myself, in fact.

"Forrest never has breakfast with me anymore," I told her. I didn't mention the other part, which still tugged at my heart: The small bunches of tiny flowers I'd find by my spot at the counter. The little wordless notes, featuring nothing more than a rainbow, or two lips formed into a kiss, followed by the letter *X*. And the one I'd found only the day before. That one, most of all, had gotten to me. A stone in the shape of a heart.

"People underestimate you, Frances," Regina said. "They think you're this mousy little bookworm. That's why you'll be such a great detective."

I figured this was supposed to be a compliment.

"Look at you," she said. "Nobody would guess what's going on in that mind of yours. You don't even have breasts."

Regina had taken a little time to think this through, she told me. Now we were ready, finally, to proceed.

My task: to gather information about what was going on between Forrest and Brenda. Some aspects of the story had revealed themselves already. What we lacked was hard evidence.

We needed concrete details concerning Forrest's assignations with Brenda—when they occurred, and where. I didn't know what the word *assignation* meant, but I could guess.

Regina reached for her knitting needles, but not to knit. She stabbed the air with one of them, waving the other like a conductor. She seemed more animated than I'd ever seen.

We could guess what happened between the two of them, she told me, but for our case to be airtight, we needed irrefutable proof. This meant a time log of their trysts. Photographs. Tapes, possibly.

I didn't need to ask Regina how she imagined we'd acquire these. I knew she would tell me.

The first question was, Where did these meetings take place? Once we established that, I'd need to stake out the spot. More than one of these, no doubt. Once I had a successful sighting, I'd get close enough to see and hear what was going on—which would be easier if the lovers didn't meet behind closed doors. As they probably wouldn't.

"One thing about my husband," she told me, "he loves fucking outdoors."

There was that word again. Coming from Regina, it had a particularly shocking effect.

There was the cottage Brenda and Kyle were renting, of course, but even if he weren't the nature-loving type, Regina doubted they'd have sex there. It would have been way too obvious if Forrest had parked his Porsche out front. He could swim over there, but Kyle wasn't working, which meant he'd be around a lot.

"This leaves us with the question: Where do they go?" she said.

On days Forrest rode his bike—purportedly to train for the big Labor Day event—he probably rode to some secret location they'd found. Then there were all those swimming days when he left the house in nothing but his trunks—gone for hours, supposedly to circumnavigate the lake.

Though houses lined parts of the lakeshore, there were wild spots too, where a pair of lovers might arrange a rendezvous. I could picture Brenda standing on the edge of Lake Catherine in one of those spots, waiting for Forrest—wearing a large hat to protect her precious complexion, and that heavy foundation makeup, with a blanket laid out on the ground. Forrest would emerge like a seal out of the water, his arms enfolding her. She'd get wet, but she wouldn't care.

Seals didn't live in lakes, of course. He'd be more like a water snake.

It was also possible they'd find a day when the Red Sox were playing and Kyle was off at some sports bar, watching the game. Then they might meet up at her rental cottage after all. Emerging from the water onto the Barnetts' small, muddy patch of lakefront, so unlike the vast green lawn of Wonderland. Forrest would make his way up the path to her back door. Brenda would be wearing a negligee with nothing on underneath.

I put fresh sheets on the bed, she'd say. She'd lead the way. As much as Forrest loved doing it on the grass, he'd make an exception then.

"If something like that happens," Regina told me, "you'll need to look in the windows. A stepladder may be necessary."

43

RENDEZVOUS

I hadn't even begun my investigation but already I knew a few things. Forrest went swimming almost every morning now, which suggested that his spot for meeting up with Brenda was more than likely somewhere along the water.

I'd taken note of the fact that though Forrest and Brenda's affair had probably only been going on for a few weeks, his body seemed even more toned and fit than usual. Of course you could chalk this up to his rigorous training regimen, but to Regina and me, this served as further evidence that Forrest was keeping himself in the best possible shape for Brenda. Billy, the handyman, had even made a joke about it. Billy was a bodybuilder. He'd taken note of Forrest's abs.

"You're looking good, man," he said, as the two of them shared a beer after Billy had finished up the mowing—Forrest shirtless, on account of the heat. "You got a girlfriend or something?"

He said this like it was a joke.

"Oh, you know," Forrest told Billy. "Just the usual. Bo Derek. Morgan Fairchild."

"I'll need you to write everything down," Regina told me. She handed me a spiral notebook small enough to keep in the pocket of my shorts.

This was when I pointed out to Regina that most detectives—every detective I'd ever heard about in books or on television, in fact—had some kind of vehicle to get around in. Even Nancy Drew drove a car—something referred to in the early books as a roadster. In the later ones she shifted to a Mustang convertible. All I had was a bike.

"That's the beauty of how you'll operate," Regina told me. "Nobody suspects a girl on a bicycle to be doing anything important. And a bicycle is compact and quiet. Unlike a car, you can lay it down in tall grass and nobody knows you're there.

"You'll hide," she said. "You'll write down everything. What you see. What you hear."

She handed me a camera—an unusually small Polaroid. Also a pocket-sized tape recorder, the kind a newspaper reporter might use doing an interview.

One more thing. Regina recognized that it could be difficult fulfilling my responsibilities as a mother's helper while conducting my detective work. For this reason, she told me, she'd step in herself to bring the children to tennis when needed.

Jilly and Hayward may have something to say about that, I thought. I kept the observation to myself.

I didn't mention this, but one of my principal concerns about Regina's plan had to do with how my own tennis lessons would fit into the new schedule—how I could make time for hitting with Jonathan while spending my days riding my bike around, looking for Forrest and Brenda.

"Maybe I'll just do this stuff on certain days," I said. "It's kind of a lot for someone my age."

Regina ignored my reservations.

"You're a smart girl, Frances," she said. "I have no doubt you'll figure it out."

What she hadn't explained to me yet was where I was supposed to go on my bicycle to locate the lovers. And what I would do, exactly, assuming I did.

44

FROM A PLACE LIKE EVERY SONG BRUCE SPRINGSTEEN EVER WROTE ROLLED INTO ONE

I hardly ever picked up the phone when it rang at Wonderland, but that day I did—adopting the words Prudence used when she answered a call. On the other end of the line, a familiar gravelly voice.

"'Emerson residence?' What kind of crap are they teaching you there?"

It was my father calling. From New Jersey. If he wasn't drunk yet, he was headed that way.

"I have a job, if you remember," I told him. "Things around here are different from back home."

"You can say that again," he said. "So how's it going in the lap of luxury? The country club life agreeing with you?"

"I'm having a great time," I told him. Given what he'd just said, I wasn't about to mention I'd started playing tennis. Or all the rest of what was going on.

"My man Howie really knows how to show a person a good time," my father said. "Excuse me. *Forrest.*" His voice had that edge to it that made it clear to me he was on his third glass of vodka of the afternoon. Possibly the fourth.

"I've been swimming a lot," I told him. Talking with my father now, I was aware that I didn't want things to sound too great. "It's been really hot here. The kids are kind of a pain sometimes."

"How's Regina doing?" he asked me.

"She's OK. You know." I'd learned long ago that mine were not the kind of parents you confided in.

"You making friends?" my father asked. This could have been the moment I told him about Regina calling me her one friend in the world, but I kept that to myself.

"Oh, sure," I said. "The kids at the club are great. We hang out all the time. At the canteen."

"I'm guessing you don't spend much time missing your old man, huh?" I could hear the clinking of ice cubes. The funny thing was that when he said this, I realized how much I actually did miss my father. In those first magical weeks at Wonderland I had loved those summer nights out on the patio—Forrest playing his ukulele and pulling quarters out of Jilly's ear, doing his Pee-wee Herman imitation, setting pints of Häagen-Dazs on the table. Four different flavors, five spoons. Playing old records for me (songs with lyrics, and a recognizable melody) and asking me what I thought about them. Asking me about the books I read, and expressing his view that one day I'd be writing books myself.

All that was before he met Brenda Barnett. Forrest, as he was now, hardly ever asked me questions about anything.

Forrest was a cheater. I might still love him, but knowing what I did now, it was impossible to respect him anymore. For all the drinking, and his relentlessly melancholy and cynical attitude toward life, my father possessed a brutal honesty I had to admire. Unlike Forrest, he refused to say anything he didn't mean, and he never told a lie, that I knew of. With my father, you knew where you stood. Even if where you stood was kind of lousy. He never tried to pull one over on you.

Maybe it was the discovery of Forrest's faithlessness that led me to question more about life at Lake Catherine. As much as I'd wanted to belong in the world of Wonderland, I was more a product of Hubbard than I'd realized. I'd never be one of those girls in the matching tennis sets—skipping out to the courts while their mothers followed three feet behind, carrying their tennis bags. Multiple racquets in case they broke a string.

Nothing unpleasant happened at Wonderland.

Only it did, of course. We just pretended otherwise.

Now here came my father, crashing into the sunlit kitchen where I had just fixed myself a milkshake. Maybe the sound of his voice reminded me who I was, still, and where I came from—a place like every song Bruce Springsteen ever wrote rolled into one.

Tomorrow—assuming I could still fit this in around my newly assigned detective duties—I'd be on my bike, riding over to the tennis court to work on my backhand with Jonathan. But for this one moment, receiving that call, I felt a wave of something—if not love, then the deepest kind of connection anyway, the recognition of a part of myself I had worked hard to keep under wraps. Maybe the most real part of me.

"How are things back home?" I asked him. I hoped he didn't hear my voice trembling a little.

"You know your mother," he said. "She thinks I'm a bum."

"You'll finish that book, Dad," I told him. I didn't actually believe this, probably, and even if he did, I didn't believe anything was likely to change in our lives as a result, but all I wanted at the moment—all I ever wanted, with my father—was to make him happy. If I could do that, maybe he wouldn't need the vodka. And if he never gave up vodka, I'd love him anyway.

"I don't blame your mother for being fed up," he said. "I doubt she could come up with a single good thing about me at the moment. She could've once, but that was a long time ago."

My parents bore virtually no resemblance to Forrest and Regina Emerson. But for a moment it occurred to me that the four of them— my parents, and Forrest and Regina—shared one thing: the experience of profound disappointment. Maybe they had all been in love when they were young. Each of them had big, hopeful dreams about the person they'd chosen to marry and make a life with. None of those dreams came true.

Maybe that's how it was with love. For a brief moment it appeared to you like this golden and glittering thing, like a treasure box you opened, filled with jewels and spilling with possibility. Then you took everything out, one piece at a time, and it all started to look like junk from a Goodwill store.

"It sounds like the good life is suiting you," my father said. "Old Howie behaving himself?" On the other end of the line, I heard a wheezing sound that didn't used to be there. I wished my father would quit the cigarettes.

"It's fine."

As much vodka as he'd consumed that day, maybe my dad picked up on something in my voice. "You OK, Junior?" he said. "If anything's wrong, you need to tell me."

And then what? *What would you do about it?*

"You know how it goes," I said to him. "There's always stuff going on."

"Like what?"

I could have said, *Like everything.*

"The usual," I told him. Why say more?

45

Here was our plan. Regina's plan. I was simply the one implementing it.

Recognizing that it would be impossible for me to follow Forrest when he set out on his bicycle, or swam—least of all times he took off in the Porsche—I would not attempt to follow him. I'd stake out places he was likely to turn up and wait there in the hope that he and Brenda would turn up eventually.

I wouldn't run the risk of having them notice me as I followed him. I'd already be there when they showed up.

Because she knew her husband so well, Regina had drawn a map for me, laying out the places that seemed to her the most likely spots where he and his lover might meet up for their rendezvous.

"Check out all the places on the map," she told me, as if doing this were no different than carrying out any of the other instructions she typed up on her daily list for me.

This felt like a tall order. There was a lot of outdoors to explore with only my yellow bicycle to get me there.

"One thing you should know," she said. "You'll probably need to do some bushwhacking. Try not to poke your eye out."

I didn't say anything, but something in my expression must have revealed to Regina how unhappy I was about my assignment.

"It won't be that bad," she said. "Spending a little time in nature will probably be a good idea for a New Jersey girl."

She thought I was just worried about mosquitoes and prickers, but it wasn't that. Maybe I worried that I wouldn't ever manage to find the two of them together. Maybe I worried more that I would.

46

The Good Kind of Obsession

Meanwhile, I kept working with Jonathan. I was getting better every day. The passion I brought to the sport probably had something to do with how totally unrelated it was to the mess going on at Wonderland, and the deep uneasiness I felt in my role to secretly spy on a man I'd loved all my life. What happened on the tennis court took me away from all that. That was the thing I loved best, probably. When you were trying to hit a ball, you couldn't think about anything else. With a racquet in my hand, my mind was like a stretch of open water on a windless day—no waves, no boats even, no swimmers. It was all about me and the ball.

I believed him when he told me I was a natural. I felt it. When I thought back to those times when I used to sit on the edge of the court, watching Olivia drag herself lackadaisically through her lesson, chewing her gum, taking ten-minute Coke breaks and giggling every time the ball went into the net—I had to smile. She had missed out on so much. She just didn't get the beauty of the game. I almost felt sorry for her.

It was right around this point in the summer—just at the moment when Regina laid out my new job, performing detective work—that Jonathan laid out his own plan for me.

"I want you to play in the Junior Girls' Tournament at the club, Labor Day weekend," he told me. "I wouldn't have believed a player so new to the game would be ready, but you are. There's no way to move forward without challenging yourself in a real match."

I'd never played in a competitive match. Then again, I'd never performed surveillance on the father of the children I was babysitting, on behalf of their mother. I felt equally unprepared for both assignments.

"You're ready for this," Jonathan told me. "You may be a little rough around the edges, but if you bring your best game, you can beat any one of those girls. The way you serve, it's like you put everything that ever happened to you into that swing. You've got the best junior serve in the club."

"Those girls have been playing for years," I told him.

"That's true," he said. "But they're just country club girls. They don't have your hunger."

I could have told him no. If I'd said that, he would not have made me play in the tournament.

But I wanted to play. More than that, I wanted to win.

I made a calendar on the back of one of Regina's notes to me and circled the date. My first tennis tournament. My last weekend at Wonderland.

47

GETTING TO FIVE HUNDRED

It was one of those days in which I had no time to get to the court, between my responsibilities at Wonderland and (more so) my new role as a private eye. All afternoon, I'd kept my eye on the clock, hoping an hour would open up when I could bike over to the club and hit balls against the backboard—maybe Forrest would take the kids out to play mini golf with him, or one of their friends would call up to invite them over—but the hours crawled along without a break. I could feel my body getting restless. I longed to move my feet, stretch my arm over my head for a serve, race to the net to return a shot, then back to the baseline to receive whatever Jonathan sent my way next.

The afternoon wore on. Then it was dinner. Jilly wanted me to read her a chapter of her book. Hayward had fixed himself a sandwich, leaving peanut butter and marshmallow fluff all over the counter for me to clean up.

Regina went to bed. Forrest turned on the game. Apart from the low sound of the Red Sox announcer, the house was quiet, finally. I stepped outside into the darkness—my racquet, borrowed from Jonathan, over my shoulder—and got on my bike.

This wasn't the first time I'd headed to the club to hit against the backboard, but I'd never shown up there this late before—close to eleven o'clock.

I might have worried that the Emersons would say something when I headed out on my bicycle in the darkness that night (assisted by my headlight), but as usual, nobody noticed. I might have worried that the gate would be locked when I reached the club, but it wasn't.

There was the backboard, illuminated by night-lights. I stepped into their glow, opened a can of fresh balls—loving the sound of the vacuum snap—and hit one hard toward the wood.

I had a good pair of sneakers now, handed down from Regina. "You should be hitting a hundred balls every day, returning every one when it comes back at you," Jonathan had told me. I went for five hundred, and when I missed one at number four hundred seventy-nine, I started over again.

It was well past midnight when I got my five hundred in a row. Pedaling home in the darkness, I knew I'd tell nobody about this. After that one time I'd mentioned tennis to Forrest—who hadn't picked up on it—I had decided to keep the secret for myself. It was almost as if I was having an affair—the kind that didn't break anyone's heart.

The odd thing was, nobody ever seemed to notice when I took off on my bike for the court—a situation not so different from how things were back home with my parents. Maybe this was how all adults were— too consumed with their own lives to pay attention to mine. This did not apply to Hayward, of course. Hayward was always watching me.

There would have been a time when Forrest would have noted my absences, but he had absences enough of his own. Many. As for Regina, she slept late in the mornings, and by the time Prudence or I had cleared away the breakfast dishes, and I was ready to bring the children to their lessons, she had taken so many pills I could have lit the house on fire and she wouldn't have woken up—except for those times, sometime after midnight most likely, when she got up to type her endless lists.

48

CHILD OF A BROKEN HOME

During all those weeks, I only heard from my father that one time. My mother had yet to call. This was a relief. After all the years of listening to the angry sound of the two of them fighting with each other—that, or their deadly silences—it felt good to get a break. I almost forgot about my parents for a while. Then came another call. My mother this time.

"I couldn't decide if I should wait until the end of the summer to tell you," she said. "I didn't want to ruin your time there, but I figured you should know. Your father and I are getting a divorce."

She said this as if it would be some big hard news.

"I know this will be difficult for you," she said.

Not as difficult as she thought. The hard part had been everything that came before.

She was still talking. My mother was not big on leaving a person space to contribute their own feelings to a situation. She had so many of hers to tell me about.

"We're still working out the details. Your father isn't what you might call helpful. He has to move out. In the meantime, I'm basically living in hell."

I didn't know what to say, but there was no need. She kept talking.

"We're out of money, by the way. If you were thinking we'd be going back-to-school shopping, I'm sorry to say it's not happening."

I hadn't been thinking that, actually. Any clothes shopping I might have done that fall would have been paid for by me. As it was turning out, my summer earnings had gone to tennis lessons. Money well spent.

"He says he's getting an apartment with some guy he knows from poker. 'Once I sell my novel, everything's going to be different,' he says. The man lives in fantasy land."

We'd been on the phone for more than five minutes by this point. She had yet to ask how my summer was going. Or anything about me. If I'd said to her, *I'm thinking of getting into drugs* or *I'm pregnant*, I doubt she would have registered the news.

At some point—mostly just out of curiosity, to see if she'd respond—I told her I'd recently taken up tennis. She said that was nice, but made no further comment.

"So that's it," she said. "I figured you had a right to know. I just didn't want you to get your hopes up."

"I have to go," I told her. "I have a job to do for Regina."

That part was true. Having had no luck locating an assignation between Forrest and Brenda at any of the first three locations on the map Regina had provided for me, I was on to the next—the remnants of an abandoned farm stand on the way out of town, on the road headed to Bangor. Regina had explained to me that in their younger days, before they had the children, she and Forrest used to go out there with a picnic basket.

There was this natural pool there that they loved, just beyond where the farm stand had stood, behind some blueberry bushes. Not deep enough to swim, but one time they'd taken off their clothes there and plunged into the water, up to their knees. Just then a car had pulled up—a couple of kids smoking pot—so they kept very quiet and remained undiscovered.

"After they left, we made love on the banks of that little pool," Regina told me.

"If Forrest brings Brenda there, I'll probably want to kill him. But he might just do that. It's just his kind of place."

49

Stupid People Having Sex

It was a hot day when I set off for the abandoned farm stand. Getting there required me to ride my bike up a series of hills on a surprisingly busy two-lane road with no shoulder for bicycles. The picture came to me, as I pedaled, of what would happen if, on my way to scope out a possible rendezvous location, I got hit by a truck. No doubt the Emersons would be sad. Forrest would probably express bafflement as to what I'd been doing, out on that highway on a day when the temperature registered ninety-five and I was supposed to be bringing the children to sailing class.

"I gave Frances the afternoon off," Regina would tell him. "Poor thing."

That would be the end of it. And maybe the end of her plans to track down evidence of her husband's affair too.

I was just thinking how stupid this whole plan was, when the remains of the farm stand came into view. Regina's directions had been perfect.

This wasn't the only part of her project Regina had planned out efficiently, though. Just behind the falling-down wall of what had once been Murchisons' U-Pick Blueberries 'N More—mostly hidden, but not entirely—I could make out the tail of Forrest's Porsche.

Still a couple hundred feet from the farm stand, I got off my bike.

My heart was beating fast, naturally. Up until now, the whole idea of my doing this had been largely an abstraction, not all that different from the fantasies I'd cooked up in my journal in the early days of summer, of sexual scenarios that weren't ever going to take place in real life. Suddenly the whole plan had stopped being a game.

I set my bike down in the brush and walked in closer, concealed in the trees. I could hear voices now. It was clear, without seeing, what they'd been doing.

"That was amazing," she said.

"When can I see you again?"

"Tomorrow? The ground's too rough here," she said. "Let's go to our other spot next time."

I watched them get up. He was buttoning her blouse for her. She was stroking his face. I reached in my pocket for the Polaroid camera.

It was in its case, and the zipper was stuck. As I struggled to get it open, the two of them got in the car.

By the time I got the camera out of the case, Forrest had started the engine. I lifted the camera into position, but it was too late. The Porsche had pulled out onto the road. I'd missed them.

I had no idea where the other spot was that Brenda had spoken about. On the map she'd given me, Regina had identified ten possible locations. It was also possible that none of these was the one.

A wave of terrible sadness came over me. It wasn't even from wishing I was the person whose face Forrest had been stroking, or my deep disappointment at confirming that the man I had admired more than any other was evidently no better than some character in a Lifetime movie or a guest on a segment of Phil Donahue. Partly I felt sad that my magical Wonderland summer was turning into this, a series of afternoons spent riding around on my bicycle in the heat of the day, looking for Forrest's Porsche. Assuming I found it, I'd be scrunched in some patch of bushes, trying to get a picture of two stupid people having sex.

50

SURVEILLANCE OPERATIONS AND A DEAD HUMMINGBIRD

Nearly every morning when I came downstairs—early, just not as early as Forrest—I'd find a note or a small, odd gift waiting for me. It wasn't just flowers now. One day a perfect, intact butterfly lay on the table by my bowl. Another day it was a single clamshell with a rhinestone ring inside, the kind you get at one of those machines at the drugstore for fifty cents. The best of all of them—not the type of thing everyone would have appreciated, but I did—was a tiny, perfect hummingbird. He must have flown into the French doors on the patio and died on impact. He was laid out on a piece of Kleenex, his beautiful iridescent wings folded against his little body. As with every one of these morning offerings I'd been receiving, a piece of paper sat next to the bird's body with the letter *X* on it.

I remembered reading somewhere that a hummingbird weighed roughly the same as a penny. Now I saw this was true.

These gifts baffled me. What did it mean that the same man who seemed to have utterly abandoned our precious friendship (precious to me, anyway), who now appeared so unaware of my presence, had taken the time to leave me these daily treasures? And what kind of a jerk was

I, to be spying on the same person who left the body of a beautiful (though dead) hummingbird next to my cereal bowl?

I had no answer to that one. I just knew that every morning when I woke up, I looked forward to finding another magical gift. This was the reason I didn't get up earlier. I didn't want to interrupt the moment when he set whatever odd thing it was he'd chosen to leave on the table for me that morning. I was afraid that if Forrest and I met now, in the kitchen, in those early morning hours before he took off for his bike ride or his swim—on his way to see his lover—it might ruin the small, good thing that remained between us. I'd rather eat my breakfast alone than risk losing that.

So I chose to lie in bed until the sun was up and I'd heard the sound of his bicycle tires going down the gravel driveway, or the French doors slamming shut as he closed them on his way down to the dock.

I made sure Forrest was gone before I descended the long staircase into the kitchen to see what he'd left for me. It wasn't how things had been when we'd sat side by side in the breakfast nook, starting our day together. But along with tennis, this was the best part of every day.

51

MAKE HER PROUD

On the surface, it might have seemed that Regina's goal, when she enlisted my services to spy on her husband, involved money. Specifically, protecting her inheritance. But I knew it wasn't money, really, that Regina cared about. From the way she talked about Forrest— the look on her face when she described the places he might take his lover, based on her own experience of having made love with him there herself—I knew her true objective was holding on to her husband.

She actually believed that if she threatened him with financial ruin, he might stick around. In Regina's mind, presenting Forrest with the prospect of forfeiting the comfortable lifestyle he'd become accustomed to—ensuring that he'd lose his home, his boat, his sports car, his golf membership, not to mention his children—served as her way of holding on to him.

I knew the truth. Regina still loved Forrest. She couldn't help it. The plan she'd cooked up, in which I was to play a vital role, wasn't really about supporting future divorce actions. It was about finding a way to stay married.

I could relate to Regina's inability to give up on Forrest. As angry as I was at him for what I viewed as his abandonment of me, I was in the same boat. As many times as I reminded myself that he was cheating on his wife, and that he'd done this repeatedly—every summer for years, it turned out—I couldn't hate him. I couldn't help smiling when he came in the door with a bagful of lobster rolls for us, or when he whipped out his ukulele, as he still did on occasion, passing around a bag of kazoos—one for each of us—and burst into one of his made-up songs. Times like those, all was forgiven. I'd forget I was supposed to be mad at Forrest, the guilt would return that I'd agreed to help his cold and unlovable wife prepare her case against him.

I never bought Regina's theory that Forrest would go after her as an unstable person or take her children away. He might have a weakness for women in tight, low-cut dresses—clearly he did—but he wasn't cruel.

And he was a loving parent. There were days when Regina barely spoke to Hayward and Jilly, days when she hardly got out of bed, and other days (many of these) when her chief form of communication with her children lay in her typewritten instructions for their lives. Whereas even at his worst—preoccupied with Brenda, and more than that, obsessed—Forrest never neglected the children. They were captivated by him. So was I.

Still, I embarked on carrying out my assignment. Regina and I were in this together now—two women who had been betrayed by the same charming, irresistible but unfaithful man. If I had lost the tender affection of the one person in this family I truly adored, as it seemed I had, I'd shift my loyalty to the one who still took an interest in me. And so the same intensity of feeling that had once fueled my total devotion to Forrest now attached itself to Regina.

I didn't want to let her down. I wanted to please her. I wanted to make her proud of me.

"These girls don't know what they're doing out there," Regina said. "They have no understanding of the sport of tennis."

Her remark caught me off guard. I remembered what Forrest had said about Regina having played tennis herself when she was younger, but it was hard to picture. Nothing in how she was now suggested a woman who'd won doubles tournaments once. These days the game seemed not simply to bore her but, more than that, to irritate her.

I could have said a million things concerning my views on tennis, a sport that now occupied my thoughts every hour of my day, much as Forrest had done once. Jonathan had recently invited me over to the club, where I got to join a group of die-hard players to watch the semifinals of the Volvo International being played in Vermont, in which John McEnroe had defeated Jimmy Connors—both of us McEnroe fans, naturally. Some of the points they played felt so exciting I could barely breathe.

With the Labor Day match and my dreaded return to New Jersey less than a month away, I worried now that functioning as Regina's detective was cutting into my ability to work with Jonathan on my tennis game.

I wanted to win that tournament.

52

ANOTHER WAY TO STAY SKINNY

It was a late afternoon at Wonderland. They were having game night at the club, and the whole family had gone over there to join in the festivities. Having seen Regina in one of her Lilly Pulitzer dresses, I figured that, for once, she must be going over with them. This left me alone in the house—always an intoxicating experience.

I figured it was a good opportunity to check out Forrest's desk. Maybe I'd find a receipt from some restaurant meal, a lock of red hair. A book of matches, even—the kind of thing Nancy Drew would come up with in the novels I'd loved when I was younger.

I heard an odd, muffled sound coming from the bathroom. This went on for a few minutes.

I tiptoed down the hall. If it was a raccoon or a possum—animals I'd observed a number of times on my bike rides around the back roads of Lake Catherine—I wasn't sure I wanted to confront it. On the other hand, I was in my investigative mode. I needed to know what was going on.

The sound was coming from the bathroom at the end of the hall. The door was shut. I hid in Jilly's room, thinking of what to do next.

Then came the sound of the toilet flushing. A few moments later, the door swung open. Regina came out. She didn't spot me. She was holding a towel to her mouth.

I'd heard about this from girls at my school. Overheard, mostly, because I wasn't one of those girls other girls told things to. I just knew this was what some girls did who wanted to stay really skinny. Usually the ones who were already skinnier than anyone else in our class.

Regina hadn't left the house after all. She'd been here the whole time, and she had just made herself throw up. She had taken off her Lilly Pulitzer dress for this. She was wearing her slip.

From my hiding place around the corner, I watched Regina walk slowly back to her bedroom. A moment or two later, she emerged, wearing the Lilly Pulitzer dress again, along with a pair of pink shoes I'd learned to call ballet pumps.

She headed downstairs. I heard the front door close, followed by the sound of her car—the Jeep—starting up. She was off to join the rest of the family at the country club, I figured. As if everything was normal.

53

Overheard over Ice Cream

The children and I were at the Caboose, getting our ice creams after sailing lessons. We had just settled into our usual spot at one of the picnic tables, with our bikes leaned up against the side of the building. I'd long since given up my one-cone-a-week vow, along with the idea of sticking to lower calorie sherbet, though thanks to tennis I had trimmed down anyway. Each of us had gotten two scoops, with jimmies.

A few tables over from us, a couple of women were eating fried clams. I didn't recognize the one whose face I could see. The other one had her back to me, but her voice was instantly recognizable, as was her hair. Hurricane Brenda.

She didn't see me. Maybe she wouldn't even have recognized me if she had. Brenda was not the sort of person who paid attention to people like me—someone else's teenage babysitter. Never mind that I was babysitting the kids of the man she was having sex with. I was pretty sure she didn't recognize Jilly and Hayward either. Brenda struck me as the kind of person who mostly paid attention to herself.

She leaned in to speak with her friend, though she seemed to make no effort to lower her voice. It was almost as if she wanted to be overheard. She was probably accustomed to getting attention, and liked it.

"I'm telling you, Lorraine. Nobody ever touched me the way he does," she said. "It's like his tongue wants to reach into the depths of my soul."

That didn't sound particularly appealing to me. But the friend seemed fascinated.

"I haven't said anything to Kyle yet," Brenda told her friend. "But it's over between us. It's going to break his heart. But I have to be true to myself. I can't live a lie anymore."

This was Brenda for you. She never stopped spewing soap opera dialogue.

"This guy's married, huh?" the friend asked Brenda.

"In a way," she said. "His wife's a nutcase."

"But it's her house, right? Her family's got a ton of money. The great-grandfather invented Scotch tape or Wite-Out or something."

"It's all pretty complicated," Brenda said. "Only it's not, really. It's like . . . we're two bodies with one soul. Once you understand that, all that other stuff doesn't matter anymore. It's just details."

I looked across the table to where Jilly sat. She was feeding ice cream to Molly, her favorite American Girl. For a moment, the picture came to me of how it would be for her if her father said he was moving out of the house and marrying Brenda. This was what Brenda meant when she talked about "details."

I remembered that, back in New Jersey, my father was going to be moving out too. Only that was different. My father's departure from our apartment would probably feel like a relief. For Jilly and Hayward—and for Regina—the possibility of Forrest running off with Brenda would bring about the end to any possibility of future happiness or joy at Wonderland.

54

I Want to Have Your Baby

Olivia's mother, Phyllis, was hosting a party for women from the club, with a special guest who promised to identify what colors they should be featuring in their wardrobes. It turned out you were either a winter, a spring, a summer, or an autumn. If you didn't know which, and favored the wrong colors, you might just have to throw out your whole wardrobe and replace it with another one. Overhearing her explaining this to one of the women at the club while I was waiting for Jilly to get out of her tennis lesson, I felt a sudden surprising wave of missing my mother. For all the ways she disappointed me, I could just hear the deep belly laugh that would come out of her if she heard this concept of what the woman called "finding your season."

In earlier days, Regina wouldn't have been caught dead at such an event either, but she'd decided to attend, probably as part of her campaign to project to Forrest and everyone else at the club the appearance that she was a regular person. As an added incentive, Phyllis had promised there'd be a bouncy house for the kids. Hayward said he was too old for bouncy houses, but agreed to go, probably because Olivia would be there, which meant he might catch a glimpse of Olivia and her friends bouncing. I knew what part of their bodies he'd be eyeing.

With the family occupied by the Color Me Fashionable party, I was left free to head to the tennis courts. It had been three days since I'd had the chance to work with Jonathan, and it was too late in the afternoon for a lesson. But I could still hit against the backboard.

I must have been hitting for over two hours. One of the night bulbs meant to light the court was out, making it difficult to see the ball. Anyone else would have called it a day by this point, but I couldn't stop.

Due to the darkness, I was missing a lot of shots. To retrieve my ball after one of these, I had to step off the court into a thicket of bushes, and beyond those, trees and brush at the far end of the tennis court.

This was when I heard their voices. I knew right away who it was.

Earlier that evening, when I headed to the court, I had no intention of carrying out one of my reconnaissance missions, so I didn't have my Polaroid camera with me. But I did have my little notebook in my pocket. Also a pencil. I had developed the habit of bringing these along with me at times when I hit balls by myself, to write down how many I'd hit and how long I'd managed to keep the ball in play. Now I took out the notebook, ready to transcribe what I heard.

"I can't bear it when Kyle touches me now," Brenda said. "It makes me physically ill."

"Oh, baby." This was Forrest. Then silence for a moment. I couldn't see, but the two of them were kissing, no doubt.

"I have to leave him. I don't even care if he takes Pumpkin. I want a divorce."

"I know, I know. But it's complicated."

"What's complicated?" she said. "I love you. You love me. I think about you all the time. We want to be together. It's simple."

I was crouched in the bushes with my notebook on my knees, writing down what they said as fast as I could. It was hard to keep up.

"It's not that easy for me," Forrest told her. "There's the children. I have to put them first."

"I love kids," she said.

They were quiet for a minute. More kissing probably. Then came Brenda again: "I want to have your baby."

From where I sat on the dirt, scribbling with the little pencil I'd picked up at mini golf, I shook my head. In case it wasn't bad enough that Forrest was having an affair, he was having one with a woman who talked like every sappy song I'd ever heard on the radio. Brenda was a pinhead.

"It's going to work out fine," she said. "Your kids love you so much, they wouldn't blame you for seeking your happiness."

"I know my kids would love you too," he told her. "In a perfect world, we'd be together, and have half a dozen more of them, and they'd all look like you. But I have to think about Regina."

"Regina?" She sounded surprised. She'd forgotten that part, evidently.

"I don't think she could manage without me. And you know, if I left her, I'd be broke. You should have a man who can take care of you."

"I don't care about money. I just want you."

"And I want you too, baby," he said. "But I need to think about my wife. Regina and I have a lot of history between us."

"We can make our own history." Brenda again.

Crouched in the bushes, I mouthed the words, *Blah, blah, blah.* The dialogue was as bad as what Jilly came up with for her American Girl dolls.

After that, Forrest and Brenda didn't talk anymore. I heard a lot of sighing and panting, followed by rustling of leaves, the sound both of them made, as if they'd just climbed the stairs of the Empire State Building and now were near the top. She cried out. So did he. Every now and then one of them said, "Oh, baby." That was about it.

All this time I'd been trying to catch the two of them together this way, but now that I had, I just wanted to get away. Only, if I got up to go, they'd hear me. And there was my racquet, leaned against the back-board. I couldn't leave it there. So I sat in the bushes instead, writing it all down.

Then Forrest spoke again, but he sounded different this time. His voice was serious now.

"You need to understand that my wife is a mentally fragile person," he said. "She tried to kill herself once."

Then came Brenda's response. Her voice took on a different tone as she spoke the words. No more soft, whispery endearments. She was all business now.

"When you think about it, maybe it wouldn't be such a terrible thing if she did it."

"Did it?" he said. "Did what?"

"If Regina did kill herself."

55

Like Bringing Home a Good Report Card

Regina had instructed me to report back to her whenever I came up with relevant findings, and though at first I'd been hesitant to share with her what I'd learned about Forrest and Brenda, it was different now. As sickening as Brenda's words had been, I felt excited to tell Regina what I'd learned at the tennis court that night.

The next morning—not a tennis day for the children, for once—I headed up to her bedroom again. She was leaned up against her pillow with a tray Prudence had made for her—half an English muffin, no butter, a glass of grapefruit juice—and her knitting. No evidence of progress on that front.

I handed Regina the notebook with my observations of Forrest and Brenda's most recent rendezvous. I studied Regina's face as she turned the pages. At one point, as she was reading, she actually let out something approximating laughter.

"I want to have your baby," Regina read out loud, delivering a surprisingly accurate Brenda imitation. She let out a kind of snort. When she got to the place where Brenda raised the possibility of Regina committing suicide, though, the bitter smile disappeared. Her mouth formed a hard, straight line.

When she was finished going over my notes, she set them on her little bed tray next to the uneaten muffin. "Great job," she told me. She could have been the coach of a girls' basketball team that just won their game in overtime.

I couldn't help myself. For all the discomfort I had felt about the assignment Regina had given me, a warm feeling passed through my body. It was almost as if Regina was my mother, and I'd brought home a good report card. Which I always did, actually. My real mother just never said anything about those.

"We're finally getting someplace," Regina said. "But we need more concrete evidence. You need to catch them in the act. And we need pictures. Recordings. The two of them, in the act."

"What do you recommend?" I asked.

Regina drew in her breath, as if the very thought brought her physical pain.

"They'll meet up on the island," she said. "I should have realized this sooner, but the island's a sacred place for me. For the two of us. I guess I didn't want to picture Forrest there with anyone but me. But if I know my husband, that's where he'd bring a lover.

"I'm guessing he'll pick her up first so they can motor over together to their little love nest," she said. Her voice, which more often than not came across as sneering and bitter, had a different tone this time, and her eyes had taken on a crazed look.

Now came the sadness. That moss was hers. So was the island. For generations it had belonged to her family. "Private property" signs lined the shore.

"We need to get you onto the island," she said. "I have a feeling that's where they go."

It had been a long time since Regina had set foot on the island. Still, she knew every inch of it.

"There's a little cove on the far side," she went on. "There's all these blueberry bushes. If you drag the boat up onto the land, it won't be difficult to conceal it in the brush. Then you can stake out the place where they're likely to go. It's all the way over on the other side. Wait in the blueberry bushes till they show up. Just keep an eye out for poison ivy. It's everywhere on that island."

Even to me, a girl with a big capacity for drama, this sounded like a wild scheme. This idea of Forrest and Brenda going to the island was just a hunch. They might not show up at all, and if they did, what if they spotted me? Not to mention, the island was a long way from shore.

"How am I supposed to get there?" I asked her.

"You know how to paddle a canoe, right?" she said.

"I guess so." I didn't add that I'd only done it once.

"Our Old Town is totally reliable," she said. "And if anything happens, you're a good swimmer."

None of this reassured me. But when you're a spy, you don't ask questions. You fulfill your assignment.

56

Moss

Though in the days since Forrest had begun his affair I hadn't been getting up as early as before, that day I made sure to be out of the house first. On the chance that what Regina imagined was actually going to take place, I had to be out of sight, out on the canoe, and around the point by the time Forrest set out to pick up Brenda and head to the island.

The trip across the lake to the island was an ambitious one. At first I had a hard time keeping the canoe on course, but after a few minutes I started getting the hang of it. The trick was alternating which side of the water you dipped your oar in, and alternating sides often enough to keep a steady course.

I started to enjoy it. Nobody had told me, but I figured out things went a lot better in a canoe if your strokes were long and you kept your paddle close to the boat. When you lifted the paddle out of the water, the idea was to turn the blade sideways, just over the surface of the water, before you dipped it in again.

Stroke, turn, dip, stroke. I got a nice rhythm going. At the moment Regina had suggested this plan, I'd been disappointed that I'd have to miss tennis time with Jonathan. But once in the canoe, I surprised myself by enjoying the experience. Even in the middle of the mess of

Forrest and Regina's marital problems (or maybe in part because of them), I experienced a feeling of peacefulness from the slow, steady motion of the paddle in the water. Lost in the beauty of the early morning—mist over the water still, the sun just coming up over the trees, a lone fisherman way out on his boat—I almost forgot the nature of my mission.

By this point in the summer, I'd become familiar with the long, sorrowful sound made by the loons when they called to each other across the water, as they were doing now. Forrest had explained to me that loons had several different calls, each distinct. One of these was a simple hello to some other loon. Then there was the mating call— longer, higher, more insistent. Then came the rarest loon call, the one signifying danger.

A pair of eagles lived at the lake. They knew not to go after full-grown loons, who possessed the ability to dive deep under the water to safety. But the babies were vulnerable. Once, sitting on the dock with Regina, watching the children play Marco Polo with their friends from a nearby house, I'd watched an eagle dive for a baby loon who'd been swimming alongside his mother.

There was a frantic flapping of wings, and a sound coming from the mother loon—mother and father both, I think—that sounded almost like a human scream. The eagle circled a few times, lower and lower. I got up from my chair, transfixed. There was nothing I could do but watch a murder taking place. An attempted murder, anyway. The loon parents succeeded in driving the eagle away, though whether they did this before he'd got his prey or after, I couldn't be sure.

The loon who called out that morning—just one, though he must have felt the presence of a fellow loon, too far for me to see—conveyed no sense of danger. He didn't seem put off by my presence either. I couldn't have been more than a few feet away from him as he sat there, lower in the water than a duck and larger, his beautiful feathers, black and white, glistening in the early morning light.

I dipped my paddle in the water again. He dove under, gone for over a minute. When he surfaced again, he did so in a whole other spot on the lake, far from the one I'd seen him in before.

It took me close to an hour to reach the island. My arms were sore by then, but it was a good feeling. The weeks I'd spent on the tennis court had strengthened my muscles and tightened my body without my having realized it was happening.

I found the cove Regina had told me about—the blueberry bushes, the tall grasses, the sandy bank where I dragged the canoe up onto land. A person would have to look hard to spot it, and more than likely, the two people visiting the island today—if they did come here, which felt like a long shot—would have other things on their minds. One, anyway.

Prudence had packed a lunch basket for me—an egg-salad sandwich, potato chips, a bottle of Snapple, and a blue-and-white-checked napkin. I had not explained to her the nature of my mission, naturally. She thought I was just taking a few hours off to have a picnic.

Now I lifted this out of the canoe, along with the Polaroid camera, the mini tape recorder, my spiral notebook, and my Stephen King book. Once on land, it took me a while to locate the place Regina had told me about, the mossy spot where she and Forrest used to come to have sex. "Make love," was how she put it. When referring to the activities of her husband and Brenda, she employed a different term.

Once I saw the place, there was no mistaking it. I'd seen plenty of moss before, but nothing like this: Tucked away inside a circle of pine trees and ferns, the moss formed a deep, spongy bed, green and damp from the dew, with the most wonderful rich, earthy smell. Even if you hadn't come to this place with a person you planned on having sex with, it was a spot that made you want to take off your shoes—take off all your clothes, even. Lie down, roll around, breathe it in.

I couldn't stay on the open patch of moss, unfortunately. If Forrest and Brenda actually did show up, I had to remain hidden. There was a large rock thirty or forty feet back, with a thick tangle of brush behind it. I could sit here with my book and my sandwich, waiting.

The morning passed. I didn't have a watch, but based on the position of the sun, and my hunger, I guessed it was probably lunchtime. If Forrest was going to bring his lover to the island, I figured he'd be here by now. Still, I'd wait a little longer. It was a long way back.

Squirrels came. I spotted a bush with wild blueberries on it, low to the ground. Just six of them, but they were ripe and sweet.

I heard a woodpecker tapping his beak against a dead tree. Then something else: the sound of a motorboat—the unmistakable low whir of a Chris-Craft—far off at first, then closer, slowing down, pulling up to the shore.

I heard the splash of the anchor hitting the water. Then voices. Forrest and Brenda. As they got closer, I could make out the words.

"It's so beautiful here. How did you ever find this spot for us?"

This would have been the moment for Forrest to explain that the island belonged to his wife and her family. He might have told Brenda about coming here with Regina, long ago. He didn't.

"I wanted to bring you someplace where I could have you all to myself."

"Oh, darling. I love you so much."

"I want to tear these clothes off you," he said.

Something about the intimacy of the scene had a surprising effect on me: two people kneeling together, as Forrest and Brenda did now on that patch of moss, the sunlight streaming down on them through the trees, the sound of lake water lapping against the shore, the smell of juniper, and that loon off in the distance, her voice long and low. For reasons I could not have explained, I started to cry. But soundlessly. I couldn't risk letting the two of them hear me.

I peered over the top of the rock. This was the first time I was actually able to really see Forrest and Brenda together instead of just hearing their voices. He was unbuttoning his shirt now. Then her blouse. He undid her bra. It didn't take him long to understand that it fastened in front. Regina wouldn't be the type to wear sexy underwear, as I knew from my perusal of her drawers at the house that day. But I understood now, as I didn't once, that Forrest was a man who knew his way around women's lingerie.

A surprising thing happened to me then. I was a girl who'd spent the last couple of years fixated on the idea of people having sex. I'd tried to figure out how they did it and struggled to understand. I'd constructed fantasies. Now here I was, situated in such a way that I could finally observe the real thing from a safe distance that allowed me a clear and nearly unobstructed view. Brenda and Forrest had taken all their clothes off. (*Almost* all. Crazily, Forrest was still wearing his white tube socks. Those, and nothing else. It wasn't a particularly sexy look.)

Now, at the very moment the secret of lovemaking was about to be revealed to me, I looked away. I couldn't bear to see it. Most of all, I couldn't bear to see a man I had worshipped in the act of doing something that still seemed to me strange and unsettling—fascinating and thrilling, but also repellent.

I turned on my tape recorder. Knowing the clicking sound my camera made, I didn't want to risk taking a picture at first. But I got up my courage once they were in the thick of it—Forrest on top of Brenda, then Brenda on top of Forrest, then the two of them, side by side, touching each other and gasping for breath. They were making enough noise by this point that I knew they wouldn't hear the Polaroid as it spit out the photographs.

There they were *in the flesh*. I'd heard the expression, but it never applied so accurately before. In the pictures I held in my hand, I could see Brenda's fingers digging into Forrest's broad, muscular back, and his mouth on her breast. Then another picture, of his head between her outstretched legs. A long, loud wail came out of them both, like a pair of loons who'd just found each other in the middle of a lake in Maine.

Well, they had.

After that, everything changed with surprising abruptness. In the movies, a couple usually lay there, side by side in the bed after sex—an actual bed, not a bed of moss. They'd whisper tender words to each other or exchange loving caresses. One or both of them might smoke a cigarette. None of this took place between Brenda and Forrest that day on the island.

When it was over, Forrest handed Brenda her underpants and bra, then her shorts.

"I hate to rush things," he said. "But I need to take my wife to her doctor's appointment."

My wife. The way he spoke the words surprised me. Not *Regina* or *her*—though he might have put it that way. Brenda would surely have known who he was talking about.

He sounded so *married*.

"When are you going to tell her about us?" Brenda asked. I heard the faintest evidence of annoyance in her tone.

"I just can't," Forrest said. "It would kill Regina."

"You know we can't be together unless you end it with her," Brenda said.

"It's just too soon. I need . . ." What did he need? He didn't finish the sentence, probably because he didn't know this himself. Or maybe he did know. He knew he wasn't going to leave his wife. He just didn't want to admit this to Brenda.

The two of them were sitting on a rock now, side by side. Forrest's shirt was misbuttoned.

"I know this could sound mean," Brenda said, "but I can't help thinking it. Everything would be so great if your wife would just . . . disappear."

"Disappear?" Forrest sounded genuinely baffled.

"You told me she's always talking about killing herself. What if she finally did it?"

Forrest sat there, facing her. He had been reaching for his pants, but now he stopped.

"What are you talking about?"

Brenda's voice as she spoke to him was oddly businesslike. She was fastening her bra as she spoke.

"I mean, wouldn't it make things easier for the two of us?" Brenda said. "If she finished things off."

Forrest just sat there in his white tube socks, staring at her.

"It could happen, right?" she said. "She was probably always going to do it sooner or later. What if we . . . you know . . . sort of helped her along with things."

"Helped her along?"

"Look at it as bringing an end to her suffering."

"I don't understand," Forrest said. Or maybe he did, but he wished he didn't.

Now Brenda sounded excited. For once she had come up with an idea she hadn't heard someone express on a show she was watching. "Suppose she showed up dead one day. Considering her past history, nobody would bat an eye."

She was on a roll now. She was talking faster. I couldn't see her face, but I could imagine it. That pale skin, with the foundation that ended at her jawline.

"Suppose Regina just turned up dead?" Brenda said. "There'd be this note next to her body where she explained she'd had enough. She hated ruining everybody else's life, but she just wanted it to be over. The pain of being alive. She'd say how sorry she was to let everyone down, but she knew she was just a drag on them, and they'd be better off without her."

"That would never happen," Forrest said. "My wife would never write a note like that."

"You're missing the point." Brenda looked annoyed. I caught a glimpse of what this woman would be like if someone crossed her in a serious way—or simply didn't give her what she wanted. Now here she was having to explain everything to him.

"What if someone else wrote this note for her? Only this person made it sound like Regina wrote it, because they knew that was the sort of thing she might do anyway; she just hadn't gotten around to it."

Forrest took a few moments to respond. When he did, he seemed to choose his words with more care than usual. On his face, a look of pure shock. Call it horror.

"You're kidding, right?" he said. "I could never . . ."

"Just think how it could be," she told him. She ran her hands over his chest. Then lower down on his body.

"It's not Regina's fault that she's depressed," Forrest told her.

"But what about us?" Brenda said. "What am I supposed to do?" He had put his pants on at this point, but her hands had made their way inside them.

"Oh, baby," he moaned. "I can't."

"Think about it," she told him. All of a sudden there was a hardness to her voice. I'd seen that part of Brenda all along. I might be young, but I understood her way better than Forrest did.

"I love my wife," he said. It made me sad to hear how weak he seemed now. He sounded like a puppy. Being trained. She'd have him peeing where he was supposed to soon. And not where he shouldn't.

"You know that's one of the things I love about you," Brenda told him. "Your loyalty. But we both know she's a sick woman, and it's only going to get worse.

"Just think," she went on. "You could have me all to yourself every day for the rest of your life."

57

CLUELESS

After they took off in the Chris-Craft, I stayed put on the island a while longer to be sure they wouldn't see me when I launched the canoe. On the way back to the house, I considered what I'd tell Regina about the event I'd witnessed that afternoon. It was more confusing than I'd thought.

On the one hand, I had irrefutable evidence that Forrest and Brenda were having sex. Not just notes of conversations. I had pictures now.

Then came the shocking part: Brenda's suggestion to Forrest that the two of them cook up a plot that would make it appear that Regina had committed suicide. She hadn't used the word *kill*, but there was only one way to interpret her words. As awful as it had seemed to me before that Forrest was cheating on Regina this way, Brenda's plan to make it appear that Regina had killed herself took the situation to a whole other level, from infidelity to murder.

Forrest hadn't said much when Brenda laid out her idea, but I had seen his face as he took in her words. He would never go along with a plan like the one she suggested.

You could look at this as a good news/bad news situation. Good news: Despite his unfaithfulness, Regina's husband still cared about her.

In the middle of a tryst with his lover, Forrest still hurried home to bring his wife to her doctor's appointment.

Still, there was no getting past the bad news, which was the sex part. The betrayal had taken place—as Regina had guessed it might—on the very same patch of moss where she herself had once made love with her husband.

And as stunned as Forrest had appeared when Brenda laid out her idea of killing Regina, he had not come right out and told her he wouldn't do it. He was probably going to do what people always did, in my experience, when something truly uncomfortable came up: pretend it never happened. Maybe this would even work, unless she brought it up again.

But if I was right about Brenda, she would.

Because the wind was up and I was paddling against it, the trip back to the house from the island took almost twice as long as it had taken getting there. It was late afternoon when I walked back into the house. My arms and shoulders hurt, but more so, my head.

The children were watching a show. Prudence was at the stove, making dinner. Just as he'd told Brenda, after dropping her off at the rental house she shared with her husband, he'd swung by the house to pick up Regina and bring her to her doctor's appointment. Now he was over at the club—having a drink with his golfing buddies maybe, or maybe he'd just wanted to take a shower. He'd need to get Brenda's smell off his skin.

Regina was upstairs now. "Those doctor visits always wear her out," Prudence told me.

"I need to talk to her," I said.

58

Green Goop

Earlier in the summer, I wouldn't have dared to approach Regina's room this way. But we were on the same team now. I was her most trusted confidante, her only friend. I knocked on her door, then opened it.

Regina was sitting on the bed, propped on her special cushion as usual. Her face was covered with thick green goop—some kind of beauty masque, I figured, designed to improve a person's complexion. The stuff covered her whole face, leaving only her eyes and mouth showing through.

I pulled my chair up alongside the bed. "They did it," I told her. "On the moss."

"You have pictures this time?"

I took the Polaroids from my pocket. Three of them. In one, Brenda and Forrest had their arms around each other, her face buried in his shoulder, one of his hands cupping her buttocks. In the next one, they were naked on the ground, stretched out on that amazing moss, and he was kissing her on her stomach. In the third photograph, Brenda was kneeling on the ground in front of Forrest. His back was to the camera. He seemed to have placed his hands on her head. The sounds that came out of them at this point had been loud enough to drown out the clicking of the camera.

Regina took a long time studying the photographs. Her mouth was drawn tight as a rubber band. This was more than a frown. It was like the kind of mask you'd see at a museum that a tribal warrior might wear when going off to confront an enemy soldier, knowing only one of the two of them would survive. The fact that she had that green goop on created an even more shocking image.

"Did you make a tape?" she asked me. I took the recorder out of my pocket and rewound. Pushed "Play."

Now came Brenda's voice.

"She was probably always going to do it sooner or later," Brenda was saying. *"What if we . . . you know . . . sort of helped her along with things."*

Now came the place on the tape where Brenda was trying to convince Forrest that killing Regina might actually be viewed as doing everyone a favor. Including Regina. *Bringing an end to her suffering* was how Brenda put it.

This was where Regina stopped the tape. She pressed "Rewind" again, to the place where Brenda said what she did about helping Regina along.

"Suppose she showed up dead one day. Considering her past history, nobody would bat an eye."

I studied Regina's face as she took in the words.

Now Brenda was laying out her idea about constructing the fake suicide note.

By the time she heard this, Regina was gripping the tape recorder so hard I thought it might break in two. Through the slick green goop, her eyes looked almost yellow. A scene came to me from one of Stephen King's novels: This was how I imagined Cujo might have looked just before he sank his teeth into the neighbor's arm. And then his face. But Cujo was a dog. Regina was a person.

At this point on the tape, their voices turned fuzzy and indistinct. I hadn't noticed this at the time, but a plane had flown overhead right about then, drowning out their voices.

"Where's my husband while she's saying this?" Regina wanted to know. Whispering now. She hissed, "What was Forrest doing while this was going on?"

"He didn't say much."

This wasn't a hundred percent accurate and I knew it.

Now comes the hardest part of the story. In fact, I knew the truth. I could have told it to Regina. If I had done that, everything might have gone differently.

I didn't lie, exactly. But in my recapping of the crucial exchange, I left out one thing. It wasn't anything either of them said as they stood there together on the moss. It was the look on Forrest's face.

This was one thing a cassette tape couldn't record. All Regina took in, when I played the tape for her, were Brenda's words. Then Forrest's silence.

I was there when Brenda had put forth her plan. I'd seen his horrified expression when she'd said it. Never mind that he had just finished having sex with this woman. I knew that Forrest would never go along with what Brenda was suggesting.

Forrest was not a murderer. He could never kill his wife, or anybody else for that matter. That's what he had been trying to say to Brenda. He just hadn't finished his sentence.

I didn't tell Regina the most important thing Forrest had said when Brenda laid out her plan.

I love my wife.

All Regina had to go on was the recording. And for Regina, the recording told a whole other story.

That day, as I stood in Regina's bedroom, presenting my detailed but dangerously incomplete report on what transpired on the island earlier that afternoon, I couldn't have known the consequences of my omission. I just knew that Regina was angrier than I'd ever seen anybody, ever—and this was me, a girl who'd seen her mother throw a pot of spaghetti at her father. All I knew was that something major had been set in motion, and I was the one responsible for making that happen. I let Regina believe that her husband was conspiring with his lover to kill her and make it look like a suicide, because doing this contributed to my sense of power. I—a girl who'd never gotten to call the shots—was now a key player in a big drama.

People were paying attention to me now. I wasn't going to be invisible anymore. I felt important and powerful, like I was the one driving the train for a change. I felt big.

Then I just felt sick.

Does it make any difference that as swiftly as I made the decision to leave out Forrest's horror at Brenda's words, I realized what a huge mistake I'd made? Is it any less terrible knowing I tried to correct the impression I'd allowed Regina to buy into, that her husband was ready to go along with the murder plan?

I knew I had to correct the false impression I'd left her with. But it was too late now. Regina was no longer listening. She was off in another world now, like a person struck by a big wave and sucked into the undertow.

"It's not what you think," I told her. "He didn't go along with her idea."

It was too late to undo what I'd done. Regina's face was twisted into a mask of so much rage that even without the green goop she would have been unrecognizable. She was wailing. She was writhing on the bed, so there was green goop on her linen sheets and her silk bolsters and all the rest of it. She was raking her goop-covered fingers through her hair, so there was goop there now too. She was moaning. Not the way Brenda had moaned earlier that day on the island, on the moss with Forrest. This was more like a loon witnessing an eagle swooping down to attack.

The green goop was all over the place now—her hair, her sheets, her arms, her neck. It was as if a whole class of kindergarteners had come over and decided to do finger painting in the bed, as if Regina's brain had been overtaken by some kind of weird virus, like rabies, that made people go into fits where they stopped making sense anymore.

"Regina," I said. "I need to explain it better."

"He said some nice things about you," I said, but she wasn't listening. She couldn't take in anything. "He said he loved you."

But Regina was in some other place now. She kept shaking her head back and forth and writhing on the bed as if she were having a seizure. She buried her face in her hands. Never mind the green goop. Never mind any of it. She had buried her face in the pillow. Goop was everywhere.

I wanted to lean over and touch her head. I wanted to put my arms around her. I wanted to do something to stop her, but she didn't seem to know I was even there anymore.

She couldn't take in my words. She couldn't take in anything. She was wailing too loud.

"Forrest didn't agree with her idea," I said. I was yelling, just so she'd hear me, but it didn't matter at this point. "It was just Brenda that said those things. Not Forrest."

"Go away," Regina screamed. "I don't want to hear anything anymore."

I tried one more time. "Please," I said to her. "If I could just play you the tape another time. You can tell he didn't go along with her."

"The tape? This tape? You think I want to hear that fucking tape ever again?" She yanked the cassette out of the machine and stuck her knitting needle into the place where a thin strip of brown recording tape was exposed. Stabbing it with the needle, she yanked it from its plastic housing. She threw the tape recorder across the room.

She lay there very still for at least a minute while I knelt on the floor to retrieve it. When she finally spoke, her voice was soft but deadly. Her eyes were so dark it was as if she had no pupils.

"Well, there's one good thing," she said. "At least now I know where I stand."

Seeing her as she was at that moment, I wouldn't have wanted to be on the wrong side of Regina for anything in the world. Her voice was a low whisper.

"I will destroy him," she said.

59

Countdown

It was the middle of August when I paddled the canoe out to the island and delivered the news to Regina of what had happened there. Twenty-three days remained in my Wonderland summer. It would all draw to a close with the Labor Day weekend triathlon and the Emersons' annual end-of-summer party with the famous fireworks display Forrest personally orchestrated every year—no expense spared. Though nobody but Jonathan and I knew the next part, this would also be the weekend of my first-ever participation in a juniors' tennis match at the club. Just a little more than three weeks until I had to go home to New Jersey. I dreaded this.

You might have thought the drama swirling around Forrest and Brenda, and Regina's response to their affair, would have cast a shadow over everything else going on in my life that summer. No doubt it should have had this effect. Chalk it up to my being not quite fifteen years old, or naive, or simply too involved in my own situation to understand fully anyone else's. But after that time with Regina—the green goop incident, as I thought of it—I carried on with my life.

I was accustomed to drama, for one thing. More than once, my father had smashed a wine bottle on the counter or thrown a glass against the wall. An entire shelf-full of bottles, one time. The year I was seven, the only time we ever got a Christmas tree—an event that thrilled me—he'd lifted it up off its stand on Christmas morning (who knew why? Was there ever a good reason for a father to upend a Christmas tree in front of his seven-year-old daughter?) and threw it out the window.

Many times, my mother had gotten in the car, tearing down the street so fast I could hear the tires screaming all the way down the block. She always came back, but I had considered the possibility that one of these days she might not. If so, left with only my father, I would have had to be in charge. Then what?

One time when I was home alone with him, my father got so drunk he fell down the stairs and I thought he was dead. One time my mother put a gun up to her head and told us she was going to kill herself.

So for me, the idea of Regina and Forrest's marriage falling apart and the two of them going to war (or Regina going to war with Forrest, anyway; Forrest wasn't the war-making type) wasn't all that out of keeping with the rest of my life. The hardest part had been recognizing how little a role I played in the family that had meant the world to me.

I had a new role now. A crucial one.

In my role as a detective, the aspect of my life I'd most struggled to overcome—namely, that nobody noticed me—was serving me well. I could hide in the bushes, lurk in seldom-frequented corners of the library, or conceal myself behind a rock and bear witness to the sight of two people making love on a patch of moss on a secluded island. As Regina had reminded me on more than one occasion, I seemed to be invisible.

Even at the country club, the place where I spent hours every day, bringing Jilly and Hayward to their lessons and taking my own, I came and went as if I didn't exist. Maybe a Chris Evert–brand tennis skirt and matching top would have been enough to allow me entry into the world of the club, but I doubted this, and anyway, I didn't own a Chris Evert tennis skirt, or any tennis skirt. In those moments when I made my way along the row of courts to the one where Jonathan would be waiting for me with a basket of balls, the only person who ever greeted me was the janitor. And Jonathan himself, of course. But even with Jonathan, I was known strictly by what took place on the tennis court.

Now, though, at least one adult had a keen interest in everything I had to say. One person paid close attention. This person was Regina.

If I could have chosen the person with whom I would find the deepest connection over my time at Wonderland, that person would have been Forrest. I would have loved more of the kinds of conversations we used to have—about books I loved, things I loved, things I worried about. But in the absence of that, I felt proud and happy that I was playing a meaningful role in Regina's life. To Regina, I was not invisible now. I was important.

I wished certain other aspects of my life at Wonderland could be different, of course—that Jilly would clear away her own dishes instead of getting up from the table every day after lunch, knowing I'd take care of them, and that Hayward would stop staring at my chest. I wished that Forrest would invite me out on the boat again. I wished that I still got to share breakfast with him instead of eating my cereal alone, with nothing but one of those odd, wordless notes left by my place to keep me company. I wished we could go back to how it had all been—how it seemed, anyway—at the beginning of the summer, back when I had ninety-two days ahead of me at Wonderland and everything seemed simple and beautiful.

As for Regina, you couldn't call her attitude toward me warm or tender. Maybe it would have been nice if what she offered me had fallen into the realm of motherly affection. But the truth was, I might not have known what to do with motherly affection if I'd received some. For the girl I was, coming from the place I did, getting to be Regina's coconspirator probably worked better.

Some girls my age might've gotten a little shaken up, hearing of a potential plot in which the girlfriend of the father of the family she worked for wanted to kill the mother. I wasn't one of those girls. What

I felt first, telling Regina about Brenda's plan, was power. What I felt after, when I saw what this had done to her, was regret.

But when it became clear to me that there was nothing I could do to disabuse Regina of her belief that Forrest wanted her dead, I gave up. I had a tennis match to think about, and my dreaded return to New Jersey, which I tried not to think about—which meant I thought about it a whole lot.

I put the rest away.

60

Queen Anne's Lace

It was only August, but you could feel fall in the air. The days were shorter, the angle of the light hitting the water no longer quite so brilliant or strong. While riding my bike to the club now, for my daily workout on the court or the interludes I carved out for myself to hit balls against the backboard, I'd see beautiful lacy flowers in bloom along the sides of the road. City girl that I was, I didn't know the names of flowers, but Prudence told me: Queen Anne's lace. When they came into bloom, you knew summer was drawing to a close.

Given her past mental health issues, you might have thought that Regina's reaction to my report on Forrest and Brenda's tryst on the island would have sent her to bed for a week. This didn't happen. But a change came over Regina after my disclosure to her—incomplete as it had been.

Regina became a woman on fire. Where, for most of the summer, she'd lingered in bed until ten in the morning or later, she seemed to have acquired a new and boundless, though manic, energy. Her rage seemed to provide her with a reason for getting up every morning. Now she was out of bed even before I was, sometimes.

Up until now—even after she'd learned about the affair, and after she'd come to understand it was more serious than Forrest's previous affairs—Regina had still maintained a certain level of affection for Forrest. Anyone could see he had this effect on her. Now, with this latest discovery, all that disappeared. Where her husband was concerned, her heart had turned to stone. Worse than that: Acid ran through her veins.

Regina's awareness of Forrest and Brenda's affair, and her belief in its seriousness, seemed to energize her. The old inertia vanished, along with her general lack of attention and fuzziness—replaced by laser focus. I could see it in her eyes. The way she looked at me now suggested an intensity and concentration I'd never witnessed in her before, centered on her hatred for the man she believed to be planning to commit murder—*her* murder.

She didn't say much about the changes in her state of mind and the revelation that had brought this about. I just watched her as she chewed on it, as if she had a rancid piece of meat in her mouth.

In the past, Regina could often be observed drifting through the rooms of the house without any particular destination or goal: Typewriter . . . chaise lounge . . . nap . . . pills . . . knitting . . . tea, interspersed with brief interactions between herself and the children that seldom lasted more than a minute or two. At her suggestion that they play a game, Jilly and Hayward would lay out the Monopoly board or deal a hand of cards, but before the game got underway, she'd get up from the table and disappear, saying she was tired, or possibly not saying anything.

For the worst possible reason, Regina seemed to be getting her act together now. For the first time since I'd known her, she made an appointment at a salon to get her hair done. She put on well-cut blue jeans and the kind of shirt other mothers wore down at the club. She suggested to Jilly that they invite a girl from the club for a playdate. Except for the weird glow in her eyes, like a rabid wolf—or what I imagined a rabid wolf's eyes might look like—she could pass as a normal person.

Forrest still brought her whatever pills she'd been taking, but though she made no indication of this to him, I noted that she seldom took any of them. She placed the pills in a little glass jar she kept in a drawer of her makeup table.

She was paying more attention to her hair lately, and wearing clothes other than caftans. She still looked frail, but beautiful. One day she even asked Prudence a question: "Do you have any children?" Prudence had worked for the Emersons for many years at this point. Until now, Regina had never gotten around to inquiring.

Prudence did, actually. Four of them.

61

Close to the Chest

Days passed, bringing us closer to the end of summer. On any one of those days, I might have knocked on Regina's bedroom door and tried again to explain with greater accuracy what had transpired between Forrest and Brenda that day on the island—not the sex part, which she understood, but what she perceived to be her husband's participation in the plan to murder her. I could have pulled my chair alongside her chaise and spoken the words: *I need to tell you something.* I could have tried to play the tape for her again.

Listen to this. Not just partway. The whole thing.

But she wouldn't have listened. And anyway, I guessed she'd probably destroyed that cassette when she ripped it out of the cassette player.

I told myself it wasn't my business. Whatever was going on between the Emersons had nothing to do with me.

I think I was angry by this point. I was mad at Forrest for not caring about me the way I thought he did. But I was fed up with Regina too. For a while there, I'd enjoyed the sense of importance I'd gotten from being Regina's confidante—her only friend. But I was sick of this now. Being friends with Regina wasn't any fun. It definitely didn't get me anyplace good. If we even were friends.

It occurred to me that what passed for a bond between Regina and me was really nothing more than her using me to achieve her own objectives. If you'd asked her about me—*Who is Frances anyway? What does she care about? What are her hopes and dreams?*—Regina Emerson would have had exactly nothing to offer by way of a response. To Regina, I existed for one purpose: helping her accomplish whatever goal she had in mind at the time. Whatever this goal might be, it served one person only. *Her.*

Eighteen days remained of my Wonderland summer. Then I'd be going home. I wasn't even sure if Forrest and Brenda were seeing each other anymore. He still left the house early every morning, but I was increasingly sure that the relationship with Brenda had cooled down, if not ended altogether, since she'd shown her true colors. I got the sense that Forrest was actually doing, now, the thing he'd claimed to be doing for most of the summer: training for the triathlon.

The weird part was, I didn't even care anymore. I was tired of feeling like a minor character in the Forrest-and-Regina drama. I wanted to be the star of my own drama for a change.

That happened on the tennis court.

My secret tennis life was taking over. Every day now my game got stronger, as did my body. I hadn't filled out in the womanly way I'd hoped I might over the summer, but something better had happened. There were these muscles in my legs that hadn't ever been defined before. Same with my arms. I hadn't gotten skinny. I'd gotten strong.

"Maybe nobody ever told you this before," Jonathan told me, "but you're a natural athlete."

He was right about this. Nobody ever told me much of anything about myself.

"I haven't ever coached a kid with more raw talent than you, Frannie," he told me. Frannie was his name for me. Nobody had called me that before.

"Talent and drive," he said. "Pure raw drive. For a player to become great, she's got to have something beyond athleticism. She needs a certain kind of hunger. You've got that."

We were sitting inside the clubhouse, sharing a bag of peanuts. From where we sat, I could see a group of girls around my age gathered around a table on the patio under a striped umbrella. They were drinking virgin piña coladas. Six dollars apiece.

"Those kids over there," he said, looking into his drink, "their parents made it all so easy for them. They want to rack up trophies, but at the end of the day they can take tennis or leave it. That's not you. I see it every time you step out on the court."

He wasn't wrong about my passion for the game. What I discovered in myself during my precious time with Jonathan—four times a week now, sometimes six, because he didn't charge me for extra sessions—was a part of me I had never known to exist until then. With a racquet in my hand—the one Jonathan had lent to me—I felt strong for the first time in my life. Maybe my role in the Emerson drama had allowed me to feel powerful, but the power I felt hitting a tennis ball was different. It came from something real, not just possession of incriminating information about two people having an affair.

Every time I went after the ball, it happened: Words and thoughts and ideas that filled my brain every other waking minute—many of them having to do with other people's lives, other people's problems—disappeared completely. I became this animal girl with one objective: smashing that ball. Winning the point.

You could say I had a chip on my shoulder. You wouldn't be wrong. My parents had handed this down to me as my big legacy: the idea that some people were the winners and some were the losers, the haves and the have-nots. If ever there was a place overrun with the haves, it was the Lake Catherine Country Club. If ever there was a bunch of have-not losers, it was my family.

In my mother's view, and maybe my father's, if you were one of those have-nots, there wasn't much you could do about it. Forrest

Emerson had felt differently about that, and you could say he'd suc-ceeded in crossing the line into that glittering territory where places like Wonderland existed and those who inhabited them carried out their lives. I'd never pictured myself being one of them. But when I stepped out on the court, I'd show them who I was.

From all those hours I'd spent there that summer—many of them watching other people's lessons—I had learned something about life as it was lived at the Lake Catherine Country Club. The kids whose lessons I studied might have good strokes. Many did. Every one of these kids had years more experience than I did—hundreds of hours of instruc-tion, probably, and parents who drove them to tournaments and clinics, hired private coaches for them, bought box seats for the family at the US Open, opened charge accounts at the snack bar that allowed them to order a fancy drink after their lesson with a little paper umbrella on top every day of the week. If one of them had a temper tantrum during a match and threw her racquet, and it broke, her parents would buy her another.

Those girls knew how to hit the ball. They just didn't care as much as I did. If returning a cross-court shot required them to hustle to the deepest, farthest corner of the tennis court, they might just let the ball sail by—where for me, it wouldn't matter if the temperature was a hun-dred and ten and I had a blister on my heel dripping blood in my shoe, I'd run that ball down just the same. It wouldn't matter that my parents back home were getting a divorce, or that a creepy twelve-year-old boy stared at my chest every morning, and his crazy mother rolled around on her bed, smearing green goop on the sheets because she thought her husband was trying to murder her. I put it all out of my mind to chase down that ball. That was my kind of hunger.

The place in my life once reserved for Forrest Emerson was occu-pied by tennis now. Only tennis was a healthier obsession.

We had just finished our lesson, my fifth that week. Jonathan reached for something now—a racquet case—and set it in my hand. "This is yours," he said. "You've worked hard for it."

"The racquet you've been lending me is fine," I told him. "I'll give it back at the end of the summer. It's not like I'll have a chance to play once I'm back in New Jersey."

"You should be playing all the time now," Jonathan told me. "By the time you go home, you'll be ready to try out for a team. And you'll get on one too."

"My school doesn't have a tennis team," I said. "It's not that kind of school. I don't live in that kind of town."

"A talented player like you can always find a game," he told me. "But you need a good racquet."

He knew my grip size, of course. "Björn Borg uses one like this," Jonathan told me. "A Bancroft. It's yours. To take home with you."

Home. Given what was going on at Wonderland now, this should have been a comforting thought but wasn't.

There were a whole lot of reasons why I dreaded going home—the end of tennis being only one of these. As complicated as things had become at the lake—a murder plot now brewing in the fantasies of Hurricane Brenda and the ruminations Regina was engaged in now, whatever they turned out to be, concerning revenge—the thought of going back to our apartment in New Jersey, my father gone, felt like exile to Siberia.

62

Almost like Being in Love

Where to begin, with the list of all the things I'd miss once I departed from Wonderland: Prudence's great fried chicken, and lobster rolls, and fried clams, and cookouts by the water. I'd miss the club, with shrimp cocktail spilling over the edge of the bowl, and those wonderful little Parker House rolls slathered with real butter, not margarine, and the clubhouse bathroom with the little individual soaps that I'd put in my pocket if nobody else was around. Ice cream cones at the Caboose.

Those things were only the beginning, of course: There was my yellow bike with the basket on the front, and my bike rides to the tennis courts or the library—standing on the pedals, pumping hard to make it up the hill to the wonderful Lake Catherine Library, and coming home with my newest Stephen King novel, stretching out on the chaise lounge with a Diet Coke or a Snapple. If the kids were watching a video—as they usually were—I'd get to read my book until it was time to set the table for dinner.

I would not miss the kids at the country club, who didn't speak to me or know my name even. Top of the list, Olivia. She'd tossed me a look one time when I was coming off the court from working with Jonathan. "No offense," she said, "but I thought I should tell you. Here at the club, we don't wear blue jean shorts. You might want to pick up a few skirts at the Pro Shop."

But I'd miss walking in the door of the club, pouring myself a glass of ice water—some days they put lemon slices in it, some days watermelon, some days strawberries. I'd miss the soft striped towels with the LCCC insignia on the front, and the hot tub, where I'd sit if nobody else was in it. Hitting against the backboard, nights, with the lights shining down on me, staying as long as it took to get to my five hundred shots in a row. Not even minding if I failed to hit one and had to start over.

The Emersons' kids were spoiled, of course—and in Jilly's case, bossy. I would not miss the interminable tea parties with Jilly and her American Girls, or Hayward's creepy way of looking at me across the dinner table. Still, I'd miss playing board games with them. Popcorn and movies, s'mores over the fire.

I'd miss swimming, and going out on the Chris-Craft, and folding laundry even.

I'd miss my little bedroom under the eaves, starry nights under the patchwork quilt embroidered with flowers from every New England state (New Hampshire, purple lilac; Maine, wild lupine), looking up at my skylight window, listening to the lake water washing up against the shore, hearing the loons call out to each other.

What I'd miss most about that room was the quiet I found there. Just twice I'd heard the sounds of lovemaking—Forrest and Regina—in the room below, but not one time, all summer, had I heard the sound of people yelling at each other the way I did every day back in New Jersey. A different kind of trouble hung over Wonderland, of course. The silent kind. But up in that little room, I'd known peace and quiet. For the first time ever, maybe.

Then there was tennis. My lessons with Jonathan had become the highlight of my days, the way my breakfasts with Forrest used to be, at the start of the summer. Now what I loved best was the court, the backboard, even picking up balls with the ball hopper at the end of my lessons.

And for all the drama swirling around them now, I'd miss Forrest and Regina. Both of them, oddly enough, though the one I would miss most painfully would be Forrest. As confused as I had come to feel about him, and as disappointed by what felt like his abandonment of me—as angry as I felt toward him for choosing a pinhead like Brenda over a girl to whom he meant the world—I couldn't help loving him. I missed that time, not so far back, when I still believed that there was one truly good man in the world, and that was Forrest Emerson. And that he loved me.

63

DISAPPEARANCES

By this point I'd been functioning as Regina's personal detective for weeks, and I wanted to be done with the job. I'd given her the information she'd asked for. Still, she couldn't leave it alone. She kept wanting more evidence. She was like a person with poison ivy who couldn't keep herself from scratching at a bloody sore. Making it worse.

She had gone off the deep end now.

Forrest had made a trip to Bangor that day to purchase supplies for the big party, with the plan of stopping off at his friend Evan's on the way home for poker night. Regina had made the surprising decision to give Jilly her bath—a ritual she'd participated in so seldom that she seemed not to get it that a silk blouse wasn't the best attire to wear for that particular task. I figured this had to be part of her campaign to reinvent herself as a good mother.

It wasn't working all that well. When I stepped into the bathroom with the fresh towels, Jilly was sitting nearly buried in the bubbles that had formed after Regina poured an entire bottle of bubble bath in the tub. She eyed her mother with a wary expression. She had brought one of her American Girls, Samantha, to join her in the tub.

"Maybe Samantha would do better staying dry," I suggested. "It might ruin her hair if you get her wet." Regina made no comment. Jilly plunged the doll underwater, then looked up at me with a smile.

When they got to shampoo time, it was up to Jilly to explain to Regina what to do next. She pointed to the bottle of Johnson's baby shampoo on the edge of the tub. "You put some in your hand and rub it over my head to make the suds," Jilly said.

She handed her mother the cup to rinse out the suds, then closed her eyes. When I did this, nights when Forrest wasn't around, I'd learned how to keep the soapy water from getting in Jilly's eyes. I'd hand her a washcloth and cup my hand around the place where the water ran down. Watching Regina pouring water on Jilly's head—a great deal of it, no washcloth or protective hand—I guessed she probably hadn't washed her daughter's hair much before this, possibly ever.

Crying now from shampoo in her eyes, Jilly stepped out of the tub. This would have been the moment for the person giving Jilly her bath to wrap her tightly in one of the extremely fluffy, hotel-quality towels that filled the Emersons' linen closet, dab her face, and put their arms around her.

Regina sat on the edge of the toilet taking it in as if this were a play and she the lone member of the audience. Jilly stood naked and shivering, and wailing, waiting for her mother to do something. I reached for her myself.

When it was time for bedtime reading, Jilly said she wanted me, not her mother, to read that night's chapter. After I'd got her tucked in, I came downstairs. Regina had the television set on—rare for her—and her cup of tea.

"My daughter doesn't like me," she said. "I doubt my son does either." She took another sip of her tea. "I can't say I blame them.

"If I disappeared tomorrow, I doubt if they'd notice."

You might have thought this thought would depress her, but after she said the words, she laughed.

64

Harvest Moon

Typically by this hour, Regina would have taken her Valium, along with whichever other medications filled the pillbox that sat on her bedside table. Often this meant she fell asleep on the couch, but with her customary regimen of pills seemingly abandoned, that night Regina seemed surprisingly alert.

She consulted the typewritten list she'd made up for the day, noting that Forrest had neglected one of the duties she'd spelled out for him. *Vanilla frozen yogurt.* As always, she'd specified the brand.

"It's not like my husband to forget something like that," she said. "He's definitely distracted. I guess we both know why."

"He's planning the big party, that's all," I told her.

"Ah, yes," she said. "The party. I wonder if he invited his girlfriend."

The funny thing was that even as she held on to the belief that her husband was plotting to kill her for the purpose of going off with Brenda Barnett, Regina's demeanor had turned weirdly chipper, though in a slightly manic way. She had tried to engage Jilly in a game with her dolls once or twice, though she never seemed able to sustain her interest in American Girl tea parties. Then there was the afternoon she'd baked a roll of Pillsbury slice-and-bake chocolate chip cookies. She'd even put an apron over her caftan. At dinner one night, she told us all about this great movie she'd heard of called *Back to the Future*, as if none of us had heard anything about it.

"We've all seen it," Jilly told her.

"Like . . . three times," Hayward added.

This particular evening Regina had made a bowl of microwave popcorn—no butter, naturally. It was as if she'd recently read a book with the title *How to Have Fun with Your Family* and she'd been taking notes.

Now she sat there, looking out the window as if this was the first time she'd ever laid eyes on the moon. It cast a shaft of light over the lake. I could hear music far off on the water. One of the neighbors must be cruising the lake in their motorboat. I could make out the sound of laughter.

"I guess I've missed out on a lot," Regina said. It seemed she was speaking to nobody in particular, though the only one there was me.

There was no way of refuting this. She *had* missed out on a lot—bathtime with Jilly only one example. Her children's whole childhood to date, another.

An odd thing happened then. This wave of protectiveness came over me. For Regina, of all people. When I thought about it, my job performance that summer had been lackluster at best. But at that one moment, I could feel myself rising to my duties. I was a *mother's helper*, after all. The person I'd needed to help wasn't just either of the children. It was their mother.

It came to me then that the whole drama swirling around us now was all Forrest's fault. Never mind that he hadn't gotten on board with Brenda's crazy scheme to fake Regina's suicide. He was the one who'd brought the Brenda mess into their lives. If he hadn't done that— if he'd been content to spend the summer having our nice breakfast talks and teaching me to water-ski—none of this mess would have happened.

At the moment, though, surprisingly, Regina gave the appearance of calm and well-being. She sat there in a pair of silk pajamas, eating popcorn and knitting, as the two of us faced the television.

"This is nice, isn't it?" she said. "The kids in bed. The two of us cozying up with a TV show. My darling husband off at poker night."

I studied her face. There was no telling what she'd do next.

"Poker!" Regina hooted. "More likely poke-her. I'd like to poke her eyes out."

She smiled and patted my leg. Nothing for me to do but reach for a handful of popcorn.

The program Regina had tuned in to watch that night was one of those TV magazine shows that focused on a true-life crime. These generally involved rich or famous people, the kind you might not think would get involved with criminal activities. People like Forrest and Regina, come to think of it.

That night's episode examined the story of a wealthy Danish businessman named Claus von Bülow, who'd married a wealthy socialite known to her friends as Sunny. One night, Sunny von Bülow was found "unresponsive," face down on her bed, leaving her in what was described as a "persistent vegetative state." The initial findings of the medical examiner had suggested that a combination of the drugs and alcohol Sunny had taken that night had left her this way. But further investigation into the case, much of it instigated by Sunny's children from her previous marriage, led the authorities to charge Claus von Bülow with attempted homicide. His mistress had testified against him. She'd put his neck in the noose, basically. The program revealed he was found guilty and sentenced to thirty years in prison but later acquitted.

Watching from her spot on the couch, Regina reached for the bowl of popcorn. She ate hers one kernel at a time.

"You think you know a person," she said. She pointed one of her knitting needles in the direction of the TV set, the handsome face of Claus von Bülow filling the screen. "Then it turns out you didn't know them at all.

"Take yourself, Frances," she said. "You seem like this sweet innocent girl. But who knows what dark thoughts and wild ideas go on in your head? You could be a pathological liar, or a thief. You could go up to your room every night and make plans to assassinate some famous rock star. For all anyone knows, you could turn out to be some kind of sex maniac."

After all the other things she'd listed, the last item on her list of my imagined madness hit home.

Had she found my journal? Slipped into my room when the children and I were at tennis, carefully removed the line of BBs laid out to alert me to any breach of security, and read all the crazy stuff I'd written about Forrest and me? Then returned the journal and the BBs to their original location, afterward?

The Regina I knew could not have made it up to my little bedroom on the third floor. I'd counted on that. Plus, I kept my journal under the mattress. She'd be too weak to lift it. But this Regina—Regina as she'd become since finding out about Brenda's plot, Regina since getting off her medications and embarking on her Destroy Forrest campaign— seemed capable of anything.

After I'd heard her speculate about the possibility of my shameful secret life, my face must have betrayed some indication of shock. Now Regina patted my knee—the furthest she seemed able to go in displaying affection.

"For god's sake, Frances," she said. "I was just kidding. Everyone knows the closest you ever get to a sexual adventure is in one of those books you're always taking out of the library. You're our quiet little bookworm!"

For a moment I felt insulted. I wanted to tell her she was wrong about that. I could tell her, *You don't even know me.* But it was better that she didn't, of course.

The show about the von Bülow case was over. Still no sign of Forrest. "I'm heading to bed," Regina said.

Partway up the stairs, she called down to me. "You're a funny little person, aren't you?" she said. "All this time I've been so worried about Brenda Barnett, but maybe it's really been you all the time who's the big problem."

After Regina went upstairs I stayed in the living room. I tried to read my book, but Regina's words kept coming back to me. I figured Forrest would make it better. I wanted to be there when he got back.

On poker nights—or whatever they were—it wasn't unusual for Forrest to stay out until two in the morning. I knew this because, nights in bed, I often listened for his car pulling into the driveway. It always felt comforting, knowing he was home.

Staying up that night, I told myself I just wanted to finish my book, but really I was hoping Forrest and I would get to have a few minutes together after his long night out. He'd pour me a glass of chocolate milk—a whiskey for himself—and ask me some question about my life. Did I believe that people were fundamentally good? If I was driving a car and I hit a deer, and he was lying on the road in a lot of pain, would I be able to hit him over the head with a rock? If I could live a long, unexciting life or a short, amazing one (like John Lennon, for instance), which would I choose?

Short and amazing, I'd say.

Same here, he'd tell me.

Now, once again, I waited for him—though no longer, as I once did, with the fantasy that he might take me in his arms or tell me I was the most wonderful girl he'd ever met. That fantasy was gone, but the place Forrest occupied in my brain was only slightly less significant now. I still saw him as the most important man in my life. I couldn't have articulated this at the time, but there was something I needed to understand, and it seemed to me that if we could just talk, maybe I'd figure out how a person I'd loved so much could behave as he did.

I didn't need further confirmation that Forrest Emerson was no Claus von Bülow. But who was he, then? What was he doing with Brenda? If he really loved Regina, how could he keep having sex with someone else?

Most of all I wanted to know, Did I mean anything at all to him?

It was after two in the morning when Forrest walked in the door. He wasn't drunk, but he'd definitely been drinking. Despite the hour, he didn't seem surprised to see me on the couch.

"What do you know?" he said. "I may have just dropped a few hundred dollars in a poker game, but I get to finish off the night with one of my all-time favorite people."

As I always did when Forrest was around, I felt my heart open up. How could I hate this man? I also believed he was telling the truth. He really had been playing poker.

"How about that moon tonight?" he said to me. "Let me play you a song." He pulled an album out of its sleeve.

Neil Young. "Harvest Moon." He set down the needle.

"Every time I hear this, I have to dance," he said. "Someday, when you meet some man who truly deserves you, I'll come to your wedding. You'll dance with your father, of course. But maybe at some point, you'll have a few minutes to step out on the floor with me."

He opened his arms. He took my hand in one of his, the other resting on my back, as a father might. A different kind of father from mine.

I could see him clearly then. Forrest Emerson had his weaknesses alright—among these, an attraction to women in low-cut dresses. A tendency for brief enthusiasms that might not last beyond a summer, likely to distract him. For a while, anyway.

But his devotion to me—the place I represented in his life—was different. This would endure beyond the summer. Forrest actually cared about me, for reasons that had nothing to do with the things people did with each other when they took off their clothes and got into bed together. Into bed, or onto a patch of moss.

In some ways, this was better. I was not all that familiar with what Forrest Emerson had felt for me, but it felt like something real. It felt like love.

That night in my little attic room, I took out my journal again. It had been a while.

I was wrong to be mad at Forrest, I wrote. *He never really cared for Brenda. That was all just about sex.*

Forrest loves me, I wrote. *I love him too.*

65

RICH PEOPLE

I'd taken the kids over to their friends Locke and Helena's house for Helena's birthday party. (Was there a single weekend in the summer when someone wasn't celebrating a birthday? Was there any party theme—unicorns, rainbows, Care Bears, the groovy sixties—that hadn't been exhausted? Was there a single child among the members of the Lake Catherine Country Club with a name like anybody I knew back in New Jersey?)

Regina had taken the children back-to-school shopping now. When they returned to Boston, Jilly would be enrolling in first grade at a private school in Back Bay. Hayward—his voice mostly changed by now—might be the only seventh grader in his class to sport a mustache. As for me, I'd be entering school the next fall almost as flat-chested as I had been before.

Back at Wonderland, an unfamiliar man sat at the dining room table across from Regina. His briefcase was open, and there were papers spread out on the table. He'd taken out a calculator.

Regina seemed to have pulled herself together for his visit. She had makeup on, and she was wearing a gray pantsuit with a pair of matching flats. I headed to the kitchen to make a snack.

"What's up?" I asked Prudence. I'd never seen Regina dressed this way, carrying on what looked like a business meeting.

"Something to do with the Emersons' money," Prudence said. "I think he takes care of their insurance policies or something. Not that those two have anything to worry about. Rich people. Who understands anything about them?"

A change seemed to have come over Forrest since that day on the island with Brenda. He had started stopping by the club to watch the children's tennis lessons, as he hadn't done since the affair began. Though I had no proof to offer Regina that the affair was over—and she seemed determined to believe it wasn't, and to accumulate more evidence— what I saw in Forrest's behavior, in these final days of summer, suggested to me that since Brenda had revealed her plan to him, he'd been keeping his distance.

It was a late afternoon, the third week in August. Forrest and I were picking up Jilly from a friend's house. Just as Forrest pulled into a gas station, we spotted Brenda's little Honda parked by one of the pumps. Seeing her car, he swerved away, back out onto the road.

I said nothing, but Forrest did. "There was someone there I didn't feel like running into," he told me. "Let's just say, I've made some stupid choices in my life."

It was a surprising admission for a man to make to a girl my age. At that moment, he almost reminded me of the old Forrest, the one who talked to me as if I was a friend, not a kid. I offered no response.

"I've always known you're wise beyond your years, Frances," he said to me. "You probably haven't missed a thing all summer. You probably didn't miss a thing."

"It's not my business," I told him. Though Regina had made it mine. This part I kept to myself, naturally.

66

Not Exactly the *Boy Scout Handbook*

Though she had not abandoned her quest to seek out more information concerning Forrest's affair with Brenda, Regina had given me the afternoon off, and Forrest was off on his bicycle, training for the triathlon. (Legitimately training, I was pretty sure. He was back to being the old Forrest now.)

I was down at the dock again, reading my book. Jilly had been invited to a Bring-Your-American-Girl-Doll party. Over by the badminton court, Hayward and his friend Jasper were having a water pistol war. I was trying to read my book, but—rare for me—I couldn't concentrate.

I was thinking about the tennis tournament coming up, and what came after that—the end of my time at Wonderland. Not that I wanted to, but I was also thinking about my parents. I'd mostly managed to keep them out of my thoughts all summer. Now the picture was coming to me of our dark little apartment. My windowless room. Lunches in the school cafeteria with Martha, my only friend, while boys threw spitballs at us and grinned. No more tennis.

I looked out to the water. As much as I could, I wanted to hold on to the picture of this moment. Sky, lake, birds, boat. The smell of freshly cut grass. Up at the house, Prudence would be making fried chicken.

Trying to distract myself—with nothing better to do—I walked over to the boathouse and pushed the door open. At first it stuck.

I'd only been in the boathouse once before, all summer—to look for an inflatable swan Jilly wanted me to blow up for her. I'd spent half an hour doing that, and by the time it was ready to float she'd lost interest. Now the deflated swan lay on the boathouse floor along with a pile of life jackets, old snorkel masks, and a broken glider Billy hadn't gotten around to fixing and probably never would. Along the back wall: a few old canoes, the Sunfish Hayward had taken out only one time all summer, a birchbark canoe Regina's father had evidently bought on a fishing trip to Quebec long ago that turned out to be too tippy to use, which Forrest was always talking about fixing up.

On the shelf by the door there was a stack of old *National Geographics* and another stack of *Good Housekeeping* magazines from the 1960s. I pulled one down and flipped through the pages. Diet tips . . . recipes for interesting things to do with Jell-O . . . advice from Dr. Joyce Brothers—none of which was likely to apply to me. *What to do if you're almost fifteen years old and you haven't gotten your period yet. What to do if your parents are getting a divorce and your father's moving out and even though he's a total screwup who gets drunk all the time, still you know you're going to miss him. What to do if the woman you work for wants you to prove her husband's having an affair. What to do if you wish somebody else was your father, and somebody else's family was your family, even if—as you know now—that family is pretty screwed up themselves.*

What to do is, you try to put it all out of your head. Think of something else. Anything.

This is when I spotted it. Tucked behind *The Ultimate Trout Encyclopedia*, on a shelf so high I had to step onto a stool to take it down.

The book contained words, but it was the pictures that transfixed me. They would probably have had a strong effect on anyone, but most particularly a girl who'd spent the last couple of years consumed with thoughts of sex without knowing how it happened or what it looked like—a girl for whom, even after spending a good part of her summer attempting to record evidence of her employer's husband's affair, the details of male anatomy remained hazy.

The illustrations featured a man and a woman in bed. No covers concealed their bodies, which were naked and assuming a variety of positions—more of these than I could have imagined.

Part of what transfixed me about the illustrations in this book was how real the people looked. They could be my science teacher, Mr. Mackenzie, or the woman behind the desk at the Lake Catherine Library. They could be anyone.

The woman in the picture had slightly droopy breasts—like real breasts, my mother's, for instance. The man featured in the drawings had a beard. In some of the pictures, he was on top of the woman, but in others she was on top of him, and sometimes they arranged themselves in more complicated and intriguing positions, not so different maybe from the knots I guessed were displayed in the *Boy Scout Handbook*, located on the same shelf.

I felt shock and fascination, both at once. Did people actually like doing these kinds of things?

I sat on the floor of the boathouse for as long as I dared, leaned up against a bunch of old life jackets, studying the illustrations. I wondered if my parents had ever done one of these things. I didn't need to wonder if Forrest Emerson had.

The Joy of Sex. I loved the title of the book. Always in the past I'd thought about sex as something dirty. Thrilling, but shameful. The idea of sex being joyful would never have occurred to me.

I flipped through the pages at random at first—naked bodies entangled in a dizzying variety of positions. Then my eyes landed on a particular page, 157. Something about the drawing there caught me up short. I put my hand inside my underpants while I studied the picture. I found the place deep inside that I could count on to make a warm, good feeling wash over me. I rubbed the spot a little. Then more.

I was breathing harder. Sitting on the old, splintery boathouse floor, I rocked my body back and forth so the feeling grew stronger. I closed my eyes. I tried to summon the image of a real person—River Phoenix maybe, or the boy at the ice cream counter at the Caboose—with whom I might imagine doing the things I saw in the picture.

Not Forrest. That was over. Maybe I'd think about nobody but my own self for a change.

I was rocking faster now. Rubbing harder. The warm feeling had spread all through my body. I was off in some other place.

I heard another sound then. This one didn't come from me. There were voices. More laughter, louder this time. Coming from just beyond the door.

I opened my eyes. That's when I saw it. A single blue eye, pressed up against a knot hole in the boathouse wall. The eye belonged to Hayward Emerson.

I heard his voice now, and that of his friend. They had probably been taking turns looking in at me through the hole.

My hand flew up to cover my mouth, as if I could stop their laughter that way. I shut my legs. No way I could pull up my underpants without standing up, naked from the waist down. Better to sit there with an old piece of tarp thrown over me.

I set the book down. "Go away," I yelled.

Then something came over me. You could call it courage, or just the refusal to be ashamed of doing something that made me feel happy and didn't hurt anyone.

"You probably do this too," I called out to the boys. "If you don't, you should try it."

The eye disappeared. Whoever it belonged to—and I knew who that was, of course—must have run away.

I considered the possibility that Hayward would make fun of me afterward. But back up at the house, as I served the children their afternoon snack, he said nothing. I poured the Coke in his glass. He muttered thank you. We went on with our day.

67

Homeward Bound

That night we had dinner out on the patio—my favorite fried chicken—but I had even less of an appetite than Regina, who picked at her salad as usual. Jilly was going on about which of her new Esprit outfits she planned to wear on the first day of school—there were three possibilities; she couldn't make up her mind. She was trying to decide whether to wear her new boots or her My Little Pony sneakers.

From the other side of the table, I could feel Hayward looking at me, but I made sure not to meet his gaze. I needed to pretend nothing had happened that afternoon. I needed him to pretend the same. This left the two of us, Hayward and me, in a position that felt almost like coconspirators. We had the goods on each other. He could reveal something deeply embarrassing about me, but to do so he'd have to reveal something embarrassing about himself. It seemed we had an understanding: to remain silent.

I studied the chicken on my plate, wondering if this was the last time I'd have a chance to enjoy it for a while. Or ever. Only I couldn't. Then Forrest set down his fork in a manner that suggested he had something important to say.

"I talked to your dad today, Frances," he said. "He's coming up Labor Day weekend. He said he can drive you back home on Monday. Save me the trip."

This might have been the moment for Forrest to deliver one of his lines about not being able to imagine life around here without me. He might even have pretended he'd be barring the door, refusing to let his old pal Hank whisk me away. But he didn't.

"We're going to miss you, honey," he said. His words felt insubstantial. He resumed eating his chicken.

It was as if a stone landed on my heart then. Or an arrow pierced it. I had known the summer was coming to an end, of course, but until that moment, I'd imagined that it would be Forrest who'd be driving me back to New Jersey. In spite of everything that had happened, I'd looked forward to our drive. I understood by this point that it wouldn't have been a replay of the wonderful time we'd had driving up in his old Porsche, back when the whole summer had stretched ahead of me—ahead of us both, was how I'd seen it—filled with the promise of times together at the lake.

Those times were behind us now. Many of them never even happened. But I figured we'd talk. I longed for this. Now I'd be making the trip in our old Pontiac with my father.

Not even three months earlier, Forrest and I had made the same drive in the opposite and vastly more promising direction. Now Forrest didn't express even the slightest indication of regret at not getting to have that time in the car with me, going back.

I should have been relieved that I'd be relinquishing my duties as Regina's advisor and personal detective. I'd give her back the Polaroid camera and the mini tape recorder and turn over my notes. I'd never know the end of the story—or if I did, it would only be the version my mother chose to tell me, months from now probably, when her divorce from my father was final. By the time that happened, I was pretty sure that Forrest and Regina would be back to their old life. Brenda would be long gone.

But a thought came to me: The following summer, Regina would get a different mother's helper. A real au pair. Someone who would teach Jilly and Hayward French, or backgammon. This au pair would know how to cook amazing French dishes for the family—soufflés, maybe. She'd be old enough to drive.

But the real problem with me had nothing to do with my age, or my lack of a driver's license. I just knew too much now, and everything I knew was everything Regina would want to put behind her.

I stared down at my plate, the untouched chicken. Nine days to go.

Maybe it's really been you all the time who's the big problem, Regina had said to me.

I was the one who'd borne witness to Forrest and Brenda's affair. I was the one who'd borne witness to Regina's descent into craziness. My presence would serve now as a constant reminder of every bad thing that took place over these past three months. If I never returned, everyone could pretend that nothing ever happened.

I knew it now, as clearly as I knew my name. There would be no more Wonderland summers.

68

Like Disney World

Labor Day weekend would kick off with the long-awaited triathlon Forrest either had or had not been training for extensively. This would be followed by a brunch at the club. But that was only the beginning of the festivities.

Every Labor Day weekend, members of the Lake Catherine Lake Association held a regatta. Forrest always decked out the Chris-Craft with flags and balloons for the occasion. This year, in addition to the Chris-Craft, he'd made the plan of launching the birchbark canoe into the lake, though to do so, he'd explained to us, would require him to attach some modifications to the canoe—some kind of outriggers—to make it steadier.

After the regatta, the Emersons would be serving food and drinks at the water for their assembled guests (many of these, no doubt). Then would come Forrest's famous fireworks display, the plans for which had been underway since the beginning of the summer and probably even before that.

"It's going to look like Disney World here Saturday night," Prudence observed, watching him carry in another box of fireworks a week or so before the big event. "With the money that man spends on fireworks, I could feed my whole family for a year."

It was the first time I'd heard Prudence offer a single critical remark concerning Forrest. I might have been taken aback, but I had other things on my mind. The tournament. And the other part, going home. Wherever home was for me now. Whatever I'd find there. Nothing good, was my guess.

69

DOUBLES

After I'd gotten those Polaroids of Forrest and Brenda together—and the tape—I figured Regina would be satisfied that we had enough evidence for her case against Forrest. But she still wanted more. Now even as summer drew to a close, with Prudence already packing up boxes of the family's possessions for their return to Boston, she wanted me to keep tabs on Forrest's every move—even the times (and there were plenty of these) when he really was just out playing golf with his foursome or running errands, most of which had to do with picking things up for Regina.

She was relentless in the way she kept wanting me to locate new evidence for her. She wouldn't leave it alone. When all I wanted now was to hit tennis balls and forget everything else.

So I had come to despise my assignment of collecting information for Regina. More than this, I had come to despise Regina. That night I wrote in my journal.

If I never see her again after this summer, I won't miss her. She's always talking about killing herself. Sometimes I wish she'd do it.

Forrest was scheduled to play a tennis match down at the club. Regina insisted that I go down to the court to keep an eye on him. By this time, I was a regular there, from all the hours I spent watching the children's lessons as well as taking my own. But as much time as I'd devoted to sitting by some court or another that summer, it was harder to justify why I'd be sitting on one of those benches again that afternoon, watching Forrest play—assuming anyone would notice. As it turned out, no one did.

Forrest wasn't a good tennis player. He would have been lost without his doubles partner, Evan. Unlike most of the men who played at the club, who each grew up at some tennis club, Forrest hadn't taken up the sport until he got together with Regina, and never had lessons. I guessed the men included him for the simple reason that he was just so likable. Though he'd probably had sex with a few of their wives.

Forrest was the athletic type for sure, but his form was all wrong. After working with Jonathan as much as I had that summer, I could have given him some pointers myself. Still, I derived a surprising pleasure watching him play. Just watching him live.

Following Forrest's match that day—with his ungainly method of reaching a ball and his odd, graceless forehand, totally lacking follow-through, as if he were swatting more than swinging—there was no way to view him as a god anymore. He was just an uninitiated and secretly insecure outsider, trying hard to fit in to a world he didn't really belong to. In some ways, who Forrest reminded me of, as I sat watching him, was myself.

Over the course of his time with Brenda, he had appeared so distracted that he barely noticed me anymore. But I wanted to believe that was over now. Partway through his match, on the crossover, he spotted me sitting on the sidelines. At one point he looked up from the service line and shot me a grin. "Let me show you how it's done, Frances," he said, grinning, as he launched into another messy serve. I pretended to be impressed.

After the match was over, Forrest and his friends headed to the snack bar while I rode home on Buttercup. One of my last bike rides of the summer, it occurred to me.

"So, don't tell me my husband was actually playing tennis," Regina said to me when I got back to the house.

He was. "No sign of Brenda," I said. No sign of her ever anymore. Brenda was history.

Regina just shook her head. She wasn't buying it.

70

A Good Friend

August was almost over now.

It felt as though I'd lived a whole lifetime since I'd begun my surveillance activities and borne witness to Forrest and Brenda making love on the moss, the day I heard Brenda's plan and shared it, disastrously, with Regina. Life went on—seemingly—as it had before. But not really. Not even close.

Sometime in the late morning—a day when the children had gotten a ride to tennis with one of the mothers—Regina received a call. Sitting with her in the kitchen, waiting for her to type up my list for the day—Prudence having taken the day off, Forrest on his way to play golf—I studied Regina's face as she held the receiver. A strange combination of emotions appeared to pass over her as she listened to what the caller had to tell her. It looked like a mixture of fury and—weirdly—pleasure. She barely said anything for the duration of the call. Just before it ended, she spoke for the first time.

"Thank you," she told the caller. "I appreciate your telling me."

"That was Pam Oliver," she said. Pam Oliver, the woman with whom, Regina was convinced, her husband had been carrying on his annual affair the summer before.

"You won't believe what that bitch said to me," Regina said. As usual, she seemed to have forgotten completely that I wasn't some forty-year-old woman down at the club, sitting on the chaise lounge next to her with a G&T in hand, or sharing a glass of wine on the patio. Now she launched into a surprisingly accurate imitation of Pam.

"'As your friend, and a wife and mother like yourself,' she tells me, 'I couldn't in good conscience hold on to the knowledge of what's going on with your husband and a certain woman who's been renting a place on the other side of the lake.'"

"My friend," Regina hooted. "That's a good one."

"She started in by telling me how she was 'always on the woman's side.'" She reached for a celery stick—her version of stress eating. Seldom a person to crack a smile, Regina had made a sound resembling laughter, though it wasn't, really.

It occurred to me that Regina had crossed over a line now. She was pacing the room, waving her hands. She might have lit the curtains on fire. Nothing would have surprised me.

"Evidently Forrest hasn't been keeping up with his golf foursome much this summer," she went on. "Pam found out this much from her husband, who told her they'd had to find a substitute the last two times they'd hit the links."

It hadn't taken Pam long to spring into action. A few weeks before this—having learned that Forrest had once again called in requesting a replacement—she'd driven past the Barnetts' place. (Their *rental* place, Regina was careful to point out.) This was when she'd spotted Forrest's Porsche parked behind the barn where the town road crew stored their equipment for the winter. Snowplows, salt, sand. Not the kind of place frequented by the people who showed up at Lake Catherine strictly in the summer months.

Once she'd calmed down, Regina filled me in on the details of what Pam had reported. The lot used by the road crew was a short walk from the Barnetts' house—no more than one hundred yards—another clear indication, Regina had noted, that the house the Barnetts were renting was hardly normal Lake Catherine caliber.

Pam had watched what happened next from a safe distance. She happened to have a pair of binoculars on her at the time.

She saw Forrest walking into the Barnetts' house. He'd felt no need to knock first, evidently. While he was still in the doorway, someone—she couldn't make out who, but it wasn't difficult to guess—extended a long, slim arm, which she wrapped around his neck as she kissed him. The two of them disappeared into the house.

Pam must have been something of a sleuth herself. She'd taken it upon herself—it was her *moral obligation*, she'd explained to Regina—to approach the window of what would have been the master bedroom. The blinds had been drawn, but the sounds emanating from the room made it plain what was going on in there.

She did not add—but Regina and I understood this part without anyone needing to point it out—that the sound of Forrest Emerson having sex (Forrest Emerson making love, if you wanted to get sentimental about it) was all too familiar to Pam Oliver. She only had to go back a year in her memory bank to remember that sound from when she'd been the one to inspire his expressions of joy. This part had not featured in her report to Regina.

On the call, evidently Pam had explained that at first she'd kept the information concerning Forrest's visit to the Barnetts' place to herself. "I didn't want to upset you," she'd told Regina. "But this morning, I saw his car over there again, and I decided that if it were me, I'd want to know.

"Of course it's up to you what you choose to do with this information," Pam had added. "It's none of my business."

This was supposed to be a golf day—the men's final round of the summer. Forrest had hoisted his clubs into the back of his sports car, letting Regina know that the boys at the club were counting on him to fill out their foursome again. She should not expect him home until late afternoon. They'd be golfing the full eighteen holes.

"I wish I could just stay home with you and the kids," he'd told her, stroking her face. "I want to put the finishing touches on my plans for the fireworks. Then I've got the outrigger to attach to your grandpa's old canoe."

The birchbark one. Too tippy to use without modifications.

As he headed to his car, Forrest turned around one more time with a wave in Regina's direction. "Love you, babe," he called out.

All of this had taken place less than two minutes earlier. Now—her conversation with Pam having concluded—Regina stood at the counter, still gripping the phone and gnawing on her celery. Her face, which had been twisted in rage moments before, took on an odd appearance now. Not glee, certainly, but not despair either. I might call it the look of anticipation an animal gets right before sinking its teeth into a piece of meat.

"Go get your bike," she said to me. She was not a woman to waste her breath on niceties. "Get yourself over to Brenda's house."

71

Breakup

Pam Oliver wasn't wrong about the location of Forrest's Porsche. He'd parked it out behind the barn where the Department of Public Works stored their snow-removal equipment. Beside the plows sat a Zamboni donated by a wealthy hockey lover, put into service every winter to clear a patch of ice on the lake for the annual Valentine's Day festival that featured a fundraising hockey game and an ice fishing derby for the townspeople—the year-rounders. In summer, nobody paid much attention to the Public Works barn. It was the perfect spot for a person to leave his car if he didn't want anyone to notice.

Always thorough in her planning, Regina had reminded me before I set out on my latest reconnaissance mission to watch for poison ivy, which grew like crazy on that side of the lake. In typical Regina fashion—as the woman who thought of everything—she had presented me with a bottle of Tecnu to slather over my ankles and shins, along with a pair of heavy socks and rubber boots to protect myself. These made the bike ride over to the Public Works barn a little more challenging, but by this point in the summer, I'd been putting in plenty of time biking up hills—not to mention chasing tennis balls.

I hid Buttercup in some bushes. Then I hiked over to the Barnetts' place—a far more modest house than the Emersons', with only a very small strip of water access, which was also overgrown with reeds and some form of algae that had definitely not spread to Wonderland.

Bending low, I made my way to the back of the house, as instructed. My plan had been to stake out the area closest to the bedroom—for the purpose of recording additional data confirming the sexual nature of Forrest and Brenda's relationship. But as I got closer, I saw that the two of them were standing on the lawn. The way they faced each other, I knew, even before I heard their voices, that this was not another one of their romantic rendezvous.

"I keep calling," she said. "Why don't you answer my messages?"

"It's not fair that I've been avoiding you," Forrest was saying to her. "I've been a coward. I should have said this to your face before now."

"I know it's hard for you," she said, reaching to touch his face. "I've been trying to be patient."

He took a step back.

"You got the wrong idea about me, Brenda," Forrest was saying to her. "We had a great time together for a while there. But I never intended to leave my wife. If I gave you the opposite impression, I owe you an apology."

"What about all those things you told me?" she said. "The part about how you woke up thinking about me. You couldn't bear a day apart."

"Those are the kind of things a person says when they're carried away," he said. "I wasn't expecting you to take it all so seriously."

A look came over her face. How had I ever imagined Brenda was pretty? All of a sudden she looked hideous.

"What are you talking about?"

"It's over, Brenda. It's been over since that day on the island. I just didn't know how to tell you."

"You . . . you . . . you . . ." Her voice was shrill. Her hands were flailing, coming at him like little birds. Or a flock of bats. "I was going to leave my husband. We were going to have this great life together."

"You're an attractive woman," he told her. "We had a lot of fun together." Young as I was, I knew he was not helping his case. Nothing Forrest tried saying was making her any less mad.

"Attractive? *Attractive?*" She was practically spitting.

"Any man would be crazy not to want you. Your husband's a lucky man."

"My *husband?* You think I want to do all the things we've been doing . . . with my *husband?*"

Forrest looked down at his golf shoes. It occurred to me that this wasn't the first time he'd faced an angry woman in the waning days of a Lake Catherine summer.

"Your marriage isn't my concern, Brenda. I don't have a right to offer an opinion on that."

Now Brenda had placed her hands on his shoulders, but not as a sign of affection this time. She was shaking him.

"We were going to Hawaii!" she screamed. "We were going to live in your house! The only thing that stood in our way was your miserable, scrawny, frigid, depressed, suicidal wife."

"You don't understand about Regina . . . ," he said. I had never heard Forrest sound this way. Pleading. He was practically crying.

Suddenly Brenda's voice became chillingly calm. "I told you I had that part all figured out," she said. "I had a plan. She just had to be dead, and everything was going to be perfect."

She'd said it. Plain and simple. There was no misinterpreting her words.

"I never wanted Regina to die," Forrest said quietly. "I would never have done anything to hurt my wife. Not in a million years."

"She's basically half dead already." Brenda's voice had gone to a whole other octave now. I felt like calling out to Forrest, *I knew she was a terrible person from the first time I laid eyes on her!* But I held my tongue, of course.

"All we had to do was work out the fine points together," Brenda said. As she spoke—yelled, actually—she was doing this odd thing. It was sort of like punching, but because the person doing the punching was Brenda, it came off looking more like tapping. She did this repeatedly, her palms landing on Forrest's beautiful golf shirt, which, I happened to know, Regina had purchased for him at a boutique in New York City, back in the days when they took trips.

Still tapping, Brenda went on with her tirade. She had even drafted the suicide note. I detected a note of pride in her voice as she told him this. She had it all set, on her laptop.

"I made the note sound just like Regina," she told him. Now she started to recite it, almost as if she were auditioning for a role in a movie. Or a soap opera.

"Please forgive me . . . I can't go on anymore . . . I just want you and the children to be happy . . . I don't want to be the weight around your neck, holding you back . . . You deserve all you ever dreamed of . . . I'll love you forever."

The words Brenda said sounded nothing like Regina Emerson. They didn't sound like Brenda Barnett either. There may have been a little of Dolly Parton in there, performing "I Will Always Love You." It was almost as if Brenda were on a stage, only instead of belting out a song, she was performing this speech.

"You wanted to murder my wife," Forrest said. His voice was so quiet, I could just barely hear him. Maybe he wasn't the brightest person, and maybe her intentions hadn't completely sunk in until now, but he finally got it. "You thought I'd be your accomplice."

"Not murder, exactly," Brenda said. "We were just going to . . . clear the way for the inevitable."

"I'm ashamed that I ever cared about you," he said. For the first time, I could see his face. He didn't look, anymore, like the stupid, love-struck person he'd been for most of the summer. He looked horrified. He took a step backward, almost as if Brenda's body—which he had made love to not so long ago—were radioactive.

"You disgust me," he said. His back was to her. "And I'm disgusted with myself for having anything to do with you."

"You're an asshole!" she screamed. "You're a stupid, pathetic, loser asshole."

Just for a moment, Forrest turned around to face Brenda for what was surely the last time. "I've got to hand it to you, Brenda," he said to her. "You're right about that."

He took a few steps toward the Porsche, then turned back one more time.

"My wife has every right to hate me now," he said. "If she knew about you and me, she'd have every reason to want me dead. I couldn't blame her if she did."

As I'd done on my successful stakeout mission on the island, I waited for Forrest to leave before retrieving my bicycle from its hiding spot in the weeds. I stayed there for several minutes, crouched outside the Barnetts' back porch while, inside, I heard the sound of Brenda weeping.

When I was sure the coast was clear, I biked back to Wonderland.

72

A Great Imagination

Later that afternoon, back at the house, Forrest was taking a shower. The children were off with friends. Regina was out on the patio.

It seemed like a perfect moment to take her aside and tell her what I'd learned.

"There's something I need to tell you," I said.

She looked up from her knitting. "Yes?"

"I just came back from the Barnetts' house. Forrest was there. But he wasn't doing anything bad. He was breaking up with Brenda, actually. You don't have to worry about her anymore."

"Oh, really?" Considering how violently she'd responded to previous reports, Regina's demeanor now seemed weirdly uninterested. Bored, almost.

"He told her she was a terrible person. He said you had every right to hate him."

Every reason to want me dead. His actual words.

Regina considered this, but only briefly. For a moment she looked out over the green lawn of Wonderland—the perfectly trimmed shrubbery, the boathouse, the dock with the Chris-Craft tied up, the words "Queen of the Lake" painted on the side—and the perfect blue lake beyond.

"I see," she said with a sigh. "Well, that's good news."

I should have been relieved. I'd told Regina the truth, and finally she understood. Only something about her reaction felt all wrong. She'd taken the news in so easily. After the scene I'd witnessed so recently, it surprised me to see Regina set aside her rage so swiftly, and with so little apparent surprise. Maybe she didn't entirely understand, so I figured I should say more.

"He told Brenda she disgusted him," I said. "He loves you."

"Oh, good." She made a little sound. So quietly I could have missed it. She shook her head. She went back to her knitting.

"You aren't mad anymore?" I asked her. "At Forrest?"

"You know the great thing about you, Frances?" she said, as I was picking up her teacup, preparing to leave. "You've got such a great imagination. You really should be a writer someday."

I stood there for a moment, holding the teacup. I had this feeling I should say something more, but I didn't know what.

"Why don't you run along, dear?" Regina said to me. She'd never called me that before.

After I left, I retrieved my tennis shoes from their spot by the door and laced them up. I grabbed my new racquet and threw it over my shoulder. I hopped back on my bike. I rode over to the club. I had my five hundred consecutive returns to accomplish. For two solid hours, I just slammed balls against the backboard for all I was worth.

73

The Happy One

It was late afternoon, a day or two after the big Forrest-and-Brenda breakup. The family had gone out on the Chris-Craft together. Forrest wanted to scope out the route the boats would take for the regatta that weekend and assess the sound system he'd installed on board: a pair of portable speakers he'd set up along the bow. He was going to blast an endless loop of a song called "Yo Ho (A Pirate's Life for Me)" out over the water. I gathered this was the theme song of a ride at Disney World, not that I'd ever been there.

So I was alone in the house again. By this time I figured I was finished with my responsibilities as Regina's detective, so I was just planning to head upstairs to read a little or maybe write what would probably be the final entry in my journal. But as I made my way down the hall to the stairs to my room, I noticed something surprising. The door to the room at the end of the hall—the forbidden room that had remained locked all summer—was ajar. I could make out a stream of light coming from inside.

Even with no one there to see me, I understood what it meant to enter this room. Hayward had explained it the first night I arrived at Wonderland.

Don't even think about going in there, he'd told me.

I stood there for a moment, just outside the slightly open door. Then I stepped in.

At first it seemed like no big deal. The room was filled with a lot of boxes, mostly. A bunch of dresses hung from a portable metal clothes rack. These appeared to be clothes from a different fashion era. Very short skirts, long slinky dresses made out of some kind of synthetic material with wild prints and plunging necklines—a kind of dress I couldn't imagine Regina wearing, even long ago. There was an embroidered coat with real fur trim around the neck and cuffs. It looked like the kind of coat someone had loved and worn a whole lot. The lining was matted and dirty, and when I touched the fabric, I could smell cigarettes. It might have been marijuana, though that wasn't a smell I knew.

There were so many boxes. Every one had been neatly labeled: *Books. Jewelry. Records. Art supplies. Scarves. Dolls. Minerals.* There were three whole boxes labeled simply *Hats*, and another labeled *Purple hats*. So many of those, they needed their own box.

Along one wall, there was a box of photographs, a few in frames. I pulled one out.

At first I thought it was a picture of Regina, though if so, this was Regina as I'd never seen her: shapelier (maybe even carrying a few extra pounds), with white-blonde hair. The biggest difference was her expression. She looked so happy.

I pulled out another picture. Here was Happy Regina again—her blonde hair flying in all directions—running along a beach and laughing. And another of Happy Regina playing a flute.

And another of Happy Regina—Ecstatic Regina, you might have called her—with a very young version of a man whose face I knew well. Forrest. Happy Regina was looking at the camera but Happy Forrest was looking only at her, with a look that was almost too much to bear, knowing what I did of their lives now.

This is what love looks like, I thought. I had not seen much of it. Ever. Also desire.

I pulled another photograph from the box. This one confused me. There was Happy Regina again—wearing the very same coat I'd noticed hanging on the rack. In the photograph, Madly-in-Love Forrest had his arms around her. (One arm over her shoulder, actually. The other on her breast.)

The two of them were so dazzling, it took me a moment to notice there was another woman in the photograph standing next to the two of them. It took me another moment to understand.

This was also Regina, another Regina, a Regina I recognized. Young, like the other two, and very thin, wearing that same serious expression I knew well. Anxious. A little sad. A little bitter.

There were two of them, then. Happy Regina and Bitter Regina. They had to be sisters.

Twins.

I must have gasped out loud. I knocked the guitar over, which had been leaned against the wall. It made a noise hitting the floor.

"You shouldn't be in here." A voice behind me. Prudence. I whirled around to see her in the doorway.

"I left the door open to do a little dusting before we close the house up for the year," she said. "Regina doesn't like anybody to come in here besides me."

"I didn't know she's got a sister," I said.

"She doesn't."

"But in the pictures—"

"That was Camille, the younger one. She died in a skiing accident a long time ago. We don't talk about her."

Only she did then. I knew, as Prudence told me the story, that she would tell me only once, then never bring it up again. I knew I must never bring it up again either.

"Camille was—oh, Camille was everything," Prudence said. "Beautiful and funny and always doing crazy things, but you couldn't ever get mad at her for that. Everyone loved Camille. Even the parents lightened up when she was around, if you can imagine. She could actually make the old man crack a smile.

"Camille and Regina were like this," Prudence said. She held up two fingers, interlaced. "Regina was the quiet one, but Camille could always make her laugh. When they were little, they'd spend all day up in this tree house their parents had built for them. They would have lived in there if they could."

"Out in front by the driveway?" I asked her.

"That's the one Forrest started building for Jilly a few years ago," she said. "The parents took the old one down years ago.

"You should have seen the two of them out on the tennis court. It was like each one knew just what the other would do and where she'd go before she got there. Their father was so proud. He liked to say those two were unbeatable."

I said nothing. Asked no questions. I was afraid that if I did, Prudence might realize she was telling me more than she should and stop.

"They were nineteen years old that summer," she said. "No matter what was going on in their lives, when Fourth of July rolled round, they always came home to Wonderland. Regina was still at Sarah Lawrence. Camille was back from one of her crazy adventures in Spain. She was spending a year abroad, attending a dancing school or something. She had this dress . . .

"Regina had been studying physics. That was Regina for you. Always studying. You'd think something happened to those two in the womb. Maybe Regina got the brains, but Camille grabbed every ounce of the fun.

"I was there the night she met Forrest. I'm talking about Camille. The family had dinner at the club that night, and I guess Camille must have taken off her shoes at some point. She got up and started dancing out on the patio.

"When they went home that night, she left her shoes at the club. That was the story. It wouldn't surprise me if she knew what she was doing. Twenty minutes later, who shows up at the door here but the dishwasher from the country club. Howie. I'm talking about Mr. Emerson. He wasn't Forrest yet. He hadn't ever waited tables before, but that night one of the regular waiters had gotten sick and they'd put him in as a substitute."

My father had told me about that summer. Their dishwashing job. He just hadn't mentioned that there were two sisters, not one. He must have promised Forrest he wouldn't talk about that part.

"We all probably knew that first night what was going to happen between Howie and Camille," Prudence told me. "I'd gone home by that point, naturally, but I saw it soon enough, when he'd come by the house to pick her up. The way he looked at her. The way she looked back.

"You should have seen those two together," Prudence said. "You know the expression, 'sparks flew'? It seemed like they really did."

After that night, Howie and Camille had been inseparable. They'd go off on walks. Pick blueberries. Who knew where? Together was all. One time Camille got Prudence to fix her a picnic to bring out on the canoe, to the island. They'd stay out there all day. Sometimes they didn't come home till the next day.

"What about Regina?" I asked. "She must have felt left out."

"She had to," Prudence said. "Camille wasn't all that understanding, being head over heels and all. She practically forgot about Regina. Right before the end of the summer—the Labor Day weekend tennis tournament where they were supposed to compete—the two of them had this terrible fight."

As Prudence explained it to me, when fall came, Camille had to head back to Spain to finish up her studies. Howie got jobs bartending in town and working at a supermarket. The Cabots hated him, of course. But when they told Camille they'd cut her off if she stayed with him, she said she didn't care.

The plan was for Howie to save up money all year. When she came back, they were going to take off and get married.

"Only she missed him so badly, she sent him a ticket to join her over Christmas. They rented a car and drove to some mountains in France to go skiing. She could handle black diamonds, and he'd never been on skis, but never mind. He'd follow that girl anywhere.

"We were in Boston when we got the call. Christmas morning. There was an accident on the mountain. Camille hit a tree.

"He was the one who brought her body home. You've never seen a more heartbroken man than Howie."

"What about Regina?" I asked. "She'd lost her sister."

"The strange thing was, I never saw her cry," Prudence said. "She just went to her room and didn't come out for a long time."

What happened next surprised everyone. Not long after Camille's funeral, Howie started spending time with Regina. By the next summer, they were married. No big Cabot wedding. They found a justice of the peace, and afterward they took off in Howie's old VW. He'd changed his name to Forrest by this point.

"They lived in a cabin somewhere in Vermont for a few years, until we heard she had a baby," Prudence told me. "Once Hayward was born, that's when her parents decided to let them come back to Wonderland. Not that they were ever happy about the two of them being together."

"What about Regina?" I asked Prudence. I figured Forrest probably never really stopped loving Camille. "Didn't she end up feeling like she was Forrest's second choice?"

"Who knows what Regina thinks?" Prudence said. "She keeps most things to herself. All I know is that man takes good care of her. It isn't easy living with a person like Regina.

"I'll tell you one thing," Prudence said to me. "Nobody ever mentions Camille's name around here. But Regina can't get rid of her things. She keeps them locked up in this room."

"What about Forrest?" I asked her.

"He never talks about it either. Though there was this one time. I guess he didn't think anyone was around. I found Forrest in here, standing by the rack of clothes. He loved that coat."

The fur-lined one with the embroidery.

"You'd better get up to your room," she told me. "Don't ever mention to either of them that I told you this. Don't let them know you were here."

I stepped back out in the hall. She locked the door again.

74

What Felt Real

That night, for the first time all summer, I couldn't sleep. I lay there in my little bed under the eaves, thinking about Regina's dead sister. Outside my window, I could hear the sound of the loons calling out to each other. And in the room below mine, the low, steady sound of Forrest Emerson snoring. I wondered if he ever dreamed of Camille.

A handful of days remained before Labor Day weekend and all the events that would take place at Lake Catherine then. A handful of days before my big tennis tournament. Though ever since I'd learned the story of Regina's dead sister, I couldn't stop thinking about her. When I stepped out onto the court that afternoon, the picture kept coming to me of the two of them, when they were young. I pictured them in matching tennis outfits—Regina at the service line, Camille at the net. And Forrest watching on the sidelines, his eyes full of love. But for Camille, not Regina.

Then Forrest, after. Bringing Camille's body back on the plane from France. The Cabots at the airport to meet the plane. Hating him for being alive. Regina standing next to them. Had she already begun to imagine herself taking her sister's place?

In the middle of the night, I took out my red suitcase. Packing wouldn't take long. One drawer's worth of clothes. The unopened box of tampons.

A few days after my departure, the Emersons would be packing up too, for their return to Boston—school for the children, and the same endless expanse of time for Regina and Forrest to carry on with their own comfortable, distant lives, uninterrupted by jobs, housework, money worries, girlfriends. Just three months earlier, it had all seemed so glamourous and wonderful. It didn't anymore.

Meanwhile life at Wonderland went on as it had, though after that day with Brenda, I detected in Forrest a new level of attentiveness to Regina—one that did not seem to extend to me as it once had.

It occurred to me then that things had played out between Forrest and Brenda just as Regina first predicted they would. They'd started their affair around Fourth of July weekend. Just before Labor Day, Forrest had ended it. In the weeks between the two holidays, things might have appeared more serious, but in the end, nothing had turned out any differently from how it did in previous summers, though his lover this summer had displayed an unprecedented capacity for plotting criminal activity, and due to this, no doubt, Forrest had displayed an above-average level of remorse for his actions this time around. Now I observed how, when Regina stretched out on her chaise lounge with the knitting project that never progressed, or a book she never finished, he'd come up behind her and massage her shoulders or bury his face in her hair.

He brought her things. Tea, of course, and her pills—though, strangely, she seemed to be rejecting these—but he brought her other things now too. Her slippers, when she'd left them upstairs. A cookie from the French bakery in town, small enough that he might have supposed she'd be willing to consume the calories it contained, which she was not.

From the moment Forrest delivered his farewell speech to Brenda Barnett, he seemed to discontinue his triathlon preparation. The event was coming up soon, but he no longer showed any sign of taking those thirty-mile training rides, the five-mile swims, his runs. He explained this by telling us that in the final days before a triathlon, it was recommended that a person cut down on the exercise, to store up energy. This meant that he was around in the early mornings again. We could have resumed our morning breakfasts together. Only we didn't.

Now I was the person who left the house at sunup. With so little time remaining before the juniors' match, I headed to the tennis court as soon as it was light to hit against the backboard and stayed there for as much time as my job responsibilities allowed. But in truth, my choice to leave the house early had to do with more than tennis. Though I couldn't help loving Forrest still and yearning for his company, something had been broken that summer, and there was no fixing it.

So there were no more pancake breakfasts or talks with Forrest over orange juice. For whatever reason—I had no idea why—the funny little gifts (a rock, a bar of soap, a ladybug) stopped showing up next to my cereal bowl. I told myself that none of that had been real anyway. What was real was my racquet. The muscles in my calves. My backhand. The ball.

Sometime that week a message came from the pharmacy. Mrs. Emerson's prescriptions were ready for pickup.

"Didn't we just fill most of these a couple of weeks ago?" Forrest asked her.

"It's good to have some reserves on hand for when we head back to Boston," Regina told him. "I just want to be sure I don't run out."

She turned her cheek in his direction for the kiss she knew he'd deliver. "On your way home, why don't you pick us up some fried clams?" she said. Not that she'd be eating any herself.

Forrest would fulfill any request from Regina now. I could tell from the look on his face. He was ready to spend the rest of his life making it up to her.

75

An Unstable Canoe

For me it was all about tennis now. If I could have pitched a tent at the tennis court I would have done it. As things were, I kept hitting against the backboard and spending time with Jonathan whenever his coaching schedule allowed. Though I had been paying him for the extra time out of my summer earnings, Jonathan taught me for free now. As always, nobody seemed to notice my trips to the court or the beautiful new racquet I brought with me when I went there.

Back at Wonderland, excitement was building for the big Labor Day blowout. Forrest had purchased a new pair of running shoes for the running portion of the triathlon and tuned up his bike. Prudence had taken the punch bowl out, ready for the party the Emersons would be hosting as the boats circled the cove, and the fireworks that would follow. Jilly and Hayward were making decorations for the Emersons' entry into the Lake Catherine Regatta. All around the lake, families were preparing their boats, stringing garlands of flowers around the masts, making signs. Everybody wanted to have the most elaborately decorated boat.

Forrest would be launching the Chris-Craft, of course. He had rented a pirate costume for the event—a tricornered hat with a feather plume, a velvet vest, and a white shirt with big puffy sleeves. Knowing Forrest, he'd keep the shirt unbuttoned.

He'd rented a dress for Regina at the same shop. "You'll be my saucy wench," he told her, flashing his customary grin. Getting Regina to join in the festivities seemed unlikely. But I could tell how hard he was trying.

Forrest's plans for this year's regatta didn't stop with the pirate out-fits and decorations. More than any of that, the big news was that in addition to the Chris-Craft, he was planning to launch the birchbark canoe into the lake for the first time in years, rather than the Old Town I'd used when I paddled out to the island.

Forrest's plan called for Jilly and Hayward to dress up as Native Americans. They'd paddle the birchbark canoe behind the Chris-Craft—Hayward in a headdress and loincloth over his swim trunks, with a tomahawk strapped to his chest; Jilly in braids and a fringed faux-leather skirt and the pair of moccasins he'd bought for her that day we drove up from New Jersey.

Regina was dubious about the idea. Then again, Regina was dubious about most ideas. In this case, she had a point. For as long as the family had owned it, everyone knew the birchbark canoe was prone to tipping. This was why it stayed in the boathouse. Only an experienced canoeist had any business taking that canoe out, and even then, the odds were strong that the boat and whoever was paddling it would end up flipped over in the water. That was a birchbark canoe for you. Beautiful but unstable—words that also applied to a certain member of the Emerson family, it occurred to me. Liable to capsize at any moment.

Typical of Forrest, he researched a solution. As hopeless as he'd been as a student, he had a knack for the kind of skills other kids probably learned from their father or their Boy Scout troop, though in Forrest's case he learned them from books he picked out at the Lake Catherine Library's do-it-yourself section.

Forrest had acquired the ability, early on, to figure things out for himself, and when there was something that mattered deeply to him—like making it possible for his children to paddle the birchbark canoe in the regatta—he'd do what was necessary to bring it about. This was one of the things I had always admired about him. One of the many. He didn't always finish what he'd started, was all. Sometimes he lost interest partway in.

With the aid of a library book on canoeing, Forrest had hit on the idea of installing a couple of outriggers on either side of the canoe to make it safe for his children to paddle in the regatta. With three days to go before the Labor Day weekend regatta, he got to work.

Forrest spent hours down at the boathouse during those final days, constructing the outrigger and then attaching it. Knowing Forrest—particularly Forrest as he was, post-Brenda, redoubling his efforts as a family man—I guessed he'd want to turn this into a father-and-son project, or father-and-daughter, or both, but Hayward and Jilly didn't seem all that interested. I was, of course. I was interested in everything Forrest did. That never changed. But I hung back now.

It was late afternoon—the children's sailing lessons had finished for the season. The two of them were up at the house, watching a video, as usual, and Regina was taking a nap. Forrest had set the canoe on a couple of sawhorses, with the outriggers he'd built (his third attempt) attached on either side with a vise. Seeing me on a lawn chair with my book a little ways off, he called out to me to give him a hand.

"You mind?" he asked. "It looks like you're really into that book you've been reading. God forbid I get between you and Stephen King."

As disillusioned as I'd become, and as angry as I'd been with him, I couldn't help it that I still loved spending time with Forrest. Now that he'd sent Brenda packing, I didn't have to pretend otherwise anymore. He would never again be the god he once was to me, but of course I wanted to help him fix the canoe.

I put my book down and headed over to the sawhorses where the canoe sat. "At your service," I told him.

From his research, Forrest had discovered an elaborate technique for sealing birchbark that involved digging up the roots of cedar trees, soaking them in water, cooking them, then scraping the bark, for the purpose of creating a gummy substance to brush over the places where water might get in. He handed me a brush.

For a few minutes we just stood there over the boat, applying the cedar gum. Neither of us spoke. It wasn't like the old days, but close enough.

"You're a very smart person, Frances," he said. "And you're the kind of girl who notices things other people might not."

He was right. I didn't know where he was going. So I just listened, brushing cedar gum onto the bark.

"You've probably noticed that for a while there I was . . ." He paused. "Distracted."

I dipped my brush back in the gum concoction and drew it over another patch of bark. I liked the smell. I liked everything about this moment.

"I haven't always been the greatest husband and father to my family," he said. "I try, but I slip up sometimes."

I wanted to tell him that I got it. I understood more than he might imagine about how the presence or absence of sex can make people do crazy things. Over the summer, I'd witnessed many of these.

"It's a little like a canoe," he said. "You can lose your balance. For a while there, that's what happened to me. But I'm OK now. Steady as they come."

He made no mention of Brenda Barnett, or the tryst on the island, or any of those other trysts that had no doubt taken place over the course of the summer now drawing to a close—and all the summers before this one. I made no mention to Forrest of having known about them. Or that I'd kept notes and reported the details of the most recent of these to Regina.

Not unlike his wife, in those times she'd confided in me about the most intimate aspects of her marriage, now it was Forrest who seemed almost to have forgotten who he was talking with. How old I was, anyway.

"I got in over my head," he said. "I could've lost everything I care about the most. My family."

I might have felt flattered that Forrest was confiding in me as he did now. What got in the way was that even as he expressed remorse for his behavior over the course of the summer, he made no mention of me. As much remorse as he expressed for betraying Regina, he seemed not to have considered that he'd neglected me—a girl who'd loved him all her life—for a stupid affair with a terrible person.

Never mind, I told myself. The important thing was that it was over with Brenda now. The important thing was that Forrest trusted me with his confession. Regina seemed happier. Everything was going to be fine after all.

"Sex can make you crazy," Forrest told me, dipping his brush into the cedar gum and moving it over the bark. "It's like a drug or something. All of a sudden you find yourself in this place you never dreamed you'd be. It's like you're in this little dinghy going through some class five rapids in someplace like the Grand Canyon, and you don't know how to get out. Things just keep happening that you never intended. You end up places you didn't mean to go."

On the island with Brenda, for instance. Plotting the murder of his wife. Or listening to someone he knew plot her murder, anyway. Someone he'd just finished having sex with.

"I just wanted to tell you I'm back now," he said. It was almost as if he knew I'd been there in the library that day, and on the island, and in the yard outside the Barnetts' rental house even.

"It's over," he said.

"That's good," I told him. "I'm happy for you."

"You know you mean a lot to me, don't you, Frances?" he said.

But the warm feeling I would have felt once, hearing these words, was gone.

76

THREE TENNIS SKIRTS. ONE WHITE.

I'm taking you shopping," Regina told me.

It was two days before Labor Day weekend, three days before my father was scheduled to drive up to Maine to bring me home.

We were having our tuna fish sandwiches in the kitchen. Jilly had set up a restaurant for her American Girl dolls in the living room, enacting a discussion between Samantha and Molly about who was the prettiest. Hayward was eating his on the deck, his eyes glued to the ever-present video game, though now and then—in a way that continued to unnerve me—he'd cast his eyes in my direction, as if he knew something about me. And he did, of course.

So it was just the two of us, Regina and me, sitting at the kitchen island. As usual, Regina had removed the bread from her sandwich, leaving only a very small portion of tuna fish. She'd taken three bites. For her this was lunch.

I hadn't planned on buying new clothes for ninth grade. I would have liked a new outfit, but getting to work with Jonathan mattered more, and the truth was, I hadn't grown out of my clothes from the year before.

"I want to buy you some nice pants and a few sweaters," Regina said. I hadn't mentioned anything about my lessons with Jonathan, but she seemed to know I didn't have any money.

She spoke the next words almost as an afterthought.

"It seems like you're spending a lot of time at the club. We'll get you a good pair of sneakers. The ones I gave you are looking a little beat up. And we can get you a couple of cute tennis skirts with matching tops. A good tennis skirt can make a big difference in a girl's life."

Regina brought me to the Gap, a very different kind of store from the one we'd visited to purchase my Bastille Day dress. When I picked out a pair of jeans from the sale rack, Regina shook her head.

"Those look like last year's style," she said, though I couldn't imagine how she'd know this. She just wanted to get me the more expensive kind. Those, and two other pairs of pants, along with three sweaters and a sweatshirt.

I told her this was enough. More than enough, more than any shopping trip I'd ever been on, though that didn't say much, considering that my mother had probably only taken me shopping twice, ever.

But Regina said no. We were going to Macy's. She had decided I should have pajamas and a nice warm bathrobe for the cold months coming up. This was Regina for you. One aspect of Regina, anyway. The problem was, you never knew which one was going to show up.

After that came the tennis shoes. Then the skirt. Three of them, actually, one blue, one green with pink stripes, one white.

When we were done with our shopping, we got lunch in the food court—hamburgers and fries and milkshakes. (For me, anyway. Regina had her usual: water.) Regina seemed more lighthearted than I could ever remember—uncharacteristically cheerful and filled with energy. For once I was the tired one.

She wanted to know what classes I'd be taking in ninth grade, what I wanted to be when I grew up.

I told her I was interested in history, World War II in particular. Reading Anne Frank's diary had inspired me to find out about the Holocaust. But what I loved best was reading. I'd finished nine Stephen King novels over the summer.

"It's probably impossible," I told Regina. "Me, actually getting to be a writer."

This was a moment when Regina might have offered some encouragement. But that wasn't her style.

"I used to love physics," she said. "I won a prize for a paper I wrote one time." I could tell she was thinking about something precious and wonderful then. Wonderful and gone. The look that passed over her face was about more than the smell of Cinnabon filling the food court. "But the truth is, a lot of things you hope in life aren't going to happen."

"I've been playing some tennis," I told her. It was the first time I'd spoken of this to anyone other than Jonathan. "I'm going to be in a tournament at the club this weekend. I'll probably lose."

"You never know," she said. "Unlike me, you just might be the kind of person who can hang in there. How's anybody else supposed to believe in you if you don't believe in yourself?"

"All those kids at the club have been taking lessons for ages," I said. For just a moment, it was almost as if she were my mother, and I was confiding in her. Something I never did with my actual mother.

Regina looked at me closely. Here was that same intense focus that seemed to have revealed itself only since she'd stopped taking all those pills. "I can picture you smashing a ball hard," she told me. "You probably have some anger in you, and if so, fair enough. Maybe a tennis court is a good place to let it out."

Or alone, hitting against the backboard at midnight. She didn't know that part.

"You're holding on to some things. If you aren't careful, you could explode. It's unhealthy keeping everything inside."

"I'm not—" I started. But her words had opened a door. Maybe Regina was right about me.

"I know what I'm talking about," she said. "I know all about anger. How do you think it's been for me, dealing with this business between my husband and that redhead?"

My head hurt. This was what I had come to hate about life with the Emersons. The way all the mess going on between the two of them always ended up spilling over into my life and becoming my mess too. I looked at the shopping bags on the floor by my chair—a few hundred dollars' worth of clothes, including the skirt I'd longed for. Three of them, actually. I wished we'd never come to this mall.

"Wear the yellow sweater with the blue buttons for dinner tonight," she said. It took me a minute to know she was talking about one of the new cardigans. We'd bought so much that day I couldn't even remember everything anymore.

"Forrest will love you in that one," she said. "Forrest loves yellow."

77

A Practice Match

It was Friday afternoon of Labor Day weekend. Just two days left at Wonderland.

"We need to spend one more session on the court together before the tournament," Jonathan told me. Our last one, maybe ever. Thinking about this left a hollow feeling in my stomach. All this time I'd been so focused on Forrest that I hadn't much thought about how much I'd grown to care about Jonathan. When you got down to it, he was probably the closest person I had to a real friend. At Lake Catherine or anywhere.

I got to the courts early to be sure I wouldn't miss a minute of my time, but Jonathan was already waiting for me. The rain was over and the court was dry, thankfully, and the sun was out, though I could feel fall in the air now.

"You're going to play a real game today," Jonathan told me. In all our time together that summer, we'd never actually done this. He wanted me to know what it felt like, facing a competitor on the other side of the net.

"I'll warm you up," he said. "Then you're going to hit with Olivia."

Olivia, the girl whose lessons I'd picked up when she quit, way back at the beginning of the summer—before I knew anything about tennis, or Brenda Barnett, or *The Joy of Sex*, or Polaroid cameras and mini tape players, or moss, or murder plots.

"Here's the thing about Olivia," Jonathan told me. "She's lazy, and she's got a bad attitude. But she's been taking lessons from me since she was six years old. She doesn't have your kind of passion, but she hates losing. She'll give you a good game."

It was the last thing I wanted—playing my first real game of tennis ever against a girl who'd practically been born with a tennis racquet in her hand. Clearly she didn't care about tennis the way I did. But she didn't need to care. She was just better, probably. She'd destroy me.

I told Jonathan I'd rather just rally with him, but he shook his head. "You need to get out of your comfort zone," he said. "See what it's like out there in the real world."

He meant the real world of tennis, of course. Which wouldn't seem all that real to some people I knew. My parents, for instance. Or just about anybody I went to school with back home in New Jersey.

Olivia was supposed to show up in ten minutes, but we were half-way through my court time before she made it. She was wearing one of her many matching tennis sets—one I'd never seen before. I felt grateful I hadn't put one of my new ones on. I'd only feel like even more of an idiot if I had.

She took her time unzipping her tennis bag. Then she took some more time retying her shoelaces. She took a long, slow drink from her water bottle and adjusted her ponytail. She flashed me a smile.

"I've seen you here, right?" she said. "You new?" I'd only been around every day all summer.

"Kind of," I said.

I'd never seen the racquet spin before, which players do before a match to see who serves first. Jonathan had to explain this part to me. Olivia won the spin.

She served three aces in a row. Game point. Finally I was able to return her serve. Forty–fifteen.

On the next point, I hit her a short ball. She missed it. After a long rally that left us both gasping for breath, I won the next point. Forty all.

The game went to me. I knew Jonathan wasn't supposed to play favorites, but I could tell how happy he was.

Next set. My serve this time. I made it to thirty–love. Then something happened.

A thought came into my brain. In my lessons over that summer, Jonathan could always spot this when it happened. "You're *thinking*," he called out to me. "You need to stop doing that. There's only one thing to do. Keep your eye on the ball. Nothing else exists."

Now it was happening again. Ideas, pictures, words, memories, skittering over my brain like static on a broken TV set. I'd be standing at the service line, ready to make my toss—racquet raised, feet firmly planted. Then this thought would make its way into my head. *What if Forrest changes his mind about Brenda and calls her up again? What if Hayward tells his mother about seeing me reading* The Joy of Sex? *And the other part he witnessed through the hole in the boathouse wall that day. Regina's dead sister. Regina herself, writhing around on her bed, getting green goop all over the linen sheets. Forrest in his tube socks, down on his knees on the moss.*

Reset. I readied myself at the service line again for the next point. Then the static was back.

What if Regina finds out I tried on her dress and snuck into the bedroom with her dead twin's things in it? What if Forrest finds out I took pictures of him with Brenda?

What if I never get my period and I spend my whole life having people treat me like I'm fourteen years old?

And nobody ever loves me. And I'm alone for the rest of my life. And when I go back to New Jersey, my father comes over to our apartment and starts throwing furniture?

That's all it took to screw up my serve.

Olivia won the match. We had time for a sudden-death round. She won that too.

I didn't know about shaking your opponent's hand after a match, but Olivia did, naturally. Seeing her standing there in her little pink skirt with her hand outstretched, I realized what I was supposed to do.

All I wanted was to be out of there.

After Olivia left, I told Jonathan I didn't want to play in the tournament that weekend. "I'm not ready," I said. "It would be too embarrassing."

"Every player has days like this," he told me. "I just wanted you to have yours before the big event. You'll be ready on Saturday."

I didn't want to do it. But they'd already scheduled my match. My name was up on the board. There was no way to pull out now.

"Don't lose sight of who you are, Frannie," Jonathan said. "I've seen what you can do. You're stronger than any of them."

78

Big Day

Saturday morning, Labor Day weekend. The sun was just coming up. I stayed in bed longer than usual. I was thinking about my first-ever tennis tournament—psyching myself up, but more so, I was thinking about this being my last weekend at Wonderland. My father was driving up from New Jersey that night. We'd have dinner with the family on Sunday. Monday morning he'd bring me home.

Forrest's affair with Brenda was over. Knowing this gave me a certain sense of relief. But I also knew that everything was different now too. The girl I was ninety-one days earlier, when I climbed up the stairs to my little room at Wonderland that first night, no longer existed.

That morning I lay in my little bed, memorizing every single thing about my room, starting with the sheets, which were nothing like the sheets I slept on back home. "There's something called a thread count, Frances," Regina had explained to me. "The first thing you need to do when you buy bedding is check the number. Eight hundred, minimum. Preferably a thousand."

I took in everything that morning: the floor where I did my nightly one hundred sit-ups, the robin's-egg-blue desk where I'd written in my journal every night—until the story got ruined; I hardly ever wrote anything anymore—the mirror where I studied my reflection, checking for some sign of womanhood that never showed up.

And more: The hooked rug next to my bed with a border of blue-birds around the edge. The milkmaid wallpaper and the lace curtains with a pattern woven into the lace (also birds), and the way they fluttered over my bed when the wind came up over the lake. The sound of the loons calling out to each other at night, and sometimes in the morning too. The chest of drawers that now held—alongside the unopened box of tampons—the stash of back-to-school clothes Regina had bought for me, which I didn't want to look at because what they signaled was the end of summer and my return to the Hubbard apartment, a place I would be sharing with only my mother now.

I thought about my journal, lying directly under my mattress, and the row of BBs still untouched, which assured me the words I'd written on those cream-colored pages would remain secret. I couldn't even bear reading them myself anymore.

As awful as it had been seeing my parents go at it with each other (that, or go silent), I also knew that when I was back home, I would miss the sound of my father's fingers on the typewriter keys. I would miss the sound of the scratched-up John Coltrane record he played, late in the night, when he'd finished his last bottle. I'd miss the hope I kept holding out all those years that things might still get better. One thing about my parents splitting up: Now it was clear, this wasn't going to happen, ever.

I looked up at the skylight over my bed. On clear nights—lying here with my book, or just lying here—I could see the stars. No stars in New Jersey, that was for sure, not that you could see, and anyway my dark little bedroom back home had no window.

This was what I thought about as I lay in bed at Wonderland for the last weekend of the summer. It felt, that morning, as if everything I loved most was about to disappear.

There was a brunch scheduled at the club, to be followed by some kind of cooking contest for the younger kids. Jilly was set to compete in that.

No brunch for me. Jonathan had told me that it was better to eat light on the day of a match—and anyway, on the few times I'd attended events at the club, the members largely ignored me, so why attend? I could hear my mother's voice in my ear, offering commentary.

Those people all have their thumbs up their ass, she would have said. *For people like them, the definition of a hard day is running out of shrimp cocktail.*

After the brunch came the triathlon. I didn't even care anymore, as I would have once, about how Forrest would do. I had no need to be there at the water's edge as he came in from the swim—an event he'd probably practiced for a lot less than he'd said he did. There was a time when I would have been out there cheering him on, but that time had passed. For me, the big event of the day would come afterward.

79

A Case of Poison Ivy

When Jonathan first brought up the idea of my playing in the juniors' tournament, I'd told him I couldn't. Now that the day had arrived, I realized how much it mattered to me. In spite of everything else going on that day, the tournament felt like the most important thing in the world now. The only thing that mattered.

I set the three new tennis outfits on my bed. I'd cut the tags off, but I'd held off on actually trying them on. It felt as if, by putting on one of the new skirts, I'd be wearing a disguise, pretending to be this girl I wasn't. Only maybe today I'd become her.

I chose the white tennis skirt—short, with sassy pleats along the hem and a matching white top. Of the three outfits, this felt like the boldest and most confident choice. I'd wait until I got to the tennis club to put it on. But as I pulled my training bra over my head, I studied my reflection. Still no breasts to speak of, but I had muscles in my arms and legs now that hadn't been there two months earlier. For once I actually liked the sight of myself in the mirror.

I could hear Forrest downstairs running the Vitamix. He was making his power shake to get him through the triathlon. Though Prudence had fixed him a mountain of pasta the night before, he was probably making the same decision I had for his own big athletic event—to go easy on the food that morning.

As I was getting dressed, I looked out the window. A figure in a hooded sweatshirt appeared to be walking toward the lake and the boathouse. When he turned sideways, I recognized that this was Hayward. Not a boy who got up at this hour, normally.

When he emerged from the boathouse, he laid a piece of paper on the picnic table by the water. From where I stood at the window, it was hard to pick out the details, but it looked to me as if he had set out art supplies of some sort. He had scissors and something that might have been glue. Also what appeared to be a marker.

Hayward worked in the semidarkness on this project, whatever it was, for a surprisingly long time. Fifteen minutes, maybe. I needed to get ready for my match, but I had a hard time taking my eyes off him. There was a sense of focus and determination about Hayward, as I saw him now, that I hadn't witnessed in the boy who spent his days—as much as possible—reclining in his gaming chair with his hand on the controller and a bowl of Cheez Doodles at his side.

Finally he seemed to be finished with whatever it was he'd been up to. He folded the paper and placed it in his sweatshirt pocket.

He did not return directly to the house. He went first to the row of bicycles lined up next to the house, zeroing in on mine. He took out the folded-up paper and placed it in the basket.

I couldn't see what Hayward did after this. He disappeared around the side of the house, but when I came downstairs, there wasn't any sign of him. He'd gone back to bed, was my guess. Hayward liked sleeping almost as much as Regina did.

Downstairs, I found Forrest at the counter in his bike shorts, finishing his shake. For him the day would start with the triathlon. But at the moment, he appeared to be facing a different challenge. He couldn't stop scratching his arms, his legs. He reached inside his running shorts, scratching wildly at his rear end.

"Damn poison ivy!" he said. "I don't know what happened, but I'm covered in the stuff."

"I've got some Tecnu in my room," I told him. "I'll run upstairs and get it for you."

The medicine seemed to help. We sat down at the counter side by side. Like the old days, but different.

"You ready for the big regatta?" he asked me. He didn't know about the rest of it.

What did I care about the regatta? No one had invited me to be on the Chris-Craft. There had been no pirate or wench or Pocahontas costume for me. I had something more significant to do: the tennis tournament.

"It's going to be really something when we launch that birchbark canoe," he said. "I don't think that thing's been in the water for thirty years. We made that baby tight as a drum, huh? And if I do say so myself, that outrigger I built is a pretty sweet setup. The kids are going to have a ball."

"I hope it's steady enough," I told him. That was the nice thing about the other canoe. You got the feeling a tornado could come and it wouldn't flip. I did not elaborate on my experience with the Emersons' other canoe, the Old Town, whose steadiness I'd become acquainted with from my trip to the island a few weeks back, when I'd spied on him and Brenda.

"Wait till you see the fireworks I've got planned for tonight," Forrest said. "Everybody may think we're just shooting them off for Labor Day, but it's about giving you a great send-off too. It's your birthday next week, if I'm not mistaken. Fifteen! Regina and I want you to go out with a bang."

I studied his face, trying to find in it some evidence of the person I cared about so much, the person I'd always believed to have cared for me, the man who just this week had confided in me about his failures toward his wife, and all of us.

Go out with a bang? Was that the best Forrest could do to express his feelings about my departure?

This was when Jilly appeared, still in her nightgown. Then Prudence, who had shown up earlier than usual to help Jilly with her entry in the Snap, Crackle, Pop Bakeoff at the club—a contest whose entrants tried to come up with new and amazing variations on the old standard recipe for Rice Krispies Treats. She made no further reference to the disclosures she'd made to me about Regina's dead sister, the secret room. I didn't speak of it.

To me it was a momentous day, but you wouldn't have known this from the behavior of anyone else here. There was Hayward, of course—his odd appearance down by the boathouse in those first hours of daylight. I'd discover what he'd been up to when I went out to my bike to ride over to the club later for the tournament. But Hayward was always weird. I felt no urgency to find out what he'd left in my bike basket.

I helped myself to a handful of almonds. This was when Regina floated in. She was fully dressed for once, in one of her Lilly Pulitzer dresses with a pair of matching flats. I figured the festivities at the club had inspired her to get her act together that morning.

I swung my racquet case over my shoulder then and headed out to my bike. *My last ride,* I said out loud, only to myself. My last everything at Wonderland. As I made my way to the rack of bikes, Regina called out to me. "I have something for you!"

I turned around. She stood there in her little print dress, skinny as ever, of course, but alert in a way I had never seen her before. She didn't appear happy, exactly, but she definitely looked excited. A person might even have described her as wired. Now she was running toward me.

Regina running. I'd never seen her do this.

"I don't want this to be our big goodbye," she said. "But we'll have so much going on tonight, and then there's your father's arrival . . ."

Don't remind me, I wanted to tell her.

"So I thought I'd give you this now." She handed me a small package, wrapped in tissue paper that I recognized as having been recycled from a gift someone had given Jilly recently.

"I finished it last night," she said. "Knowing you were leaving this weekend. Something to remember me by."

As if I'd forget.

The moment she put the package in my hands, she turned around, heading back to the house. I got the impression Regina would prefer that I open her present when she wasn't around. Expressions of emotion were never easy for her.

After she left, I stood there for a moment. I remembered the small folded-up item Hayward had placed in my bike basket. He'd placed it there and then disappeared. Like his mother, it appeared he preferred that I open whatever it was he'd put in the basket at a time when he wasn't around. Maybe he didn't even want me to know he was the one who'd left it there for me.

Two unknown offerings awaited my discovery that morning. Which to examine first?

I reached for the paper Hayward had set in my bike basket and unfolded it.

It was a page ripped from *The Joy of Sex*—an illustration featuring one of the more surprising positions in the entire book.

The image had been altered. In the place where the faces were—the woman and the bearded man—Hayward had glued a couple of pictures around the same size, but cut out from a magazine. I recognized which one: my July issue of *Seventeen*. For the man's face, he'd substituted the smiling, clean-shaven face of Michael J. Fox.

For the woman, he'd chosen the picture of a girl also featured in the magazine. From my close examination of this issue (I'd basically memorized it), I recognized this girl. She was not one of the models. She'd written an essay they published about why she didn't smoke marijuana. The least cool girl in the entire issue.

You could have said this girl bore a passing resemblance to me. He'd glued this picture onto the body of a woman on all fours, with large full breasts and thighs, rear end jutting out to meet the penis of the man now bearing the face of Michael J. Fox.

Written across their bodies in marker, four words:

You want to FUCK?

I couldn't move. I was still holding Regina's package. Assuming whatever it was she'd made for me carried a more benign message, I felt glad I'd saved this one for last. I thought of that scene in the *Sleeping Beauty* movie I'd loved as a child—the Disney version that Forrest and Regina had taken me to at a drive-in when I was little (my parents not being the type to take me to the movies, let alone a drive-in). It was the scene where the evil fairy bursts into the christening of the baby princess and puts a curse on her. The good news being that one more fairy remained at the christening that day, who had yet to offer her gift. She'd chosen to cancel out—or lessen, anyway—the harshness of the curse with a benevolent gift of her own. This would be what saved Sleeping Beauty. This was how I viewed the still unopened package from Regina now—as my one chance at undoing the curse of Hayward's terrible offering.

I unwrapped Regina's package. It took me a moment to understand what this was, though I recognized what it was made of. Mohair.

It was a piece of knitting, roughly five inches square, made from the yarn I'd seen looped over her knitting needles all that summer. At first I thought it was some kind of a hat maybe, or a scarf, but this item was smaller than that. Regina's gift to me was more along the lines of a pot holder. If pot holders were made from white mohair yarn.

I stuffed it in my racquet bag and set out for the court.

80

Secret Admirer

I gave little thought to Regina's gift. She had made me something odd, but all her gifts to me over the years had been strange. There should be no surprise that of all the things Regina might give me, she chose a white mohair pot holder.

It was that morning's other offering that occupied my mind. Then it came to me as I was pedaling up the hill, the truth that Hayward's sickening collage revealed.

All those weeks I'd been finding little presents next to my cereal bowl. Heart-shaped rocks. Flowers. The tiny beautiful body of the dead hummingbird. All that time I'd believed it was Forrest who'd left them for me, and that they served as proof that in spite of everything, Forrest still thought about me. Forrest still held me in his heart.

Now I knew: It wasn't Forrest who'd been thinking about me on all those mornings, or Forrest who'd left me the strange little gifts. It was Hayward. The heart-shaped rock, the butterfly wing, the shell, the dead hummingbird; they weren't love offerings after all, or if they were, the love was being offered by a person whose interest and affection I considered completely unwelcome.

Those gifts weren't a testament to anyone's love for me. Maybe it was more accurate to say that those little gifts I'd looked forward to—and found—over most of the summer were just evidence of a sick obsession. Nobody needed to explain to me what an obsession looked like, or the things it made a person do.

81

Itch

On my way to the club, I passed the Barnetts' rental house. Their car was out front with a couple of bicycles attached to the rack on the back and a row of suitcases lined up beside it, along with a cooler and some fishing equipment and a pet carrier. Though most summer people chose to stay through the Labor Day weekend, it appeared that the Barnetts were leaving Lake Catherine early.

I watched as the two of them stepped out the door, Brenda holding her husband's hand as they made their way toward the car, Kyle with his golf clubs over his shoulder, Brenda carrying the dog. She no longer appeared beautiful, or anything close.

Her legs appeared red and swollen and covered with scratch marks, but the worst was her face—which looked puffy and covered with runny sores. One look and I understood what had caused this, though given how much time had passed since Brenda and Forrest's rendezvous on the island, it seemed she must have an above-average sensitivity to poison ivy. She probably had more than a few sores on her butt too.

Brenda stood scratching herself as her husband lifted their suitcases into the trunk of their car. She set the dog in the carrier, put on her sunglasses, and settled into the front seat beside Kyle Barnett, who reached over to her now and gave her a peck on the earlobe to avoid her swollen and oozing cheek.

I guessed this was how it went with peoples' marriages. One day you might be lying on some moss with a man who wasn't your husband, saying you couldn't live without him. You might even think you wanted to have a baby with him. If you were a truly terrible person, determined to achieve your goal of nabbing him for your next partner, you might even come up with a plan to kill his wife.

But if it didn't work out, you and your husband might just head back to Connecticut like nothing ever happened, with no more than a nasty case of poison ivy on your rear end (just my guess) to show for it all.

82

Just like in *Carrie*

I didn't want to get to the club too early, so I stopped at a point along the road where a large boulder known as Elephant Rock loomed over the lake. I sat there for a while, thinking over Jonathan's advice to me—a whole summer's worth of instruction reduced to a single thought.

It's all about the ball. Put every other thought out of your mind.

The club was decked out for the festivities; brunch-goers were milling around outside near the pool with their Bloody Marys, golf carts whizzing off to the links. As I had done in gym class all the previous year, I changed in a bathroom stall and not—as the other girls were doing—in the locker room.

Through the door I heard the sound of their laughter. One of them was talking about a boy she liked, scheduled to compete in the sixteen-and-unders, who'd put his tongue in her mouth when they'd kissed out at the gazebo. Somebody mentioned Jonathan's name. "He looks like Rob Lowe," she said.

"I heard he's gay." This came from another of the girls. Apart from Olivia, I didn't know any of their names.

There was a lot of high-pitched shrieking then. Somebody asked if you could get AIDS from touching a person's tennis ball, if they had it.

"I hardly ever took any lessons with him anyway," one of them said. "He spends all his time with that lame-o girl that wears drawstring shorts."

That would be me.

I had changed into my new skirt by now, but I couldn't leave the bathroom until they were gone. I sat on the toilet for a long time, waiting for them to leave. Finally I heard the locker room door slam, followed by quiet. I figured it was safe to come out.

Jonathan stood on the edge of the court, waiting for me. "Don't lose your focus, Frannie," he said to me. "You're going to do great."

The game began. I lost the first point, then came back for the next one. Five minutes in, I had found my rhythm. For the first time in my life, maybe, my body was doing everything I asked of it. My racquet felt like a part of me. All I had to do was see the ball and get to it, and I did this.

A medium-sized crowd of people had gathered—parents of the players, mostly, but also members of the club, though I knew without looking that there would be nobody on the sidelines rooting for me except Jonathan, though he couldn't openly play favorites. Once or twice when I made a particularly good shot, I heard some voice calling out—a fan of my opponent, invariably—but my eyes never left the court. There might have been music playing somewhere, or the sound of a golf cart, a whistle coming from the pool when the lifeguard needed to let some kid know not to go out in the deep end, a whirring noise from over at the snack bar as the bartender fixed the first piña colada of the day in the blender. I tuned it all out.

It was the last set of three, and I was up, two and O. We were changing sides when one of the mothers from the country club, who'd been watching from the sidelines, approached me.

"I thought you might want to know, honey," she whispered. "I think you had an accident." Her eyes went to my skirt, those crisp white pleats. On the hem, and more than likely spreading across the back, I could feel dampness. I knew what it meant. Plain as a target, probably. Bright red.

I hadn't noticed. I couldn't see the blood, but now I could feel it seeping through the crotch of the built-in underpants in my new skirt, a thin trickle making its way down my leg.

"It's all over the back of your skirt," the woman told me.

I could have asked for a time-out. But what then? I had no other clothes to change into—nothing but my blue jeans. If I'd had one of those Chris Evert tennis jackets the other girls wore when they came out onto the court that matched their skirt, I might have tied it around my waist to conceal the growing stain. But I had nothing.

An odd thing happened then. It came to me that I didn't care. They all hated me already. I didn't fit in. Everyone at the club—everyone but Jonathan—viewed me as a loser. What difference did it make if the whole country club saw that I had blood on my skirt?

"I'm OK," I told the woman.

I took my place at the service line.

I did not look at my skirt again, but I knew the stain was probably growing as the match progressed—the evidence, at last, of the thing I'd been waiting and praying for all summer that had finally taken place at the worst possible moment. With nothing I could do about this, I willed my brain to put away the thought and concentrate on the ball.

When it was over—final score, 3–6, 6–2, 6–5, winner: me—my opponent approached the net to shake my hand. I'd been so focused on the match I never got her name. Afterward, the head of the juniors' program presented me with my trophy: a girl holding a racquet aloft, reaching high for an impossibly high shot. Until that moment, I'd never won a prize for anything.

I just wanted to get off the court, stuff a wad of toilet paper in my underpants, get on my bike, and ride someplace far away, away from everyone.

I zipped my racquet into my case and walked back toward the locker room to retrieve my clothes. I didn't even want to change in there. I could take my shower back at Wonderland. All I wanted was to disappear.

Then there was Jonathan, running toward me with a giant grin on his face and his arms open wide. He picked me up—never mind the blood on my leg—and spun me around a couple of times—me, still holding my trophy, with a stain the size of a giant Rorschach test covering my skirt.

"You were great out there," he said.

He started talking about the match then, mentioning specific points, shots the other girl had made (her name turned out to be Kate) that had seemed to him un-gettable, only I'd gotten them. My second serve in the last point of the third set was amazing, he said.

"You were really in the groove by then."

After a few minutes, he explained he needed to congratulate his other students, losers as well as winners.

"There are a couple of other kids with matches coming up," he said. "But you know who my favorite is."

83

A Place Little Girls Aren't Supposed to Be

I made my way down the hallway toward the locker room. I dreaded going back in to face those girls, but I had to pick up my clothes.

I faced two doors. On one side was the door to the women's locker room. Beside it was the door for the men. On each door, a little stick-figure image announcing the gender of those who belonged there.

Something came over me then. You could call it an irresistible impulse, my body taking over for my brain. I placed my hand on the door to the men's locker room. I turned the handle. I stepped in.

I heard the sound of showers running and the slamming of locker doors. The air smelled partly of sweat, partly deodorant. Steam filled the room.

A lone figure stood at the row of sinks with his back to me. There was enough steam to obscure but not completely obliterate him.

He wasn't wearing a towel. He wasn't wearing anything. I saw only the back of him, but I knew who this was. Those well-muscled calves. His strong back, every muscle defined. Naked buttocks. When I'd seen him making love with Brenda on the island that day, I'd looked away. This time I didn't.

Forrest didn't see me right away. He was shaving. There was a tattoo on his left buttock—a name, with a heart surrounding it. *Regina.*

I have no idea how long I stood there. Maybe as long as a minute. Possibly less.

I guess he must have spotted me in the mirror then. He set down the razor and turned around.

He stood there facing me. Naked.

"Oh, Frances," he said. "You aren't supposed to be here. This is a mistake."

Only it wasn't a mistake. Seeing my face, Forrest must have understood that. I'd chosen the door to this locker room.

Always in the past, lying in my bed, when I got to that big moment in the stories I constructed, this had been the problem. No picture came to me, of the man, and what he would look like. Now here stood a man in real life, a few feet away from me, facing me head-on with a real-life body.

"I had to drop out of the triathlon," he said. "I guess I didn't train hard enough."

"I won a trophy today," I told him. He was still standing there. There was a towel on the sink, but he had not wrapped it around himself. I had never seen a man's penis in real life before. Not like this. I did not look away.

"Oh, sweetheart," he said. Another man might have exhibited embarrassment at being discovered naked this way. Not Forrest. The look he gave me then was not unkind, but it crushed me. "Little girls don't belong in here," he said.

I wanted to tell him I wasn't a little girl anymore. *Look at my skirt,* I could have told him. The blood was everywhere now.

I turned and ran.

84

MOHAIR

The blood was still pouring out of me—more blood than I'd imagined, times I'd imagined some version of this event. More blood was coming out of me now than a person could soak up with a wad of toilet paper.

Then I remembered something.

In the girls' locker room—where, strangely, no other girls seemed to be present—I reached inside my racquet bag and took out Regina's gift to me, the mohair pot holder. I stuffed it in the built-in underpants of my tennis skirt. Mohair turned out to be a lot more absorbent than toilet paper was.

I rode back to Wonderland, my golden first-place trophy in my bike basket, my whole body shaking. The tears were coming so hard I could barely see the road.

Back at the house, the only one around was Prudence. She was occupied making appetizers for the big party that night—a Martha Stewart cookbook open on the counter. She paid no attention as I raced upstairs to my room.

Alone at last, I stepped out of the stained tennis skirt and briefly examined the blood-soaked pot holder. Naked from the waist down, I took the familiar but untouched blue box out of the drawer. Squatting on the toilet, I peeled off the wrapper and unfolded the thin paper sheet bearing the instructions for inserting a tampon.

I pored over the instructions—the tidy drawing of an elegant female hand, fingers grasping the tampon inserter, accomplishing her task as if this were a pencil placed into a pencil sharpener.

I must have spent half an hour trying to figure out how to put the cardboard tube into my body. I couldn't get the tampon inside. Over and over I tried. *No.*

I was an idiot. I should have bought pads instead for my first time.

In the end, I pulled the small white fluffy tampon out of its tube. I wrapped it in toilet paper to make it more substantial and stuck the whole thing inside a fresh pair of underpants to soak up the blood.

I could have washed the white skirt. With cold water, the bloodstain might have come out. But I couldn't bear to deal with it. I wrapped the bloody evidence in a bunch of ripped-out pages from one of Regina's magazines and some granola bar wrappers. I stuffed the ruined skirt in the trash along with Regina's gift of the mohair pot holder that had evidently taken her all summer to finish—red now and heavy with my own blood.

I changed into my jeans.

Downstairs I found Jilly—just back from the club herself—showing off her second prize medal for her Marshmallow Surprise Rice Krispies Treats to Prudence and modeling her Pocahontas costume. Hayward leaned against the counter, still wearing his hoodie and sweatpants from the morning. When I passed through the kitchen, he gave me a look. I pretended to act like a person who had no clue he'd been the artist behind the *Joy of Sex* collage.

"Where's the skirt you had on before?" he asked.

"What's it to you?" I said.

The regatta wasn't due to start for several hours. In the meantime, the children grabbed a bowl of Doritos and settled themselves in front of the television—Jilly in her faux-leather skirt and fringed vest, a string of beads around her neck, Hayward's feather headdress untouched on the seat beside him, along with a plastic tomahawk and his faux-leather loincloth. Someone, probably Prudence, had applied warpaint to Hayward's face. The fact that he'd allowed this surprised me, but Prudence—and Prudence alone—seemed to inspire respect from Hayward. Jilly had lipstick on. It didn't matter what the costume was, Jilly found any excuse to apply lipstick.

Off in the corner, Regina sat at her desk, typing furiously—more pages of instructions for the tasks each of us was to undertake, no doubt, pertaining to the upcoming festivities. Not even my father, bent over his typewriter at midnight, working on his novel, displayed greater concentration. Regina did not look up.

When he'd first mentioned the regatta plan, Forrest had spoken optimistically about the two of them—himself and Regina—leading the parade in their costumes, pirate and wench, with the children following behind in the canoe, like a couple of Disney characters. Watching Regina now, seated at her typewriter, preparing some new document or other for us all, I had a hard time imagining that she'd be putting on the wench costume Forrest had picked up for her anytime soon, if ever. Even for the new and strangely more sociable Regina, this seemed unlikely.

Following his unsuccessful attempt at completing the triathlon and his brief stop at the tennis club for a shower and a shave—a part of his story that day I'd witnessed firsthand—Forrest had not shown up back at the house. He was making a trip to the liquor store, Prudence told me, and to the party store to pick up decorations—flags, balloons, party hats. Down at the dock, the Chris-Craft and the birchbark canoe were already festooned for the big event.

I figured I'd head back up to my room to replenish the blood-soaked toilet paper stuffed in my underwear and finish packing—all thoughts of my recent victory on the tennis court evaporated. I had cramps, but the awful feeling in my stomach was about more than having gotten my period. All around me, I could feel endings. As much as I had wanted to get my period and be done with my childhood, now that it had taken place, I felt an unexpected sense of loss. Six hours into this experience, I already hated being a woman.

85

Ahoy, Matey

The regatta was due to begin just before sunset, followed by fireworks, and because the Emersons' was the best spot anywhere
on the lake for viewing the parade of boats, friends had been invited
to watch it from the dock. Jilly had lined up her dolls along the edge
of the water as spectators, along with an assortment of trolls. Though
the sun wasn't down yet, Billy had set out the tiki torches, with extra
picnic tables and chairs for the guests and an assortment of kazoos and
noisemakers.

At six o'clock, Prudence went down to the shore with the first
trays of food—a light meal of cold cuts and an array of Buffalo chicken
wings, potato skins, stuffed mushrooms, and miniature quiches. I wasn't
hungry, but I figured I'd head down to the lake anyway. A distraction
from packing.

There was Forrest, back from town and setting up the grill. The
costume he'd rented had turned out to be a little cheesy, but Forrest
had improved on it significantly. Despite the heat, he'd put on a pair of
riding boots (he'd made a brief attempt at playing polo a while back)
and tied one of Regina's silk scarves around his neck (Hermès, probably; she'd explained to me about those). He'd drawn on a beard, but
the mustache he wore was attached with some kind of glue. The effect

reminded me briefly of the man in *The Joy of Sex*. He'd substituted a white tuxedo shirt for the polyester one that came with the rental costume and left it unbuttoned, with the sleeves rolled up. You could see the hair on his chest.

Guests were starting to arrive by now—couples I recognized from the club, mostly, along with their children. Pam Oliver was there, though not her husband. "We're separated," she announced, within the first sixty seconds of her arrival. "Thank God Almighty, free at last!" she crowed.

Olivia's mother, Phyllis, had also shown up, along with her husband (the one whom she had described to Forrest as in need of training on how to be a more attentive partner). He was a pleasant-enough looking man, who eyed Forrest warily, with the air of someone who recognized the possibility that his host and his wife had a history.

"Methinks ye could use a G&T, matey," Forrest said, greeting him, but it seemed to me that alcohol was unlikely to solve Terry's unease. Phyllis's outfit (low-cut, with a heart pendant tucked between her breasts) looked like something a woman might choose if she wanted to attract men's attention—one man's attention, anyway, but it wasn't working.

Their daughter, Olivia, had not accompanied them. I figured there was probably another party going on someplace else that night—a cooler one for the young people. I just wasn't invited.

It was no big surprise to me that Regina had not come down from the house for the arrival of the guests. Even for the new, friendlier Regina, this would have been too much. Forrest was the life of the party naturally, admiring the women's outfits, serving drinks, making jokes about his abysmal failure to complete the long-awaited triathlon, and slapping the backs of those who had.

"Ahoy, me hearties," he said as he greeted his guests.

The father of one of the girls who'd participated in the tournament came over to me.

"That was some match you played today," he said. "You're quite the dark horse, aren't you? That last set was a shocker."

I didn't know what that meant. Was he referring to my final killer approach shot at the net or the blood on my skirt? He moved on to talk with someone else before I had time to come up with a response.

As usual at gatherings like this one, I stood off by myself watching everyone—the husbands talking about sports, the wives talking about their children, the children running in circles on the vast lawn of Wonderland, wearing glow-in-the-dark bracelets, tossing Barbies in the air, blowing bubbles, tumbling and laughing on the soft grass as fireflies danced around them.

Out in front of the firepit, some friend of Forrest's—one of his golf foursome, most likely—had set up a boom box. Now Bruce Springsteen blasted out over the water, "Glory Days." On the dock, a group of women started dancing. They were mostly moms, and they danced like moms, except for the ones—and there were a couple of these—who danced like moms who wanted Forrest Emerson to notice them. *File this away for next summer,* maybe.

I could smell hamburgers on the grill. I caught sight of Prudence circulating with a tray of appetizers. A quarter moon hung over the water now. It was a perfect late-summer evening. But not really.

I looked over to the boathouse, thinking about the terrifying and wonderful book inside. The pictures in that book had alarmed me, but they had also provided so much excitement and stimulation over the course of the summer. That book had served as a part of my Wonderland education (that, along with tennis lessons—an unlikely combination).

The thought came to me that I could tuck *The Joy of Sex* under my sweatshirt and bring it up to the house, place it in my suitcase under the new Gap wardrobe Regina had purchased for me. If I brought it home with me, I could study that book whenever I wanted.

This brought me back to Hayward's unwanted gift to me of the collage. I hated that he had ripped out that drawing from the book that had come to matter so much to me. To Hayward, *The Joy of Sex* was nothing more than a dirty book, whose illustrations might offer a moment's titillation and inspire an obscene note. For me it represented something entirely different. It was a guidebook to a country I'd never been to, and might never find. I wasn't even sure I wanted to go there. But I wanted to know about it.

It was clear, from the fact that *The Joy of Sex* had been relegated to the boathouse, that nobody in the Emerson family valued it. The book had likely been sitting under spiderwebs on the shelf for years—ever since Forrest started sleeping in his solitary bedroom probably, with only the occasional visit from his wife. *The Joy of Sex* would probably sit on the shelf, unopened, for many more summers. This seemed like a waste.

Watching the Emersons' friends arranged around the picnic tables, laughing and scarfing down appetizers as their pirate host refilled their drinks, Hayward and his friend Jasper shooting off rubber bands at random guests, Jilly serving deviled eggs to her dolls, I concluded that the person who should have this book was me. Taking ownership might be a fitting way to mark my entry into womanhood that day. Back home in New Jersey, the book could serve as a reminder of my strange and complicated summer. One good part.

It was dark in the boathouse. If I'd fallen, climbing up on the step stool to bring down the treasured volume, I'd be caught red-handed with a book no fourteen-year-old was supposed to be reading. Though to me, the book was—along with all those Stephen King novels—the best reading experience a person could have asked for that summer.

Once I retrieved the book, I headed up to the house to stash it in my room. The sun was low over the lake now. The regatta hadn't started yet. Billy had lit the tiki torches.

I found Regina in the kitchen. As expected, she had not put on the wench outfit. She had no intention of riding in the Chris-Craft with Forrest.

The sight of her took me by surprise. She was standing over the counter, where Prudence had lined up the desserts she'd be bringing down to the lake: A carrot cake, a sponge cake, a Boston cream pie.

Regina had a spoon in her hand. Not a teaspoon. A soup spoon. When I saw what she was doing I froze.

Regina was digging into the Boston cream pie. She wasn't taking some delicate taste from one small corner. She had plunged her spoon right in the center of the pie. She was stuffing in giant mouthfuls. Even as she worked on swallowing the cream pie already in her mouth, she was digging her spoon in for more. Chocolate oozed from her mouth. Whipped cream dripped down her neck, onto her clothes.

The sight of her brought to mind that day she'd writhed on her thousand-thread-count sheets in green face masque goop. Only this was even stranger. Green goop was messy, but it wasn't fattening. Now the same woman who refused a single butter cookie her husband brought her from the bakery, out of concern for her figure, was ingesting great, gasping gulps of the richest dessert Prudence ever made. She could have been a dog who hadn't been fed in a week. Or a coyote come upon fresh carrion.

When she looked up from the pie and saw me watching, a look of shame came over her. I might have just stashed a book that didn't belong to me under my sweatshirt, but the crime Regina was committing was—for Regina at least—ten times more heinous. She wasn't just ruining a dessert intended for her guests; she was consuming calories in triple-digit numbers.

No words came out of her. No way they could. Her mouth was full; Boston cream pie and whipped cream were oozing down onto her chin.

There seemed only one thing to do then. I reached for a spoon myself. I stepped closer to the counter. I dug into the pie and took a bite. I licked my lips. I tried to act like this was normal behavior. I, the girl who struggled, herself, trying to figure out what normal was. The two of us stood there at the counter for several minutes until the last of the pie was gone. Finally Regina spoke, though her speech was slurred.

"This will be our secret," she said.

I ran up to my room and put the precious book in my drawer. Then I headed back to the waterfront. I knew Forrest would be needing me to help get the children loaded into the canoe. More than this, I wanted to get out of there.

It took longer than we bargained for, getting the boats lined up. Over an hour, at least. As much of a charmer as Forrest was, he possessed none of Regina's skill at getting a job done efficiently. Every time a few boats got in line, someone else would need to come in between them, requiring a lot of jockeying for positions. One family's Boston Whaler got tangled up in someone else's anchor. Another couple had trouble getting the engine started on their Grady-White. It turned out they needed fuel, which took another half hour.

The guests were getting restless. Children were cranky. A few people were drunk now. Prudence brought down the desserts—remarking, as she did, that her Boston cream pie seemed to have disappeared.

86

Birchbark

The regatta was supposed to get underway right at sunset, but it got to be eight thirty and Forrest still hadn't managed to get the boats in line and out on the lake. By nine o'clock quite a few of the families gave up and went home.

Hayward was off with a couple of boys he knew, setting off the smaller fireworks, the kind that just make a noise and freak out people's dogs, two of whom had started howling loudly, one of whom had grabbed a large steak off the grill and run off with it. This required another interruption to get the animals back under control.

Through it all, Forrest remained cool and unflappable. There was only one boat left to place in the lineup—the birchbark canoe.

Only where was Jilly? Minutes before, I'd seen her playing tag with her friends, all of them wearing their pink and green glow necklaces.

"She went up to the house to get her Teddy Ruxpin," one of the other children told me.

Then I saw her. Jilly was back with her toy, but she was weeping and shivering on the grass, her face buried in the fur of her talking bear.

Whining was nothing new for Jilly but this seemed different—the kind of crying you'd expect of a person if they'd just lost their dearest and most beloved friend on earth. I had never seen Jilly like this before. As if this night marked the end of the world.

Catching sight of her, her father knelt down on the grass next to her, wrapping her in a blanket.

"You don't have to go in the canoe if you don't feel like it," he said. But she got up and made her way to the dock, holding Forrest's hand, her lipstick smeared and her feather askew. She looked like a zombie.

Overtired, no doubt. It was past nine o'clock.

"Come on, Hay-man," Forrest said. "Let's get this show on the road. One pass around the bay and we can call it a day. Then we'll come in and let off the fireworks."

Jilly had settled down now, though she wasn't her usual self. "Look out for your sister, son," Forrest told Hayward, as the two of them pushed off. He took one last look at the outriggers he'd attached to the birchbark canoe. "Looking good," he called out. "Steady as you go."

Everything looked magical then. The tiki lights were burned out by this point, but the strings of white Christmas lights remained illuminated, though the best part was the moon, reflecting silver on the water, and the fireflies. From the speakers blasting on somebody's boat—another Chris-Craft—Bob Marley was singing "One Love."

"Avast, me hearties," Forrest called out to those on shore as his boat took off. "Shiver me timbers." No Pirates of the Caribbean theme music and no wench on the prow, but never mind. All by himself in the darkness, Forrest cut a dashing figure.

Out on the lake, the Chris-Craft made its way in slow circles around the cove. Alongside it, the children, in their costumes, paddled the birchbark canoe, Forrest keeping a close eye at all times. I watched them from the shore, my eyes on Jilly. Once in the canoe, she had perked up a little, probably due to all the attention she was getting.

Forrest had just called out to them, "Time to head back, everyone!" when the trouble hit—the wake from the Bob Marley–blasting Chris-Craft the probable culprit. The birchbark canoe started to lean sideways.

Someone said, "Oh shit." A woman next to me, holding a pitcher of margaritas, let out a shriek.

"Dad!" Hayward called out. He tried righting the canoe, but it was too far sideways.

Suddenly the children were in the water. All around, darkness, but I could hear their voices. And Forrest's: "Someone help me!"

Half a dozen guests raced into the water. Those who didn't stood at the edge, shouting. It was hard to make out where the children were at this point; there was so much splashing and yelling.

Forrest had wasted no time diving in after them. Hayward had managed to swim to shore already, but Forrest scooped up Jilly, cradling her head as he carried her to dry land.

They were back on shore within a matter of minutes—Jilly crying in huge, gasping sobs, Hayward warming his hands by the bonfire, teeth chattering. I stood, watching, the way I always did. Partygoers gathered around the children, handing them sweaters. Someone had run to the boathouse for towels. Forrest sat on the grass with Jilly in his arms. She was alright. So was Hayward. But I think he was crying.

The Chris-Craft sat abandoned a little way out in the lake at the spot where Forrest had jumped ship. The birchbark canoe floated upside down a little beyond it.

Only Billy remained out on the lake now. He'd taken the Emersons' smaller boat, an old Boston Whaler, out in the direction of the island, far enough that he must not have seen what was going on closer to shore—the canoe capsizing, the wild scramble to rescue the children.

It was Billy's job to set off the fireworks. Never mind the somber mood that had overtaken the gathering, the stunned silence that followed the wild commotion. Celebration of any kind was the last thing on anyone's mind, but all Billy knew was that he'd been instructed to set off the fireworks at nine forty-five. It was nine forty-five now.

Suddenly there was a giant popping sound, and the sky lit up with a shower of red and blue and green sparkles. Then more popping. Another shower of light, even more spectacular than the first one.

I had always hated fireworks, but never so much as I did that night. I thought about the loons out on the lake, how it must be for them, hearing that awful barrage of what sounded like gunfire. So many fireworks filled the sky now, you couldn't even see the moon anymore.

The show went on and on. Every time I thought it was over, another explosion of light bloomed over the water. Not that anybody seemed to be paying attention. The guests, some soaking wet, were gathering up their things—shoes, coolers, children—and heading to their cars.

Prudence approached me, looking troubled.

"I'm worried about Regina," she said. "Loud noises always set her off. When people do target practice around here, one gunshot is enough to send her to bed."

"I'll go check on her," I said.

I walked back up to the house. Behind me, I could still hear the explosions, one after another, as if a war were going on. Like the end of the world.

87

Touched for the Very First Time

Up at the house now, I checked the kitchen first. The ruined chocolate cream pie was gone. Maybe Regina had thrown away what little was left of it.

I climbed the stairs to her room. I tapped lightly on the door and called her name. No answer, but I figured maybe the fireworks—still exploding—drowned out my voice. I called out to her again, louder this time. When there was still no answer, I pushed the door open and stepped inside.

Regina was lying on the bed with her hair fanned out on the pillow, no blanket covering her. Instead of the sweatpants and T-shirt she'd been wearing when I'd seen her earlier that night, she was wearing a negligee—silk, probably—so sheer you could see the outlines of her body underneath, making visible every rib and the dark circles of her nipples on her tiny breasts. One thin arm was draped across her chest. The other hung down over the side of the bed.

Her eyes were open. So was her mouth.

I ran back down the stairs, down the hill, past the crying children and the last of the guests in the remnants of their soaked costumes. I ran straight to Forrest. I could barely breathe.

"It's Regina," I said.

The ambulance arrived: flashing lights, men carrying medical equipment, followed afterward by a stretcher with a still form over it, a blanket covering the form underneath. Prudence had taken the children somewhere—to her house, probably—so swiftly that Jilly's precious American Girls and the rest of her toys remained lined up in their doll-sized chairs along the edge of the dock, facing out to the water as if awaiting the next act in the show.

The few party guests who hadn't left yet were crying. Mostly they just disappeared as quickly as possible once they got wind of the news. Forrest had gotten into the back of the ambulance with Regina's body. Through the window in the back of the ambulance, I caught sight of his face for only a moment as he took his place next to the stretcher, still wearing the fake mustache and beard. The ambulance pulled away. I was alone.

Not surprisingly, nobody had remembered about me. I knew I should cry. I wished I could cry. But a terrible feeling of numbness had overtaken me.

Alone now, I went back inside the house. All around were untouched platters of food. Hours since I'd last eaten anything more than a few spoonfuls of Boston cream pie, I reached for a miniature lobster roll. Then another. My favorite food, or one of them, anyway. I tasted nothing.

I did what I'd seen my father do then. For the first time in my life, maybe, I understood why my father did what he did, why he kept pouring himself another drink, knowing it would never lead to anything but trouble, and still unable to stop himself. I poured myself a glass of the only alcoholic drink I knew anything about. Vodka. I hated how it felt on my lips, but I didn't care. I drank it down.

As much as I can remember, I sat there for a long time, though it's hard to know how much time passed. I thought about Jacqueline du Pré and Maria Callas and my mother. Every heartbroken woman I'd ever heard of, most particularly Regina. Also my own self.

I put on Madonna.

The pirate hat lay on the floor. Forrest must have thrown it off at some point as he was racing up the stairs to Regina, after I'd come to get him. Now I put the hat on. I guess I was dancing.

Still numb—and drunk, no doubt—I played that CD all through the night. It was still playing when I saw the lights of the taxi pulling up to the house. It must have been early morning by that time. Like a dead man, Forrest walked in, still wearing the pirate costume, though the mustache had come off and at some point he'd buttoned his shirt.

"There was nothing they could do," he said. He put his arms around me, or maybe it was I who put my arms around him. We were two desperately sad people offering each other whatever comfort we could. Which wasn't much.

88

Morning After

I must have fallen asleep at some point. When I woke up—morning now—my head was throbbing. A deep red circle stained my thousand-thread-count sheets. In all this time I still hadn't managed to locate a sanitary napkin.

There are occasions when something terrible has happened and you wake up the next morning and for a moment you don't remember what it was that happened the day before. The not-remembering part only lasts a few seconds, and when it passes, and it comes to you what you'd forgotten, it's as if you have to live through the terrible discovery all over again. For a moment, I thought I'd dreamed the whole thing. Only I knew I hadn't.

From the stairs, as I approached the kitchen, I heard voices. One was Forrest, who probably hadn't slept at all that night. The other was my father, who'd just pulled in after driving almost eight hours through the night from New Jersey to pick me up. I could tell from the sound of his voice as he greeted Forrest that he hadn't heard the news.

He was saying something to Forrest about a tollbooth and a song that came on the radio as he was crossing the border into Maine that reminded him of a time when the two of them had hitchhiked to the Catskills with a couple of girlfriends and someone's pet bird.

Forrest interrupted him. *"Hank,"* he said.

Even my father, as absorbed as he generally was in the events of his own life, must have recognized something on Forrest's face.

"Oh god," my father said. *"Regina?"*

The two of them were sitting at the kitchen counter. Forrest had his head in his hands. My father had his arm around him—the kind of gesture I'd been the recipient of from him only once or twice, myself, ever.

"I know you loved her, Howie," my father said. He was Howie again. He'd never stopped being Howie, was the truth.

89

SOMEONE MOVED THE BBs

The plan was for Forrest to pick the children up from Prudence's house later that morning, once he pulled himself together. He'd need to explain what happened. As if anyone could.

The celebration dinner for my last night at Wonderland was canceled, of course. "Frances and I should get out of your hair, Howie," my father told Forrest. He didn't argue. Regina's parents were driving up from Hilton Head. Having to deal with the presence of one low-life from New Jersey was probably enough for them.

Forrest headed out to get Jilly and Hayward. No time for good-byes. My red Samsonite suitcase was packed. My father carried it down to the car.

"Take one more look around the house in case you forgot anything," he said.

I considered the *Joy of Sex* book I'd stolen the night before from the boathouse, which I hadn't placed in my suitcase yet. I thought about Hayward, but not the Hayward who'd ripped out the page of the book, just one day earlier—how was this possible?—and left it for me with that sickening note. For a moment there, to me, Hayward was just a little kid whose mother was dead, and a big wave of feeling sorry for him came over me. Then I saw Hayward's blue eye, looking in at me that day as I studied one of the illustrations of the now familiar couple making love and touched myself.

What came to me, remembering this, was not anger toward Hayward so much as sadness for him. Like me, he was probably still struggling to figure out sex, and bodies, and what people were supposed to do with each other—besides roll around on poison ivy with someone else's wife. Only now, in case that wasn't enough, his mother had killed herself.

Hayward wasn't a bad person. Like me, Hayward was just trying to figure sex out. Sex and everything else. No big surprise, he hadn't found any answers. Neither had I.

I put the stolen copy of *The Joy of Sex* back on the boathouse shelf. One summer, a few years from now, Hayward might go looking for it himself. Jilly too, though at this point that was harder to imagine. Jilly was just a little girl. It occurred to me that those were the same words Forrest had used just one day earlier to describe me.

I would have liked to say goodbye to the children, but the truth was, they weren't going to be thinking about their babysitter at this point. I would have liked to say goodbye to Jonathan too, but my father wanted to get on the road.

I left my tennis trophy in the closet of my room. But I took my racquet.

I was out the door already when I remembered one more thing: the journal with the birds hand-tooled into the leather, where I'd written my most secret and thrilling stories in those first weeks of summer.

After I'd learned about Forrest and Brenda, I'd been unable to write stories like those anymore. Since placing it in that hiding spot under my mattress with the row of BBs alongside the edge to alert me if anyone touched it, I hadn't written a single one of the crazy sexual scenarios that had filled the pages of the book during those first weeks of summer, back when Forrest Emerson had seemed like the most perfect man in the world. I'd written one rant about how crazy Regina was, and a few entries about tennis. Nothing more.

"I'll be right back," I told my father. "I forgot one other thing."

Upstairs in my little room, I lifted the mattress off the slats of the bed. I reached in to retrieve the beautiful leatherbound book Regina had given me back in June to memorialize what it felt like to be me that summer.

It wasn't there.

I lifted the mattress higher. Maybe the journal got pushed further back, scrunched up against the wall. But no.

My journal was gone.

90

The Pane Is Unbarable

We couldn't leave town yet after all. The police wanted to talk with me. Because I was the person who'd found Regina's body, and because, other than her husband, I was the one who'd spent the most time with her in the weeks leading up to her death, they had a few questions for me.

Sitting in the front seat of our Pontiac, next to my father, I looked out the window at the now familiar landscape: Red, white, and blue begonias lining the drive. My yellow bike parked in its spot. For once my father had turned the music off in the car. No cassette playing. Neither of us spoke.

It seemed pretty obvious to everyone at that point that Regina's death was a suicide. Everyone knew she'd been depressed for years. Everyone knew there had been pills and doctors and a hospitalization or two. For years they'd heard Regina talk about killing herself.

"It's just a formality, but we'd like your daughter to answer a few questions," one of the police officers who stopped by the house that morning had told my father. "Stop by the station on your way out of town."

They'd found a typewritten note next to Regina's body. In it, she'd expressed her love for her husband and children, and her parents, and Prudence—even me. The note said how sorry she was. The pain of living had just become too great.

There was just one problem with this note.

The investigator who'd come down from Augusta to assist the local police led me into a small room then. We were alone, just the two of us.

"I know this has got to be hard on you," he said. "At your age, a girl should be thinking about hanging out with her friends and getting on the cheering squad."

Not exactly, but never mind. No need to elaborate.

"We understand that Mrs. Emerson chose to use a typewriter when she wrote her daily reminders to the family," he said. "I get that part. But the spelling in the final note we found next to her body struck us all as pretty unusual. Particularly for a college graduate. I gather she went to one of those Ivy League schools."

He passed the note across the desk to me. I scanned a few sentences.

The pane is unbarable. You mene evrything to me. I just reched the point ware there is no way out . . .

I knew someone who spelled this way. It was Forrest, of course. Forrest, who was barely literate. From someplace deep inside me that I didn't even know existed, a wave of pure, hot protectiveness rose up in me.

"Regina took a lot of drugs sometimes," I said. "Last night she probably took more than usual. Maybe that made it hard for her to write very well."

Officer Reynolds nodded, but he looked dubious.

"We've obtained some examples of communication written by Mr. Emerson to members of the club the Emersons belonged to, as well as samples of his communications with others in the community," the police officer said. "It appears Mr. Emerson is greatly challenged by writing the English language."

"Forrest is a smart person," I said. I didn't see where he was going, but I sensed trouble. "He's good at a lot of things. He's just a really bad speller. There are kids like that at my school."

"Nobody's arguing this point, Frances," Officer Reynolds said. "The Emersons' cook also provided a few notes written to her by Mrs. Emerson's husband. The kinds of errors displayed in the alleged suicide note appear virtually identical to the kinds of errors we've noted in Mr. Emerson's writing."

"I don't know what you're trying to say," I said. But I did, actually.

"We have to wonder if somebody other than Mrs. Emerson might have written this alleged suicide note," Officer Reynolds said. "Someone who wanted to leave the appearance that Mrs. Emerson had taken her own life."

I could feel myself starting to get dizzy. We were seated at a desk as we spoke. I held on to the sides of it.

"Regina acted funny when she took her pills," I repeated. "She probably took a lot of pills that day."

Wasn't this obvious? She took so many pills they killed her.

He nodded and wrote something down on his notepad.

"Do you know anything about a recent change to the Emersons' life insurance?" he said. "We've learned that an insurance agent paid a visit to the family home recently to amend the family's policy. When I spoke with Mrs. Emerson's father this morning, he mentioned that it's his understanding this revision came at the suggestion of Mr. Emerson. You may have been present for his visit?"

"Some man with a briefcase showed up one time. I don't know about life insurance," I said. "I'm fourteen."

I was turning fifteen the next week. But suddenly I wanted to be younger. Young enough that nobody would ask me these questions.

I wanted to be gone, actually. Anywhere but in this room, at this police station, talking with Officer Reynolds.

There were more questions. Many of these.

Now I knew what it meant when girls in my class talked about cramps, and how weird they felt when they got their period. In all this time, there had been no opportunity to get to a drugstore and buy sanitary pads. For twenty-four hours now, I'd been stuffing wads of toilet paper into my underwear. I could feel the blood seeping into my pants.

"And how would you describe Mr. Emerson?"

Describe him? (Handsome? Funny? Wonderful? My favorite person in the universe?)

"Nice," I told him. "You know. The usual."

"Was he a good father?"

"Oh, yes." I did not add here that I wished he had been mine.

When Officer Reynolds asked me to characterize Forrest's relationship with Regina, I told him about how considerate he was to her all the time. How patient. "He was always keeping track of her pills," I said. "Every time she needed some pills at the drugstore, he picked them up for her."

Uh-huh. The officer gave me a look.

"And how would you characterize his relationship with you?"

"Good," I told him. "Forrest always . . . took an interest in me."

"Took an interest?"

"He listened to me," I said. "He paid attention."

"Would you say Mr. Emerson loved you?"

"Not in a boyfriend-girlfriend way. He just . . . loved me."

The one he really loved was Regina, I told the police officer. A thought came to me then, supporting this.

"He even has a tattoo with her name on it," I told him.

Interesting. "Where on Mr. Emerson's body is this tattoo located?" he asked.

I had to tell him then.

"He showed you his naked buttocks?"

Oh god. Nothing was coming out the way I wanted it to.

"It wasn't like that," I said. "I want my dad," I told the police officer. I don't know if I'd ever said those words before, or if I'd ever had that thought.

"We're almost finished," Officer Reynolds told me. "You can see your father in just a few minutes."

I wanted my dad right then. Not in five minutes. Or maybe I just wanted to get out of there.

"One of our other officers is talking with your father," Officer Reynolds told me. "I gather the two of them—your father and Mr. Emerson—grew up together. It seems Mr. Emerson had some run-ins with the law when he was younger."

I told him how Forrest's family didn't have much money. Of course, everything changed for him once he married Regina.

"That's when he changed his name," Officer Reynolds said. "Did that ever strike you as odd?"

The room felt hot. The blood still coming out of me felt warm and sticky in my underpants. I tried to think about the tennis court where I had my lessons with Jonathan.

I'm standing at the baseline, preparing to serve. I keep my eye on the ball. Nothing else matters.

"We understand how young you are, Frances. But it appears you played an unusual role in Mrs. Emerson's life over the course of this past summer. Not the normal kind of job for a babysitter."

An unusual role?

"I'll be honest with you," he said. "We found a notebook on the bed, next to Mrs. Emerson's body."

He took it out now. The little spiral notebook I'd kept in my pocket when I was pretending to be Nancy Drew. Back when this whole thing seemed like an exciting game. Or a play I got to be in. With me in the starring role, for a change.

"This notebook seems to document the details of some sort of relationship between Mr. Emerson and a woman named Brenda. Would you know anything about this notebook?"

I just sat there.

"You probably know from watching television that law enforcement professionals are able to determine the identity of the author of a document based on the expertise of a handwriting analyst," he told me. "It wouldn't be difficult to prove that you were the author of these notes. That this was your notebook."

"She just wanted me to find out a little information," I said. I could feel everything tumbling down around me.

"We found a set of Polaroid photographs. Of Mr. Emerson and a woman who isn't Mrs. Emerson. We haven't identified her yet, though I'm guessing you may be able to assist us with that. I'm guessing this may be the 'Brenda' referred to in these notes you appear to have written. We're also in possession of a tape recording. Also made by you, perhaps."

More blood. It was still seeping out of me.

"I'm sorry," I said. I wasn't actually apologizing to the police officer, though that's what he thought, probably. I was sorry the things I said made Forrest sound like a bad person. I was sorry I hadn't done a better job with the questions. I was very, very sorry I had misled Regina when I first told her about Brenda's plan to make it look like she had killed herself, sorrier than I could ever say that I'd let Regina believe Forrest was in on that plan.

It didn't matter that I'd tried to explain, afterward. It was too late by then.

"It's all my fault," I said.

"Nobody's blaming you for anything," the police officer told me. For a few minutes there, he had sounded like the principal at my school when you got called in for detention. Now he was nice again. He sounded like someone who felt genuinely bad about all I'd been through. He passed me a box of Kleenex. They'd probably taught him to do this at police school.

"I've got a daughter about your age," he said. "We all know you're young. We just need you to help us. Concerning this Brenda, for instance."

"She's a terrible person," I said. "She said some awful things. I thought Regina should know about it. To protect her."

"It won't be difficult to locate Brenda," he said. "We'll be speaking with her, I have no doubt."

This was the moment I could feel myself giving up. There was no way of figuring out anymore which things to say to help Forrest and which ones would only get him in more trouble. By this point, I'd already observed how some of the things I'd said, hoping to make him look better in the eyes of the police officer, ended up having the opposite effect.

Maybe it would be better to lay it all out. The main thing was that Forrest hadn't killed Regina. It seemed to me at the time that maybe the best strategy was to explain the whole story so the police officer would understand.

"Brenda told Forrest that Regina would probably kill herself someday anyway," I told him. "She told Forrest they should encourage her to do that."

"And you told Mrs. Emerson about this?" Officer Reynolds said.

I nodded. "But Forrest wasn't ever part of that," I told the officer. "When Brenda said she wanted to kill Regina and make it look like she killed herself, Forrest didn't go along with it. He got mad at her."

"So Brenda and Mr. Emerson were carrying on some kind of relationship?" he asked me.

"I guess you could say that."

"And where did this take place?"

"There was this patch of moss," I said. Among other locations.

A deep wave of weariness came over me. More than that, exhaustion. I'd barely slept the night before. I had a hangover. Nothing I told Officer Reynolds came out the way I meant it to. Everything I said made it worse. I was still bleeding. Regina was dead.

I couldn't try anymore. Didn't care.

Officer Reynolds placed his hand on my shoulder. "You must be hungry," he told me. "Have some M&M's.

"And when you told Mrs. Emerson about Brenda's idea that she and Mr. Emerson should 'encourage' Mrs. Emerson to take her own life, what did Mrs. Emerson have to say?" he asked me.

I had no response to offer him. The blood had soaked through the wad of toilet paper. My blue jeans would have a stain in the back now. Out in the hallway, my father, who always said the wrong thing even when he hadn't had a drink, was probably telling one of the other officers about the time he and Howie stole their high school mascot, a stuffed bobcat, and set it on some railroad tracks. For some crazy reason, I heard the voice of Teddy Ruxpin repeating that one dumb sentence, over and over. *Can you be my special friend?* Jonathan, beside me on the service line, reminding me to breathe. Madonna, singing about being touched for the first time.

"Just because Forrest and Brenda had sex," I said, "that didn't mean he wanted Regina to die."

I'd said it now. Maybe I hoped that once the words were out, Officer Reynolds would stop asking all these questions. Maybe I thought I'd feel better to have it out and finished. But I only felt sicker.

"I think I have to throw up," I told him.

91

It was hours later when they finished with us at the police station. On our way out of town, I asked my father to stop at a drugstore so I could buy sanitary napkins. I didn't care anymore that they weren't as cool as tampons. I didn't care if the person at the cash register looked at my face as I bought them and knew what it meant that I was doing this. Even if the cashier was a boy, or a man, I didn't care about that either.

We were heading back to New Jersey now. It occurred to my father that we hadn't eaten anything for a long time. Before hitting the Maine Turnpike, we pulled into a diner in some little town. Not a town like Lake Catherine. The kind of town we were more familiar with, where people drove old cars and played bingo at the VFW hall. Or went nowhere, more likely. The kind of place where people like us would live if we lived in Maine instead of New Jersey.

There was a family at the next booth over: a father and a mother and three kids—a couple of them were teenagers, one who looked close to my age. I noticed them because they looked happy. They looked like one of those normal families that go out for pancakes on a Sunday afternoon, and afterward, go to a ball game or something. Or they just hang out and don't worry about much.

There was something about this family that made it hard for me to take my eyes off them. Even at a moment like this one—after spending three hours being interviewed by a police officer in the aftermath of Regina showing up dead—I couldn't help looking at them.

It sounded like they were talking about an exhibition Red Sox game in which one of the New York Mets had hit five balls over the wall in a single night. I didn't understand what they meant when they called it the Green Monster, or any of the rest of what the son and the father were talking about in the booth next to ours. I just liked the sound of their voices, the easy, comfortable way they talked to each other. The parents' backs were facing me, but the way the mother had her hand on the father's arm made me know these two people liked each other.

Across from them, the younger son was making a stack out of sugar packets and trying to knock them down by blowing on them with his straw—just the kind of dumb, pointless thing a kid his age would do. He looked happy and normal too. Not like some boy who'd stick a picture of Michael J. Fox over the drawing of a naked man that he'd ripped out of a sex book and put it in the bike basket of somebody who didn't even like him.

I tried to imagine I was sitting in that other booth instead of the one with my father. Now he was lighting a cigarette.

I was listening so hard to what was going on in the next booth, with the normal family, that I didn't hear the waitress asking me for my order.

"You ready, hon?" she said. From the sound of her, this must not have been the first time she'd asked.

"I'll have the pancakes," I told her.

"I don't blame you for staring," she said. "They're our local celebrities. You'd never know to look at him that he'd be the type to write all those weird, twisted stories, right?"

I had no idea what she meant. This was when the dad got up to go to the bathroom or something, and I saw his face for the first time.

It was Stephen King.

92

Home

Three days later I started ninth grade. It would have felt strange wearing the clothes Regina had bought me at the mall that day, so I threw them out, same as I'd done with the bloody tennis skirt. I mostly wore my same Cyndi Lauper sweatshirt and jeans, alternating with an old T-shirt I'd rescued from a box of my mother's old clothes from her hippie days. Janis Joplin and Big Brother and the Holding Company.

As expected, my father had moved out of our apartment by the time I got back to New Jersey. My mother had found a job at a package store. Given the nature of the business, we figured she would probably see my father as often as she did back when he still lived with us, but this turned out not to be the case. After all the times my mother used to beg him to quit drinking, he'd joined AA.

For a while then, nobody said much about Regina's death or any of the rest of it, though I gathered Forrest had called my father up one night at his new apartment that he shared with his friend Bud and ended up crying on the phone for a couple of hours.

My one and only friend at school, Martha, had a boyfriend now, so she wasn't that interested in hanging out with me anymore. My breasts filled out enough that the training bra actually served a purpose, finally. I even got a real bra after that. I figured out how to use tampons.

As I had guessed, my high school had no tennis team, but it turned out there was a tennis program starting at the local Parks and Rec. I showed up for the first session with the racquet Jonathan had given me. The tennis player kids in Hubbard didn't look anything like the ones back at the Lake Catherine Country Club. One of them made a remark about my racquet. How expensive it must have been. I didn't go back.

I had not forgotten Forrest's words to me, that I was going to have an amazing life, but this no longer seemed likely or even possible. Sometimes, when I woke up in my dark little room in the apartment I shared with only my mother now, it felt as if the whole summer I'd spent at Wonderland was just a dream. Except Regina really was dead. That part was real.

Over and over, my mind returned to those last days at the lake. Two images haunted me.

I couldn't get the sight of Regina out of my head, as she'd been that last night, standing over the kitchen counter, shoveling in giant spoonfuls of custard and chocolate and whipped cream as if she was in a Boston cream pie–eating contest.

There could be only one reason why Regina, a person who lived with a deathly fear of gaining a pound, would have eaten that pie the way she did that night.

She knew she wasn't going to be around in the morning to step on the scale.

This was probably her last act on earth before she went upstairs and swallowed the pills. Remembering how she'd stopped taking her pills that August, it came to me that she'd probably been stockpiling them for weeks.

There was something else I tried not to think about, but I kept coming back to it: the leatherbound journal Regina had given me with the birds on the front and all those stories I'd written inside about sexual scenarios I dreamed up that never really happened. I kept replaying that moment when I'd lifted the mattress off my bed to retrieve my journal and found it gone.

Somebody had taken it. They'd read what I'd written on that thick, creamy paper, about a man who strongly resembled Forrest telling someone meant to be a slightly older, sexier, more beautiful version of me, that he couldn't keep his hands off her. Avowals of love in the library stacks. Open-mouth kisses. Sex behind the tennis court. Sex on moss.

My journal was out there someplace. I had no idea where.

I couldn't stop thinking about how, if it wasn't for me, none of this would have happened. Forrest would be off in Boston, thinking up an idea for some crazy new company. Jilly would be signing up for Brownies. Hayward would still be a jerk, but Regina would be alive. I wouldn't be walking around feeling like I'd ruined their lives.

I told myself Regina had always teetered on the precipice. My discovery, just days before her death, of what took place with her sister may have offered an explanation for the mystery of what led her to that point. She'd probably never been alright after that. Her relationship with Forrest was founded on the knowledge that she was the replacement for a dead woman. His favorite.

She'd talked about killing herself for years. Still, I knew what it was that had led her to making her final decision when she did, to do it again. Only this time she made it work.

This was my awful secret. I'd carry it around with me forever. Who wouldn't go crazy, believing that the man she adored was going along with his lover's plot to kill her?

Now the police were investigating Forrest. And because the way Regina chose to end her life implicated her husband as a possible murderer, I could be responsible for destroying Forrest's life too.

93

After

It was late November when my father told me the news: The police had arrested Forrest, charging him with Regina's murder. Bail denied.

In the charges she filed, the district attorney for Franklin County, Maine, asserted that Forrest was a serial cheater and sex addict with a long history of deceit and betrayals. The DA alleged that Forrest's motive lay in his desire to end his marriage and his intention to create a new life with a woman named Brenda Barnett. She pointed to the fact that just weeks before her death—with her husband's encouragement, no doubt—Regina had named her husband as beneficiary of a three-million-dollar life insurance policy in the event that she died before him.

Now more accusations spilled out over the pages of the *Portland Press Herald* and beyond: the theory that Forrest had stockpiled sleeping pills with the intention of giving his wife—whose pill usage he oversaw—a lethal dose. In an attempt to replicate the manner in which Regina would have crafted a suicide note—and to avoid handwriting analysis—he'd typed the letter meant to look like a suicide note.

But Forrest had made a grievous mistake, the DA contended. Given the spelling errors in the note he allegedly laid beside his wife's body—errors of a kind Regina herself would never have committed—he identified himself, a man known to have struggled with literacy, as the true author of the note.

Then he'd administered the drugs that killed her.

Now Forrest Emerson was charged with first-degree murder, locked up in a jail, awaiting trial.

94

Trash Folder

My father and I were having lunch at the diner he used to take me to on Sunday afternoons, when he filled me in on what was happening. This diner gave you two hamburgers for the price of one and your first beer on the house.

"The case won't hold up in court. Everyone knows Regina talked about taking her life for years." He didn't know yet—because I hadn't told him—about the Polaroids I'd taken, the tapes, the spiral notebook in which I'd documented Forrest's comings and goings that summer, including Brenda's words to her friend that day at the Caboose about the plans to make a life with Forrest. And more.

The next Sunday—lunch with my father again—he told me the latest news. The police had succeeded in getting a search warrant for Brenda Barnett's computer. It had taken them all of ten minutes to locate the draft she had written of what she'd constructed as Regina's suicide letter, located in her trash folder. (I had figured this out long before: In addition to being a really terrible person, Brenda was also a stupid one.)

On the basis of the draft of the fake suicide note, along with corroborating evidence in the form of the photographs I'd taken, Brenda Barnett had now been charged as an accomplice to murder, facing a sentence of twenty-five years to life.

95

A Regular Nancy Drew

It was late April when the trial got underway.

When the call came from the DA's office, informing me that I was required to show up in court to testify, I considered running away. If I said the wrong thing, I would incriminate an innocent man I'd loved all my life. I was terrified of saying the wrong thing again.

My father tried to keep it from happening, but in the end I had no choice. The two of us drove up to Maine together—a very different ride from the one I'd taken just short of a year earlier with Forrest.

For my court appearance, I wore the only dress I owned that seemed like something a person would wear when testifying at a murder trial—the blue Fourth of July party dress Regina had bought for me. It was a little tight by this time. I'd finally developed breasts.

The public defender assigned to represent Forrest, Ted Storm, looked as if he'd graduated from law school ten minutes earlier. Though I'd been called to testify as a witness for the prosecution, the plan was that in his cross-examination of me, I'd manage to convey a different side of the story—one that would support his client's innocence.

He said little about what might be asked of me in court. "Should be pretty cut and dried," he'd told my father and me when we'd spoken on the phone a few days before coming up to Maine. Ted Storm was one of those people who gave you the impression he was opening his mail while you talked with him. Maybe, at the same time, he was watching a ball game with the volume off.

"There's something you should know," I told Forrest's lawyer. "I think it's important."

Then I told him about the night—Regina's last—when I'd seen her eating the Boston cream pie. I described to him how I'd seen her in the kitchen, not long before her death, shoveling spoonfuls of pie into her mouth.

"One thing everyone knew about Regina," I said. "She was terrified of gaining weight. Regina counted every calorie that went into her body. But she was scarfing down that pie like there was no tomorrow," I told him.

Like there was no tomorrow. It was a phrase that applied with chilling accuracy to that night.

"I don't get the significance here," Ted, the lawyer, said, sounding bored.

I tried to explain. "The only way Regina would have let herself eat that pie was if she knew she was about to kill herself," I told him. Meaning, it was Regina who took the pills. Nobody gave them to her. Here was proof of Forrest's innocence.

To support my theory, I told Ted about the scale in Regina's bathroom that she weighed herself on two times a day. The celery sticks she kept in sealed baggies in the refrigerator, that she gnawed on at mealtimes. The way she removed the bread from her tuna sandwich, eating only the filling, and hardly any of that either.

I was talking very fast. Too fast, probably, because I was excited. I had spent a lot of time thinking about my theory. Offering it in court would give me a chance to right the terrible wrong I'd committed the previous summer when I'd led Regina to believe that Forrest had been in on Brenda's scheme to murder her.

It was too late to save Regina. But offering my testimony about the Boston cream pie might be my only chance to make things right for Forrest.

At some point during my speech about the pie, the name Karen Carpenter probably came up. The word *anorexia*, which I'd learned about from reading *Seventeen*, and another word (also learned from the pages of *Seventeen*) that actually applied to Regina, as I'd learned that time I saw her leaving the bathroom with the towel over her mouth: *bulimia*.

"Once she knew she was going to kill herself, it didn't matter anymore," I told him.

I was crying by that point. I probably sounded like a crazy person. Even my father—a man who believed in Forrest's innocence with every cell in his body—seemed not to understand the significance of what I was saying. I was so worked up, I could barely get the words out.

Calories. Bathroom scale. Whipped cream.

"Slow down, honey," the lawyer said to me. Then he addressed my father, in a tone that made me understand he considered my dad the only person worth speaking to here. "When a witness comes across as hysterical, it doesn't play well with the jury." *Hysterical*: a word applied when a person, usually female, expressed strong emotion.

I tried one more time. "Regina was so mad at Forrest that she wanted to make it look like he killed her, so he'd get into trouble," I said. "She wrote a note that looked like what he might write if he was faking her suicide. She was faking a fake. The police believed it!"

I managed to get this all out without crying, finally, but I was gasping for breath.

Ted Storm was gathering up papers strewn over the table and putting these into a folder as he spoke. "You need to calm down, honey," he said. "I don't think we'll bring this chocolate cake business into the case."

"It was a pie," I told him. "Not cake. Pie."

Lawyer Ted shot a look at my father. "It's always complicated putting a kid on the witness stand," he said.

"But I got to hand it to you, Hank," he said, chuckling. "This daughter of yours is a regular Nancy Drew."

96

The *Merriam-Webster Spell-Checker*

We were not allowed to pay a visit to Forrest in jail. Seeing him in his suit—too big for him now—as he approached the witness stand was the first time I'd laid eyes on him since the morning after Regina's death. He was thinner, but even now, after months in jail, he carried himself as if he were walking across a golf course or hopping into his Chris-Craft.

Under oath, Forrest admitted to engaging in an extramarital affair with Brenda Barnett, as well as having had numerous other affairs over the years, with women whose identities the police had been able to track down—an aspect of the case that eventually resulted in at least three divorces among members of the Lake Catherine Country Club.

"I'm deeply ashamed of my behavior," Forrest said. "But being unfaithful to my wife is not the same as killing her."

"Objection." The DA stood up. Her name was Vivian Latournier.

"Strike from the record," the judge agreed.

About the suicide note: It was true, Forrest said, that he could barely write a sentence in the English language. All his life he'd depended on his friend Hank—meaning my father—to help him when it came to writing.

But he wasn't an idiot. Putting aside the fact that he loved his wife—he'd said this again: *I loved my wife*—if he was going to fake a suicide note, he wasn't so stupid that he'd leave it filled with the kind of errors that would point to him as its author.

"I keep a book called the *Merriam-Webster Spell-Checker* in my bureau drawer for times I need to be sure my writing isn't too bad," he said. "Go look. You'll see it there."

Not likely. The Cabots had long since moved Forrest's possessions out of Wonderland.

97

Cut a Deal

Brenda Barnett took the stand next. She had cut her beautiful hair—her best feature, I realized now, which meant she didn't look remotely pretty anymore. Also, she appeared to be pregnant, though not so far along, I calculated, that Forrest could be viewed as a possible father to her child.

Now came the shocker. In exchange for the prosecution dropping all charges against her, Brenda had turned state's evidence, testifying for the prosecution that it had been Forrest Emerson who had laid out the plan to murder his wife in such a way as to make her death appear as a suicide.

"The man was obsessed with me," she said, shaking her head. "He kept begging me to marry him. I told him that as much as I cared for him, I couldn't bear to be involved in any way in such a heinous crime, or bring about the death of an innocent individual."

She still sounded like a character in a soap opera. "That's when I broke off the relationship," Brenda said, looking regretfully in the direction of the jury.

Vivian Latournier didn't stop there: Now came the pills. She set forth the picture of Forrest having premeditatedly hoarded Regina's medications over the weeks prior to her death for the purpose of delivering a fatal dose. Supporting this claim, she presented pharmacy records indicating that he'd filled her prescriptions three times.

I knew the story, of course, for all the good it did. It was Regina who'd ordered those extra doses, Regina who'd called in her prescriptions.

I sat in the front row, taking in Brenda's testimony, feeling sick. In the DA's account of what transpired that weekend, Forrest had set up a boat regatta for the express purpose of keeping everyone out of the house long enough to ensure that Regina was dead. He had even made sure to include his children in the spectacle by outfitting a canoe for them. Not only that, he'd placed his own children's lives at risk by putting them in a boat that was certain to tip over, as a device intended to keep all guests at the dock, away from the bedroom where, at that very moment, his wife lay dying of the overdose he'd delivered to her not long before.

When the DA got to this part, I glanced in the direction of the jurors, several of whom shook their heads.

It was hard to look at Forrest as he was now, seated at a long wooden table next to the only lawyer he could afford—a man so young, he appeared to be dealing with acne. Now Vivian Latournier called me up to the witness stand. I took an oath to tell the truth.

As he always had—with the exception of during his brief and disastrous affair with Brenda Barnett—Forrest listened intently to every word I said. Even when I found myself delivering what I came to see was coming across as incriminating testimony, I saw no sign of anger or resentment on his face. Only sorrow. Only regret.

Forrest and I had not exchanged a single word since the night of Regina's death. Now was the first time we'd been in the same room together since then.

The DA wasted no time. "We understand you kept a diary while you lived at Wonderland," she said.

A diary? Maybe they were talking about the little spiral notebook I'd kept in the pocket of my shorts, where I'd scribbled down times Forrest went off for his swim or his bike ride, and the rest of it. If so, this was bad, but I knew already that the police had found the notebook on Regina's bed, the first day of their investigation.

Only it wasn't my little spiral notebook the DA was talking about. She reached for an oversized manila envelope. Slowly, she pulled out my long-lost leatherbound journal. Somehow it had ended up in the hands of the police. Someone must have given it to them.

The room started to spin. I knew well what that journal contained. I wished I were dead.

"That journal was just . . . crazy things I thought up," I said. "I used to like making up stories." *Used to.* That was over. Like riding my yellow bike and playing tennis. Like my summer in Wonderland.

"You like making up stories, Frances?" the DA said. "Maybe you're making up more stories now?"

She opened my leatherbound journal. There were those birds on the cover, those thick, creamy pages. Vivian Latournier shifted her stance in such a way that she was partly facing me, but more so directing her performance to the jury. She began to read out loud from the pages I'd written the summer before. Her voice was low and husky.

"His finger made its way down my neck and my chest. Then further down."

"'Don't ever change,' he told me. 'I love you just the way you are.'"

There was more, but I tuned out the rest. Page after page of the words I'd written in my little bed that summer, looking out at the stars. Pretending something was happening that wasn't.

"This is your handwriting, isn't it, Frances?"

"You don't understand," I said.

I looked out to the people assembled in the courtroom, starting with the members of the jury, looking uncomfortable. Regina's parents. Prudence. Pam Oliver, even. My mother hadn't come with us to Maine, but there sat my father. He didn't look angry, or shocked, even. Just heartbroken. Then I spotted someone I hadn't expected to see there: Jonathan. Unlike my father, my tennis coach—my friend—did not look down as he heard the words I'd written in my journal that summer.

Not unlike how it was when I was playing my match at the tennis tournament—the one and only tennis match of my life, which definitely wasn't going well—his eyes met mine. I could hear him speaking to me, though he wasn't really, of course. *Forget everything else. Just focus on your breath.*

Eyes on the ball.

From somewhere far away, I heard the voice of Forrest's public defender, Ted, utter the word, "Objection." He said it as though it were a question.

Overruled.

The DA turned another page of my journal. She started reading again.

"As we were clearing up the dishes in the kitchen after dinner, he leaned over and whispered in my ear, so nobody else could hear him. 'I wish I could take you out on the lake tonight,' he told me. 'Just the two of us in the moonlight. I think about you all the time.'

"'I'd love that too,' I said. 'I never stop thinking about you.'

"'I want to wrap my arms around you and never let go.'"

It all seemed so long ago now. Feeling that way. Wanting to be with Forrest Emerson that way, without even knowing what being with Forrest that way would look like, without knowing what sex actually was. Just knowing it was something important.

Then wanting to please Regina. Wanting to do whatever it was that might make one of them love me, when it felt as though nobody ever had.

I looked over to Jonathan again. I pictured myself hitting my five hundred balls against the backboard. I remembered how strong I'd been then. I didn't feel strong anymore.

"I made all that up," I said.

"You told Officer Reynolds you'd seen a tattoo on Forrest Emerson's buttocks," the prosecutor said. "Did you ever see Forrest Emerson's naked body?"

"It wasn't what you think."

"So even though you took an oath to tell the truth, you're telling us now that you lie. Is that right, Frances? No wonder it's hard for the rest of us to figure out when you're telling the truth."

Where was Forrest's lawyer now? Wasn't this a moment for him to object?

"I'll remind you again that you're under oath here. There are serious consequences for lying in a court of law." The prosecutor stood in front of the witness box, but in such a way that the jury could see her, shaking her head. "Were you in love with Forrest Emerson, Frances?"

"Yes," I told her. I could have added *I still love him. Just not the way you think.* But I left it at that.

"And did Forrest Emerson ever suggest that your feelings were reciprocated?"

There had been that day we sat together by the lake, after he broke things off with Brenda. He'd put his arm around me. And so many other times, too, that had meant the world to me. It wasn't just the words he said. It was how he treated me.

"You don't understand," I said. Even I could hear the tone of pleading in my voice.

The previous summer, when I learned about Forrest's affair, I had come to believe that I never mattered to him after all. But I knew now that Forrest actually did love me. In a different way from how I'd described in my journal, was all. A more precious way, actually. More real.

That's when our eyes met in the courtroom, Forrest's and mine. Just for a moment. He nodded almost imperceptibly. You couldn't call the expression I saw on his face one of happiness, but I saw kindness there. Other than Jonathan, he was the only person I could find in the courtroom that day displaying any sign of true kindness. They were the only ones on the planet, possibly.

I didn't dare smile at him, but the faint trace of a smile passed over Forrest's lips. He closed his eyes as if what he saw now was something he'd prefer not to behold. His future.

Now came the part none of us could have anticipated. As terrible as things were, I didn't know yet they could get worse.

The DA having set forth, through the testimony of Brenda Barnett, a scenario in which Forrest Emerson could have held out no hope of a future with her, the question hung in the air: Why, then, would Forrest Emerson have killed his wife? There was still the motive of the insurance money, of course. But the DA chose to go further. Having worked to establish the portrait of Forrest as a man obsessed with sex, she evidently wanted to portray him as setting his sights on a new relationship, now that Brenda had rejected him. Once he'd gotten his ailing and demanding wife out of the way.

This was when Vivian Latournier turned back from addressing the jury and faced me again, pointing her finger directly at my heart.

"Is it not possible, Frances, that you saw yourself as having a future with Forrest Emerson?" she asked me. "The man whose wife had entrusted you with the care of their two young children just weeks before? You thought if she was out of the way, you could replace her? Isn't it possible that Forrest Emerson encouraged you to believe this, by telling you he loved you?"

No. No. No. No. I wanted to say the words, but none came out.

"You stated on record that Forrest Emerson has a tattoo on his left buttock. What kind of a man displays his naked body to a fourteen-year-old?" she demanded.

"It wasn't like that—" I said.

Now Vivian Latournier started to read from my journal again— words I'd forgotten until now, written sometime early in the summer, after that boat ride together probably, describing a picture of Forrest and me, some unspecified date in the future, when the children were off at boarding school maybe, and Regina simply . . . gone. A fantasy featuring the two of us heading out to the island on the boat, his arms around me as I took the wheel.

Then came another of my journal entries, written late in the night, a time—one of the many—when I'd felt frustrated by Regina's endless demands.

"If I never see her again after this summer, I won't miss her. She's always talking about killing herself. Sometimes I wish she'd do it."

"Perhaps there were two people who wanted Regina Emerson dead that summer," the DA said. "Her husband was one. Weren't you the other?"

Up until this moment, Forrest had been sitting quietly at the table next to his attorney, listening to the testimony without apparent bitterness or rancor, making notes occasionally. But when the DA spoke these words, Forrest rose up out of his chair and shook his fist.

"For god's sake, let her alone," he said. He didn't yell, but the anger in his voice was almost frightening. You might even describe it as murderous. In my whole life, nobody had ever stood up for me as Forrest Emerson did at that moment.

"Frances didn't do anything," he said. "She's just a kid. It's all my fault. Everything. If it wasn't for me, my wife would be alive today."

98

LIFE

The verdict was guilty. First degree.

I wasn't in the courtroom when they sentenced him. Life in prison with the possibility of parole with good behavior after thirty-five years.

Jilly and Hayward went to live with their grandparents. Age seven was a little young for this, but the moment Jilly reached fourth grade, I gather, the Cabots shipped her off to the same school in England where members of the royal family send their children. Hayward was there already.

It was over a decade later when I got a letter from Prudence, filling me in on more recent developments. By this point, Jilly was off to Sweet Briar College in Virginia. Hayward had attended his grandfather's Ivy League alma mater—his admission secured, perhaps, by a donation that made possible the construction of the Cabot Center for Business Studies.

Hayward had dropped out of college, but he had gotten a job on Wall Street through some family friend, where he made a lot of money. He had a lot of money already, of course.

Then one day I opened up the newspaper and there he was in *The New York Times*, charged with securities fraud. Around this time, women started coming forward, accusing Hayward of drugging them for the purpose of sexually assaulting them. He was ultimately found guilty on multiple charges of rape and sentenced to prison, though unlike his father, he'd been able to hire an expensive attorney, who had gotten him out on bail, pending appeal.

The Cabots held on to Wonderland, but except for the occasional weekend, Prudence told me, it sat empty nearly every summer after Regina's death. What was left of the family came up on Memorial Day and the Fourth of July. Never Labor Day, for understandable reasons.

Jonathan Gleason, my beloved tennis coach and friend, died of AIDS at the age of twenty-nine, the year I turned nineteen. By that time, I'd long since put tennis away. I didn't even know what became of the Bancroft racquet Jonathan had given me—long out of date by this point, but once my most prized possession.

My mother had a stroke at the age of fifty-one and died two weeks later. I think all those years of holding on to so much bitterness ate away at her heart.

My father finished his novel. More surprisingly, he sold it to a small publisher in Berkeley, California. He called the book *Wonderland*. In it, he told the story of a couple of boys who grew up almost like brothers in a tenement apartment building in a rough New Jersey town, and of the summer they got jobs at a country club in Maine, where one of them fell in love with a beautiful girl from the other side of the tracks—and, much to her parents' chagrin, married her. In the novel, the boy saves his beautiful, deeply troubled wife from jumping off some rocks in a quarry in Maine. Wishful thinking, you might call it.

Though my father's novel wasn't a bestseller, it sold well enough that he was able to get himself a little condo in south Jersey, where he lived—sober, mostly, with only a couple of slipups—for a few good years before his death at age fifty-nine of lung cancer.

I went to college on a full scholarship and earned a degree in physical therapy, all thoughts of playing tennis long evaporated. I got a job right after graduation at a rehabilitation center for veterans of the Gulf War. As much as I had loved making up stories once, I did not pursue that secret dream of mine. Those pages I wrote that filled my leather-bound journal the summer I was fourteen (quasi-erotic juvenilia, you might call them) represented my one magnum opus. You could say I lost my focus, my hunger maybe—that's what Jonathan had called it—or simply my faith in myself.

Those ninety-two days at Wonderland—the hours I spent out on the tennis court, and hitting alone against the backboard until close to midnight, refusing to stop until I'd returned five hundred shots in a row without missing one of them—I had known, briefly, what it felt like to be in charge of my own destiny. When I fired a tennis ball over the net, I felt strong and worthy, without needing anyone's approval, and it didn't even matter if a girl with a closet full of tennis outfits, whose mother was on the board of the country club, called my shot out when it wasn't. I knew who I was and what I was capable of. I felt powerful.

But in another way, what I experienced over the course of that Wonderland summer was a terrible abuse of my own power.

You could say that I brought about the ruin of Forrest Emerson's life. You might even say I'd led Regina Emerson to kill herself as an act of revenge against her husband. He had betrayed her, alright. And I had betrayed him. For that I could never forgive myself. Because of that, I believed I had no right to happiness or joy. For a long time, I lived without much of either.

99

You Weren't Supposed to Come in Here

Just two times over the years that followed my Wonderland summer, I communicated—briefly—with Forrest Emerson. Sometime around my thirtieth birthday, I sent a letter to the correctional facility in Maine where he was incarcerated.

It was a short note. I wrote to say I was sorry for whatever role I may have played in bringing about his conviction for Regina's murder. I did not go into the details. *I would give anything to change what happened,* I wrote. *I don't expect you to forgive me.*

Ten more years passed before I heard back from Forrest.

Then one day, a long friendly letter arrived, written in pencil, the return address featuring a string of numbers that identified its origin as a correctional facility. In his letter, he wrote about his activities at the prison. As a man who'd always been good at picking up unlikely skills (fly-tying, outrigger construction, harmonica playing, magic tricks, tree house design), he had become intimately acquainted with the contents of the prison library.

I probably know every book in that place by this point, he wrote. *I've read more of them than you might think. The interesting thing is that, for once in my life, if I start something, I finish.*

It took me three years, but I got through Moby Dick. *Though as always, what I love even more than reading is working with my hands. I've gotten pretty good at carpentry. I build stools for the children of some of the guys here. Every one a little different, with their name carved on the top. They're always a big hit.*

In this letter, Forrest wrote of his sorrow over what had become of Hayward and his regret that he hadn't been around during some crucial years to guide his son to a better path.

When a kid loses his mother at age twelve, he wrote, *and they send his father away, and he spends his teenage years with a couple of stiffs like Suzanne and Colson Cabot supposedly looking out for him, it's not surprising he loses his way. My daughter did a lot better. She found herself a nice partner. A woman! Maybe her old man didn't leave her with the highest opinion of men. She and her wife have twins. I guess this makes me a grandfather!*

For a long time there, Jilly didn't want to see me, he wrote. *Then just a couple of months ago, she showed up here. Best day I can remember.*

She told me something you should know. She'd been keeping it secret all these years. Then her own kids got to be the age she was when everything fell apart, and I guess she decided it was time to stop pretending.

When I got to this point in Forrest's letter, I took a deep breath. I knew I'd read the rest, but I had to take a moment first. I had done all I could, all those years, to keep from revisiting that night.

You must remember when we were all running around, trying to get the boats lined up for the regatta, and it was taking so much longer than I'd intended, he wrote. *What I didn't know was that in the middle of it all, Jilly had decided to go back up to the house.*

Jilly had this habit of going into Regina's room just to sit on the bed, to be around her mother, even if Regina was sleeping. It's funny. Regina always thought the children didn't care about her, when the truth was, all Jilly ever wanted was for Regina to pay attention. That Saturday she'd climbed the stairs to her mother's room to show her the certificate she'd earned for her entry in the Rice Krispies recipe contest. Regina had been sleeping, as usual, so after a while she'd gone downstairs again to join the rest of us down by the water.

I took Forrest's words in slowly, the way a person does when she's reading a horror story—Stephen King, maybe. You know something bad is going to happen. You're preparing yourself for it. Part of me wanted to put down the letter, knowing what came next. But I kept on reading, of course—that neat and oddly still-familiar handwriting. No evidence of spelling errors now.

Evidently Jilly had left one of her toys upstairs in Regina's room. You probably remember that talking bear of hers that drove us all crazy. She wanted to bring her bear down to the water. She went back in the house, up the stairs to Regina's bedroom to get it.

The door was closed, but she opened it. Regina was on the bed. Nothing so unusual about that. As you know, Regina spent a lot of time in that bed. But even to Jilly, young as she was, something looked different about her. Also, she was wearing that negligee. This wasn't usual for her.

So Jilly went up to where her mother was lying. Regina's arm was dangling off the edge of the bed, she told me. She knew something was wrong.

I guess she said something to Regina. Then she yelled in her ear to wake her up.

Now came the hardest part of the story Forrest recounted in his letter to me.

Regina was still breathing at this point, he wrote. *Jilly remembers that part. Her mother even spoke to her. She just didn't make much sense. Regina told Jilly to go away. She told her not to tell anyone what she saw.*

"You weren't supposed to come in here," she said.

So Jilly left. She picked up the bear and got out of there. When she got back to the water, we were still lining up the boats. She started to cry, and I came over to comfort her. But Jilly never said what had happened at the house.

When she kept crying, and shaking, I thought she was just tired and cold. I said she didn't have to go in the canoe with her brother if she didn't want to, but she insisted. I think she wanted to pretend what she saw in her mother's bedroom never happened.

Later, of course, when the rest of us found out, Jilly felt this terrible guilt that she could have saved her mother, if she'd just told me. She lived with that for years. Right up to the day she came to visit me here. All this time she's been holding on to that story, not telling anybody.

I knew what that felt like. I'd done the same.

I guess her brother had his story too, Forrest wrote. *You must have recognized that Hayward had a thing for you that summer. I knew he was leaving you all those funny presents, but I figured it was just puppy love. Then I got all tangled up in that Brenda business, and I stopped paying attention to anything else.*

Hayward must have snuck into your room, Frances. He knew you kept some kind of diary. A journal. He figured out where you hid it.

No doubt he read every word without understanding that sometimes what a person writes in a journal is a far cry from what actually happened. It probably made him nuts, reading what you wrote.

The picture came to me then, of Hayward as he'd been that summer. His body, softened from too many bags of Cheez Doodles. That one blue eye peering in at me through the hole in the boathouse wall as I touched myself.

After Regina died, when the police came, they found your journal in his room.

Writing about the journal, all those years later, Forrest displayed no anger or reproach for the stories I'd made up. That was like him. Judged as he'd been all his life, Forrest Emerson was never one to judge anyone else.

What you wrote should have been kept private, he wrote. *Those were your secret thoughts. They should never have been read out loud in a court-room or taken as proof of some kind of inappropriate relationship going on between you and me. A person should be free to write down anything she wants. You could never have dreamed your words would end up being read out loud at a murder trial.*

He was right about that. Not in my worst nightmares.

You were always a special girl to me, he wrote. *Of course I loved you, but not the way they made it sound.*

I guess I just wished you were my daughter. Or maybe I just wished your father was doing a better job of being your dad.

I sat at my kitchen table, reading the note. I had fixed myself a cup of tea, but I hadn't taken a sip. I realized I was weeping—the first time I'd done that since the night of Regina's death.

What I want to tell you is this, Forrest wrote. *We all contributed to what happened that night. It wasn't just you telling Regina what you saw going on between Brenda and me.*

It wasn't Jilly, not letting me know Regina looked like she was in bad shape while we might still have been able to save her, or Hayward stealing your private journal and letting the police get their hands on it. Maybe those things contributed to their ideas about me as some messed-up guy who was putting the moves on a fourteen-year-old, in addition to fooling around with somebody else's wife. Maybe none of it made any difference.

The truth is that Regina had big problems long before you came to Wonderland that summer. Her sister's death had something to do with it, for sure. So did the way their parents raised the two of them. A woman who decides to kill herself for the express purpose of sticking her husband with a murder rap—to punish him for having an affair—is not a woman who was OK before that.

Now came the part of the letter where he spoke of the person whose name he had never mentioned before. It seemed to me his handwriting changed at this point. I could almost feel how tightly his hand must have gripped the pencil as he wrote her name.

Regina told me once that all her life she'd wished Camille was dead. Then Camille died—

Camille. He'd finally spoken of her. It was all such a long time ago now.

I can't tell you to forgive yourself, Frances, he wrote. *I can only tell you that I forgive you.*

I hadn't even known it, but I'd been holding my breath as I read his letter. Now my lungs filled with air.

I'll put it differently. You never needed to be forgiven. None of this was your fault. You just landed in our lives at an unfortunate moment in time. I'm not saying Hubbard, New Jersey, is the greatest place for a girl to spend the summer. But you would have done better sticking around there instead of falling down a rabbit hole called Wonderland.

If anyone needs to apologize, he wrote, *it's me.*

He signed his letter *Love, Howie.*

I read that letter three times. When I was finished, I folded it and put it away. I felt no need to read the words again. I'd taken what I needed from them.

100

WHEN YOU LEARN THE GAME YOUNG

At the time I received Forrest Emerson's letter, I had recently turned forty. My daughter, Jess, was three years old.

Maybe as a result of my experiences when I was young, I had never cared much for children. Over the thirteen weeks that constituted my Wonderland summer, I viewed the job of caring for the Emersons' kids as a necessary irritation I'd endure for the gift of getting to spend my days in the bright and shining presence of the person who represented for me everything I could hope to find in a man. Lover or father. I barely knew what those words meant.

After my time with the Emersons ended—after I'd betrayed the man I loved best in the world—I let go of my fervent longings. My hunger, as Jonathan had called it. I think I ceased to believe that love was possible for me. I could no more realize my old dreams that I'd play at the US Open or write a novel. Or have the money to rent a house on Lake Catherine.

Not that I wanted to return there, ever.

Jess was conceived—a calculated plan—through the unwitting sperm contribution of a man I had no interest in spending further time with, let alone marrying. We went out together, if you can call it that, the year I turned thirty-six, for exactly as long as it took me to get pregnant, at which point I broke it off with him, feeling no need to divulge news of a baby on the way.

By the time Jess was born, both my parents were dead. As was true about much of my life, this too—the raising of my one precious daughter—is something I've done on my own. I decided it was better for a girl to have no father than to have a father who would end up disappointing her, as the two most important men in my own young life had done.

Not long before my forty-fifth birthday, an odd thing happened. Walking past a tennis court—a public court, not some private club—I got the idea of signing up for lessons. Though age had taken its toll on my knees, and no doubt my stamina, it turned out that I had not altogether lost the passion for the game I'd first discovered the summer Jonathan invited me onto the court.

What do you know? I had not lost my serve. I started playing regularly. I won a few doubles tournaments in our town, then made it to the regionals.

Not long ago, in the locker room, after a tournament in which my partner and I took second place—the New England women's over-fifty division—a woman we'd competed against made a friendly observation that took me by surprise.

"I can tell from the way you hit that you learned the game young," she said. "It's different when you pick up tennis later in life. There's always something about those players who started out at some country club."

In her eyes, I must have seemed like one of those people who grew up in a place like Wonderland. Well, I did, in a manner of speaking, I might have told her. I grew up in a place called Wonderland. But it wasn't how she imagined.

A FEW LAST WORDS, AND

ACKNOWLEDGMENTS

I embarked on this book in the aftermath of completing the many-years-long endeavor of following a complicated fictional family through two separate novels over fifty years. That project—rich as it was, and consuming—had me filling a whiteboard the size of a wall with names and dates, big events and small, in the lives of more than a dozen characters.

The one thing I told myself when I set out to find my new story was that this time around, I would narrow my focus to a relatively short period of time, a single place, and a handful of characters—one in particular. Without any deliberation, and for reasons I could not reconstruct, I chose Maine as the site of my story. It may be this simple: I love the state of Maine. I love lakes, and houses that look out onto lakes (though vast family estates, not so much). If I was going to be spending time someplace for as long as it took to bring a book to its completion, I wanted that place to be one for which I felt a deep affinity, as I do for the state of Maine.

But a novel really begins with a character. As is so often the case in my work, I was drawn to exploring the experience of an adolescent—in this case, a young girl, just at the moment in her life when she's crossing over from child to woman, but stuck in the middle.

I remember inhabiting that place.

I may possess a big imagination, but as a woman whose own teen-age years ended in the early 1970s, I knew better than to try to capture the world of a fourteen-year-old girl in present-day American life. With no clue yet as to what would take place in the story I'd be telling, I chose to set my new novel in 1986—not the year I was fourteen, myself, but a moment in time that represented the last days before technology began overtaking our culture. I wanted to explore the life of a young person without a telephone in her hand, or a set of earphones.

Not without reason, I gave her a tennis racquet.

I want to mention here that when I am writing a novel, I hardly do anything else besides work on that novel, but over the course of the summer in which I began this particular piece of fiction, I allowed myself one other activity: private tennis lessons. Not every morning, but for many of them, I got out of bed a little after five a.m. and made the eighteen-minute drive to the house of my tennis teacher, who has, in her backyard, a wonderful tennis court surrounded by nothing but fields and woods and a great old peach tree.

For fifty-five minutes (with the five minutes remaining in the hour devoted to picking up tennis balls), my teacher and I faced each other across the net as she put me through my paces. And for those fifty-five minutes, something wonderful happened: The concerns that filled my days—including about the book I was writing—disappeared. For those fifty-five minutes, my world was about one thing: the ball.

It's important to add that I am not a great tennis player, or even an above-average one. Though I first took up tennis at age thirty-five, I abandoned the game soon after, when I discovered that the youngest of my three children possessed what I did not: real talent for the sport. I became that mother who comes up with the money for racquets and lessons and drives her child to tournaments and sits on the sidelines, holding her breath.

More than thirty years went by before I took my old racquet out of its case and set foot on a court again. I wanted to see if there was any point still in trying to get a ball over the net. When I did, I decided to give myself the gift of private lessons. This is when a gifted teacher entered my life.

I learned a lot about hitting a tennis ball that summer, but one of the things that came to me over the course of those early mornings on the court—with the sun just coming up, birds calling out to us, and my teacher's dog sunning herself on the sidelines—was how much I was discovering out on the court besides footwork and how to improve my stroke. I got stronger, for sure. I learned some things about breath, and focus, and human psychology, even, but I also found myself revisiting the girl I was more than fifty years earlier, whose family would never have belonged to a country club. The girl I was never played sports well but cast longing glances at those who did—most of all, at that other kind of girl who owned little white tennis skirts. This was the kind of girl I longed to be and never would become.

I will go so far as to say that in addition to learning how to serve, that summer, and to execute a backhand stroke that wouldn't put terror in the heart of any opponent, ever, I learned a fair amount about myself out on that tennis court. A great portion of what I learned on the court—not simply the tennis part—I owe to my teacher and friend, Tami Vezina.

For those fifty-five minutes, my mind ceased its whirring. I thought about nothing—I, a woman forever analyzing situations, relationships, problems, work, the troubles of the world, the future, the past. With a racquet in my hand, it all went away. Here was the greatest gift of those lessons I took: the stillness I found there.

Stillness followed by inspiration. Because after my lesson was over, and for the eighteen minutes I spent driving home, the girl I'd been long ago, who longed to play a sport, never mind play it well—the girl who longed to belong somewhere, and never felt she did—seemed to be sitting in the car with me.

This is where the character of Frances came from, and how I came to give to her my love of tennis. And because I was writing a work of fiction, not memoir, I gave her something I did not possess, which was great natural aptitude for the game and fierce competitive hunger.

Other parts of my young character's story connected more closely to my own young life: the experiences of being a babysitter (an activity that occupied nearly every weekend of my years from ages twelve to sixteen) and of having an alcoholic parent, of feeling like an outsider, and longing to be part of somebody else's family rather than the one I was born into. I gave my fictional character the same kind of odd sexual preoccupations I had possessed, myself, at her young age. And one more thing: Having known, briefly, the experience of writing every night in the pages of a secret notebook, I gave this character of mine a journal.

In my real-life journal-writing history, my nights of committing my deepest thoughts to the pages of a notebook ended at twelve years old, on the night I opened that notebook to discover a two-page letter pressed between the pages, right where my most recent entry left off. The letter was written by my deeply loved and wildly invasive mother, who had evidently read my most recent journal entry, in which I had dared, for the first time, to write about my father getting drunk.

In her letter to me (brilliantly written—typewritten, in fact), my mother responded to what I had put down on those pages concerning my father getting drunk by listing for me all the extraordinary aspects of being his daughter—all he'd taught my sister and me about art and music and poetry. She reminded me how much he loved me, of course. In her handwritten postscript, she'd gone so far as to figure out what percentage of the day my father was actually under the influence of alcohol (her math calculations visible in the margin of the letter). No big surprise: The percentage was relatively low. My father was definitely sober more often than he was drunk.

One thing that happens when I create a fictional character and begin to fill up her world is that my obsessions—some of them obsessions of the moment, some lifelong—come to the surface on the pages of my book.

This is where I can let them spread out and live. I get to explore, fictionally, themes and experiences that haunt me. And sometimes I get to imagine what it would be like if the things that happened in my own life—my real life—had turned out differently. Case in point: What would my life have looked like if I had turned out to be a terrific tennis player at the age of fourteen instead of a totally average one five decades later? More than that, what would my life have looked like if my boundless fascination with the secrets of other people's lives had made me not simply an annoying busybody but someone who had contributed to a full-on tragedy?

I'll go back now to the part about sex, and a young girl's sexual coming of age, and the confusion that's likely to swirl around just about everything to do with sex, particularly if she has nobody to share it with.

A small but memorable moment from my life as a young teenage babysitter came to me then. I was thirteen or fourteen probably. Ten thirty or eleven o'clock on a Saturday night, sitting in the front seat of a car as the father of the children for whom I'd babysat that night drove me home.

He'd probably had a drink or two. Back home, his wife would be getting ready for bed. Would they have sex? These were the kinds of questions I thought about in the front seat of that car.

But for that brief moment in time—as long as it took to drive from the house where I'd performed my babysitting duties to the one where I lived with my parents, where my father was probably up in the attic, working on a painting and getting drunk—it was just the two of us, the young husband and father, and me.

It was a moment that seemed filled with quiet sexual energy and even danger—as, some years later, I would think of that moment, from the perspective of the young wife and mother waiting in bed while her husband drove the babysitter home. At the point in my life when I embarked on exploring Frances's story, I'd known that moment from two perspectives.

All of these images and obsessions went into this novel. And a few more besides. Tennis skirts, tampons, Chris-Craft boats, American Girl dolls, *The Joy of Sex* . . . my love for my first bicycle. My love of moss, even. And my unlikely love of tennis. (Unlikely, because my love for the sport has so little to do with how I play the game.)

I accomplished a few things over the course of the summer when I dreamed up the summer home I named Wonderland. I got better at tennis. I formed a deep and lasting friendship with my tennis teacher, Tami. And just as Labor Day weekend approached, I finished my first draft.

What I needed at that moment (more, even, than a great tennis teacher) was a wonderful editor. Celia Johnson proved to be that person. To me, one mark of a great editor is the ability not simply to assist a writer in improving and refining what's on the page, but the gift of imagining what's not there yet, but might be. Celia accomplished this, not just once, but through two successive drafts. She read this book in its earliest version, and what she had to say threw the door open for a whole new vision of the story.

I need to express my deep gratitude, as well, to my highly perceptive and generous agent, Caroline Eisenmann, who agreed to represent my new book, and me, at what felt like a crossroads in my writing life—decades in, but feeling a need to embark on something I'd never tried before. As much as I appreciate Caroline's support and encouragement, and her enthusiasm, even more than that, I appreciate her for her willingness to tell me what I needed to work harder on, and what I needed to let go of. Caroline is that rare kind of agent who still reads and offers serious critiques of her client's manuscript. Every page. It's a gift I treasure.

For many years, I've turned to women I've known, outside of the publishing world, to serve as my early readers for books not yet in their final stages. This time around, it was a former writing student—and a fine writer herself, who has gone on to publish the memoir she began years ago at one of my workshops—to whom I sent a very early draft of this novel. Mary Black—former high school principal, Harley rider, and a lover of the psychological thriller—did not simply read that draft. She offered astute notes, many of which informed the work that came after.

My good friend Pam Dawkins—and a longtime tennis player, also a mother of tennis players—read an early draft of this novel and corrected the tennis errors. Would that she could do the same on the court with me.

I want to thank my longtime friend Shonna Humphrey, former director of the Maine Writers & Publishers Alliance—a native Mainer, and a marvelous writer—for her insights into the era of her own adolescence in Maine, growing up in a community that bears virtually no resemblance to the one I invented for these pages. For all the things I got wrong about Maine, I offer my humble apologies and the flimsy excuse of being a New Hampshire native, myself, and never a member of any country club. Nor was Shonna, for sure. But oddly enough, it was her Maine—that very different part of the state from the one in which this story takes place—that I held in my mind's eye, lying just beyond the edges of the rarefied little fictional town I created in these pages. Among other things, this turned out to be a novel about class. I took a girl from one social class and dropped her into another world. Not mine. Do that, and something interesting is sure to happen.

I also want to acknowledge, here, a writer I have never met—a Mainer as well—but one whose books and characters have populated my imagination for a very long time, Stephen King. I like to think of my character's devotion to Stephen King's work, and his brief cameo appearance in this story, as my small homage to a writer I deeply admire on all kinds of levels.

Closer to home, I am indebted to Carmen Johnson and her team at Amazon, who dove in and got right to the heart of my story with laser vision and helped me find my way through what can be (but wasn't) the painful final stage of cutting and editing. I offer huge gratitude, as well, to Megan McKeever, my Amazon editor, for her close and perceptive work on that crucial draft, and Jaye Whitney Debber, who did a fabulous job of making sure I got the details right. If you ask me, copyeditors rank among the unsung heroes and heroines of book publishing.

Finally, as always, I offer up my undying appreciation to the women and men who have continued to read and support the books I write for over fifty years now. Nobody inspires me more to keep telling stories. I have never had to come up with an answer to the question, "If a tree falls in a forest and no one is around to hear, does it make a sound?" because I've been fortunate, as a writer, that there have always been wonderful readers out there in the woods letting me know, "I heard what you wrote."

You heard and understood. For a writer, there may be no greater gift.

ABOUT THE AUTHOR

Joyce Maynard is the *New York Times* bestselling author of thirteen previous novels and five books of nonfiction, as well as the syndicated column "Domestic Affairs." Her memoir, *At Home in the World*, has been translated into eighteen languages. Her novels *To Die For* and *Labor Day* were both adapted for film. She is a fellow of MacDowell and Yaddo artists' residencies.

When not running her hotel/retreat center, Casa Paloma, in Guatemala—where she mentors women in the telling of their stories—she makes her home in Northern California and in the state of New Hampshire.